Welcome aboard Orca!

When the

Wind

Blows

Maggi Ansell

Extraordinary adventures with a deadly twist

Would you like to order a book, or make a comment to the author?
Please email wtwb@shaw.ca with 'Book' in the subject line or visit
www.maggi-ansell.com

Note for Librarians: A cataloguing record for this book is available from Library and Archives
Canada at www.collectionscanada.ca/amicus/index-e.html
ISBN 1-4120-9922-6

*Printed in Victoria, BC, Canada. Printed on paper with minimum 30% recycled fibre.
Trafford's print shop runs on "green energy" from solar, wind and other environmentally-friendly
power sources.*

PUBLISHING™

Offices in Canada, USA, Ireland and UK

Book sales for North America and international:
Trafford Publishing, 6E–2333 Government St.,
Victoria, BC V8T 4P4 CANADA
phone 250 383 6864 (toll-free 1 888 232 4444)
fax 250 383 6804; email to orders@trafford.com
Book sales in Europe:
Trafford Publishing (UK) Limited, 9 Park End Street, 2nd Floor
Oxford, UK OX1 1HH UNITED KINGDOM
phone +44 (0)1865 722 113 (local rate 0845 230 9601)
facsimile +44 (0)1865 722 868; info.uk@trafford.com
Order online at:
trafford.com/06-1679

10 9 8 7 6 5 4 3 2

Dedications

To the memory of Senior Pilot, **Peter Hope**
To Rescue Paramedic, **Angus McDonell**
To Aircrew Officer/Winchman, **Ian Callaghan**
Crew of Queensland Emergency Services Helicopter, *Rescue 521*

Angus McDonell
Ian Callaghan
Peter Hope
Rescue 521 crew
Photo: Brisbane Courier-Mail

To Pilot, Lt. Cdr. **Robert Spratt** and the crew of US Navy Hercules,
Nalo 817, who flew into the cyclone to pinpoint *Orca* for the rescue
helicopter

Lt. Cdr. Robert Spratt

Acknowledgements

Many thanks for...

Reviewing and editing suggestions:
**Wilma Doxtdator, Julie Huot, Lisa Phillips,
Catherine Smyly, Michael Smyly**

Cover preparation: **Shawn Sanders:**
www.shawnsandersphotography.com

Line drawings: **Robin Ansell**

Photos:
Brisbane Courier-Mail, for *Rescue 521* photo
Townsville Bulletin, for post-rescue photos
Julie Huot, for author photo
Caribbean Utilities Company, Ltd. (CUC)
Para-Tech Engineering Company: *www.seaanchor.com*
Peter Phillips

Also many thanks to family and friends who offered letters and
pictures received from us on our travels, since our records perished
with Orca

~~~~~

*For Alex, Mitch, Libby & Jessie,
the next generation of adventurers!*

ORCA

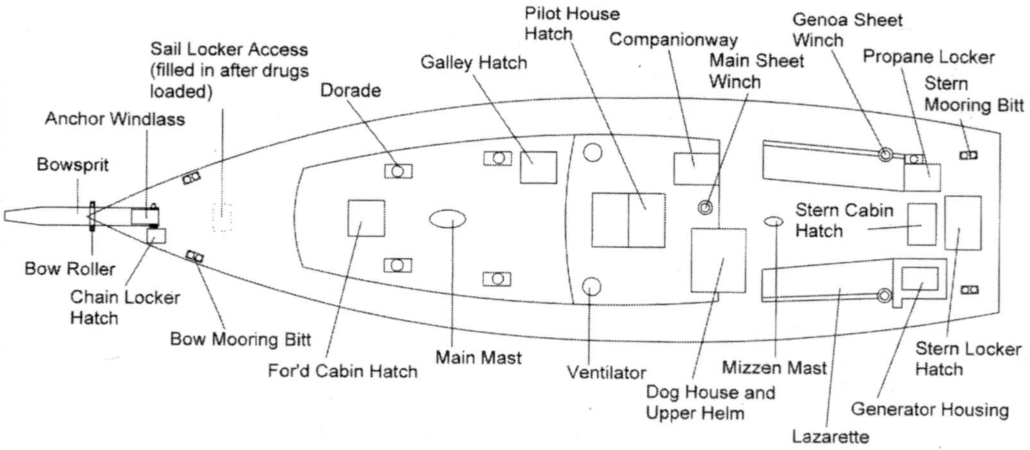

Pilot House
Hatch
Companionway
Genoa Sheet
Winch
Sail Locker Access
(filled in after drugs
loaded)
Galley Hatch
Main Sheet
Winch
Propane Locker
Stern
Mooring Bitt
Dorade
Anchor Windlass
Bowsprit
Stern Cabin
Hatch
Bow Roller
Chain Locker
Hatch
Bow Mooring Bitt
For'd Cabin Hatch
Main Mast
Ventilator
Mizzen Mast
Stern Locker
Hatch
Dog House and
Upper Helm
Generator Housing
Lazarette

Deck Plan

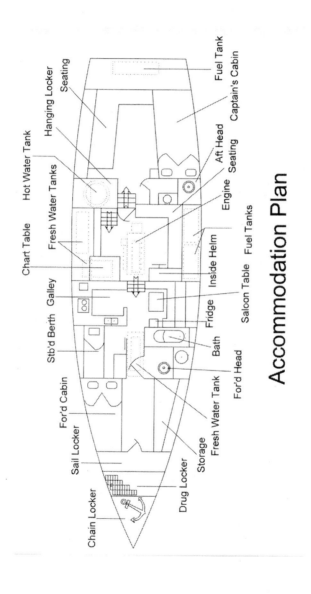

Accommodation Plan

Chain Locker

Sail Locker

For'd Cabin

Stb'd Berth   Galley

Chart Table   Hot Water Tank

Hanging Locker

Seating

Fresh Water Tanks

Drug Locker

Storage

Fresh Water Tank

For'd Head

Bath

Fridge   Inside Helm

Saloon Table   Fuel Tanks

Engine   Seating

Aft Head

Captain's Cabin

Fuel Tank

Foreword

My love affair with the sea began in England at the tender age of five, shipping out with the trawlermen from Whitby on the North Yorkshire coast. I also learned, from these professionals and sometimes the families they left behind, what a cruel mistress the sea could be. Ignorance is bliss and, in skippering my own yacht, I've often been referred to as Capt. Bligh.

I was delighted that, with *Orca*, two very good friends realized their dream, but I was also disappointed. I lost two very able crew members. In more than fifty years of sailing, not many people have made that grade in my book.

For those who only sit by the fireside and dream, 'When the Wind Blows' is a fascinating nautical travelogue, well worth the read. For the day sailor, it is required reading before pointing your bow at the horizon. 'Blue Water' veterans will be in awe at what Robin and Maggi experienced and survived.

It is my secret hope that some little thing that helped, rubbed off from Capt. Bligh.

Jeff Parker
Grand Cayman, 2006

Introduction

The family of an enterprising mechanical engineer can expect an interesting and varied life. Work demands took Robin, me and our two children Lisa and Bill to several locations in the UK before moving to Sarnia, Ontario, Canada, in 1979, where we happily embraced the Canadian way of life and became Canadian citizens.

In 1984 we made a temporary move to Sirte Oil Company, a Liquid Natural Gas plant in Libya on North Africa's Mediterranean coast. The children remained in boarding schools in the Toronto area, visiting Libya for wild holidays.

Following his five-year term in Libya we returned to Canada, this time to B.C. In October, 1989, Robin accepted a job in the Cayman Islands with Caribbean Utilities Company (CUC), where he became Vice President of Engineering and Planning and I worked for Caribbean Publishing Company.

In the sub-tropical paradise of Grand Cayman, the opportunity arose to tender for a confiscated drug boat. Robin, whose plan to enter the merchant marine when he left school was met with a parental veto, found his youthful dreams of setting sail for distant horizons, turning into reality.

It has long been a matter of irritation to Robin that I underestimate my abilities. He has spent a lifetime encouraging and supporting me in many ventures, including learning to swim at age 33 (my greatest personal achievement, overcoming a phobia of water). With his support, I also learned to scuba dive, gained a private pilot's licence and then a degree from the University of Toronto when I was over 40. It was natural for Robin to believe I would be a competent sailor too, even if I didn't start until age 46.

To quote Silbar & Henley's classic song title, Robin has always been the 'Wind Beneath my Wings'.

Shunning nautical superstition, we renamed our vessel *Orca*. Later you will discover the irony of discarding the original name of the vessel!

In order to write an accurate account of the last hours of Orca I contacted the Rescue Helicopter crew; the US Navy Hercules Pilot; Australian meteorologists; the Maritime Rescue Coordination Centre in Canberra, Australia; the EPIRB (Emergency Position Indicating Radio Beacon) centre in Maryland, USA; the National & Meteorological Library & Archive, UK, and every other agency which played any part. I did this with the express intention of writing it for the Reader's Digest *Drama in Real Life*. The condensed version was published in Reader's Digest Canada in May, 1999, and in Reader's Digest Australia, and Reader's Digest New Zealand in July, 1999.

~~~~~

Orca's Route: Cayman to Australia

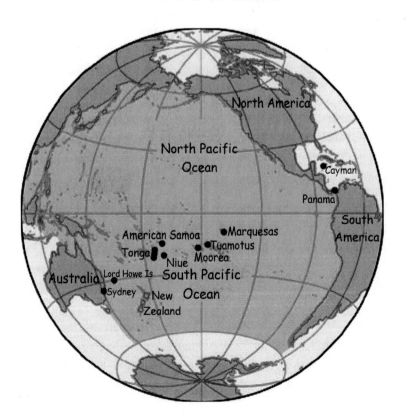

Contents

1

Temptation — Grand Cayman, British West Indies

"Drug Alley, they call it!"

Robin sweeps his arm in a gesture of introduction towards a row of dilapidated boats resting on chocks along the west side of the desert-like expanse of Harbour House Marina, in Grand Cayman.

"This is where all the drug boats are stored when they've been confiscated by the government."

The midday November sun blazes down. In the shimmering heat we wander along the row of broken dreams: small sailboats, home-built boats, antique boats—all in degrees of disrepair with vestiges of yellow, plastic police tape attached. I shake my feet to loosen the gritty sand and chips of old anti-fouling paint working their way between my bare, sandaled toes and step over the old paint-rollers, brushes, sanding disks and beer cans littering the ground.

"Have all these boats been caught running drugs?"

"Yes. They've come from Panama en route to the USA. They come via the Cayman Islands to throw suspicion from their Panamanian roots." Robin rolls his eyes. "What the drug runners fail to realize is that the Cayman authorities are naturally distrustful of all vessels from Panama."

"What happens to them?"

"The crew is removed, tried and jailed; the cargo is disposed of and the boat is impounded."

I don't think Robin has driven me 8 km from town during our lunch-hour, just for an entertaining stroll in the sticky heat. I wait expectantly, head on one side and smile at him.

"A new yacht came in a while ago," he says, casually.

OK, now he *has* managed to tweak my interest. "What was it carrying?"

"Oh, 900 kilos of cocaine," he says nonchalantly, "worth US$172 million dollars."

"A hundred and seventy-two million dollars? My God! What happened to it all?"

"Ah ha! The police have it under lock and key, still wrapped in oilskin packages. They unloaded it at the government dock, motored the yacht round to North Sound and hauled it out at the Marina here."

For once I'm speechless: overloaded with information swirling in my brain. "So which one had all the cocaine on it?"

Robin darts a meaningful glance further along the row, but instead of telling me, he draws a small slip of paper from his pocket.

My life is about to change because of a three-sentence announcement in The Compass, our local newspaper:

> *FOR SALE by private tender: 17-metre yacht. Viewing at Harbour House Marina by arrangement with the Manager. Sealed bids to the Cayman Islands' Government offices by noon, December 1st, 1990.*

"So *this* is what it's all about. I thought you seemed extraordinarily well informed."

"I do my homework," says Robin looking off into the distance, "it won't do any harm to take a look at it. Let's get the keys from the manager."

"You mean we can go on board?" I glance behind as we walk back to the marina office, keen to know which vessel it is.

We poke our heads into the gloomy interior of the plywood and corrugated iron shack, thinly disguised as an office and boat supply shop. Slowly our eyes adjust. Crowded, dusty shelves support paints, resins, fibreglass, shackles, chains, nuts, bolts, zincs, tools, mouse traps and a few mouse droppings. A cat snoozes in a coil of rope on the floor. Roger, the manager, sits behind a desk littered with stained invoices and old coffee cups, the telephone to his ear.

Harbour House Marina

He drops the phone in its cradle and examines us. We must look incongruous. Robin, with his neatly-trimmed, brown hair and short beard, is dressed in grey pants and a white, short-sleeved shirt with the Caribbean Utilities Company (CUC) logo on the sleeve. He has a brightly-coloured bow tie—his personal trade mark. I'm wearing a summer dress suitable for the office, and sandals.

"You've come for the keys of the latest drug boat," Roger says in a rich Devonshire accent. I smile at him. Robin has obviously planned this meeting as a nice surprise for me. "Be careful," Roger continues, chuckling, "don't fall orf. We don't carry insurance for you, y'know!"

Outside, we squint from the brightness of the sandy yard and walk past the boats again. On our right are a couple of non-drug, long-term nautical inhabitants still waiting for work to be completed, long after money for restoration has run out. This time we walk further than before; past piles of rusting, corrugated iron, paint pots, old batteries, torn disposable overalls, cardboard and strips of paint-spattered masking tape. There's no end to the richness and diversity of the environment.

One man is spray-painting his boat. A cloud of spray hitch-hikes on the air and envelops us.

"Nothing toxic here." I smirk, but Robin's not listening.

"This is it!" His eyes are aflame as he points towards something the size of a dinosaur.

"My God! You've got to be kidding." We stand beneath it, dwarfed by the hull. The tip of the mahogany bowsprit at the front of the yacht is 4 metres above the ground. Orange streaks from rusty deck fittings stain the once-white hull and blue keel.

"What's it made of?" I ask, still stunned.

"Ferro cement."

"A concrete yacht! Won't that be a little heavy?"

"I'll have you know," replies Robin, "some very fine yachts have been made from ferro cement, especially in New Zealand."

Stepping away, I bend my head back as far I can to look at the masts. "My God!" I say again. My vocabulary is somewhat limited in times of stress. "How tall are those masts?" I feel a moment's unsteadiness as a small white cloud drifts past, giving me the impression the mast is slowly falling over. I put my hand out to touch Robin for support.

"The main mast is 18 metres," Robin is in his element, "the mizzen mast is only 12 metres. It's a ketch, you see."

I trail Robin round the vessel as he inspects the exterior. The stern is buried in a stand of mangrove trees and we have to fight our way through a tangle of scratching branches. A beautifully carved wooden nameplate spans the transom, showing the name and port of registry: *Cowes, Isle of Wight, England.*

"Uh-oh! I hope this is not an omen, Robin. You used to work in Cowes, Isle of Wight."

Robin continues with his own musings. "We'd have to re-register under the Cayman registry, of course. Let's find a ladder and go aboard."

Languishing in Drug Alley

The keys jingle in his hand as he searches the boatyard for a typical 'Caymanian' ladder—two 3-metre 2x4s with irregularly spaced pieces of wood nailed across, for steps. Whistling through his teeth, he leans the heavy construction against the hull, quickly climbs up and steps onto the deck. I follow, challenged by the wide spacing between the rungs and the need to clutch at my skirt.

Chained to the handrail at the stern is a rusty, fold-up bicycle that has seen better days. An ancient Zodiac inflatable dinghy wheezes its last breath as I poke its crumpled form with my foot. Interesting algae have colonized the puddles in the black fabric. I peer into the murky depths and can see squiggling creatures.

"The mosquito larvae like it here." I say, but Robin is busy.

"The equipment looks a bit grim, doesn't it?" I continue as I straighten up.

Against my better judgment, I'm beginning to feel a tiny bit interested in this leviathan and rather sad at the state of the gear.

Our tour of the deck starts on the starboard side. "Deck's recently been repainted," Rob observes, "and isn't it interesting that she has black masts."

"What's special about that?"

"They don't show up at night under searchlight; they're not so reflective as bright shiny aluminum if you're trying to avoid detection."

We step up 40 cm onto the upper deck, which forms the roof to the main cabins and to the midline of the yacht. The sails are still in place on the booms, but the black Sunbrella sail covers have chafed through where they are bound by rope lashings, exposing the sails to degrading sunlight. A couple of small heaps of guano on the deck indicate that some birds have found convenient roosts.

"They should have taken the sails off," Rob muses. "Hmmm. All the sail covers are black too!"

I stare up at the main mast again, towering aloft. "Hey Rob, it's got steps all the way up, can I climb it? There must be a heck of a view from up there."

"We're not doing any climbing before checking the state of the rigging wires supporting the masts," replies my ever-practical husband. "Anyway, you're wearing a dress."

At the bow, the anchor chain locker lid is set into the deck. Robin opens it and peers inside. "Lots of rusty anchor chain but no sign of an anchor."

"Come on!" I urge. "Let's look inside. I want to see what the accommodation is like."

"All in good time."

Robin continues his inspection, returning along the port side of the yacht. I should know by now, there's no way I can rush him, just because I want to satisfy my curiosity.

At the stern is the 'dog house' covering the deck steering station. It has a one-metre diameter spoked wheel, bound in fine rope and finished with a Gordian knot (see Glossary for terms). It is superb

Outer steering station   Companionway

craftsmanship—evidence of many hours at sea and much patience. Behind the wheel is a series of instruments I don't even ask about, for fear of a detailed description which will delay us.

"Shall I turn the wheel?" I'm eager to do something.

"Try it gently." Robin replies. "The rudder didn't look fouled when we were below, but you never know." I turn it as far as it will go to port, then to starboard and back to the middle.

"Three and a half turns each way," I report, "and the rudder is in midline position when the Gordian knot is at the top."

Hooray! At last he has completed his tour and inserts the key into the lock of the companionway cover. A couple of clicks release the lock and Rob pushes back the hatch top. He slides up the duck boards—which act in lieu of a hinged door to the interior of the vessel—and places them aside.

I can't explain it, but as I'm about to go inside, I feel a shift in my long-held negative opinion of boats. Not a tectonic shift, but a shift all the same.

Heat billows up from the interior accompanied by a strange, unpleasant smell—something mixed with diesel fumes.

"What's that?" I say, wrinkling my nose.

Robin is impervious to unworthy comments. Our eyes scan rapidly and eagerly as we cautiously step down the three-step ladder into the cockpit containing the inside steering station. Here there is a small traditional wooden wheel. The interior of the cabin is striking, crafted in polished mahogany; the bench seats on two sides look like church pews, although their royal-blue velvet seat cushions are tossed on top in an untidy pile.

"I love all this rich woodwork, it's really beautiful!" I say, as I run my hand along the silky contours.

Chart Table

Nautical charts and books of sailing instructions are strewn haphazardly on the chart table, with pens, pencils and scraps of paper everywhere. Cupboard doors hang open. A bundle of multicoloured electrical wires protrude from a control panel behind the chart table, like a bunch of tendons, veins and arteries left hanging, where equipment has been removed and the wires severed. A bicycle seat, flashlight, pop cans, tubs of bearing grease and a few baseball caps complete the scene.

"I guess it's too much to expect the drug police to put everything back in order when they've searched." I say.

Galley with remaining food

Two steps down from the inner steering station brings us to the galley and dining area. On the starboard side in the galley is a double stainless-steel sink, with crockery still in drying racks. There is a gimballed propane stove with pots and pans stored beneath. Above and behind the stove, small shelves are crammed with provisions: peanut butter, flour, cashews, parmesan cheese, herbs, salt, syrup, pancake mix, there's no end. Trails of food run everywhere, mixed with rodent droppings.

"Yuk, look at this," I say. On one of the counters a dirty fridge is bolted to the bulkhead.

Robin makes a brief inspection, not of the inside of the fridge, but of the back. "This is a special nautical fridge," he tells me, "it runs on either 12-volt batteries or bottled gas."

"Oh, perhaps we can clean it up, then." Opposite the fridge there's a new microwave oven set in mahogany surrounds. "This would be useful too," I say, this time to myself.

Captain's locker.

In the dining area across from the galley is a mahogany pedestal table fixed to the sole of the yacht. Set into the pedestal is a miniature mahogany door with antique brass fittings. This *Captain's locker* is stacked with partially full bottles of liquor—gin, vodka, rum, brandy and tequila.

"Hey, shall we have a drink?" I ask. "Maybe I could fix something to eat too if you're hungry. There's lots of food and we haven't had lunch yet."

Robin smiles indulgently and continues exploring. Moving forward, we find a single cabin on the starboard side. Sliding open the louvered wooden door reveals a comfortable-looking bunk, again finished in polished wood. A non-opening port light lets in the sunshine. Bedding and clothes are strewn on the bed and tumble onto the floor, books fill the shelves of the cork-lined walls and a goose-necked reading lamp sticks out over the bunk.

"Just imagine lying here reading when you're off watch—that would suit me." I say.

"OK. If you like that, wait till you see this." Robin says as he peers through a narrow open door opposite the single cabin. I squeeze past him and look in. A splendid turquoise half-bath claims pride of place, complete with a showerhead. There's also a little stainless steel sink and a toilet. "Nothing but the best for you," he continues, "you can even have baths!"

Turquoise half-bath

"This is great! I'd thought life on board had to be Spartan, but I think I could handle this."

A few steps further and we are in the forward stateroom in the bow of the yacht. A double bunk fills the starboard side, with drawers and doors to storage space underneath and on the port side a tabletop and more storage. At the far end of the cabin is a child-sized door set 35 cm off the sole. I cautiously open the door and see coats and clothes hanging inside.

I lean into the locker, push the clothes aside and feel beyond. There's a 60- by 45-centimetre hole in the wall, into a further storage area, maybe it is the sail locker. If I climb in past the clothes, I wonder if I might find myself in the Narnia of my childhood.

I return to the present. Everywhere brass fittings and handles compliment the rich woodwork. "There was no expense spared when this was built. It's lovely."

We retrace our steps over the shiny, cork-tiled floors back up the two steps to the inner steering station. Robin lifts two large brass rings set into the floor and removes two floor sections, creating a 2-by 1.5-metre hole, revealing a massive new Volvo engine. He whistles, hops down into the 'engine room' and looks around. "Good God!" he says. "There's enough power here—165 horse power and it's turbocharged. I bet the drug-runners put this in so they could outrun the authorities."

While he is admiring the engine and checking the layout, I go towards the stern, past the steps that would return us to the deck, to the last area to explore. Two steps down, on the port side, is the louvered door of a wood-panelled two-piece bathroom. The toilet is set high up on a pedestal.

"Hey Robin, guess what? We've got a *real* throne in here! Why is it so high off the floor, with a step up to it?"

Robin peeps in. "Well if it weren't, it would be below sea level and the ocean would siphon into the yacht through the heads."

O.K., I'm not a nautical engineer, but it makes sense. I'm learning.

Together we gaze into a spectacular master stateroom spanning the stern of the yacht. Beneath the tangled mess of clothes, bedding and books, there is a large double bunk, with inset mahogany cupboards beneath, spilling out more books and sailing directions for many parts of the globe. There is also an upholstered seating area for five to six people and a large clothes closet. Two portholes on each side of the stateroom have little curtains to draw across when in port. It is all so charming, like a miniature house.

Am I beginning to get a warm fuzzy feeling already? Did I say *we've* got a real throne? This is ridiculous; no way could we afford to buy something like this under normal circumstances. Yet I start to picture it as our home. Settle down, I tell myself, this is a pipe dream and anyway, it won't belong to us.

Back on deck, I force myself to concentrate on a few areas of peeling paint and flaking varnish, and imagine all the renovation work that needs to be carried out.

"I suppose we'd better get back to work," I say as Robin re-secures the lock on the hatch. "We're really late."

He descends the ladder ahead of me, as a gentleman should. We take a last look from below, and then return the keys to Roger.

"Had a good look then, did you?" Roger is trying to gauge Robin's feelings but he's wasting his time. Robin's expression is not easily read.

"Yep," Rob answers, "thanks for letting us see her." Now it's Robin's turn to probe. "What sort of price do you think she'll go for at tender?"

"Ah well," Roger appears lost in thought for a moment, scratching his chin. He then throws out a preposterously high figure. I say nothing.

"And where are the anchors and radar?" Robin asks.

"That's a long story," says Roger, "I'll tell you when you're here another time."

We get back into the oven-hot car, turn on the air conditioning and head for town.

"What do you think?" Robin asks.

"Well, if you want to put in a really low bid and you can afford it, go ahead," I say, and put all thoughts of boats out of my mind.

Robin obviously does a lot more research and thinking than I do. Unlike me, he's not impulsive. A few days later, as we leave for work, he casually says, "Tomorrow's the deadline for the sealed bid for the yacht. I'm going to write a cheque for 10% of my bid price and take it down to the Government Offices today."

Is this what he really wants? Could I feel happy owning a boat? What a liability! Why am I even considering it? If I'm honest, I'm disturbed at the superior feeling it's giving me.

"OK," I say, "that's fine. Don't forget to be home in good time tonight. We're going out to dinner."

Harbour House Marina view to North Sound

2

A Monstrous Christmas Gift

Thursday, December 20th rolls around and we're not prepared for Christmas. When it's hot and sunny all the time, it's difficult to get into the mood, even though our children have arrived for the Christmas holidays. I've taken the day off work, to do some baking.

"Can we borrow your truck and go diving?" Billy, our son aged 21, is up bright and early and has decided the order of the day. He is entering the Air Force as an officer, and while waiting for his call-up papers, has been working as a waiter in a restaurant in Waterloo, Ontario. Lisa, our daughter, and her boyfriend, Pete, both 22, have just arrived from university in Guelph, Ontario. With only a couple of weeks at their disposal, they need to put their days in Cayman to good use. Scuba diving in these beautiful waters is top priority for all of them.

Today is also decision day on the sealed bids for the yacht. We have money tied up in the bidding procedure, money which I could very well use for this Christmas season. I'd like to buy diving accessories for the kids. It's been niggling at the back of my mind, so at 10:00 a.m. I call the government office to see if we can pick up our deposit.

A lady with a sense of humour—a rare commodity among some government officers—answers the telephone and I explain my plight.

"Yes," she says, rustling through some papers, "I understand. There was a decision made this morning about the tenders. Just a minute and I'll check the file."

"Uh—no," she says, "you can't have your money returned."

"But it's Christmas!" I plead.

"Sorry, in fact you owe us money; your husband was the successful bidder. We need the balance of the funds by 31st December. You are also responsible for the Marina storage fees immediately. I hope you enjoy your yacht and your Christmas."

I know instantly that my life will never be the same. Where is a massive yacht going to fit into my world? The children are out, so I can't tell them the news. I'll just have to call Robin straight away.

"Hi Mags!" says Rob's voice at the other end of the line. "What's up?" I have his attention, as I rarely call him at work.

"Are you sitting down?" I ask, my heart thumping. "Get ready for a shock."

"What's the matter?"

"You're the owner of a huge yacht."

"Really?" Robin's voice rises an octave. "That's great!" He knows I wouldn't play a cruel joke on him.

I pitch the next question. "Does that mean that now we own the yacht and everything that is on it?"

"Yup—well, when we've paid the balance."

"Then we'd better get to the marina as soon as possible to tell Roger, before anything disappears from it, now it belongs to us," I say. It's never too soon for practicalities.

"You're right. I'll take a cheque to the government offices at lunch time and get home a soon as I can. We can go before it gets dark and then we can start inventorying it at the weekend." Now it's Robin who's racing ahead.

Against my better judgement, I'm excited. We suddenly belong to the 'yachting set', a group of people I'd hitherto thought were rather overtly affluent. They, of course, won't know that we don't really belong in their bracket. Our new status could be hard to live up to.

Robin arrives home with a fistful of boat papers and we start sorting through them, piecing information together. When the kids come in an hour later they whoop, holler and dance around when we give them the news—they have a million questions. At 5:00 p.m. we're heading to the marina, crammed in our Nissan Patrol.

Roger, the manager, has already been notified that we're the new owners and has a bill prepared for the moorage fees. Sometimes he can be really on the ball. "You'll have some fun with her," he says knowingly, "just a bit of work to do."

We drive through the marina and pull in between two neighbouring boats.

"Which one is it?" the kids are impatient.

We walk up to our acquisition and pat her bulky cement hull. "This one!"

"Holy Shit!" says Billy, his eyes like archery targets.

"You're kidding!" says Lisa. "You don't even sail, Mum!"

"Wow, this is great!" Pete, who has the most sailing experience, is already assessing cruising possibilities.

Saturday can't come soon enough, so we can see what we have and start cleaning up. In fact, not everyone waits till Saturday. At supper on Friday, Billy admits that they've all been to the marina and climbed aboard to inspect everything possible without actually going inside.

I don't have to drag anyone out of bed in the morning. Breakfast is early, then boxes, garbage bags and all the cleaning materials we can lay our hands on are stuffed into Robin's car and my truck. I include notepads and pens for list making and the boys pack lunch and beer into coolers.

This is the first of hundreds of trips to the marina we'll be making over the next year.

It's another clear day and not yet too hot. On board, Lisa and I start with all the clothing, bed linen, towels and sundry rubbish. Stripping the beds and emptying all the closets and drawers, we create two massive piles. One is to throw away immediately and consists of unappealing items, like pillows, toiletries and underwear. The other pile is for 'launder then check', including sheets, towels, blankets and good clothing, like T-shirts and shorts.

"You're not thinking of keeping any of that are you?" Billy is horrified when he sees our efforts. He wants nothing to do with it.

"Suit yourself." I tell him. Lisa and I can see the bargains that are to be had. So now we only need to share stuff between four of us, not five. The former crew really had good taste in designer casual wear.

Billy and Pete work on the noxious job of bagging and throwing out all the food. After running extension cables to the nearest power point, they use the yacht's shop-vac to suck up trails of flour, nuts, other packaged foods and, of course, the ubiquitous rodent droppings. Canned food gets tossed, as do all the half-full liquor bottles from the Captain's locker. It's a pretty disgusting job and although we've thrown open all the hatches, it's hotter than Hades inside. At least that's the excuse given for the copious amounts of beer being quaffed.

Robin is busy boxing up books, sailing directions, charts, tools, boat spares, rigging spares, engine spares, lifejackets—everything that will be useful to us in our new life. It all has to be transported home for assessment, logging and storage, to give us room to work in the yacht.

We've been hard at work all day and we still haven't emptied the interior. At dusk we head home to get cleaned up.

"Anyone for a gin and tonic?" Pete offers to mix us a drink to sip while we're getting showered and dressed to go out for a celebratory dinner at a Mexican restaurant. The table talk accompanying our Coronas and enchiladas is, 'the sailing adventures we will have'. Funny how we've managed to embrace a new life, just like that.

Sunday finds us eagerly returning to the Marina and Robin and the boys take the sails off the booms and pack them. As befits a heavy vessel weighing 36,000 kg (40 tonnes) the sails are correspondingly large, heavy and difficult to handle. Lisa and I soldier on below decks.

"What's that gluey smell?" Lisa asks when we're poking around in the forward cabin.

"It's what gave away the crew," I say, "and perhaps what saved the yacht from being totally wrecked by the drug squad. In Panama, an artificial dividing wall was built in the sail locker in the bow. The drugs were loaded through a hole cut in the deck into the concealed compartment. The hole in the deck was filled in and painted over and they made a panel to hide an access hole at the back of this closet. They glued on thick cork tiles to match the lining of the hull, to disguise the entrance. Amazing that we can still smell the contact cement, isn't it?"

Lisa frowns. "What happens if we find any more drugs?"

"I don't think we will. Drug dogs have been over the entire yacht, but if we do find anything, then we hand it in. If there is any more, I certainly hope we find it here in Cayman and not when we're entering another port."

"It's not funny, Mum."

"It was certainly quite a haul and somebody put a lot of money and effort into making this a drug-boat, what with the huge engine and repainting the waterline."

"What do you mean repainting the waterline?"

"Oh, didn't Rob show you? Come outside and have a look."

We climb out of the confines of the yacht and down the Caymanian ladder, glad of a break and some air.

Drug locker

"Come here you guys!" Lisa shouts to Pete and Billy, "Look at this."

It is clearly visible. The waterline at the bow was repainted about 20 cm higher than the natural waterline and slants back to rejoin the original about 4 metres towards the stern. Even thick applications of antifouling paint haven't fully disguised it.

"This way it wouldn't be immediately obvious that the yacht was nose-heavy," says Robin. "With 900 kilos of cocaine in the bow, it substantially alters how she sits in the water."

"They certainly tried to think of everything," says Pete.

"Yeah, but I guess they were too cocky, believing the Cayman authorities were naive," Billy chips in, "they obviously didn't do their homework. I imagine every boat coming directly here from

Repainted waterline

Panama gets the third degree."

At the end of an exhausting day, most of the interior and the deck lockers are now empty. Our house and carport are filled with boxes and gear, all smelling of diesel fumes. It's hard to believe all this stuff fitted on the yacht.

In the evening, after a take-away supper of some particularly fine Jamaican jerk chicken, we sit around with beers, musing over the day's activities.

"So who actually were the crew?" The kids are keen for the full story.

"Well," I say, repeating some of the history Robin has researched and information we've gained from newspaper reports, "as far as we know, they were all Americans from Florida. Two fellows and one girl: the captain, Kevin Shawn McNulty; Alfredo Carmona and Frances Fox. They posed as friends out cruising. Hence the womanly touches, like the artificial flower displays, pretty curtains and wall paper on some walls, which were intended to lend an innocuous air to the ship's complement."

Robin takes a drink of beer and continues the tale. "The girl, Frances, tried to say she didn't know what was going on and only found out when the drugs were loaded in one of the San Blas Islands and she could do nothing about it because she was not in control. Judge Harre didn't wear that. He said that it defied belief that a crew member would be recruited in a haphazard fashion without some confirmation of the crew member's commitment to the enterprise."

"Where did they get the yacht from?" asks Pete.

"We're not sure of that yet," says Robin.

"How did they actually get caught?" Pete continues.

"There's more than one story going around about that," replies Robin. "One was that the authorities had a tip-off from somewhere, another is that the harbourmaster on duty was suspicious of the way the yacht was sitting in the water, and a third was that the customs officers boarding the vessel had a drug dog with them that marched smartly to the forward locker and just sat there. The officers could smell contact cement, from the recently glued cork tiles. The last theory was that the captain, in return for a break, owned up and told them what drugs they were carrying and where they were."

"There was probably a bit of truth in all the stories," I add.

"So what happened to them, where are they now?" Lisa asks.

"They went to court, were tried and convicted of drug-smuggling," continues Robin. "Judge Harre sentenced them all to 11 years with no parole, for possession with intent to supply 900 kilos of cocaine."

"They're here right now, just up the road in Northwood Prison," I add, "probably having a ball. Northwood is affectionately called a holiday home. It's fairly well populated and every weekend families go to visit their nearest and dearest and have a bit of a party."

"Well who stole all the equipment off the yacht when it was in the Marina?" asks Billy, frowning, "they had no right."

"The marina gave us a copy of the initial inventory so we know we've lost radios, radar, another dinghy, outboard motor and anchors," says Robin. "But it's really rather funny. Several months ago, the police launch went out through the North Sound passage. As you know, the passage has a severe dog-leg in the middle and the marker lights aren't anything too special. When the launch returned, it missed one of the outer marker buoys and powered in over the reef. Well, it didn't get far as it blasted right up on top of the coral and sat there, for all to see.

"They were embarrassed, naturally, so radioed to someone to come and pull them off the reef immediately before they became the laughing stock of the island. Now there is minimal tidal difference in Cayman, perhaps 30 to 40 cm, and it was low tide. Instead of waiting for the tide at its height, a cable was hooked to the launch and it was dragged off, lacerating the hull. As soon as it cleared the reef it sank in the channel, in 6 metres of water. Not good for the electronic equipment."

I take up the story. "Apparently the Brits gave them a new launch but there was no money in the budget for fancy electronic equipment. Then along came the drug boat with all her gear and the local wharf rats swarmed her and stripped off all the electronics, together with anything else they fancied. They rationalized that the yacht belonged to the government, so it was OK."

"How could they do that?" Billy thumps his beer down on the table. He has a strong sense of ethics and has a hard time believing that people in authority can manipulate the circumstances to make dishonesty appear honest.

"Quite easily," says Robin, shuffling some leaflets he's been looking at on his lap, "they have ultimate power. We know exactly what's been taken, of course, because of the yacht inventory. This is why we've spent two days removing everything from the yacht, except the standby generator and that's chained down. The really amusing thing is," he continues, holding out the handful of papers to Billy, "we have all the instructions and installation diagrams."

"So what happened to all the cocaine?" Lisa asks.

"Ah ha," says Robin, "officially, it was all taken to the municipal dump and burned in front of the MLAs, the Governor of the Island and select invited guests."

"They must have been as high as kites if they were standing downwind," says Pete, "and unofficially?"

"It's rumoured that some found its way back onto the streets. With such huge sums involved, it must have been very tempting. I don't suppose we'll ever really know."

"It may not seem much like Christmas," adds Pete, "but this has got to be the best Christmas present you guys have ever had!"

"Let's hope you're right." I say.

3

Marina Rats and Other Low Life

Christmas is over. Lisa and Pete have reluctantly returned to Guelph and we throw ourselves energetically into our task. We have persuaded Billy to stay and work for us on the yacht, rather than return to wait tables in Canada and sleep on the floor of a friend's apartment. We get the better part of the deal as we have such a lot to do and he is a willing worker.

One disadvantage to having the boat on land, is that we're not the only ones who can board the vessel. We are host to a legion of cockroaches, one of the creatures I most dislike. I set down a batch of roach-bait cans under stairs, inside lockers, under the sinks and in the engine compartment and hope for the best.

Unfortunately, they're not our only uninvited guests. While searching in a locker for some rags to use, I come across a fluffy nest with tiny babies snuggled inside.

"Robin, quick, come and look, I've found the sweetest little black mice in a nest!"

"Black mice?" Robin rushes to where I'm standing admiring the little ones curled together like chubby punctuation marks. "Don't touch them, they're not black mice, they're baby rats."

He quickly pulls on some thick work gloves, grabs the nest and takes it down into the bush and despatches the young.

"That's bad news," he grumbles, "it means there's a mother somewhere and you know how quickly these things reproduce."

We think no more about it for a week or two, until one Saturday morning we arrive and throw back the hatch cover and are met by a disgusting smell.

"What the hell is that?" I ask, sniffing around.

"Something's decomposing." Rob frowns in disgust. "I wonder if it's a rat?"

"It reminds me of that putrefied turtle we had in Libya." says Bill. "You know, you brought the dead one home from the beach and put it inside the front gate and thought the ants would clean it up. People used to cross the street rather than walk by."

We split up and start checking lockers and storage areas.

"I've found it!" I say, looking into the locker which housed the baby rats in their nest. "God, it stinks."

"Here it is!" I can hear Robin's muffled voice coming from the stern heads.

"There's one in the bilge." Billy brings his great news.

In total we find four decomposing bodies, but it is a mystery as to why they died. We didn't set any traps or rat bait. Perhaps they ate the cockroach bait, or ate the cockroaches which had eaten the bait. Either way, we're glad they're dead. All we have to do is get rid of the lingering smell.

A few days later, instead of improving, the smell is getting worse. We rip out all the floors of the cupboards and remove the heavy, insulated covers to expose the engine.

"I thought so," says Billy, who has volunteered to jam himself in the engine compartment to check. "I can see another body under the Volvo." He scoops it up with rubber-gloved hands, drops it into a bag then continues searching with his flash lamp.

I can't take the stench any more and have to rush out on deck before I lose my stomach contents. Soon Bill emerges and he's retching.

"Oh God," he says, "I've found another one, but I'm not sure I can reach it. I have to press my face right up against the engine and I'll have to pull it out at eye level with a hook. Something like a scuba tank J-rod would be good."

Robin finds a suitable hook and poor Billy disappears once more in the bowels of the yacht. Some time later he re-emerges with a foul-smelling polythene bag.

"The worst thing was, Mum," he explains, "when I hooked into it I pulled the head off and I could only tease out little bits of putrid meat and fur and limbs, it was so friable. Then I had to check it to see if I'd got it all." He always did rather like biology at university.

The 7th and final rat is located in a locker on the deck. Now we well understand the origin of the phrase *I can smell a rat*.

We clear out all roach bait and decide to bring 'TP' (Tropical Pussycat) to live on board, to act as the RRCO—Resident Rodent Control Officer. Despite our concerns that she might run away, she settles in well and immerses herself in her job.

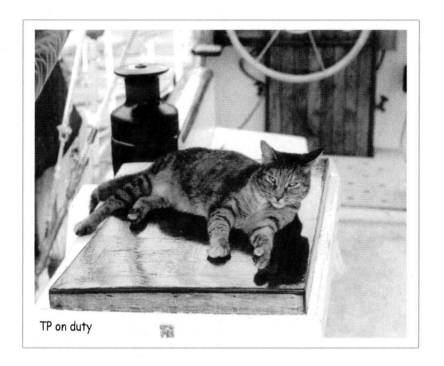

TP on duty

Our first official visitors are Chris and Nik van den Bok, my bosses at Caribbean Publishing Company, complete with a video camera for the 'before' record. They are the start of a long list of visitors intrigued with the yacht, its history and our ambitious restoration schedule. It's amazing how they can watch us work and happily join us in a beer or glass of wine, without feeling the slightest urge to pick up a tool and scrape! It's a pleasure to see them all and to know they're interested.

The Marina is a blend of fascinating characters. The qualifications for working here are various, including a desire for a slow pace of life; the ability to drink Old Milwaukee for breakfast, lunch and dinner; preparedness to use ancient unguarded equipment in the machinery shed; adeptness with such things as oxyacetylene and, above all, an irrepressible sense of humour.

Rudi, a well muscled, shy 'Honduranian', lives aboard a little vessel by the harbour wall with his girlfriend. They have no running water or sanitation. He works for Roger and also for himself, on the side, in order to save money to send back to his wife and children in

Honduras. His burnished brown skin is complimented by the gleaming, chunky gold chains circling his bull neck and the gold glinting in his smile. Rudi is one of the few who saves Old Milwaukee for supper, probably because his girlfriend provides him with plenty of real calories in the shape of food. She also always keeps him dressed in neatly-pressed khaki shirt and pants.

Rudi performs many tasks around the Marina. In fact he's a skilled craftsman in numerous areas. He drives the Travelift to haul boats into and out of the water and we've seen him in the bush, oxyacetylene torch in hand, converting an old fridge side into a hood for his car.

One day while I'm at work, Billy is toiling inside the galley on a thankless task, trying to chip unsavoury one-inch ceramic tiles and grout from the walls and counter surfaces. Without warning he is pitched off his feet and the yacht is rocking, as if in the grips of a major earthquake.

He rushes on deck as the yacht continues to pitch violently and sees the Travelift on the starboard side. He races forward shouting, "Stop! Stop! Stop!"

Rudi has snagged the bowsprit side-stay with the Travelift and is frantically shifting from forward to reverse in a desperate attempt to free himself, oblivious to the fact that someone is on board. He almost falls out of his driving seat with fright when he sees Bill.

"What the hell do you think you're doing?" Billy shouts.

Rudi sits shamefaced, admitting defeat, then together they devise a plan to extricate the Travelift from the side stay.

"God, Mum!" Billy says when I arrive after work, "I thought he was going to pull us off the chocks. Come and look, I think he's cracked the bowsprit. This crack wasn't here before was it?"

The bowsprit, formed from a one-piece slab of mahogany, measures 30 cm wide, 10 cm thick and 4 metres long. It has a crack running from the side stay attachment to the pulpit attachment.

"No, it's a new crack—it's pink inside, not weathered, so it's newly exposed wood. We'd better report it to Roger."

I exert a little friendly pressure and Roger humours us and comes to see. Billy is looking like thunder.

"Nooh, not our responsibility," attempts Roger after rubbing a well-practiced thumb over it, "it's an old crack."

"I don't think so," I say calmly, "if you look closely the crack is pink and there's no flaking of varnish along the crack line. We'll expect to be reimbursed for the replacement."

Roger bristles.

"That bow sprit supports the self-furling jib, which acts as the forestay for the main mast," I continue, although he knows this perfectly well, but probably hopes I don't. "If the bow sprit breaks we'll be dismasted."

Roger mumbles something about coming to an agreement.

"Yes, we will." I state firmly.

The situation is defused. "Don't worry Bill, they'll pay for it, but we really don't need the extra work. We'll have to import a piece of mahogany."

Rudi remains sheepish and aloof when we see him, but we continue to be friendly. He's a nice guy—an intriguing part of our neighbourhood.

Work moves along slowly on the longest and worst job of all, scraping off the old blue anti-fouling bottom paint, centimetre by centimetre, metre by metre. It's a soul-destroying task, as all the little dimples and dents in the ferro hull must have individual attention. We wear overalls, gloves and face masks, but still the toxic dust covers us. For weeks our bath and shower water is cobalt blue. Billy toils on, with intermittent help from Robin and me.

A constant joy for Bill at the Marina are the puppies. A bitch has found it a safe place to give birth. As soon as they are big enough, every day they greet Billy ecstatically. They romp and play, are cuddled and cradled and sleep in the shade of the hull while he works. They pull the power cable around like a snake, run off with paintbrushes and sandpaper—every mischief they can devise.

Two months into our restoration, Billy receives his call-up papers. He and I make a trip to Miami, Florida to shop for everything he needs and all too soon he has gone. We'll miss the hundreds of hours of work, like those spent on the hull and the galley; the painstaking sanding of all the paint from the mahogany portholes and rub-strips and, of course, ridding us of the rats. All the nastiest jobs he tackled happily, often in the suffocating heat and without complaint.

Things are quiet around the house and yacht for a couple of weeks and we have to readjust to our extended workload. There's no more night-diving for me either now Billy's gone. Others in the Marina miss him too. The growing puppies rush to greet the truck, but wander off when Billy doesn't get out.

Billy and puppy

Not all the visitors we receive in the Marina are known to us. One Saturday, Rob is happily installing a new Northern Lights standby generator and I'm busy mixing some of the two-part Philadelphia Blue resin that we're using to coat the ferro cement keel, for good protection. I can only mix up two tablespoons at a time, because the temperature is a lot higher than 21° C and the mix cures in about 15 minutes. Applying it with a scraper, I can cover a 30-centimetre square before it chemically hardens. Our keel is 85 square metres, so I have many days' work ahead of me.

The mix is just ready when a large man with a Dutch accent comes along and starts to chat. I excuse myself and continue with my task for a few minutes. Our visitor, a minister of religion, has a disturbing request.

"I'm a prison visitor," he tells us, "and I regularly visit the captain of this vessel at Northwood Prison."

We're shocked. What on earth is he doing here?

"Captain McNulty has asked me to bring you a message. He would like you to visit him in prison."

I feel as if I've been doused with a bucket of cold water. What possible reason could he have for wanting to see us?

The minister asks us to consider the request and let him know the answer. He then walks away, leaving us staring at each other in disbelief.

"Is this legitimate, or sinister?" I say. "Do you suppose he's going to tell us about more drugs?"

"I'll think about it," says Robin, "but I don't like the sound of it. How suspicious is it going to look if we go to visit the captain of the drug boat that we've just bought?"

The weeks rush by and Robin ticks the jobs off his long list: renew electrical wiring; overhaul the engine; recast the rear portion of the keel and remove a fake waste-handling system.

I reupholster all the sitting areas, including cutting new seat cushions and mattresses from foam. I sew matching curtains, mend worn sail covers and make new ones. I also repair sails, using the Sailrite sewing machine we ship in from Miami.

Robin checks the rigging minutely, laboriously washes it all with acid and replaces a couple of turnbuckles. Now it is safe to climb the steps of the masts. What a wonderful view we have when we stand 23 metres above the ground at the top of the main mast! North Sound in one direction and across the island to the sea at South Sound.

Acid washing the rigging

If we have any energy left after supper in the evenings, I sort and catalogue the multitude of charts we have and Robin sorts through batches of papers. Gradually we piece together parts of the jigsaw of the yacht's history and also start planning our own first cruise across the South Pacific. It's all a game for me—we'll never actually do it.

"Well, it looks as if the yacht has been all round the world, but not with the three crewmembers who are in Northwood Prison." Robin tells me. "There are all sorts of papers from before their time. The yacht was built in the UK in 1978, and cruised round the world with a family on board. I think it was stolen in the Indian Ocean."

"What happens if the original owners ever find out and want the yacht back—are they the legal owners, or are we?"

"I wouldn't worry too much about that," he says, "we have legal title to it from the Cayman Government. Anyway, I would think if they had any insurance, they've long ago claimed the insurance money. I'm more concerned whether she'll be recognized in Panama. It is a singular design. Maybe the people who went to the trouble of making it suitable for drug-running will want it back and take it by force. The area's riddled with pirates."

It is fascinating unravelling the mystery, but I don't want to entertain the idea of being caught by an irate drug lord.

One evening Robin brings a large roll of paper into the living room and carefully opens it on the floor. It measures 4 by 2 metres.

"What's this?" I scrutinize the white markings on the dark blue paper.

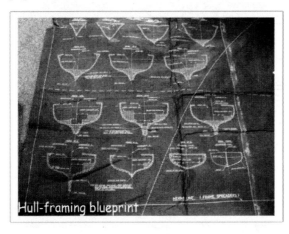

Hull-framing blueprint

Rob is grinning. "It's the blueprint of the boat's hull framing! We are the happy owners of a New Zealand-designed Hartley Tahitian, only this blueprint is of the 13.7-metre version and ours is a stretch model. It's nice to know what make she is."

A few days later, the minister turns up again and I can't say we welcome him wholeheartedly. He repeats the request, yet he won't tell us *why* the captain wants to see us. We had put it out of our minds, but now that he has reintroduced the topic, we are feeling distinctly uncomfortable about the whole thing. I wish he would just leave us alone. Robin politely asks him not to bother us again, but we can't help wondering what is going on. It will be good when we move away from the marina.

This Saturday is a milestone for us. We have finished the

preparation of the hull and are ready to start applying the white epoxy top coat. The two parts must be mixed together well, poured into a tray and quickly applied with rollers, before the paint cures. It is incredibly sticky. Robin is more successful at applying it than I am, possibly because it takes such a lot of muscle power to overcome the friction, in order to get it on the hull. The temperature is far too high and curing is too rapid, but we have no choice but to continue. So I mix and Robin applies. By the end of the day we think we've done well on the first side. It looks superb.

On Sunday morning we are keen to look at the results of our handiwork and walk round to the port side of the yacht.

"Oh no!" I have to bite my lip to stop it trembling. The hull is sporting a rash of bubbles. "Oh Robin, what's happened?"

Robin's shoulders droop. He inspects one of the blisters. "I'm not sure; it seems as if it's cured on the outside but not on the inside. I don't know if it's temperature and humidity related, or whether it wasn't perfectly prepped underneath."

There are more than a hundred small blisters, over an area of about two square metres.

"We'll just have to scrape them off, fill the holes, rub them down and repaint," he says.

It is a laborious, disheartening job, but thankfully, the rest of the paint looks great. Subsequent coats go on without a hitch, so the bubbles remain a mystery. During the painting I only once drop the whole tray of paint. Robin glances down from his painting position on the scaffolding, says nothing, then returns to his task. It is an atrocious mess to clean up.

During the many hours I spend working alone on the hull while Robin is at work, I often have the benefit of advice from Emile. He's a tall Romanian Canadian with curly grey hair and is the sign-writer in the boatyard. He also knows everything about all aspects of boat building and repair and freely shares his opinion. I admit that my knowledge is inferior to everyone in the marina—I'm not a sailor or a boat-builder—so I'm easy prey for do-gooders. I really *do* like hearing the opinions of others on the job at hand, but once Emile starts talking, there's no stopping him. At first I listen with rapt attention, but after fifteen minutes or so, I have to make my excuses and continue with my work.

Funnily enough, he never bothers Robin. Emile does give me a compliment one day though, when he says I'm the '*hardest workingest woman he's ever seen*'.

Mostly, the marina workers let me get on with my business—I'm allowed to use any of the tools and equipment in the big sheds. It is a constant battle, though, to keep the use of the large oil drums and planks, or the scaffolding for the few days of hull painting. Often our first chore of the day is to round it all up before we can start.

Mr. Miller, a dour, elderly gentleman well over 70, is the antifouling painter on many of the vessels. I can see him from the corner of my eye, watching me work without making comment as I apply masking tape for the thin grey stripes I want on the white hull just above the waterline.

Centimetre by centimetre, I pull out the tape and stick it to the hull, making sure I follow the original line. Mr. Miller can't tolerate watching any longer. He strides over and without a word snatches the masking tape out of my hands, unravels it in an expansive gesture, strides about six metres along the hull and slaps it on.

"You can't do it bit by bit," he spits out and promptly stomps off leaving me to continue. He's never spoken to me before and has never said a word since. But, as I say, I like advice.

It is November 1991, and we have completed the major tasks necessary before we leave the marina and hit the water. As well as the boat work, we have to pack up and leave our rental house so the landlord can move back in. This time we're renting an apartment at Governor's Harbour because it has a dock where we can berth our 36,000 kg gem. It will be wonderful to have the yacht right outside our patio doors, so we can spend even more time working on her, without all the travelling.

The new bowsprit is finally being installed and bolted through the ferro cement, using two kilos of special caulk to seal it to the deck. We've renamed the yacht *Orca* after the whales around the west coast of Canada, as she is black and white, bulky and of a similar shape to a killer whale.

She is now registered on the Cayman registry and proudly flies the Cayman flag from the mahogany and brass flagpole at the stern. Emile does a superb job of sign-writing *Orca* on port and starboard bows in black, and *Orca George Town CI* on the transom in black and gold lettering. He adds the gold as a gift for me. It looks magnificent!

Bow signwriting

Robin has re-commissioned the engine and it is running smoothly. All that is left before launching is to apply the antifouling paint.

"Shall I call the Police and ask for the equipment back that they took from *Orca*?" I ask Robin. We have spent so much money so far, it would be good if we could get back the radios and radar.

"Yes, why not, it can't hurt."

"Good Morning," I say positively when I'm put through to the right police department. "My name is Maggi Ansell. I wonder if you remember the drug boat that went to auction last December?"

"Yes."

"You remember the accident with the police launch on the reef and a lot of the equipment was commandeered from the drug boat to furnish the new launch?"

"Yes."

"Well. we now own the yacht. Did you ever install any of the equipment of the new launch?"

"No." He's not being very forthcoming.

"So, as we have all the installation diagrams and operation manuals for the equipment, I wonder if we could have it back?"

I hear a chuckle at the end of the line, before he answers.

"No."

There's not much more to say, but I say it. "Well, if you change your mind, this is my telephone number and we could come to the police warehouse and pick it up."

I never receive that call, but one police officer does come to the marina and gives us something very valuable. It is a picture of the unloading of the drugs with the hundreds of colourful waxed packages being pulled from their hiding place and stacked on the quay.

Unloading drugs

4

Launch Parties and New Docks

Launch Day! How we've longed for this. Monday 23rd December 1991, just one year after we acquired the yacht.

Our bowsprit negotiations with Roger come to a satisfactory conclusion when he deducts $800 from our last bill for marina fees, so we are happy.

It is such a momentous time that we organize a party. Invitations go out to friends and acquaintances who have visited us at the marina during the year and cheerfully watched our progress.

Robin takes the day off to get things ready. I'm detailed to be in charge of bringing the 'bar' and food in the back of my Patrol.

Ready to roll

At noon our friends arrive. A lot of Robin's colleagues at CUC have contacted me in advance to see if I will lend them bowties without Robin's knowledge. We have a hasty bowtie-tying session before they present themselves. One or two end up looking more like aeroplane propellers, but the intent of support is there. Robin is so involved with *Orca* and the tasks at hand that I'm not sure he recognizes they are wearing his 'signature ties' until much later.

The Travelift is positioned round the yacht and the giant strops secured under her belly. Four or five friends are on board with Robin, to man the fenders and throw mooring ropes. The rest of us watch, drink and take photos. With Roger in the driving seat—this trip is too important to trust to Rudi—the strops are tightened, the last chocks knocked away and a cheer goes up from the onlookers.

"Wagons roll!" *Orca*, at the upper end of the weight range for the Travelift, slowly progresses across the boatyard to the launching slip. Cautiously, Roger positions the lift straddling the slipway—there are only a few centimetres to spare on either side and he doesn't want an unscheduled entry into the water, especially with an audience. Peering out from the middle of the drinking crowd, I watch Orca lowered into the water, my fingers at my mouth, while the others continue with their partying.

Moral support

Orca is floating free of the strops. Robin rushes from cabin to cabin below decks, to check that no water is entering though any of the stopcocks, but all is well and he returns topside, to oversee the mooring. The Travelift backs away and willing hands receive the mooring lines thrown from the deck and snug them up on the bollards on the dock.

Lining up the lift

I initiate the ritual of 'blessing' the vessel with champagne, spraying it over the hull, rather than smashing the bottle. I then leap aboard and fling my arms round Robin.

"We're floating, we're floating!" is all I can manage. Robin is grinning like an idiot, too overcome to say anything. It will be impossible for others to imagine how happy he is feeling, but *I* know. Designated bar tenders go into action opening bottles of Champagne—or whatever is the preferred tipple—for everyone to join in a toast. Our glasses are constantly refilled.

It's time for everyone to clamber on board and tour the interior. Food and drink are flowing freely, in every sense of the word and several people don't bother to return to work. Those who do have had a much-extended lunch hour. Heck, it's Christmas Eve tomorrow! People are lounging on the seats, making expansive gestures and slopping wine onto my new upholstery, but I'm too excited to care.

Some of the revellers drift away, leaving the stalwart. Robin, by this time being well fortified and deservedly relaxed, is ready to try the motoring capabilities of *Orca*. He offers them a trip, fires up the engine and motors a short way inland along the canal. It's a short way, because the canal becomes shallower and with a big 'clunk' *Orca* connects with an infamous rock. Nonplussed, our fearless captain executes a multiple-point turn in a restricted width of canal, testing the forward and reverse gears and finally moors in our appointed slot along the canal wall.

Orca is allowed to stay here for the next two weeks, to await the extraordinarily high tide we'll need to get over the extensive sandbar in North Sound, about one nautical mile from the entrance to the marina. It offers less than 1.8 metres of clearance at high tide. Although the difference between Cayman's tides is only a matter of 30 to 40 cm, a high tide will be invaluable as *Orca* has a 2.1-metre draft. The benefit to waiting is that it will provide us with a wonderful excuse for a full-blown party.

On 4th January, 1992, we arrive at the marina early. Our dock at Governor's Harbour is already decorated with black and white balloons, black and white streamers and tables set out under sun shades. The food is organized, drinks are on ice. We have boxes of black T-shirts and white T-shirts printed for the occasion with *Orca Launch Crew*. For us, it's a once-in-a-lifetime occasion.

Heading for home

Seven of our yacht club sailing friends act as 'launch crew' on board, and Robin's boss, Bruce, has offered to use his powerboat *North Star* to act as a support vessel. We arrange with him that if necessary, he'll take the end of our spinnaker halyard, motor off and use it to pull us over about 30° to reduce our draft.

Our new neighbour at Governor's Harbour offers to bring his triple-decker, 14-metre sport fishing vessel, so if necessary he can rush up and down creating a huge wash to help lift us over the bar! Who are we to turn down offers of help?

At the marina Robin is even quieter than usual, checking out the systems and preparing everything for our epic voyage.

"Ok, I guess this is it," he murmurs.

Uncharacteristically, I'm too nervous to say anything at all. I flit from place to place ineffectually. Fortunately, our crew is so experienced they just get on with the job at hand. Lines are cast off and slowly we glide along the canal.

Everything is going well as we approach the sandbar. At the first sign of drag, Robin uses full power and *Orca* dredges her way through the top layers of sand. Looking astern, we can see it churning in our wake. Robin continually checks the instruments for signs that the engine is overheating, but after a few minutes we break free and shortly the elevated engine temperature drops and we're clear.

"Hooray!" We whoop and cheer and holler and I break out the champagne—the rest will be plain sailing, or rather plain motoring. We only have 6 nautical miles to go across the sound to Governor's Harbour and our crew take turns helming.

This day ranks amongst the happiest of our lives. Months and months of hard work have paid off—we not only own a yacht, it is watertight too! Only 13 months ago, we had never

Happy Day

heard of a ferro-cement drug boat. I should never doubt Robin's determination and ability to complete a project. I love him so much for his strength of character. I hope I'll be an asset to him.

Our voyage is uneventful. Guests are arriving for the party on the dock and for the second time in two weeks Robin and I are floating with happiness. *Orca* has come home. The afternoon passes in a blur of food and drink and happy chatter peppered with advice and sailing stories from those who have gone before.

Once the excitement has passed, we realize there's still much to be accomplished before we are ready to start voyaging. One of the first jobs is to re-attach the self-furling gear which had to be disconnected for *Orca* to fit into the Travelift. The mounting point is way out on the end of the bowsprit.

Before we start, Robin asks, "Have you got the pin?"

"Yep," I say, patting the breast pocket of my shirt, "it's right here."

First we drag the heavy self-furling drum as close as possible to the required position and tie it off to the pulpit. Robin then grunts and heaves and grunts some more to get it perfectly lined up. I lean over the pulpit to get close to his ear, to give some advice.

"Plop!" My mouth falls open as I experimentally feel my breast pocket, hoping the pin is still there. It is a fruitless task, as I know it has dropped into the water and sunk without a trace in the silt below.

"Oh God! You *haven't* dropped the pin have you?" snarls Robin.

I try to think of an excuse for my carelessness, but none comes quickly to mind.

"I'm sorry," I say, with tears threatening, "it just slipped out."

"Bloody stupid place to put it, wasn't it?"

"Yes. Well next time, do the job yourself, if you're so clever."

I leave the battle area, distressed, but the pin is etched in my mind. I have a sneaking suspicion that I've seen a second pin with the boat spares we inherited, it's just a matter of locating it. I find the pin and we install it together—it's an impossible task to complete alone. This time it goes without a hitch and all is forgiven. I immediately order another spare from the manufacturers.

We happily slip into the routine of office work and boat work. One task I've set myself is to keep up with varnishing the dozens of metres of brightwork. To this end I buy gallons of varnish and in some places achieve nineteen coats. It looks magnificent. But nothing is safe from the relentless Caribbean sun which destroys hours of hard labour with ease. At first, I inspect the mahogany minutely every week and sand down and touch up as necessary, but it becomes evident that this will take the rest of my working life.

There has to be a better way.

"What can I do to protect the woodwork?" I idly ask Robin one day.

"Why don't you cover it?" Simply said, but expensive and time consuming. So I order a whole bolt of grey Sunbrella from Miami and make patterns for covering everything made from wood. It turns out to be a 'work in progress' for the next four years, as I have a multitude of other chores. I start by making covers for the highly-varnished wooden pods for the winches and the tops of the deck hatches. The downside, however, is that we only get to see the beautiful woodwork when we're actually sailing and the covers are off.

Just after we arrive at Governor's Harbour, we notice a couple on a yacht anchored some way off our dock among the few other boats moored there. We've watched them several times, rowing ashore in their dinghy and walking off. One evening we hail them and ask them to join us on board for a drink and snacks. Steve and Susie are from Australia—seasoned sailors in *Trochus*, an 8-metre Vega. After a few meetings with this delightful and knowledgeable couple, we offer the use of our rented facilities for laundry and showers, but they remain fiercely independent.

A trip to Miami gives us a respite from responsibilities. We visit boat shows, chart shops and boat chandlers; we buy gear, books, charts and storm sails and, my favourite, a hand-held GPS. We never once get near a regular mall—those days are over. In the evenings we visit Jazz Clubs for some cool relaxation.

Back at the dock, when Steve and Susie offer, we gratefully accept their help to reinstall the unwieldy sails—any advice they like to give is thoroughly welcome. We spend several hours working together and enjoying a few beers.

A calm day is needed to install the self-furling genoa which has just been returned from Miami with its new sacrificial Sunbrella edge—a 40-cm wide strip of ultraviolet-resistant material which will, when the sail is furled, prevent exposure to the sun. It rolls up smoothly, without a trace of sail showing anywhere. We also re-install the fully battened mainsail and flake it onto the boom. It is the first and last time the sail flakes in such a beautiful conformation.

One day, Robin arrives home from work with some news.

"There is an article in the newspaper," he says, "*Orca*'s captain, Kevin McNaulty, has had his sentence reduced from 11 to 9 years."

"What? Why would that be?"

"He appealed his sentence, apparently, and because he had fully cooperated with authorities, it was reduced. Judge Harre wants other drug-runners to learn that if they are helpful, they will get lighter sentences."

This opens up an old wound. Any mention of the drug runners induces a visceral response in me.

"It makes me wonder what he wanted with us," I say, "whether it would have had any bearing on the case."

Installing the genoa

While we are in Governor's Harbour, I have my first boat accident. I trip when stepping aboard and my right leg slips between the dock wall and the concrete hull. It is at this moment that the wind decides to blow, pinning my thigh to the dock. I crawl back onto the dock and inside the house. I haven't broken any bones but it turns out that my thigh muscle has been squashed and the sheath split. It is excruciatingly painful but I recover in a couple of weeks without anything more serious than an odd-shaped thigh muscle.

"You've got to be more careful," Robin warns me, "we can't have

you injuring yourself when we're sailing."
Oh, yes, I think, *we're supposed to be going sailing.*

Robin is attending a course on celestial navigation run by our local yacht club and has booked me on the next course. We must know how to navigate using a sextant and the positions of the heavenly bodies. I borrow numerous library books, to learn the theoretical side of all things sailing. I even read from cover to cover, Adlard Coles' book *Heavy Weather Sailing*. What a chilling read it is! Little do I realize that I'll be writing Chapter 26 for the fifth edition.

We've only been a few months in the townhouse at Governor's Harbour when our landlord wants to sell the property. Once again we will have to move and find somewhere to moor *Orca* and *Spirit of Carmanagh*. Being the good citizen that I am, I offer to show prospective clients around, to save him employing a real estate agent—who knows, maybe he'll share the commission he would have had to pay.

I should have had it in writing. I do a good selling job to some prospective clients who buy the property but the landlord is not parting with any cash, not even a bit off our rent. I guess that's what one expects from a wealthy old boy.

Skinflint that he is, he cycles from his house to the townhouse to check the hydro meter monthly and gives us a handwritten bill, rather than go to the expense of putting the hydro meter in the name of renters.

We broadcast to friends and colleagues that we are looking for a home. One of our yacht club members owns a lot on a canal in North Sound Estates and we view it, undeveloped and secluded. The lot is full of stately casuarina trees.

"It will be perfect, I love it!" I say.

"Yes, it's great, isn't it? We'll have to hire someone to build a dock and erect a shed for a sail locker and storage area."

I can't imagine what we did with our time before the yacht. This business is taking over the whole of our lives.

Orca at Governor's Harbour

We agree with the landlord to cut short our rental to allow the purchasers to move in and will leave in July, 1992.

"But where are we going to stay when we leave here and put *Orca* on her own dock?" I naively ask Robin.

He gives me a penetrating look. "We'll live on *Orca*, of course."

"But she's not ready."

"Whether she's ready or not, we're going to live on her in July."

It is at this point that I admit I've only been pretending we're going sailing. I love working on the yacht, restoring her beauty, I love the parties, the attention of our friends and she will make an enchanting miniature home, but are we really going long-distance sailing?

Preparations have suddenly become serious and focussed. I start to plan things like storage of food and clothes and try to imagine waking, showering, breakfasting and leaving for work from *Orca*. It is more difficult than I like to admit.

5

The Government Frowns and Sea Trials to Cuba

Construction of the dock and shed is delaying our work schedule. Grand Cayman is becoming more environmentally aware, which is good. We already have permission to drill a 30-metre deep outfall well and install a septic filtration system to take waste from the yacht. Work is well under way when we discover the rules have

Dock construction

changed. No one used to need planning permission to build a shed. Now, in order to prevent people from living in shacks instead of condos and hotel rooms, there are new regulations. So we apply for 'post construction' planning permission for the shed and receive a letter that we are to be inspected.

"Well," says Robin after reading, "it's not only the planning department representative coming, but all thirteen of our elected island MLAs. What an honour!"

"Perhaps it's because we're the first people applying to live aboard on a canal attached to our own dock, instead of in a marina."

On the appointed day we are feeling apprehensive, but ready to receive our honoured guests. We believe our argument is sound.

"There's a line of cars coming down the road." says Robin, "Action stations!"

I feel my heart rate increasing, we've invested so much time and money in this venture. I can't imagine having to throw it all away now, for the sake of a shed.

I put on a welcoming, if sycophantic, smile as they pull into our driveway. It has been specially constructed to weave through the Norfolk pines and bougainvillea bushes, so the shed, dock and yacht are invisible from the road. It is interesting to watch their faces as they climb out of the cars—eyebrows raised in surprise and a few frowns. The females straighten their fine dresses and gingerly step in high-heeled shoes onto the rough, scrubby terrain. Eleven MLAs are present, plus the man from the Planning Department.

"Good morning." Robin says, and launches into a description of what we intend. He is so firmly persuasive that they actually walk around and view the site for the septic system and the well, rather than perform a 360° sweep with their eyes. They enter the shed by turns and register surprise that the shed is dry-walled, has air-conditioning and a telephone.

"The cladding and AC unit are to regulate the temperature and humidity of the stored items," I explain, "and the telephone is the master unit for the portable handset we have on the yacht."

There is another concern. Our shed has a full-length 2.4-metre wide screened-in porch.

"It's so we can sit in the evenings and work without interference from mosquitoes." They are our biggest pest on the island. The MLAs then eye with suspicion the large fridge-freezer in the porch and think we may really be planning to live in the shed.

"Why would we want to live in a shed, when we have beautiful living quarters on board?" I ask one of the women, who is beginning to annoy me. It may not do my cause any good, but I will not sit back and let her get away with her implications. "You must come and tour the boat and see for yourself."

She declines and I feel an urge to slap her. Fortunately, I control myself. Robin is looking at me with an expression that says, "Now don't do anything silly."

There is one man who is eager to inspect the yacht. He is a seafarer of old and is pleasantly impressed with what he sees and wishes he could come along on the voyage. He particularly admires the bathroom and the fact that we have air-conditioning running from our shore power. Hopefully, he will give a favourable report to the others. He and the ship's cat, TP, form an instant liking for each other, which may go in our favour.

Camouflaging shed

They've seen enough and the cavalcade retreats to their respective air-conditioned offices in town. In hindsight, perhaps I should have offered coffee and donuts.

"Phew! I'm glad that's over," says Robin.

"I'm really disappointed that more of them wouldn't come on board," I say, "but I guess we can only wait and hope."

In due course post-construction planning permission is granted, to our massive relief. I suppose it didn't hurt that the man from the Planning Committee was one of our son Billy's good friends at the University of Waterloo and that they are drinking buddies here. I laugh with Robin about it. We gave no indication of recognition. Nor did we refer to the few occasions we'd found the same handsome young man, complete with Rasta curls, wandering around in the morning in our house with the kids, following a party the night before. We'd also really enjoyed being guests at his beach wedding!

True to Robin's prophecy, we move onto the yacht in July 1992, six months after launching *Orca*. I have to admit that he is right and with only a few minor adjustments—mostly attitudinal on my part— it is a very comfortable arrangement, especially since we can have hot showers and baths. In really warm weather, however, we usually have cold showers at the end of the dock where we have erected a

From the sublime to the ridiculous

shower head. No curtain—no neighbours!

One evening I'm busying myself on board when the phone rings.

"Hi Mum!"

"Lisa, it's great to hear you! What's news?"

"I've been accepted to do my M.Aq. (Master of Aquaculture) at Simon Fraser University, B.C. and guess what?"

"What?"

"I'm doing my thesis on turtles and the turtle farm in Cayman says I can work there next summer. Can I stay with you?"

"What a crazy question. Of course! What about Pete, can he come too?"

"He hopes to come for two or three weeks."

This is indeed great news and something to look forward to.

Shortly after, we have more good news. Billy has a brief leave before his Air Force posting and is coming to stay. He's desperate to see how 'his' yacht is coming along. When he arrives he can't wait for us to take *Orca* out for a sea trial.

At the weekend, when the weather looks good, we prepare for an open-water sailing trial, our first outside the reef. There's a surprising amount of stuff to do, to break the physical and mental ties to shore. It is the weirdest sensation after being attached to the dock, to have our comfortable home move away from the shore with us and be at the mercy of the elements. Somehow it doesn't feel right. I'm sure we'll get used to it.

First we have the challenge of getting *Orca* out of the canal. We certainly won't be reversing, because *Orca* adamantly refuses to go backwards in a straight line. So we must turn her manually, but including the bowsprit, she's 17 metres long and the canal is only 15.2 metres wide. With a series of bow and stern lines, we haul *Orca* around, trimming the neighbour's scrub bush on the opposite bank.

Once we've crossed North Sound and safely negotiated the infamous dog-leg passage through the reef, we emerge unscathed into the Caribbean Sea.

"I'm heading due north," Robin tells Billy, "as we have an easterly wind. That will give us a good beam reach for sailing." A kilometre outside the reef, we turn into wind, put the engine in idle and raise the mainsail. So far, so good. Next we unfurl some of the genoa and we are confident enough to cut the engine. Gradually, we let out more genoa and soon are scything smartly through the water, heeled over to port. Finally, we raise the mizzen sail.

"Wahoo, this is fantastic!" exclaims Bill, as he takes the helm for the first time.

"Shall we have coffee and cookies?" I ask, and go below to work in the little galley. I stand still and listen for a moment—I can hear a disturbing noise and return on deck.

"Rob," I say as gently as possible, "there's a kind of liquidy noise below."

"Maintain this course, Bill. I'll go and see what's happening." Robin disappears below. In a while he returns. He's discovered a major design fault of the yacht.

"Is it serious?" I ask, dreading to hear something bad.

"Yes and no," he replies, "we're taking on water through the drain beneath the bath. Since we're heeled over, the sea water is siphoning in and collecting below the sole, hence the slopping sounds. I don't know how much water we've taken on. We'll have to turn back."

At least it's an opportunity to practice a tack. We sail back to North Sound on a reciprocal course then start the engine, ready for when we drop the sails. Nearing the channel, we're going way too fast. Great rollers lift the stern and rush under us so we're surfing in. Robin struggles to keep the nose in line, but a swell picks up the stern and tries to turn us broadside onto the reef. *Orca* is sluggish, perhaps because of the water we've taken on board. Robin jams the throttle fully forward, lays hard on the helm and just in time, the bow comes round and we race into the dog-leg at about 8 knots. Robin is sweating and I have white knuckles. Billy is carefree, oblivious to any potential danger.

"Wow," he says as the rolling wave bears us aloft into the channel, "this is exciting!" He has total confidence in his father and never once feels threatened.

Now there's another job to add to the never-ending list; replacing the anti-siphoning loop and valve and modifying the bilge pump arrangement.

"I wonder what the previous owners did when they sailed with a system like that?" I ask Robin, as I think about the practical implications.

"They probably motored most of the time so they weren't well heeled over."

"Oh well," Billy adds, "It's certainly been a useful sea trial, but it's a pity it was so short."

Dockside, things are really moving along. Robin has installed a new nautical fridge-freezer that has a door safety-locking device. We donate our dual-purpose gas fridge to a Honduran boat going home. We've also taken delivery of an Avon dinghy and an 8hp outboard motor. Looking ahead, we realize that when we anchor offshore in foreign ports, we are likely to be some way from shore and the prospect of rowing long distances over open seas is not a welcome one.

A big disadvantage to being in Cayman and having to import all the equipment from the States, is the hassle of getting goods through customs. It always works in the end, with documents in triplicate and bundles of red tape, but it's really tedious. There are big line-ups and the customs officials are invariably churlish. I don't know why, I just think it's part of their job description. We've never tried to import anything illegally, but they manage to give us the impression that we're guilty of something the minute we walk through the door. I've tried various approaches: bright and breezy, sickeningly sycophantic, snarling and sullen. The results are always the same. I so dislike it that I decide we should take turns clearing goods through customs.

Unpacking the Avon

I particularly love the new dinghy we import. It is well worth the hassle and releases us from the dock. We can take off, picnic and sup a glass of wine at the end of the day in surrounding canals and mangrove swamps and watch the wildlife—birds, crabs, fish, jelly fish and turtles—so relaxing and it helps us to unwind. It is on one of these occasions while Rob is sitting in the dinghy by the dock waiting for me, staring down into the water, that he suddenly shouts.

"Hey Mags, come quickly, we've got a tiny seahorse!" By the dock piling, is a perfect little specimen about 6 cm tall. It is suspended upright, just below the surface of the water looking—I hate to say it—cute! I'm not sure I really believed they existed until we had our very own.

"The yacht club is holding its 'round the island' race in April," Robin says one day, "shall we take *Orca*?"

"Yes, if you like, it'll be a chance to do a bit more sailing, but we won't be racing."

So, rather tongue-in-cheek, we tag along and have lots of volunteer crew. In fact we don't even know half the people who come on board. In a good fresh breeze the yachts assemble outside North Sound and serious contenders jostle for the best position before the start line, while we hang around at the rear without a hint of jostling. As usual, we're well provisioned with essential supplies because this could take a while.

At 8 o'clock the racers shoot across the line, the crews yelling orders at each other—they must be having such fun. We are sailing clockwise round the island. As Cayman is 35 km long and 11 km wide at its widest point, the race is 100 to 115 kilometres long, depending on the number of tacks required to catch the wind.

We have to sail a much looser course offshore than everyone else, so when winds are light and nearly everyone has disappeared from sight, we boldly employ our 'bronze spinnaker' (the engine) as we're not racing. In this way we can pass another slow vessel that is ahead and inshore of us. Through binoculars we can see they look rather incredulous at our turn of speed. If they'd mugged up on their nautical messages, they would see that we have our motoring cone hoisted.

I consider taking the helm, for practice, but there are many other offers and the autopilot takes care of a lot of the work. I'll do it another time.

The first to cross the finish line takes 4 hours 18 minutes in a J36. We take 9 hours and 17 minutes with help from the engine. It's been a good day and we confirm our belief that *Orca* is not a racing yacht. This knowledge is partly responsible for declining an invitation from the Jamaican navy to join a Cayman to Jamaica race! She does have her advantages, though. Being commodious, she is proving popular with party goers, but we really need to take a longer run, so we're going to plan a trip to Cuba.

Our first sail to Cuba was in October, 1990, on Jeff Parker's yacht, *Zag*, a Morgan 36. We were the first yacht to sail to Cuba from Cayman for many years and were part of an official delegation in order to promote friendly relations. Originally, it was to be a deputation of five yachts, but the other four dropped out because the weather forecast was poor. After the arrangements had been made we felt we couldn't let the Cubans down, so went ahead on our own.

We were an unlikely bunch of diplomats: Jeff and his American-born girlfriend, Carolyn; Robin and me; two young blonde American brothers, Peter and Matt; and Billy, who'd never sailed before. The sail to Cuba was indeed ghastly, with mountainous seas in gale-force winds. Captain Jeff, an ex-Olympic Laser sailor is a powerful and knowledgeable captain. He was sea-sick for the first time in his life because of the salt water he'd swallowed.

The 135% genoa was pulling the port gunwale under water.

Although we were harnessed and clipped to a safety line on the high starboard side, Billy had resigned himself to the fact that we would surely drown. Each time we blasted through a wave rather than over it, a flood of seawater swept over the deck. We just raised ourselves a little out of sitting position, to allow the warm water to flow beneath us.

Just as Jeff said, "We should change the genny," it blew, top to bottom with a crack like a cannon. When all sails were shortened, things were more bearable. Peter volunteered to stand in for the Captain, so Jeff could go off watch. Carolyn spent the entire 28-hour trip curled in foetal position in the well of the yacht. She even missed the excitement when a super-tanker stopped to allow us to continue passage across its bow. Jeff thanked the captain for his courtesy but declined. In those conditions we couldn't guarantee safely crossing ahead, and so would take our chances beating in to wind to take their stern.

Much to Billy's surprise and delight, we survived the journey and docked at Cayo Largo, an island to the south of the main island of Cuba. Carolyn immediately recovered and was in fine form to tuck into the lobster cocktails and knock back a couple of 'Cuban Sunrise' drinks, made from Havana rum with a few drops of exotic fruit juice. Customs and Immigration officials boarded the yacht and processed our passports. Americans, at that time, were forbidden by President George Bush Senior from entering Cuba, so instead of stamping their passports the accommodating Cubans just slipped a paper inside which could be removed when leaving.

We spent an amazing week as guests of the government who stopped at nothing to make us comfortable. They assigned us a guide and translator, Piry, from the Tourist Association and a 'heavy' Mr. Sierra, who we think was really a KGB protector! They turned out to be great fun and good drinking companions.

We were wined and dined, flown to Havana free of charge for an official open-air dinner and a floor show at the Tropicana Night Club; and taken on tours of the city and of the countryside. Back in Cayo Largo we were guests at a different hotel each night for dinner and dancing. We were also taken to an iguana paradise, a crocodile farm and topless beaches, much to the delight of the three young men. They assured us that they took long walks on the sandy beach because it was 'so much finer' than the sand in Cayman.

Soviet Antonov AN2 Biplane

To top it all, we had a low-level flight over the island in an old Russian AN2 biplane, with a huge single radial engine up front. When they discovered Robin and I had pilot's licences, they insisted we fly the plane. Robin did a magnificent job and wasn't fazed by the fact that the instruments and dials were in Cyrillic. Fortunately the T-panel was standard, so he could fly using the airspeed indicator, turn and bank indicator, altitude and giro heading instruments. He was having such a good time, flying at 60 metres above the island, I declined to take over, which is probably why we are all living to tell the tale today.

I began to think I could get used to the life of a diplomat! Our uneventful sail home was something of an anticlimax, but welcomed as everything went smoothly.

The trip we plan in June, 1993, on *Orca* is much shorter. Out of courtesy, we inform Mr. Sierra of our impending arrival. We will be seven on board again, Jeff and Carolyn; another young American protégée of Carolyn's, Steve; my boss—Chris van den Bok, and Tony Walsh, a Cayman Airways mechanic from whom we bought *Spirit of Carmanagh*. All are excellent and experienced sailors and not afraid of hard work.

Our first challenge, as always, is to turn *Orca* by hand in the canal, necessitating a couple of people on the other side in the bush to receive lines and haul her round. Nothing like a good workout to start the voyage.

Turning in the canal   Photo: CUC

We sail through the night and when we get close in the morning, call to give our ETA and ask for permission to dock. An eight-piece band is playing on the jetty just as before, and our reception committee is waiting. There are a few members of the Tourist Association, including two attractive young women, one of whom, Suzanna, is the wife of the Governor. The Customs and Immigration guys are waiting with a grinning Mr. Sierra, who is looking ready for more partying.

Carolyn leaps ashore with a tray of cold beers for the orchestra

Cuban welcome

and they beam their appreciation. We unload boxes of gifts: washing powder, hand soap, liquid dish soap, razors, toothbrushes, toothpaste, clothes, powdered milk—so many things that we take for granted, they lack. They can only shop at the government store and the shelves are usually pitifully empty.

Sadly, we only have two nights and one day in Cuba this time and all sleep on board. We do a little exploring, photographing the pelicans on the dock and manage to do some duty-free shopping at hotel shops.

On our return journey as we approach Cayman we are becalmed. The sails flog and the boom bangs from side to side, so we drop the sails. We are also at the mercy of the long-shore current so have to motor. When Robin starts the engine, a terrible grinding, growling sound comes from below decks.

We heave-to and roll around in the swells while Robin lifts the floor sections and carries out an inspection. He determines that it's coming from the prop-shaft coupling. Cayman Kai and West Bay are on the horizon, so we aren't completely at sea. We proceed with great caution through the dog-leg passage and across North Sound into the canal system. By the utmost good fortune, it isn't until we turn into our own canal that there is a loud bang and the coupling separates. With only two hundred metres to go, we coast gently along to a full stop at our own dock.

Once *Orca* is secured, we have to jump into vehicles and drive to town to clear customs and declare our 12 bottles of 9-year old Havana rum, 12 cases of Hatuey beer and 150 Cuban cigars that we admit to on our entry documents. There are some good perks from a sailing trip to Cuba.

Yet another expensive and time-consuming task is added to Robin's list. For each job we tick off, we add two more, but far better that it happens here than in the middle of the Pacific. I am concerned about mishaps like this. What would we do? Then I remind myself that Robin is capable and can make anything work. He would be thinking, while I would be panicking. So in his quiet, efficient manner, Robin draws a design for a new coupling, has it fabricated and installs it. It works well.

It is a welcome break when Lisa and Pete arrive for a short holiday before Lisa starts work at the Cayman Turtle Farm to gather material for her thesis.

A British Navy ship is visiting port and the yacht club organizes a rafting-up picnic party in North Sound near Cayman Kai, and invites naval personnel to attend. *Orca*'s presence is requested. As she's the heaviest vessel, they're thinking we should anchor and the others all stream off our port and starboard sides, like wings.

We start out early so Pete and Lisa can do some sailing and arrive at the appointed spot in plenty of time to set our anchor. In ones and twos the other yachts raft up. The Navy brings a launch and anchors on its own, the crew swimming across to join us on the yachts. We're all having a rip-roaring time, moving from party to party on the boats. I'm in one of my favourite places at the top of the mast to photograph some of the yachts on our port side. When I turn to do the same for the starboard side I can see that the boats are straining at the mooring lines.

Pete helming

"Hey Rob, that's funny!" I yell down to the deck, "Those yachts are drifting away from us. Release the lines!"

We are now in two distinct rafts and then it dawns on us. One of the yachts on the starboard side has set its anchor. Far from them drifting away from us, it is *Orca* drifting away from them. Because it is so shallow, we were lured into not laying out enough scope and the combined windage of all the yachts is sufficient to cause us to drag.

"Oh, what the hell," the other captains say, "there's lots of room!" So that's the way we stay.

In August, we're invited to a lunchtime pool party with Bill and Sheila Church, and Marilyn and Brian Limbrick. I have a great idea. "Let's take Spirit of Carmanagh, so we don't have to drive."

Lisa and Robin agree, so we have an opportunity to put our sailing and navigating skills to the test in the Com-pac. Unfortunately, Pete has returned to Canada, taking his sailing skills with him, otherwise we probably would have been all right.

All is well getting there in daylight and mooring to the canal wall near their house. We have a terrific party—in and out of the pool, great food and too many gin and tonics. It is after dark when we have to jump down into Spirit and return to our own canal. Only a matter of 4 nautical miles across the sound from their canal to ours. Rob pulls the starter cord on the outboard and off we go. The return journey is altogether different from getting there in daylight.

"Do you know where we're going?" Robin asks.

"Sure, that light over there," I say, pointing to a minute twinkling in the distance, "is the only street light on Ann Street at the end of our canal."

The only problem is the light keeps moving and we eventually figure that maybe it's attached to a little fishing boat.

"Well, *I* think you're going round in circles," says Lisa, who's not at all amused and is getting rather snipey. I think it's funny.

For some reason Robin is wearing his Tilley hat as if it's sunny, then suddenly it seems to be floating away on the water. We try to motor round to do a man-overboard test and retrieve it, but give up. The next thing we know, we run aground on a sand bar, although we only have a 35-centimetre draft.

"No problem," says Rob, as he steps out into water not quite up to his knees and just pushes us off.

Somehow we find our way home, but we're not sure how. It doesn't say much for my navigational skills, perhaps I need to hit the books.

Shortly before Lisa returns to university, we take delivery of 250 metres of 2.5-cm triple-strand line, as required by the Panama Canal authorities for transiting the canal. It is now September, 1993, nearly three years since buying *Orca*. The pretending is over. Robin makes one more of his prophetic statements that scares me. "We're leaving in December."

Our Aussie friends, Steve and Susie are setting off at a similar time, and while we'll not be sailing in tandem, we'll be in touch.

For old times' sake and to buy a few items we are *absolutely* unable to manage without, we make a trip together to Miami and Fort Lauderdale. We shop and party. I'm painfully aware that this will be our last care-free time, before the big day.

Lisa with line

On our return, we continue planning possible sailing routes now we have dozens of new charts. I assemble lists of stores and clothing we will need. As the immediacy of this voyage is closing on me, I have a feeling that perhaps I'm not physically fit enough to undertake the trip, despite the fact that I'm always working. I have a cracking idea.

"I should join a fitness club, Rob," I say to him one day, "so I can be stronger and fitter for this trip. I don't want to let you down."

"You'll be alright," he says.

But there's no dissuading me. I sign up and start my exercises. The beginning routines are pretty wimpy, so I increase everything— more weights, longer duration. I'm especially pleased with my efforts on the Pec Deck aimed at increasing my upper body strength ready for hauling those lines. The day following one strenuous workout, I wake with the feeling that someone is sticking a lance in the side of my neck. I'm only a little concerned at this point and take a few painkillers, which normally I scorn, and trust it will go away. Tomorrow I'll wake up and be back to normal. But the stabbing pain turns into a constant pain in the neck and no matter which way I move or lie down, I can't rid myself of it.

I usually avoid consulting doctors, but that is what I eventually do and am advised that the solution lies in physiotherapy twice a week, to be stretched on the rack. I do as I am told, but as the weights and stretches increase, so does the pain. I'm assured by the nurse that it will feel worse before feeling better. I only carry on with this lunacy for a couple of weeks before I call my sister, Di, in England. She is a nurse in London, married to a surgeon. I lament my situation and explain my problem. She is horrified and immediately makes an appointment with a private surgeon in London. Although the USA is closer, I have no family there.

Things happen so fast. Within two weeks I'm on my back in the UK after a severely damaged disk has been removed and my cervical spine fused via keyhole neck surgery. Just what the doctor ordered for a strenuous sailing life.

Poor Robin, his plans are wrecked. My misery at his disappointment doesn't help my recovery. This is *not* what we need at this stage and now our departure will have to be delayed. In trying to be a better support, I've become a liability. My family are wonderful, but it's a miserably long 10 weeks' convalescence before Robin comes to England to collect me, just before Christmas, to take

me home. Before we leave, we attend the local Frinton & Walton Yacht Club's Christmas dance. It is so exciting to see each other again!

I'm left with just one unforeseen and annoying problem. During surgery, my vocal cords were damaged and I can't speak in anything other than a hoarse whisper. Pretty limiting for an inveterate chatterer. When I voice, or rather rasp, my concerns to the surgeon he has a wonderful solution when I complain that I won't be able to shout to Robin on the yacht. "Buy yourself a whistle," he says. I imagine myself talking in whistles, like one of the Marx Brothers.

I return to Cayman to no job and no income—I lost that when I was off sick for more than two weeks—and Robin at last resigns his post as Vice President of Engineering and Planning at the Caribbean Utilities Company.

This time it's real. We're counting down to March, 1994 when we'll be on the high seas looking for adventure. If I keep up this positive thinking I might even believe it myself. We have found a purchaser for our land, dock and *Spirit of Carmanagh*. There's no rush—the purchasers are happy to take over when we leave.

I do find it amusing that on returning from England we are living in the shed! Robin, with the help of friends, hauled out *Orca* while I was away, ready to clean and anti-foul the bottom. I hope the MLAs aren't thinking of doing a spot check.

My first job, in the wonderful warmth of the Cayman sun, is antifouling the 85 square metres of hull. I enjoy being in the marina again, seeing our old buddies. The puppies seem to have grown and gone away. Emile is happy to see me back—someone to talk at.

Since our first year working on *Orca* in the boatyard, there have been some wonderful changes. The garbage has been cleaned up, not just pushed into the bush. It is a pleasure to work in a clean, healthier environment and be rid of the eyesores.

After completing *Orca*'s anti-fouling, we again have to wait for an exceptionally high tide before returning to our dock. We now need to devote all our time to final preparations, including notifying all and sundry of our imminent departure.

In February, 1994, we make a final trip to Miami. Just to challenge ourselves, we inadvertently shut the keys in the trunk of the rental car at the hotel in Fort Lauderdale. We hire a taxi to drive us back to Miami to the car rental company for spare keys. Unbelievably, they don't keep spare keys. However, they have the key code. We hop back into the waiting taxi, find a locksmith who can interpret the code, get a key cut and drive back to Fort Lauderdale. The taxi hire for a few hours costs more than our hotel and air fare combined.

We return to Cayman with more gear totalling over US $5000.

As we are soon leaving the country, this time we don't want to pay import duties. Customs, therefore, impounds the equipment while they check the veracity of our story; that the items will be installed on the yacht and leaving with us. We invite them to come and see *Orca* and suggest that as they're coming, perhaps they would like to bring the equipment with them!

Stormy day in the canal   Photo: Peter Phillips

6

Ready or Not—Leaving Grand Cayman

I never really believed today would arrive; that we would be setting off from Grand Cayman for Panama at the beginning of our voyaging life. Yesterday we drove to Georgetown to get our exit papers from a solid, unsmiling official at the Immigration Department. This saves half a day of motoring in *Orca* from the north of the island, to George Town on the south. Now we can leave direct from our dock.

The culmination of three years' toil is a dream come true for Robin but I'm reserved, even though I know his strengths and abilities after 27 years of marriage. I admire his dedication and determination to see a project through. Although we've made many moves around the world together, this is different.

It is a bright, clear day and Robin is lost in thought, probably putting ticks on his mental check-list that everything is ready. We're keeping our departure low-key and both are tense. I'm making small talk to some friends on the dock who've come to wave farewell.

A car draws up to the dockside and Jeff gets out. The other door opens and out bounces Carolyn, our 'five-foot nothing' friend and a bundle of energy. She's excellent company; an experienced sailor who will crew with us until we have passed through the Panama Canal. She has always wanted to go through the canal.

"Hi guys, put these on," she says, skipping forward with some new extra-large T-shirts in her arms. We slip on the shirts and admire our new outfits, with '*Orca*, World Cruise' emblazoned across the back and embroidered on the left sleeve: 'Captain', 'First Mate' and 'Crew'.

"Carolyn! They're delightful, thanks a lot." I give her a big hug.

Jeff empties the car and loads kit-bag and boxes on board. Carolyn has brought enough prepared food to serve a platoon.

"We don't want to be bothered with cooking," she explains, "so we can eat this finger food." Carolyn is a Cordon Bleu cook.

"That's fantastic, now I know we'll eat well!" Although at the moment, I can't imagine ever feeling hungry.

I remove some of the contents of the fridge to make room for the delicacies. Carolyn stows her bags and belongings in the forward cabin, then presents us with a large denim bag she's made and embroidered with *ORCA*, which she ties to a wooden cleat.

"There's never anywhere to put garbage on deck," she says, "and we're not throwing anything overboard."

It's time to leave. We've already turned the yacht; the engine is purring and cooling water intermittently splashes out into the canal. Jeff and Carolyn are hugging and engaging in a slightly tearful farewell on the dock. When Carolyn hops on board, her cheeks are damp and shining, but she's grinning.

"Jeffrey just asked me to marry him!" She doesn't know whether to laugh or cry.

"Oh dear," says Robin, "that's putting the pressure on us to get you to Panama safe and sound."

"Have you got your patch on?" I ask Carolyn. She turns to show me. We're all wearing identical anti-sea-sickness patches behind one ear.

"I put it on last night," she says.

Someone takes a couple of snapshots for us on our cameras, for the record. Ironically, the film was later double exposed, the second shot being of undersea corals.

Orca in the corals

The mooring lines at the dock are cast off and thrown on board for us to stow. We slowly chug to the end of the canal, wave, and turn to starboard to reach North Sound. After 6 nautical miles we pass through the reef where the fated police cruiser ran aground years ago.

"I hope the new police launch is using the equipment they wouldn't let us have back." I say.

"I doubt it," replies Robin, "it'll be auctioned off."

The Caribbean Sea at last! Next stop, Panama. The sun is intense in a blue sky dotted with white woolly sheep and we have 15-20 knots of wind, so raise the mainsail, genoa and mizzen and set off at a good clip on a port tack.

"This is fabulous," Carolyn says, as we cut through the water creating a bow wave and listen to the gentle swoosh and occasional slapping of waves on our hull. Carolyn brings out a big bottle of sun screen.

"Don't forget this," she says, squirting us liberally on our exposed arms, legs and faces. Caps and sunglasses are the order of the day, although I soon reject my sunglasses. I'm not used to wearing them and find them irritating.

Carolyn is at the helm after we've trimmed the sails to our course and Robin is resetting one of the autopilots. He then tries the other one before he breaks the news.

"I'm afraid the autopilots aren't working properly. We're going to have to hand-helm." The news is a severe blow. One worked perfectly well on all our previous trials, the other we hadn't re-commissioned. We vote to continue. If we return now, we'll never get away. Hand-helming will necessitate a change in our pre-arranged watch schedules.

"As we're new to this, do you think there should be two of us on deck at all times?" I ask. We have a discussion and decide that we should maintain a 4 hours on and 2 hours off watch, around the clock. Gruelling. One person will helm and the second can rest on the lazarette bench close by in case help is needed, especially for sail adjustments, while number three sleeps below. This is baptism by fire, or rather by water. Gone are those luxurious nine hours of sleep we used to have at night.

Five miles SSW of the island, we call Port Control on the VHF Radio to advise them of our departure from local waters. The port controller is most perturbed. He wants us to return for port clearance.

"Negative," Robin says and explains, "we obtained our clearance documents yesterday when we came to the office. We are not returning."

Robin's patience pays off and the controller concedes that we may continue. There isn't really much he can do about it. Our first hurdle has passed without too much stress. Gaining clearance in and out of ports, we're told, can be an onerous task and a bureaucratic nightmare.

A few hours out of Cayman, while on a port tack and heeled to starboard, I'm in the galley making tea when I make a startling discovery. We have bolted the fridge to the sole of the boat, with the door opening to starboard, instead of towards the stern. It's a bit late in the day for enlightenment when a lurch springs the 'safety' catch. A cracking sound is followed by meats, cheeses, cans, butter and fruit cascading off the shelves. It bounces and slithers across the varnished cork floor into the furthermost corners of the saloon and galley.

"Help!" I yell up the companionway. "The fridge door has broken open." Fortunately, we have no eggs in there—they are safely swinging in a little hammock in the starboard berth which is being used for storage. Carolyn comes to the rescue, yet try as we might, we can't stuff the contents back in and shut the door while we are still heeled over at that angle. If we open the door a crack to put one thing in, something else drops out. What can't go back now, will have to wait till later. Now we know that if we have to open the fridge, we must be upright or on a starboard tack.

"I guess Robin's first job in Panama will be to rotate the fridge," I say to Carolyn.

Our joy at the great breezes is short lived. After the first 24 hours we lose all wind and have to motor for the next four days on calm seas with long swells. It is unbelievably tedious to continually roll from side to side to side to side as the swells pass beneath us. The only consolation we have is that if we judge the rolling moment just right, we can open the fridge to remove food, little by little, slamming the door shut in between, in time with the motion. We now keep a wide webbing belt buckled securely around the fridge's mid region to prevent a recurrence.

Poor Carolyn still suffers from initial mal de mer. Even with a patch, she's sick for the first couple of days, so has that major discomfort to add to her tiring schedule. Never once does she complain and always presents herself on time for her helming stint, only indulging in brief skirmishes to the side rail. She bravely forces down food from time to time and drinks to keep hydrated, but none of this lasts long in her stomach. While on support watch, she curls up in her favourite foetal position on the deck, harnessed to the safety rail. Robin and I are successful in warding off those terrible waves of nausea.

We follow our watch schedule closely but when it is my turn to go below for two hours, sleep won't come despite the fact that I'm desperately tired. All too soon I must go on deck again. We divide the helming into half-hour chunks at night, and while acting as support watch, we can read by torchlight or lie back and study the stars. When we're away from land they seem unbelievably close and so dense it's hard to pick out familiar constellations.

Standing at the steering station for prolonged periods of time gives us all backache. The wheel is on the port side of the vessel, not in the middle, so because of the contours of the deck we are constantly unbalanced, bearing more weight on one foot than the other. Robin brings one of our tall, swivel-seated bar-stools from below and saws off the legs to the required uneven lengths and lashes it in position at the steering station. This relieves some of the stress as we can now sit down to helm.

Carolyn helming

From the moment we set off from Cayman, we wear our full safety harnesses which fit over our shoulders and round our middles with a quick-release buckle. Attached to the buckle by a carabiner clip is a Y-shaped webbing tether, the other two arms also terminating in carabiner clips. We clip onto anything secure, like the rigging, or the safety 'jack-lines' running at deck level from stern to bow on both port and starboard sides. This way we are able to move around the deck safely yet remain attached.

There is a fourth soul on board; TP, the cat. She's never been on the high seas, for when we went sailing she stayed at home in the shed. I worry that she might be frightened and jump overboard, so before we leave I doctor her with a piece of a Gravol tablet. The outcome is that she's virtually unconscious for two days, stretched out on our bunk. On the third day the princess awakes.

"Hey, it's TP," says Robin as he catches a glimpse of her peeping over the companionway step, "she's woken up at last."

"Oh fantastic!" I was secretly afraid I might have overdosed her. I slowly move towards her, not wishing to frighten her. "Come on TP." She delicately jumps out onto the deck, puts her little nose in the air, twitches her whiskers and then settles down in some coils of line by the steering station. I slip below and check her dishes and litter box under the companionway stairs. Yes, she's used them all, so she's getting back to normal. She doesn't show any signs of mal de mer, so hopefully, during her enforced sleep she has acclimatized to the motion of *Orca*.

"Hey, I'm starving!" says Carolyn after a couple of days.

"Hooray! you're over your sea-sickness." We celebrate by eating chicken legs and a big bar of chocolate.

"Thank goodness you're back to normal," Robin says, "I was beginning to worry about what I would say to Jeff. Now, if you can conjure up some wind, we'll be in good shape."

But there's not even a whisper of a breeze to fill a sail, so the engine continues to consume diesel as we proceed towards Panama. Occasionally Robin tries one or other of the autopilots again, but to no avail.

Despite our initial teething troubles, there is something magical about being out of sight of land. We only see one other vessel, a Greek cruise ship coming up behind us. In case he hasn't seen us, I call the captain on the VHF radio and explain who we are and ask if he has us in view, to which he replies, "Don't worrrry my dear—I can see evvverrrything!" Fortunately at this point we haven't started conserving laundry by walking around naked.

It is 17th March, day five of our trip and we should be getting close to Panama. We're all eagerly scanning the horizon.

"Land ahoy! Yeeeha!" Carolyn hollers at the top of her voice, holding the binoculars to her face and stabbing a finger into the middle distance.

Approaching Colón

"Where? Let's see." I train the binoculars on the horizon and can just discern a smudge of land.

It's not long before Robin says, "Isn't that little black dot a container ship way ahead on our port side?" Indeed it is. It's not long before we spot several larger dots, all converging on the same point. Next, we can see cranes on the skyline.

It is an overwhelming feeling spotting Cristobal Harbour after our trials and we can hear vessels talking to Port Control. When we are 5 nautical miles off the outer breakwaters, Robin waits for a slot in the incredibly busy radio traffic to call Cristobal Signal Office on Channel 16.

"Cristobal Radio, Cristobal Radio, Cristobal Radio, this is Zulu Charlie Foxtrot 1585, S/V *Orca*. Over."

"S/V *Orca*, go ahead."

"Cristobal Radio S/V *Orca* is a 17-metre ketch, 5 miles off the breakwaters, inbound from Grand Cayman, and requests entry to the harbour for transiting the Panama Canal. Over."

"S/V *Orca*, can you see the Hapag-Lloyd container ship one mile to your stern?"

"Affirmative." The vessel looks like a 12-story apartment block. It has not escaped our attention that it is rapidly bearing down on us and will soon be blotting out the sun.

"Increase your speed and you may enter ahead of the vessel."

Robin eases the throttle forward for the first time in four days, but instead of a corresponding increase in speed, the revs fall off and our speed drops. I am blissfully unaware of the problem as Robin keeps it to himself. He doesn't show signs of being under stress, but has instantaneously assessed that he must not touch the throttle further. He picks up the microphone and calls Port Control again. "I'm having a problem and can't increase speed. Over."

"OK S/V *Orca*, please make a 360° turn to port and then enter behind the vessel. Over." The Port Controller is skilfully feeding us seamlessly into a giant dynamic system, just like an air traffic controller.

"This is S/V *Orca*. Will make a 360° turn and follow the Hapag-Lloyd vessel through breakwaters. Over." Robin concentrates on his gentle turn.

"S/V *Orca*, once inside the breakwaters, proceed two and a half miles south and anchor at the Flats on your port side."

"Where are we going?" I ask when I realize that we're turning away from the entrance.

"Port Control has asked us to let the big chap through first, so we don't hold him up." Robin says.

Orca seems very small and insignificant as we pass between some of these leviathans, no doubt waiting for pilots. Without further incident we enter the breakwaters, then Robin confesses that we can't increase revs and will risk losing more if he touches the throttle.

My heart rate rockets, but he calmly continues helming.

"What's wrong then?" I ask.

"Probably the rolling motion has stirred up some sludge in the fuel tank and it's been sucked into the fuel line, causing a blockage." He thinks for a moment and then continues, "We may not have more than one chance at anchoring, so we'd better get it right."

I move forward to get things prepared.

'The Flats' is actually Colón Harbour, adjacent to Cristobal Harbour, where small vessels anchor while waiting to transit the canal. Fortunately it is a very large anchorage and we choose a location well away from other vessels, furthest from the yacht club. We head into wind, release the anchor and allow the chain to run free to the required length and shift into reverse to gently set the anchor. Thank God for lots of room. It passes off without a hitch.

"I'll just hoist the Q flag," I say. As we've just entered the country, we may not leave the vessel until we have been boarded by the quarantine officer. Our little yellow square fluttering in the light airs will tell them which vessel to approach. This is just fine with us, as we're all super-tired and not thinking of going anywhere for a while.

As soon as the engine is switched off, Carolyn, with her wonderful natural effervescence, goes below and returns with an ice-cold bottle of the Rolls Royce of champagnes, Dom Perignon, and champagne flutes on a silver platter!

"Where did that come from?" I ask Carolyn, knowing full well that she must have brought it aboard. "We've never aspired to Dom Perignon before!"

It's 1:30 p.m. Robin raises his glass and offers a toast. "To teamwork and the crew—thank you both for everything." He grins and relaxes his shoulders for the first time in several days.

"Yes, thanks Carolyn and Robin for a safe passage. What a great bunch we are!" Our first leg of the voyage has been accomplished.

TP pokes her head outside. Looking around, she decides to join us as the gross motion of the boat has stopped. Perched on top of the companionway hatch, she observes her surroundings. There's plenty to keep us all entertained while we wait for the quarantine officer.

"Ugly buggers, those Panamax vessels, aren't they?" Robin says as he leans back on the lazarette watching the traffic. "How any self-respecting nautical engineer could lay claim to that design is beyond me, but of course they're made to just fit in the Panama Canal, with 30 cm to spare on either side."

Familiar names are emblazoned on the container vessels: Evergreen, NYK, Maersk, Hyundai—bulk carriers plying to and fro and car carriers loading and unloading at the docks. It is an amazing clearing-house for vessels travelling the world.

We recline on deck, sipping champagne and chatting. Carolyn brings out smoked salmon to accompany the champagne. The little breeze in the anchorage ameliorates the heat of the sun.

"This is the life," she says, chomping into a delicious mouthful.

Dom Perignon

7
Challenges of Colón—Panama

"I'd better start work on the autopilots, to find out what's the problem." Robin frowns, disappointed that there are already more jobs to tackle before we get to the Pacific. "We can't arrange for a transit until we know how much has to be done."

"Just take a few minutes' break, will you?" I say.

"I think we have company coming." Carolyn points to a small launch heading our way.

Robin helps the quarantine officer on deck and invites him below. There are many questions to answer about who is on board and what goods we are carrying. I resist the urge to be chatty and tell him that *Orca* used to be a drug-running boat. As soon as he disembarks, I pull down the quarantine flag.

The Flats

"OK, let's go to the yacht club and find out where we have to complete the immigration formalities," says a more cheerful Robin.

The champagne is working and we've found the energy to continue. The dinghy is already inflated with the motor padlocked in place, waiting for its first real assignment. We attach a spare main-mast halyard to three hitching points on the dinghy, then winch the dinghy up and over the side safety lines to lower it to the water. Our new system works well—it's a good thing something does.

The three of us step down and get comfortably seated, Robin at the tiller, and motor to shore to tie up at a finger quay. The Panama Canal Yacht Club is contained within a compound, surrounded by chain link fencing topped with barbed wire. Armed security guards are present 24 hours a day, so for transiting yachts the club grounds and anchorages are very safe. We find we need to go into town to complete the necessary paperwork. The yacht club provides us with a sketch map of the area, showing all the relevant offices that we must visit to register, to obtain cruising permits and sundry documents.

The minute we step outside the compound, however, we are fair game to a legion of muggers and pickpockets indulging in what appear to be two of Panama's national pastimes. Ample warnings are posted at the yacht club: 'Never walk alone; never walk out after dark; never wear watches or jewellery; never wear a fanny bag so it can be seen; always carry a stout stick'.

Robin picks up a suitable stick and, like the three musketeers, we set off on the half-hour trip to town, keeping our heads down, walking briskly and arrive without mishap. The government offices are remarkably well run and we swiftly pass in and out of the various dark and sombre-looking rooms. Officials are courteous and helpful—something officials in Grand Cayman could do well to emulate. This is quite remarkable, considering the vast amount of traffic they have to deal with.

We leave town with a fistful of documents, all stamped and double stamped with purple official seals.

On our return journey to the compound, we feel a little bolder and look around us.

"This used to be a beautiful city," says Carolyn, an archaeologist by training and interested in buildings and all things ancient.

"Yes," agrees Robin, "it reminds me of when we were in Cuba—same style of buildings and sadly, in a terrible state of disrepair."

"Look at those streets over there," I say, swinging my head in the general direction without pointing. Dozens of little block shanties are jammed together on either side of dark alleyways, with skeins of laundry hanging between the balconies."

We breathe a collective sigh of relief when we are back safely inside the compound. The young security guard smiles then continues playing with a little puppy which he indicates is his buddy.

"I could murder a beer," says Robin.

"Good," I say, "Carolyn and I have been wondering who would have to suggest it first." Inside the yacht club, the bar is rather like an English pub. There's a big U-shaped bar, plus an area with tables and chairs.

"Let's sit at the bar," says Carolyn and places our order.

I take a handful of popcorn and put some into my mouth and chomp down. Crack! It sounds loud enough for the whole bar to hear, but no one notices. I fumble with a napkin and then say, diffidently, "Robin, I'm sorry, but I've broken a tooth." I gingerly probe around with my tongue and discover half a molar has disappeared. Robin looks at me but makes no comment.

"What a great start to the trip! Now I'll have to find a dentist. The good news is, it doesn't hurt."

I enlist the help of the barman who gives me the name of a reputable dentist in Colón. He offers to phone to make an appointment for me. How accommodating—I hope he works on commission. There must be a lot of people passing through who need dental services.

"I've got an appointment in a couple of days," I tell the others, "that's pretty good, isn't it?"

Back on board we all have the same idea, voiced by Robin. "Well, I'll probably have plenty of time for work now, so I reckon a glass of wine and some of Carolyn's filet mignon for supper and then beautiful, beautiful sleep."

Even I sleep soundly and in the morning after a hot shower, we are much refreshed. Robin and I are starving and ready for one of his breakfasts—eggs, bacon, toast, marmalade and tea. He even produces fresh mushrooms and tomatoes. Carolyn has brought her own special coffee maker—she's more of a 'coffee only' girl—doesn't know what she's missing!

It's straight to work for Robin. Trouble-shooting the autopilots and re-siting the fridge have the highest priority. Carolyn and I take ourselves off for a mooch around, to keep out of Robin's way. He's never liked people hanging about, firing off questions when he's working and trying to solve problems.

I visit the dentist, who doesn't speak English and I don't speak

Spanish, but with his nurse's smattering of English, we manage. It transpires that I must have the tooth crowned and it will take about six weeks to complete. This is bad, because we are further delayed and will probably have to miss the Galapagos Islands and go straight to the Marquesas. But it is good because Rob has a chance to complete the work without being rushed. We'd like to have the single sideband radio working too, that Cayman customs wouldn't release in time to install before leaving.

"I won't be able to wait to go through the Panama Canal with you," laments Carolyn.

"I know, but I've got an idea. Let's hang around the bar and see if there's a boat looking for a line handler and perhaps you can join them."

Spending time in the yacht club bar—even if it's only to keep clear of Robin while he's working—means we can strike up conversations with lots of yachties passing through. Carolyn chatters even more than I do and gets loads of offers to go through the canal on small yachts. She cleverly sidesteps them until she has one from a big, expensive yacht—one in keeping with her aspirations and her appreciation of the good things in life.

Visiting the yacht club has other benefits. One day an American base ex-commander invites several boat owners to Sunday brunch at the American Servicemen's club on the base. He sends a little bus to pick us up and we are given a grand tour. The buildings are surrounded by beautiful flower gardens, lawns and exotic flowering shrubs. Everywhere cheeky monkeys swing in the trees. Brunch is spectacular—everything imaginable to eat. Although we haven't been away from home very long, it feels like we've been in a different world for ever. We enjoy chatting with the guys on the base. For them, it must make a welcome change from routine, meeting people from other parts of the world, which, no doubt, is why they invite us and we all benefit.

We have exhausted the environs within safe walking distance of the yacht club and Carolyn would like to see Panama City, so we persuade Robin to take a day off from boat work. The express bus is surprisingly cheap and comfortable and is air-conditioned, which is a boon in this humid climate. It's a scenic 2-hour trip, through tropical rainforests and we glimpse all sorts of exotic flora among the trees, plus ubiquitous monkeys, colourful macaws and noisy parrots.

Panama is bursting with people. Shopping along the main street is fraught with danger, or so we are warned, because we will most likely be pick-pocketed. Carolyn seems oblivious to the possible dangers and wanders around, wallet in hand. She's fascinated by the cheap, good-quality denims for sale. Robin drags her closer to us, saying he isn't going to have to admit to Jeff that he hasn't looked after her. We make our way to the Hotel Internaçional, where things are somewhat calmer and cooler inside. In fact, it's ominously quiet, but Carolyn manages to attract attention and places a long-distance call to Jeff. She returns to us flushed, a little moist-eyed, but happy.

We have the choice of the fast bus back, or the slow bus, but the more we think about it, the more we want to get home and relax with a beer, so the fast bus it is. It only costs $6.

Two weeks disappear in a flash and it's time for Carolyn to leave and fly home to make wedding arrangements. The big yacht that will be her home for the next couple of days as they transit the canal, sends a dinghy to collect her. She's travelling light, with just one kit bag.

"What about all your clothes?" I ask.

"I've left them for you; I only brought them as throw-away gear." Carolyn is dismissive of the two dozen superior-quality T-shirts, so I accept them graciously—they'll be great for both of us. We don't prolong the parting. We've already thanked her profusely for all her support, her catering and her wonderful company. Just big hugs all round and then she's gone, zipping across the water with a wave, on her way to another adventure.

We will miss her high spirits and vitality; her cooking and champagne!

One late afternoon in the anchorage, a sleek Australian motor-sailer pulls in, slows ahead of *Orca*, rattles out its anchor and chain and drifts back, much too close to us for comfort. We hail the craft and explain to the captain in the nicest possible way, that he has just dropped his anchor on the top of our line, that we have considerable scope out as is demanded by the depth of water and we do have a 40-tonne vessel. We mention it because if the wind changes and we swing, he will be in the unenviable position of being swiped by us. We suggest perhaps he could move a little further away, as there is plenty of space in the anchorage.

The red-faced middle-aged captain responds that he and his crew are much too tired to move. However, despite his reluctance, upon consultation with his crew, it appears they do have enough energy to move and re-anchor. I think the red-faced man would have had energy enough to complain, had something unpleasant happened to his boat.

Over the weeks, we savour the delights of Colón. It is a city of contrasts. Brand new expensive 4-wheel-drive vehicles of the rich squeeze down filthy alleyways between the shanty buildings. Amid the grandeur of the Spanish colonial architecture lie hills of rotting waste. A dirty, very fat lady with elephantiasis bends to the task of sorting through some garbage. We can't fail to notice that she has no underwear. Such indignity for her. Only once, we see a garbage truck backed up to one of these mountains but as Robin points out, it is difficult to tell if it is collecting or delivering.

Colón is one of those places where, despite an initial scepticism on our part, we can obtain absolutely anything and everything we desire. We learn not to be fooled by the tiny shops with up-and-over garage-door-type shop fronts. Inside, there will be a knowledgeable artisan who, if he can't help you, will readily point you along the right road and accompany the directions with a carefully-drawn sketch map. They are the most accommodating people. They don't deal in fancy sealed packages with just half a dozen screws in each shiny bag; they have the real thing that we remember from hardware stores in the days before everything was regulated and packaged. Banks and banks of wooden drawers of various sizes worn smooth and shiny from the handling of generations, with bright brass knobs or handles and full of every conceivable fitting and fastener. Or the floor may be littered with coils and coils of wires, ropes and cables, but just name what you want and it's yours. In this manner, after only two or three tries, we are able to acquire 10 metres of 5-centimetre wide copper stripping to act as grounding for our single sideband radio.

"Well now I have a chance to get the SSB working properly," Robin says, happily. "Not only the copper grounding-strip, but we've found the right impedance coaxial cable to connect the SSB self-tuner to the main mast backstay. It's not the common TV coax, that you can find everywhere," he explains.

Taxis are used for all our excursions outside the compound, with the exception of my frequent visits to the dentist when I run all the way there and back, brandishing a stick like a lunatic gringo. Despite the fact that they look decrepit, taxis are reliable and cheap and the drivers take good care of their passengers. They'll take us anywhere and wait for us, for only a minimal charge and are expert at finding the most obscure locations. Many speak good English and will act as translators too and it's an easy job to call a taxi from the yacht club bar telephone. We just have to dial the number and say, 'Yatt cluub por favor'.

With so much electrical equipment on board *Orca*, Robin thinks it will be advantageous to have a second battery bank, so he does his research and with the help of local merchants, finds that we can buy four, deep-cycle batteries direct from the manufacturer in Panama. Weighing about 40 kg each, we can't carry them home on the bus, so we make plans to fly to Panama. We hope to take a taxi from the airport to the manufacturer, pick up the batteries and inveigle the driver into bringing us back to Colón. We are ever optimistic!

On the little aircraft to Panama, an *Embraer 110 P1 Bandeirante*, most of our co-passengers are big men with black overcoats, black tall hats, large dark beards and carrying black briefcases—wealthy businessmen with big interests in the Colón Free-Trade Zone, probably off to seal another big deal in the city. It's rather sobering later to learn that shortly after our journey, on 19th July, 1994 the aircraft was blown up by a bomb, killing all 18 passengers and 3 crew.

At Panama airport we find a taxi driver willing to take us to the battery manufacturers and wait while we conduct our business. So far so good. We have to go to the rear of the building to pick up our purchases from the loading bay. I ask the driver to back along the side alley, to the rear.

"Help me lift these into the trunk, will you?" Robin asks the driver.

He looks down at the batteries, then at us as if we're mad, his voluble tirade in Spanish is accompanied by energetic gestures. We *think* it might mean that he's not *totally* comfortable carrying them in his taxi.

I try my persuasive powers. "*How much* to the Yatt Cluub in Colón?" He grudgingly settles on a price. Probably it was a ploy to bargain for more money. Works every time. We don't mind, in his place we'd likely do the same. It's still a heck of a deal.

With the weight of the batteries in the trunk, plus us in the back seat of a vehicle with questionable suspension at best, the driver can hardly see over the dashboard. It is of no consequence, however, as he knows his way. Racing over hills and squealing around corners, he's no longer concerned about carrying batteries.

The guard at the yacht club compound also needs his palm greased, to allow the taxi to drive in to deliver our booty right to the dock. What admiring eyes there are when we unload the cargo! I guard them with my life while Robin fetches the dinghy from where it has been moored.

"What's all this stuff?" I ask Robin, when he arrives with the dinghy covered in a fine grey powder. The air seems to be rather hazy too. We look around and find the source of the problem.

"It's a cement boat. They're unloading cement powder into those trucks." Robin points across the harbour. Everything downwind is covered in a thin film of cement dust. After Rob ferries the batteries to *Orca*, two at a time, we have to hose down the dinghy. Fortunately, *Orca* is upwind of the cement unloading and saved from the covering.

One day, there's a buzz in the yacht club bar. Apparently the young Swiss single-hander we've spoken to a couple of times, was walking outside the compound alone and was stabbed and mugged. He lost his wallet, but not his life although he suffered painful wounds to his buttocks. Good job he was attacked from the rear.

It's on this day that we meet the owners of *Sara of Hamble*, John and Andy Cossey. They're from Britain and we strike up a conversation. They too, have a ferro-cement boat and have travelled extensively in her. It is a fortuitous meeting, because they ask if we'll transit the canal with them as line handlers.

"That's great, we'd love to!" It will be wonderful to have first-hand experience before taking *Orca* through. TP is happy about the arrangement and agrees to stand guard on the yacht for the two days we'll be away.

The experience is a good one and the pilot they are allotted is jolly. We overnight in man-made Gatun Lake between the two sets of locks and have quite a party; eating, drinking, singing and playing musical instruments. Our hosts are musical and we are not, but that doesn't deter us. We even encourage other people in the anchorage to join in the noise-making. After a safe passage through the Canal, we return to Colón by bus hauling two 38-metre lines the Cosseys borrowed from another yacht.

It is a red-letter day when our SSB radio is operating with its new grounding strip and backstay aerial for the self-tuner. I'm elated because now we can keep in touch with the world. The new batteries and switches are in place and the automatic pilots both function. On our trip from Cayman to Colón, the first had failed because the plastic coating of the wires was worn, causing a short in the circuit. The second autopilot, which we hadn't re-commissioned, had a toothed drive-belt, with missing teeth. As a result, the helm didn't turn when the autopilot did, and no course corrections were made. So with a new toothed belt and several spares, we are now well supplied.

"Let's check out the arrangements at the dock." I suggest when we're talking about refuelling *Orca* before the Pacific.

As we drift along the channel in the dinghy, we pass a mast sticking up out of the water close by, marked by a small buoy. It seems that a yacht sank there, but it is too costly to move it.

A vessel tied up along one side of the quay is refuelling. The fuel hose is lying across the stretch of water from the adjacent quay, kept on the surface by floats. We watch as a man tries to manoeuvre his dinghy underneath the hose, to reach his yacht on the neighbouring quay. He shouts invective at the boat being refuelled. Eventually he squeezes under the end of the hose. Moments later he's out on the deck of his gin-palace, hurling abuse and brandishing a handgun. It seems to be an example of American diplomacy at work.

"I think we'll wait to refuel in Balboa," Robin says, "I believe the access is better."

This scene reminds us of advice we received when we originally asked Billy about carrying weapons on board. Being well trained in arms he offered us the following:

"Don't carry a gun on board unless you're prepared to fire first— invariably pirates are well used to using guns and unless you shoot first, they will easily disarm you and use your weapon against you. It's a lot harder to shoot than you might think. You've got to be prepared to kill another human being, face to face. Your nature is to hail a vessel coming alongside, to see what they want—not to shoot."

This advice confirms our decision that we won't carry any arms. We have cause to remember this a few days later, when we are in Balboa.

At last it is time to arrange our canal transit. The admeasurers arrive to measure *Orca* in every conceivable direction for calculating her potential cargo-carrying capacity upon which the computations for fees are based ($40 admeasurer fee). We complete the paperwork for customs and make a trip to the Port Captain to arrange a transit time ($250 fee for 17-metre yacht). We are given *Orca*'s certificate and Ship Identification Number 344265, which should be used on every subsequent transit of the canal. All the officials are unfailingly helpful and polite.

We already have our four 2.5 cm, 38-metre long lines; multiple fenders; suitable mooring bitts—all checked by the admeasurer—and just need to have four line handlers, (hire fee $40 each). A proper meal must be provided for the transit pilot as well as shelter from the sun and rain. The final requirement is that a speed of 5 knots must be maintained throughout the passage.

It isn't difficult to find four line handlers hanging about in the bar and we hire three men; Jacques (French), Franz (German) and Carlo (Italian)—no kidding about the names. Our fourth is an American girl named Nancy, who's long since said goodbye to her girlish years.

Before departure, Robin puts on his scuba gear and dives into the filthy chemical mix of water at The Flats, to check the anchor and keel. He makes sure that nothing nasty has befallen us while we've been anchored for six weeks and checks that the log impellor isn't fouled. We're heeding the warning that maintaining a speed of 5 knots is essential. If we don't, we'll incur a fine of $295 for an aborted passage plus a further fee for re-scheduling.

8

Sea to Sea—Panama Canal Transit with Nancy

It's 4:30 a.m. and I've been awake for ages. I have to get up and start moving although we prepared everything possible last night. I make a mental check. Our lines are looped neatly on the safety lines, two fore and two aft and tied off on mooring bitts. Each has a bowline tied in the free end. The fenders are to hand and the dinghy is ready to go. Food has been prepared.

I try to climb across Robin to get out of our bunk without waking him, but he rolls over and sits up. "I guess this is it," he says, running his hands over his head and yawning. He swings his legs over the side of the bunk and pads away to the bathroom. I pull on my good shorts, shirt and deck shoes.

I check outside the hatch. It's still dark with no stars visible, so it will be another dull day. Not a bad thing for a crossing instead of the baking sun.

"Breakfast!" calls Robin. "Just cereal and tea this morning, I knew you wouldn't be able to eat much."

"Thanks." I slide into a seat at the saloon table and tackle my muesli. As soon as we finish, I wash and stow the dishes.

"Just going to make sure we've done everything," Robin says as he heads on deck.

I make the bed and check all cabins one last time to see that everything is securely lashed and all locker doors and drawers are fastened. We haven't moved for a while and I have to get back into the habit of having everything secured for a passage. I flit from task to task, like a butterfly, while Robin is systematically working through his list, outwardly calm.

Soon we'll be setting off across the largest ocean in the world, during which time we'll be the furthest away from land that is humanly possible on this globe. When I think about it a knot forms in my stomach and I have to drag my attention back to the present. Have I got enough food prepared for the pilot and the line handlers? I locate my menu and read it quickly. Chicken, ham, beef stew, salads, fruit, eggs, bacon, muffins, cookies, cheeses, breads... I think that should do it.

Robin pokes his head in the companionway.

"I've launched the dinghy and I'm just off to get the line handlers. I promised to pick them up at 5:30 a.m."

The outboard motor starts and the sound fades into the distance. We are instructed to be ready to accept the transit pilot at 6:30 a.m. so I hope the handlers haven't overslept. In fifteen minutes I look through the porthole and see the dinghy approaching with three people on board. Nancy, the tall blonde American lady and Jacques, the small dark Frenchman, climb up onto *Orca*.

Nancy immediately slips below to stow her knapsack and to find out which is her cabin. An old hand indeed. It seems she hasn't yet had time to perform her facial routine with sundry potions, so she commandeers the bathroom with the best light and the big mirror. Jacques is leaning up against the rigging; he leisurely rolls a cigarette and starts to smoke, his eyes slowly scanning *Orca*. In contrast to Nancy, he is a man of few words.

Just after 6:00 a.m. Robin is back with Franz, the German with his shock of curly blond hair and commanding eagle-like nose; and Carlo, a gentle, round Italian. They help Robin winch the dinghy on board and stow it. We have quite the cosmopolitan crew and they are straight into their duties, which is reassuring.

"I'm going to take the guys round the deck to show them the gear, where's Nancy?"

I jump below and tap on the bathroom door.

"Nancy, Robin's waiting for you on deck, he wants to run through things with you."

"OK, comes a muffled voice, sounding more like Uh-Kuh, as if she's flossing her teeth."

"She's just coming Robin." I relay the message to a serious-looking captain.

Nancy emerges, amidst an aura of cosmetic vapours. "I'll have to finish my face in a minute."

She's back downstairs in short measure. "It's important for me to look after my skin—it's very greasy," she explains.

I can see that is so as I peer into the oversized pores of her face, which is thrust close up to mine for inspection. I go back on deck to speak to Franz, Jacques and Carlo.

"Would you guys like to come below so I can show you where everything is? Then you can just look after yourselves. Would anyone like tea or coffee?" I show them the bathrooms, coffee and teapot and a basket of muffins.

The trio look around briefly and I point out where they can bunk, but they are anxious to get out on deck.

At 6:30 a.m. everything is ready. The dinghy is stowed and Robin has the engine running. All that is left is to winch up the anchor using the hand windlass. I'm secretly pleased to have more sailors on board to help with the heavy work.

"Should see the pilot soon," Robin comments, but there is no pilot launch heading towards us. There is, however, a sinister-looking black launch circling the anchorage. Inside are three men, beside the man at the helm. They have binoculars and notepads and appear to be checking each vessel.

"It's the Drug Enforcement Agency launch," Robin says. They have a base on the opposite side of the canal, at Fort Sherman. "They're looking for someone."

That's all I need to hear—are they looking for *Orca*, now we've been measured and registered to transit the canal? Have they cross-matched our details and found a match with the drug yacht when it was here previously? My mind buzzes with possibilities. I can't imagine what Robin is feeling. After a few more circuits, the DEA launch zooms off. Obviously it's not our turn to be apprehended.

"There's not much point in burning all our diesel here." Robin says as he shuts down the engine after half an hour of idling. We settle down to wait and the guys smoke. I hand round some cookies and more coffee. Nancy is in her element and chatters idly. I try to be polite and listen. Robin is lost in his own thoughts and the men have their eyes closed, resting.

7:30 a.m. passes; 8:30 a.m. passes. Pilot launches rush hither and thither to other vessels, but never approach us.

"I wonder if they've forgotten us?" I say cheerfully. It's a bit like being the last one picked to play on a ball team.

When we've all but given up hope, at 9:30 a.m. a pilot launch in the distance is heading this way, creating a massive bow wave for such a little vessel. Robin fires up the engine and as the launch draws alongside we rock quite violently from the combination of bow wave and wake. A solemn-looking rotund man scrambles aboard carrying a knapsack. He's sporting a blue-peaked white cap and a blue and white horizontally striped T-shirt with a radio grafted onto his right shoulder. His new navy deck shoes show beneath a pair of immaculate pale blue jeans. He's busy shouting into his radio, then says, "Who's the Captain?" He looks round at our motley crew. Robin introduces himself.

Waiting for the pilot

"Anchor up NOW," he orders, Quick! Quick!" We jump to our feet and mill around in all directions like a disturbed nest of ants. I go forward with Jacques and Franz to start winding up the anchor and then leave them to it. They are perfectly capable without me overseeing. The pilot has dumped his gear below in the inner steering station and stands beside Robin.

Franz cups his hands round his mouth and shouts back to Robin. "Anchor's free."

"Move out towards the lock," the pilot commands. Robin engages forward gear and advances the throttle. The pilot's radio squawks and crackles and an unintelligible voice speaks. The pilot responds. As we near the perimeter of the anchorage the pilot directs, "Circle round the anchorage slowly."

First the pilot is three hours late arriving, then he hustles us unmercifully and now we have to circle round to waste time. For another hour and a half we go round and round the anchorage, waiting for the order any moment to steam towards the lock.

Occasionally the pilot communicates with the disembodied voice on the radio, in between bursts of white noise. He is not a man to be engaged in conversation, unlike the amiable pilot we had on *Sara of Hamble*.

The line handlers have slumped back into a snooze, unable to maintain a high state of alertness and possibly to make up for a sleepless night. Nancy, her make up in place, is still chattering, although even I have given up all pretence of listening or making intelligent responses.

The radio squawks—the magic words have been heard.

"Go straight to the lock. Quick, quick." The pilot is anxious and we all jump to attention as finally we get our steaming orders at 11:00 a.m. Robin is being very restrained. He says nothing, but I know he is under stress. We can't just push the throttle wide open, because then we'll have to jam her into reverse to try to stop ramming whatever is in front of us. Also we've discovered that if we aren't patient in transferring from forward to reverse gear, *Orca* refuses to make the transition and coasts along in neutral.

"*Orca* is a ferro cement vessel," Robin patiently explains to our pilot, "she weighs 40 tonnes and takes time to get under way and a corresponding amount of time to stop. We are not a racing yacht." Perhaps the pilot has spent more time on lightweight launches than on vessels of substance.

At last we're leaving Limón Bay and the anchorage called The Flats, which has been our home for the past six weeks. It's good to be doing something positive. Franz, Carlo and Jacques are on deck at the ready and Nancy is somewhere below decks. I find her in the galley washing up a couple of spoons. "You need to squeeze just one drop of washing-up liquid onto a damp cloth—it saves water you see," she says.

"Yes, thanks. Could you go up on deck please, to be prepared?" I can't understand her reluctance and am beginning to regret letting her line-handle, despite her professed experience. She's certainly experienced, but at what? Maybe manipulation.

Orca heads towards the approach walls of the canal and the lock gates. In our application for transit we have chosen centre-lock position. This means we'll have a vessel on either side to which we will raft up. We have our big fat fenders dangling over the sides to prevent direct contact with the other boats.

The pilot urges us on. Our companion boats are already in position and we must glide in between them, each taking the other's lines and cinching them up extremely tightly, so we will react as one vessel in the lock, not three. In front of us is a large 38,000 tonne bulk carrier, the *Osland*, which is probably carrying grain. As soon as our stern is clear, the massive lock gates start closing and we are barely tied to our companion vessels when the water under and around us starts to boil as millions of gallons rush into the chamber to raise us up in the first of three steps, to the level of the next lock.

There is massive turbulence with great whirlpools and eddies, but we are securely fastened. I recall tales of insecure yachts being dashed against the rough concrete lock walls, snapping masts and suffering untold damage.

In 12 minutes we've reached the level of the next lock and the steel lock gates open. The cargo ship is pulled forward into the second chamber.

"Cast off lines, full steam ahead," the pilot yells, as do the pilots on our two companion vessels. This is where the line handlers really prove their worth. Our three vessels simultaneously retrieve lines from each other and surge ahead singly—or at least the other two surge, we are a little slower. We still haven't convinced the pilot that if we rush ahead, we'll ram the cargo ship before we can stop. He appears somewhat irritated, as if he's involved in a race and it will go against him if he's the last one. Robin remains stoic and although the pilot is in overall control of the vessel all the way through the canal, he would never take over the helm.

Inside the second chamber we re-raft with our companions and quickly gain the level of the last chamber to repeat the performance. In less than an hour we've risen 26m in three stages to the level of the manmade Gatun Lake. The lock gates open and we motor out behind the bulk carrier. Our companion vessels, with which we spent such an intimate time in the locks, pass us on either side and pull ahead without a backward glance.

Our male line handlers tidily stow the lines and fenders and the pilot once again urges Robin to all speed. He reminds us of the consequences of not maintaining 5 knots to make the crossing.

Robin calls to me, discreetly. "Hey Mags, have you noticed anything?"

"You mean apart from the fact that Nancy is lazy?" I reply. Robin raises his eyebrows, then continues. .

"The throttle is open as wide as it will go and we're not actually making 5 knots. I know the prop needs scraping, but I've just realized that we're in fresh water now, so we're riding a lot lower in the water, causing greater drag. I'll try to obscure the log from the pilot's eyes, so he can't read our speed."

We have about 10 nautical miles to go in the lake to the anchorage where we will have to stay overnight. The speedy million-dollar yacht with its snooty crew from our port side will be able to complete the transit in one day, but we can't reach the Miraflores locks before they are used for traffic coming from the Pacific.

"Anyone want some lunch?" It's time to feed the crew.

We tuck into cold chicken, ham, potatoes, salads and cold beer, that is, all except the pilot and Robin who steadfastly stick to their tasks; Robin urging *Orca* onwards and the pilot urging Robin. I can only persuade the pilot to drink a juice.

The weather has deteriorated into a persistent and annoying drizzle and after lunch the crew take the opportunity of catching up on their sleep in the cabins below.

There are a couple of other boats in the anchorage when we arrive, but we anchor without incident. It is beautifully calm. Our pilot looks tired and is happy to jump into the little launch which has appeared from nowhere, to whisk him away for the night.

"I'll be back at 10:30 a.m.," he says, "be ready."

Robin breathes a sigh of relief. "I could do with that beer now!"

While the beef stew is heating for supper, the line handlers swim in the fresh water of Gatun Lake. I keep watch for alligators from the upper deck—oh yes, there are freshwater alligators. I dole out fluffy towels as they return to the boat.

Refreshed, they snack on chips, nuts, beer and wine until supper time. It has stopped raining and we sit around on deck, swapping stories and generally relaxing for the evening, then one by one, drift off to bed.

We're up bright and early. A couple of the guys have slept on deck. They take the opportunity before breakfast of having another swim. Robin and I don masks, snorkels and fins and dive over the side with knives and scrapers to clean barnacles off the prop and rub off some of the growth from Colón Harbour. Our brief stay in the freshwater has done wonders to kill off the saltwater marine life attached to the hull. By the time we've finished, the brass prop looks shiny instead of covered with a thousand tiny sea anchors. We climb the steps to *Orca*, to prepare breakfast.

By the time I've dressed, Robin is already cooking eggs and bacon for the crew.

"Gee, that smells good!" Nancy follows her nose into the galley and looks over Robin's shoulder.

"Got to start the day right," he tells her, "you've still got lots of work to do."

I'm not sure the subtle hint will work on Nancy.

We eat breakfast on deck and drink scalding tea and coffee. The men, as usual, are quiet, but Nancy is happy to fill in any voids in the conversation.

"This is how you should sandpaper your mahogany," she says, and offers to spend some time working on part of the stern handrail. I fetch a piece of the required grade of sandpaper, so she can start straight away. She also gives me her good advice on varnishing techniques, which I must take note of so I can apply them later.

At 10:30 we are ready and waiting, but our pilot is late. When he arrives he rushes aboard trailing his rain gear.

"Full steam ahead," he instructs. We must reach Pedro Miguel lock by 12 noon, or we won't get through before they open the gates to traffic from the Pacific. We have 6 nautical miles to cover.

I stand next to Robin, anxiously looking at the log as he plunges the throttle forward. The line-handling trio have raised the anchor and stowed everything securely. Nancy is nowhere to be seen.

"Look Mags, we're making over 6 knots!" Robin grins. "No problem today, it must have been cleaning the prop that did it and the freshwater killing the seawater life on the hull."

He whistles tunelessly through his teeth. It's a treat to see him happy.

"This is my first solo crossing of the Canal," our young pilot admits, "the first time I've been in charge of a vessel." Thankfully he's loosening up at last. Now he realizes that we'll be on time, he's relaxing. It seems a stressful job. The radio on his right shoulder continues to emit squeaks and he mutters into it from time to time.

We motor through Gaillard Cut, the narrow channel blasted through the mountains of the intercontinental divide, scanning the horizon for the marker buoys. We must ensure we keep in our appointed lane so we don't interfere with oncoming traffic. It would be fascinating to see the semitropical landscape on either side of us and catch a glimpse of exotic birds and monkeys, but the cloud is very low and it is gently raining again. Not an auspicious start to the day we first view the Pacific. At least the pilot and Robin are sheltered by the new awning I made in Colón.

I serve coffee and cookies to the crew and pilot. Shortly before we reach Pedro Miguel Lock the cloud starts lifting and we can just make out Gold Hill on our port side, 202 metres above sea level. There is not much transiting traffic today and we're the last few vessels travelling towards the Pacific. This time we motor to the forward part of the lock. On the downward trip through the locks, small vessels are moored in front of the giant ships. The line handlers are at the ready and we raft up on our starboard side to what looks like a naval party boat on a trip. Lots of doors opening and shutting along the side and children running in and out. They all look very happy—a contrast to my nagging unease as I contemplate the Pacific.

There is no one on our port side, so only one pair of line handlers is necessary, which is useful, because Nancy is once more ensconced in the bathroom performing her daily magic before she's unleashed on Balboa. I dart about with big fenders which I try to stuff between our companion vessel and my prized varnish work. The massive steel lock gates swing closed and we begin the descent from our lofty 26 metres above sea level.

There are just the two of us in this mighty chamber. I pick up the literature book and read: "In this first step we are going to be lowered 10 metres." As I speak, the water disappears as the plugs are removed from our giant bathtub. We can measure our progress as the wall seemingly grows beside us. In a few minutes the gates opens to reveal the small man-made Miraflores Lake, 2 kilometres wide, across which we must motor to the last two-stage Miraflores Locks where we'll be lowered a further 16 metres to the Pacific Ocean.

"The last set of lock walls are taller than at the Caribbean end of the canal," I continue reading snippets of information from my booklet, "to contend with the much greater tidal differences of the Pacific; up to 4 metres as compared to less than one metre tidal difference in the Caribbean."

It seems no time at all before we have entered, lowered and exited the remaining two locks.

The line handlers release and retrieve lines and fenders for the last time and a pilot launch comes alongside, matching our speed as we motor. Robin steadies the pilot as he steps down into the moving launch.

"Many thanks for all your help," we shout at his departing figure. Hopefully he feels his first assignment was OK and will be more confident and relaxed on his next.

The fresh water of the lakes and locks is behind us and we're in the salty Pacific. We pass under the Bridge of the Americas—the 1653-metre section of the Pan American Highway reuniting North and South America, which was divided during construction of the canal. I ask one of the handlers to pop the cork on a bottle of ice-cold champagne and we all have a glass to celebrate, plus of course, a traditional glass for Neptune—not that I'm superstitious.

Once under the bridge, we enter the Bay of Panama with the mighty Pacific Ocean ahead of us. I silently hope it will be peaceful for us. On our port side is the area with mooring buoys where we may tie up. It's almost full, but Robin manoeuvres to an available mooring and Franz expertly uses the boat hook to pick up the floating line which we attach to our mooring bitts.

The men have left everything typically ship-shape and Nancy has managed to repack her facial restoration kit and other gear into her huge knapsack and hefts it up on deck. We pay the line handlers their US$40.00 each—Nancy at the head of the queue—and blow an air horn to hail a passing water taxi to take them to shore.

Nancy is holding back. "I've line-handled on many boats and have never enjoyed my time as much as on *Orca*." She's flattering us. "Are you sure you won't let me crew all the way across the Pacific to the Marquesas? I could do all your varnish work."

Politely, but firmly we decline. Cruising is new to us and we'd rather learn it without the responsibility of unknown crew. We have faith in each other's abilities and a third person does not fit into our plan. Carolyn was wonderful from Cayman to Colon, but we knew each other well and had sailed together several times.

I once heard of a captain threatening bodily harm to a casual crew member who ate all the captain's favourite peanut butter. It gets that serious. I imagine it wouldn't be long before we got tired of her and slipped her overboard.

Robin checks the security of our mooring and we collect our papers, money and shopping bags before locking up the vessel and calling a water taxi to ferry us to Balboa Yacht Club. It will be May 1st, tomorrow, a public holiday and the yacht club office will be closed. We must pay ahead of time for the fuel we will require to top up our tanks before leaving and for our club fees and mooring fees.

We pay our mooring fees—$35 for two days; our Club Visitors fees—$15; and our fuel bill, we telephone for a taxi to take us to the local 24-hour market. We must complete our provisioning and stock up on the last few fresh items.

After shopping, we sit back in the ancient taxi en route to the yacht club and Robin asks, "Have you got the passports? Once we have an exit stamp, everything will be in order."

Or will it?

We carry our bags through the car park to the Immigration Office. Robin hands over the passports, the 'Zarpe' customs clearance and the port clearance which we obtained in Cristobal.

The official reads the documents, stamps Robin's passport and returns it. He then flicks through mine, stamps it and holds it out, but just as I lean to take it, he snatches it back for a second look. "Your visa is out of date."

We originally obtained a 30-day visa on entry to Panama, not knowing that we'd have to stay six weeks. We seem to have missed extending our visa although we did change our yacht permit from 'for transit' to 'for navigation in Colón waters'.

We are so close to leaving and yet still so far away. We have no 'Paz y Salvo' and no 'Visa de Salida'—that seems to be the problem. Robin is protectively clutching his passport to his chest, while I try to argue with the official that we are leaving tomorrow and there is no point now to getting an extension. Oh! The paperwork that would be involved and the making of excuses for our oversight is more than I care to think about. He is upset. It is his duty to see that all papers are in order and we've been in the country illegally for the past few weeks. He's obviously considering his options.

I'm not about to see all our plans fall through for one minor discrepancy, so while he is remonstrating and waving my passport, I reach across his desk, take a firm grip on it and give a sharp tug.

"Thank you so much," I say, smiling falsely. "Goodbye."

With that, we smartly turn around and walk swiftly down the ramp, along the boardwalk to the water taxi and jump aboard without a backward glance. I imagine it is a little too much trouble to follow and apprehend us. After all, it is almost time to close the office and tomorrow is a government holiday.

We're feeling rather more comfortable once the water taxi is under way and settle back to look around us.

"Look at that yacht!" Robin says, as we pass a familiar-looking vessel. "It belongs to that couple we spoke to at the refuelling dock."

We idly wonder why it is tied up in Balboa. Later we learn the couple were anchored off Cocos Island, alone, when a power skiff came alongside with three men in it. They boarded the yacht and in a scuffle, the husband was shot in the leg with his own gun but the wife was left unharmed. Presumably the men were not dedicated pirates and became scared. The couple were lucky to escape with their lives.

Safely aboard *Orca* once more, we vow not to leave. We can't hear our name being called over Channel 16 on the ship's radio, so presumably we're not *wanted* persons.

Pacific bound

"That settles it," Rob says to me, "we're not going ashore for supper tonight."

The food that is left over from the transit provides an ample supper with a glass of wine.

We mull over the last couple of days and realize that we've come through Panama unscathed. *Orca* has retained her anonymity and has not been snatched back, so we can lay that ghost to rest.

All we have to do is fuel up tomorrow, and then the world is ours.

9

Apprehension and Facing Reality—Pacific Ocean

"Only 4,000 nautical miles to our next landfall," Robin cheerfully reminds me as we are at last leaving Panama. "That's 8,000 km, further than from Victoria, B.C. to St. John's, Newfoundland. We're finally on our way round the Pacific!"

I don't really need to be reminded of the fact.

It is noon. Dozens of pelicans rise and dip in precisely choreographed, wave-like formations as they escort us from the Panama coastline. A rusty-chested martin flies aboard for a free ride, clamping its feet onto the mizzen backstay. TP hasn't seen it yet. She is tucked into a small corner behind the steering wheel, hypnotized by the perpetual rise and fall of the water, never taking her eyes from it. It's a task to which she devotes herself for the next several weeks. I'm not sure if she's happy or not to be in motion again. I've given her a tiny crumb of Gravol this time, so I don't knock her out. We started sea-sick pills last night and will continue for a day or so, till we're acclimatized.

The sky today is peacock blue, the sun fierce. A welcome change from the drizzle of the past two days. The only air flow is created by our passage as we motor across oily-calm waters, with the autopilot now steering proficiently. Dressed in long-sleeved cotton shirts and wearing caps, we are in good spirits and anticipate wind once we're away from land influence. Then we can raise the sails. Robin whistles his tuneless whistle. He is highly optimistic about the voyage—his dream of the last four years is finally coming to fruition.

Occasional patches of garbage float by; plastic bags, blocks of polystyrene, waxed cartons and rotting vegetation, all intertwined with straggling fishing net. A legacy left by ocean-going vessels.

Bang! My heart thuds. I rush to look over one side of the yacht, fearing the worst.

"Just a small deadhead." Robin is reassuring. "It's nothing

compared to the stuff round Vancouver Island, so stop worrying."

We wait expectantly for a couple of hours for some wind. The sails are ready to hoist and everything below decks is strapped down and secured, prepared for rough weather. As we round the outer sea buoy, Panama is only a smudge on the horizon behind us, fast disappearing into the haze. The largest ocean in the world stretches before us and we will be crossing the equator into the South Pacific to reach our first destination, the Marquesas Islands, French Polynesia. This will be the longest leg of our voyage in circumnavigating the Pacific. We will be isolated on our 17-metre home for more than a month.

As the distance from land increases, so does the magnitude of the Pacific Ocean swells and the yacht starts to roll: left … right … left … right … port … starboard … port … starboard … one roll about every 2 seconds. A phenomenon that will stay with us for most of the next five weeks. Where is the wind?

The enormity of our undertaking dawns upon me. Anxiety and the continual rolling motion combine to make me feel queasy. I take another sea-sick pill and give a fraction more to the cat, who doesn't seem too happy either. I glance at Robin and smile—a weakly smile that refuses to involve my eyes. I don't think he's fooled.

The engine is running smoothly, though, so we have no worries. Yet I worry. What if we meet pirates? They're pretty common on this Panama coast. *Orca* was commandeered by pirates in the Indian Ocean and then used for drug running. What if the engine fails when there's no wind? How will we manage in a storm? I try to think pleasant thoughts and imagine brilliant skies, tropical fish in clear waters and the sandy beaches of our destinations, but I cannot banish the endless vignettes of disasters passing through my mind which invariably involve tumbling in bubbles, rolling, gasping for breath and being drawn into the depths below. I've always had nightmares about drowning, which is why Robin and our children insisted that I learn to swim.

I know this is self-destructive, but there is a fine dividing line between worrying uselessly and thinking through scenes so one is prepared in case of need.

I can feel a breeze on my face and see cats' paws on the water.

"OK, let's raise some sails," says Robin as he's already moving forward to undo the restraining clips on the mainsail. It's good to have something positive to do. Once the mainsail and genoa are set and the autopilot is fine tuned we turn off the engine. Sailing at last! The throb of the diesel engine is replaced by the swoosh of the water passing the hull as *Orca* cuts a swathe through the sea.

Like a smothering blanket, night closes in rapidly after the sun disappears below the horizon. I choose to take first watch as there's no way I'll be able to sleep yet. Robin goes below to rest and I am left alone. He has that wonderful ability to switch off, relax and sleep.

I slowly turn 360° to scan the horizon, checking for boat traffic. Pinpricks of light from the occasional vessel approaching Panama pass by on our port side and shrink into the blackness. One by one they disappear towards the land, warmth and company that we are leaving behind. For a moment I wonder if we should turn around and follow them back. Instead, sliding my safety harness clip along the jack-line running from stern to bow, I look past the doghouse to check the shape of the sails. I need something to focus my mind on. Perhaps I should sheet in the genoa just a bit? If I can improve the shape of the sail a little, I can adjust the autopilot to steer slightly closer to our optimum direction, which could reduce our journey time.

I collect the winch handle from its slot by the lazarette seat and manipulate my harness lead to allow me access to the winch. As I try to insert the handle into the winch top I fumble, and it flies from my grasp—plop!—straight over the side.

Adrenaline courses through my system instantly up to my shoulders and down to my feet and icy fingers clutch at my stomach. In disbelief, I stupidly watch the spot where the handle disappeared willing myself back in time a few moments, so that I might be more careful. How did I allow this to happen? I can't believe it. What will I tell Robin? We don't have too many spare handles. I return to my watch position and scan the horizon again for signs of vessels. I shiver, it's cold.

After three hours, Robin relieves me from my watch and I go below to the cabin to lie down in the darkness, but it is impossible to sleep.

The noise of the water rushing past the porthole right by my ear is so loud and so 'liquid', sloshing and slapping at the hull. When the yacht heels over, the lower part of the porthole is actually under water. It is only strengthened glass set in a mahogany frame—what if

Captain's bunk

it can't withstand the pressure? Sleep won't release me from reality.

Somehow the hours drag by. We rotate watches once more before the sky lightens in the east. Robin looks grey and tired. Perhaps he's really as anxious as I am, but he knows he has to be strong for both of us. I'm sure I look ghastly. I daren't look into a mirror, I know a haunted face will be staring back.

The day passes and I feel like a zombie. We raise and lower sails, trying different combinations to increase our speed. Sometimes the engine is on, sometimes off. We check and recheck the security of our equipment.

Life is ordered by the clock. I prepare some food. We try to eat—we need energy, but have no appetite.

Something is wrong with my face. I can feel two heavy weights tugging down the corners of my mouth. My throat aches and my lower lip keeps trembling. I bite it hard to keep it still. Surely this is not what sailing is all about?

TP now watches the water from a new vantage point on the cabin roof. I feel sure she will slither off when we are rolled by a big swell. Man-overboard drill for a cat is not possible.

The sun sinks into the sea while I am on watch again with the rusty-chested bird and cat for company. The cat has lost her appetite too, she hasn't eaten and doesn't give the martin a second glance, although it's well within reach. During the day we raise the staysail and sheet it in tightly along the midline to try to reduce the rolling motion. It doesn't seem to make much difference. At night my eyes ache from lack of sleep and from staring into the blackness. There is nothing to see, except our phosphorescent path, reaching back, like an umbilical towards the security of land.

Aeons pass before my watch is over, but finally I can wake Robin. I hand him a cup of tea, give the night report, then stumble below to wedge myself on the bunk, jamming my feet against the weather boards and my head against the hull, to counteract rolling. It's our second night on the Pacific and we've only gone about 50 nautical miles. I'm desperately tired. I drop into an uneasy twitching sleep, born of exhaustion.

My dreams are hallucinatory. I don't know if I'm really on the yacht or at home experiencing a nightmare. I toss from side to side, willing myself to wake up to sanity, wanting to be rid of the violent sea scenes that plague me. Something grabs my shoulder. I sit bolt upright, as if powered by a gigantic spring. It is Robin waking me. "Please, please tell me this is all a horrible dream." I beg. "I can't do this."

It isn't a dream, of course. *This* is reality. We are on the ocean and must survive several weeks before reaching land. I realize I have to confront and accept the truth. I have to be strong, for Robin's sake. We are a partnership. We are not turning back, this *is* our life now.

Breathing slowly and deeply, I dress in warm clothes, strap on my safety harness and climb the steps to poke my head out of the companionway opening onto the deck. I clip myself to a safety point and step out. Robin hands me a steaming mug of tea and a digestive biscuit. His strength is palpable.

"Thanks." I murmur. I scan the horizon and then look up to the heavens. The stars are like billions of gems scattered across black velvet, intensely brilliant. Why didn't I see the stars yesterday? The ocean is like liquid velvet, with silvery phosphorescent traces.

"Look there!" Robin points over the side. "We've got company." A group of porpoises is swimming alongside—playing in and out of our wake, creating their own mercurial trails. We're not alone—it's comforting to have them here.

My mal-de-mer has passed and I sense the tiny beginnings of an inner calm. The icy fingers that have been clutching at my stomach are thawing and loosening their grip.

A fair breeze fans my face and is gently filling the sails. It is breathtakingly beautiful out here at night. I reach for Robin's hand, squeeze it and smile my first real smile for two days.

"We'll be fine," I say.

TP on the Pacific

10

It Always Happens on My Watch—36 Days at Sea

The nightmare of my first two days from Panama is over and we settle into a routine on board. The SSB becomes a lifeline to me as I can keep in contact with other yachts crossing the Pacific. Morning and evening I tune in to the yachties' 'net.' Usually I just listen. It brightens my day and I can get the latest news in the early morning before Robin relieves me from my watch. Although we should use our official call signs, like 'Zulu Charlie Foxtrot, One-Five-Eight-Five', yachties call each other using boat names.

'Sea Squirt, Sea Squirt, Sea Squirt, this is Heavenly Body. Over.'

Each day, regulars to the net call in their longitude and latitude, local weather and sea conditions and relate items of interest. This morning it is *quite* interesting.

"I've got a painful red rash all over my groin and penis," the sailor confides.

My eyebrows shoot up into my hairline as I reach to turn up the volume on the SSB.

Two South African doctors sailing across the Pacific carry on a long-distance practice. They recommend treatments for minor ailments and give instructions to the single-hander who has amputated the top of his finger in a winch. Amazingly he heals without infection. The greatest indignity, however, with a radio doctor is that there is absolutely *no* privacy.

"Hey, Rob, I hope *we* don't have to call in about anything personal!" Robin's answering glare suggests that he wouldn't do it in a million years. He'd be stoic to the last.

We—that is the other boaters and I—follow with undivided attention the plight of the poor sailor and his rash. Twice a day we have graphic updates. Robin doesn't listen to the boat chatter, but nonetheless is happy for me to relay information to him. Weeks later we meet the unfortunate young man on a Tongan Island at a gathering of yachties. Robin whispers to me through clenched teeth,

"*Don't* make any comments and *don't* ask any questions." As if I would! There will just have to be a big gap in my medical knowledge, that's all.

Occasionally, to pass the time on night watch, I lie on the deck looking up, to identify familiar constellations and stars. "There's good old Orion the hunter," I say out loud to no one in particular, "and Taurus the bull." They are my personal favourites, as they are so easy to identify. I can see the Pleiades, Castor and Pollux the heavenly twins and Sirius the Dog Star—all these old friends make me feel close to home. They look down over the family we've left behind. In a few months we'll be looking for the Southern Cross and a whole new batch of stars from the southern hemisphere.

Each morning we plot our position on the chart and can see how far we've travelled in the previous 24 hours. It's often disheartening. During slack periods in the day, we read books and at midday Robin practices taking noon shots with the sextant, so he can calculate our longitude and latitude. Having the GPS is so easy, but if anything should go wrong with it, we would have to use traditional celestial navigation.

"I'm doing some laundry, have you got anything?" I ask one morning. With the slack winds, motoring day after day can be mind-numbingly boring. Relief comes in the shape of tasks such as 'laundry in a bucket', using our precious fresh water, although I know we can always burn precious diesel to convert sea water into potable water. Robin, helpfully, lessens my chore and the strain on the water by wearing as little as possible. He has another way of reducing water use. One day the dark clouds actually offer precipitation, but no wind.

"Yippee, it's raining!" He rushes below for soap and moments later is luxuriating on the top deck in a mass of bubbles and lather, singing loudly. "Come on Mags," he calls, "it's lovely."

I reluctantly strip off and join him. Vigorous soaping action keeps me warm for a few moments, but then I have to wait for the rain to rinse off the excess foam and soon I'm freezing. I really must work on adding a bit of body fat to give me some protection from the elements. Robin looks as though he's enjoying a Finnish sauna. I'm more concerned with getting dry and warm again.

Avoiding laundry

Later, a tantalizing smell of baking wafts up from the galley. Robin pops his head out of the companionway. "Surprise!" He produces a perfect loaf from behind his back and holds it out for inspection. It's his first attempt.

"It looks fabulous," I say, "there's nothing like the smell of freshly baked bread, can we try a slice now? No wait a minute, let me take a picture first."

Robin has the patience and strength to knead dough and is practicing his art. He's also considering cakes and cookies, which he happens to like eating. It helps to fill in time. I concentrate on breakfasts and suppers. Baking is not therapeutic for me; I prefer meat, vegetables and rice which can all be cooked together in a pressure cooker, in about 15 minutes, on the propane stove. We have a great variety of frozen meat on board—pork, beef, chicken and lamb which can be cooked this way. We also have enough cheeses to open a delicatessen, but no fish. We anticipate catching some along the way.

Captain's loaf

"It's time to put out a fishing line." Rob says one morning.

"Good idea. The people on the net are always bragging about the fish they catch."

We dig out our hand-line and tackle box and assemble a lure on a long line, trailing it from the stern of the yacht and wait. Nothing happens during the few minutes we watch, so we leave it and go about our business. A bit later, we pull in a very light line. No weights, no hooks and no lure.

"Never mind, we'll try again." I say, but the same thing happens. On our third attempt we wait with the line. It doesn't take long.

"I think we've got something!" Rob says.

"Quick, quick, haul it in."

No time to reel it in carefully, so using chain-mail gloves we were given by Bill—remnants from his work at a meat-packing plant for a summer job—we haul in the line, hand over hand and it piles up on the deck. I lean over with a huge landing net ready to scoop up supper, but as the head appears out of the water and the line takes the weight of the great fish the line breaks. A beautiful turquoise and yellow mahi mahi, (dorado or dolphin fish) plops back into the water.

"You let it go." says Rob, looking at me with disappointment.

"I couldn't get the net under it." I retort.

Now we have no fish, but we do have a bird's nest of line on the deck. Robin tries to untangle it, but soon stomps off in disgust. There are obviously more important things demanding his attention. He's not at his best with trivial tasks.

I take up the line and work on it for an hour and a half until it is all back on the hand reel, tangle-free. I assemble a lure—a silver spoon this time—and a large multiple hook, plus more weights. The line slips out behind the yacht. After I watch it for a while, I can see something black sticking up out of the water. I call Robin. "What's that in the water?"

"Uh-oh. Looks awfully like shark fins to me." He confirms my suspicion. "Reel it in carefully, there's probably a fish on the line." Indeed there is and a shark is trailing it. The shark draws closer, but when only 15 metres away, it disappears taking the fish and gear with it, severing the line.

We decide not to throw away any more equipment. Obviously we are not competent fishermen. When I tell of our misfortune on the yachties' net, a voice advises me: "You've got to use a much heavier line with a 6-metre steel trace at the end so that it can't be bitten off." Oh well! Something for the shopping list when we get ashore. Meanwhile, we give up fishing—well almost. We employ a simpler method.

When the sun has risen each morning at the end of my watch, I make a quick round of the deck, checking equipment and making sure all is well and sometimes I pick up a stranded flying fish. It has a remarkable armour-plated carapace which protects it as it dives back into the sea from great heights, and its fins pull out into extraordinary semi-circular 'wings'. Best of all, they are delicious and help to make up for our lack of fishing skill. Often we can see a shoal leaping from the sea and flying a considerable distance to outwit predators such as the mahi mahi.

One day, fairly early in the morning we are both below decks, when we hear a strange series of noises above our heads. "Floop,

floop, flop", several 'floops' in quick succession. We pop on deck. "Squid!" We say simultaneously. Nineteen young squid, about 12 cm long have jet-propelled their way onto the deck and are stranded. Delighted, we pounce on them and Robin takes them below to clean.

"Hey, fresh calamari for breakfast!" he says. Indeed we enjoy a sumptuous feast with enough for two more meals.

Saloon

I hate giving bad news. Rob has so much responsibility, but being the engineer, he's the only one who can diagnose and correct certain problems. "I'm sorry, but the log's not working," I tell him. The log, which shows our speed through the water, isn't giving any reading. He takes out his multimeter and checks the electrical connections, but all seems well.

"I expect the impellor's fouled," he says. The tiny propeller, the size of my little fingertip, is situated on the belly of the boat, about two-thirds of the way between bow and stern. It spins as water flows across it. Robin checked it before we left Panama. "I'll dive under the yacht and check it again," he says.

"You can't. Now your ear infection is getting better it would be stupid to go into the water just yet. *I'll* go over the side and check it, I don't mind."

Rob turns off the engine and after a considerable time we coast to a standstill, rolling with the swells. I am wearing a long-sleeved leotard—to protect my skin from tiny jellyfish stings—and my harness with a line tied to it, so in the event of an accident, he can winch me up. Sitting on the side of the yacht, I put on my fins and spit in my mask, rub saliva round the inside of the glass and lower it into the water to rinse it, using the snorkel as a handle. I fit my mask and am ready. I'm also wearing a weight belt, to help me sink. Without it, hovering a metre or so beneath the surface is impossible.

I lower myself into the refreshingly cool water. Looking down into the depths, I slowly pirouette, scanning the area below me. Shafts of white light pierce the top blue layers of water like sunlight through cathedral windows. Further down, the blue intensifies to a midnight-blue colour, then there is nothing to see. I shiver a little. We are an insignificant piece of flotsam and below us are hundreds of fathoms of ocean, home to unknown creatures. I remember the winch handle I dropped overboard a few days ago and can visualize it plunging down into the depths. I hold onto my lifeline and poke my head into the air.

"The impellor should be about in line with this port hole." Robin says, indicating the position.

"Right, I'm ready. Don't let go of the line." I take a deep breath, and clutching a little brush in one hand and my dive knife in the other, I am prepared for weed, barnacle or adversary. At the first attempt I can't find the impellor and have to surface to breathe again.

"No good. I'll go again," I gasp, holding onto the boat as I catch my breath. I dive once more. It's strange to be peering and feeling along the underbelly of the yacht underwater after knowing it so intimately on dry land. There's a green filmy build-up of algae below the water line already—I could write my name in it. By the time I find the impellor I'm out of breath, break surface, and gulp in air.

"OK, I've found it; I'll do it this time." A headfirst dive, a flip of the fins below the surface and I'm searching again with my hands. It's incredibly noisy down here, the yacht creaks and groans and cracks. Ah ha! Here it is. I give the impellor a few gentle rubs with the brush and a couple of twiddles. There don't appear to be any barnacles to be cut off so I spin the tiny blades again to make sure they're free and with bursting lungs, surface.

"I can't go down again, Rob. If it works it does, if not, too bad." I have a mental image of eyes watching me from the depths; I've certainly made enough commotion to attract something. But I'm in luck, I don't have to go over the side again, the log is working.

For the past 12 days the engine has been running. When I wake ready for my watch at midnight, something is different.

"Hallelujah!" I shout, when I check the wind speed. "We've got 15 knots of wind." I step outside. Robin smiles and hands me some hot chocolate. He has the sails well set and we are cutting a furrow through the water, making 7 knots. "Isn't it fantastic to hear just the water instead of the engine?"

This is an exceedingly good moment and we're both elated. Before Robin goes off watch, we celebrate by opening a bar of his favourite Cadbury's fruit and nut chocolate from my hidden store of special treats. After 24 hours, however, the wind drops and the swells take over, tipping the boat and spilling the meagre breezes from the sails. We're back to motoring again.

"We might as well take advantage of the doldrums," Robin says as we slop around, "and go up the mast to check the state of the halyard in the guides. We've hauled the sails up so often, there's bound to be wear up there."

"Can I do it Rob?" I ask after a moment's reflection. I've been up the mast many times on dry land—18 metres high with metal steps set into the sides about one metre apart. "Remember that poor man who had a heart attack when he was at the top of the mast? His wife couldn't get him down and had to motor the yacht for several days before she reached land, with him swinging from the mast in a bosun's chair. What a nightmare. You could run the boat without me, but I couldn't without you."

"If it makes you happy." Robin says and clips the halyard from the mainsail onto my harness. He winds the rope round the winch and as I climb, he takes up the slack, so that if I fall, I can't go far. The deck at the base of the mast is 3 metres above sea level. At 21 metres up I'm at the top of the world. I look all round and can see nothing but endless blue sky touching endless dark blue sea. It's all rather magnificent. I have to keep a firm grip, because *Orca* rolls 30° to port, then 30° to starboard, although it seems a lot more from up here. I daren't look straight down when I'm hanging out over the water. I make an inspection under Robin's shouted guidance from the deck and all seems well. Bit by bit he releases the halyard as I climb down.

"Let's check the chart," Robin says, "tomorrow is a milestone; sometime we should cross the equator."

It's 2:00 p.m. we are nearly there. I stand on the top deck and look all round with the binoculars but sadly, there is no line around the middle of the earth. Robin is whistling through his teeth, as he takes the cork out of a chilled bottle of champagne. He pours three glasses. One for me, one for him, and one for Neptune. The ritual is fun and a perfect excuse for a glass of bubbly for the first time in weeks. The sea looks like a blob of mercury. No air movement, not a ripple. The engine is purring. We dribble a glass into the sea, to appease the great sea god and hope for good winds.

"Cheers Mags, we've made it so far!" Robin says, chinking his glass on mine. "I love you, thanks for coming along!" He gives me a bear hug. We are now in the southern hemisphere. I sip the champagne, savouring each drop. A warm glow spreads through me from my stomach to my shoulders, to my fingertips and feet. Everything is tingling. There are no disasters tonight to mar our tranquillity.

"I don't know where the hell these trade winds are," Robin moans a few days later.

"Yeah, so much for consistent 10—15 knots from the south east." Sometimes the breeze reaches 7 knots and we start hauling up sails in anticipation of strengthening winds, but then they die away and the sails are flogging … flop … flop … flop. It is only marginally cheering that none of the Pacific sailors ahead of us has any better winds, we're all complaining. However, their lighter vessels will sail in lighter breezes.

Near the equator it is so hot during the day, that we can't step on the deck without footwear, yet when the sun sets, it rapidly becomes very cold and we're often muffled in sweaters, jackets and woolly hats. One night I am sitting on watch, reading a book by flash light. There is no moon, no boat traffic and all is calm, then THWACK!

Something slams into my shoulders and head. I catapult off the lazarette seat, a sledge hammer pounding in my chest. It is like being flogged with a huge wet towel. But there is nothing out here! Or is there? What the hell hit me? Giant squid, giant octopus? My pulse is racing as I very cautiously shine my lamp behind the lazarette where I was sitting. I expect to see the tip of a tentacled limb, but wedged in the gap between the mast rigging and the seat back is a huge grey creature. It's quiet and not fighting, so I won't disturb Robin. I move to the starboard seat and keep watching. My book has lost its appeal. Toward the end of my watch, I make a cup of tea and rouse Robin.

When daylight arrives the creature recovers. With huge effort, it squeezes out from behind the lazarette, waddles to the foremost part of *Orca* and flaps up onto the pulpit. It stays for three days.

"It's a male Brown Booby," Robin says, reading from our bird book, "it's called that because it allowed sailors to get up close and kill it for food. Do you fancy some Booby meat? It's probably the closest thing we'll get to fish and it will be easy to grab him."

"How could you say that?" I'm disgusted. "Look at it sitting there, you couldn't call that sport."

Robin delights in teasing me where animals are concerned. It is a magnificent bird, with a delightfully dumb expression.

"It is a member of the pelican family and has a wingspan of 1½ metres," Robin continues, "and mainly eats flying fish."

It isn't frightened of us as we go about our daily tasks. It's rather fun having an independent pet aboard and I'm glad that Brown Booby does not appear on the yacht's menu. Perhaps he was responsible for our feast of flying fish, driving them out of the water. TP doesn't pay him any attention.

Booby on pulpit

Day after day of slatting sails has caused considerable chafing. "Look at the mainsail," Rob says one morning after a routine check, "there are slits in it where it's rubbed on the shrouds."

"Oh Great! Now we've got to take the whole bloody sail down." I grumble. It's a huge job.

"Well, if we don't repair the slits they'll soon get worse and the whole sail will shred."

I do *not* need to be told this. I *know* it, but it will be a major undertaking.

I am not wrong. It's an atrocious job. The 83-square-metre sail is thick, heavy and fully battened. There are four horizontal pockets at intervals through the length of the sail which contain plastic battens or 'stiffeners' laced into them in order to help the sail maintain a good shape and to prevent sag.

First we have to unlace these pockets, remove the screws which hold the battens in place and slide out the battens. Next we must release the sail's leading edge sliders from the slot in the mast and lower the sail to the deck. We're left with a massive heap of sailcloth slithering everywhere as we roll from side to side. We spread it out bit by bit and mark the areas which have to be repaired, so that I can first prepare patches to sew on.

"I think we'll bring the sewing machine out here as it's calm," I say, "and you can manipulate the sail while I stitch." Robin runs a long cable from the generator to the sewing machine and we're ready. I sit on the deck with one leg straight out, the other leg bent so I can operate the foot pedal. We laboriously stitch the patches over the slits. Robin has to crawl around carefully pulling the sail over the concrete deck, so I can turn the corners of the patches. We also have to contend with the Pacific swell which repeatedly rolls Orca from starboard to upright to port, one roll every few seconds. Stitch stitch … hang on to machine … stitch stitch … hang onto machine. It takes all day and is well past supper and into first watch when we finally have the sail reinstalled and are eating baked beans and poached eggs on toast.

"OK Rob, you're right, I *am* glad we did it!"

My earlier fear of being alone on the ocean has been replaced by chronic frustration at the inability to sail and the amount of work required just to keep things in good shape. "If there were a dock out here, I'd tie up, get off and never come back." I say the next day.

"Don't worry," Robin says, in an atypical burst of emotion, "so would I."

At sunset, I gaze at the sun sinking behind the horizon. Every evening I watch for the elusive 'green flash', the somewhat mythical phenomenon that is reputed to occur the instant the last of the sun sinks below the horizon. The sea is glassy and there is not a wisp of cloud to be seen. Often, although the sky appears cloudless the sun passes behind a thin band of cloud, barely visible, on the horizon.

I try not to blink. The sun has nearly gone; going, going, and WAHOO! I see it! A ballooning, intensely luminous green flash right on the horizon lasting only a second, but burned in my memory. Just when I need some morale-boosting, nature obliges with one of her marvels.

A couple of days later one of the other boaters on the net complains bitterly about a squall. "The winds are too strong and gusty." Far from being a nuisance to us, we love it. Up to 25 knots of wind is perfect for *Orca* and we fly along, heeled well over, the mahogany toe rail running through the water. This way we can make up for some of our many slack days. In one squally period we cover 180 nautical miles in 24 hours—a record for us!

During my watch in the early hours of the morning, the rain feels like steel needles blasting my face. I keep an eye on the wind-speed indicator in case I need to get help putting another reef in the sails. Every 15 minutes I scan the horizon. Are those lights I can see off our starboard bow? We haven't seen lights for weeks and I stare intently. They are lights! Which way are they going? I use the binoculars, but can't make out red or green running lights, which would tell me the direction of the vessel. I stand still and line the lights up with a fixed point on the boat. There's no doubt. The lights are getting brighter, but are still in the same relative position. That means only one thing, they're coming directly this way.

I leap down the companionway and shake Robin. "Quick, quick, there are lots of lights out there and they're coming towards us!" He is instantly awake and jumps into foul weather gear and harness. By this time, it looks to me like a cruise ship approaching. But that can't be so, this is not cruising ground. Robin grabs the microphone and starts transmitting over the radio.

"Unknown vessel, unknown vessel, unknown vessel," he gives our approximate location, "this is Zulu Charlie Foxtrot One Five Eight Five, Sailing Vessel *Orca*. Over."

He tries several times, with increasing urgency but there is no response. No time for further calling. I can see the lighted bridge of the huge vessel. Robin fires up the engine and pushes it to full revs, makes a 90° change in course to port—a recognized manoeuvre to indicate that we know we are on a collision course and are diverting.

But the vessel seems oblivious and is still following us. I continue calling the vessel as Robin helms. Still no response.

"I've got to turn inside his turning circle when he's really close." Rob shouts. Through the rain we can see the phosphorescence from its bow wave—a 4-metre high waterfall. We can see inside the bridge, about 10 metres above the water. There's no one there. I fling the microphone back into its holder and hang on to a supporting wire.

"NOW!" screams Robin, above the din of the squall. He yanks the wheel hard over to starboard. *Orca* is reluctant at first, the engine fighting to counter the effects of the wind on the sails before she executes a smart turn and the mainsail boom thwacks across the deck as we tack and the sails balloon from the opposite direction. For a few seconds we are on a reciprocal course to our assailant, port side to port side before the vessel shoots past our stern. As it retreats we can even see a helicopter on its deck.

"It's one of those bloody factory-fishing boats, Korean or Japanese." Robin is disgusted. "They don't keep watch or man the radio—all they do is follow their fish finders."

The fishing vessels are concerned only with chasing huge shoals of tuna, until the tuna stop to feed. Then the mother ship deploys her small boats which skirt round the shoal, dragging nets, like sheepdogs circling sheep, until they have the shoal trapped. A mere sailing vessel doesn't get in the way of this multi-million dollar industry.

We resume our course, turn off the engine and are back to racing along in the squall. "There was no name on the boat," I say, "so we can't report it."

The squall blows itself out and we slow down. For many nights we watch closely for more fishing vessels. Although we do see another one in daylight it is stationary, its tenders working the sea. We are not a target this time.

Some days later we are barrelling along in a squall during the day and are making good headway. CRACK! I rush up from below at the sound and join Robin on deck. "What's happened?"

"A gust has ripped the bottom section off the genoa," he says, pointing. "We've got to get it down quickly." A 6-metre long 60-cm wide section is attached only at either end. It's alternately ballooning then deflating, snapping with the sound of a whip.

We both move forward on our safety lines. I release the halyard metre by metre as Robin hauls the flapping beast to deck level, where we lash it as securely as possible to the pulpit and side safety lines. There is no hope in such rough conditions of removing it and fighting it along the deck to take it below. Limited now to the mainsail, mizzen and small jib sails, our progress is severely reduced and we feel the effects of the 3-metre lumpy seas created by the winds.

We return to the galley and are making a sandwich and heating soup for lunch when we hear a distressing voice.

"MAYDAY, MAYDAY, MAYDAY!"

This short sentence has the same effect as a bucket of iced water thrown in our faces. Immediately we jump to the radio to listen.

"Cease all communications on this channel until further notice," the voice continues, "we have a MAYDAY situation, I repeat, a MAYDAY situation. There is an EPIRB (Emergency Position Indicating Radio Beacon) alert." The broadcaster gives the location. "All vessels within range please call with your positions and intentions."

It is an unwritten rule that a sailor will always go to the aid of another sailor unless it puts his own vessel in jeopardy.

"This is Zulu Charlie Foxtrot, one-five-eight-five, S/V *Orca*. Over." Robin delivers our coordinates. Three other vessels also call in with their positions.

"S/V *Orca* you are closest to the distress signal. Will you please give us an estimate of your time of arrival from your current position?"

Robin has already been making detailed calculations and the prognosis does not look good.

"The direction from us is close to wind and we have just lost our genoa. If we motor flat out all the way, we would hope to make contact in four days. Over."

"Stand by *Orca*." We stand by the radio and await instructions. Some time later we are called again.

"S/V *Orca*, the French Navy is going to respond, you may resume your course."

The Navy is sending a high-powered vessel from their naval base at Papeete, Tahiti in the Society Isles. It will arrive within two days. We breathe a huge sigh of relief. The sailor has a chance.

An EPIRB can be activated accidentally and unless it's a properly-registered 406 EPIRB, there often is no way for the authorities to tell real from false alarms. However, this was a real emergency situation, with a happy ending. An American single-handed sailor lost his vessel in the storm and had to take to his life raft.

We continue on our course, but sadly for us, the squall blows itself out after another day.

"We'd better mend the genoa," Robin says, "while we have a break in the wind." We drag the bundled, torn genoa down below decks, where we set up the sewing machine on the saloon table. We must re-stitch the 6-metre slit and reinforce it with a long strip of additional sailcloth. Manipulating the 124-square-metre heavy sail in the confines of the saloon is challenging. After many broken needles and when my patience has just about frazzled, we finish. All that remains is to take the sail back to the bow and refit it into the self-furling gear.

Our 8000 km tribulation should soon be over. We have eaten well and are quite physically fit, yet have lost a lot of weight over the past five weeks. We still have plenty of food, including some 'fresh' vegetables, fruit and eggs.

"We've burned 1800 litres of diesel fuel so far," Robin says, "but the good thing is we still have 450 left!"

In total, we have had five 24-hour periods when we sailed well, without the engine. The rest of the time the engine was on for part or all of every day.

"Well, there has to be better to come." I say.

On 6th June, we're sailing calmly. It is 6:00 a.m. As soon as it's fully light I make my regular tour of the decks, but I'm not particularly bothered if we have flying fish or not. We'll be reaching land today! Robin is up early and busy with his daily chores.

Although I don't feel hungry this morning, I cook eggs and bacon. Robin will appreciate it. Then I devote myself to scanning the horizon. TP is lively. She can sense the proximity of land, especially with the abundance of land birds that now fly the skies. She is acting like a young kitten, but eventually settles down in her coil of rope.

"Land! Land! I can see some clouds on the horizon. Come and see!" I shriek. Robin joins me on deck and looks through the binoculars.

"You're right, let's hope it's Nuku Hiva."

A grey smear appears beneath the telltale clouds and gradually grows in height and breadth. Sighting land after 36 days at sea is the most indescribably wonderful feeling.

"I'm going to get showered and changed." I say. Bouncing down the steps below decks, I think I can be lavish with water today.

Back on deck, we go through unfamiliar routines of preparing to enter port and anchor. Robin has already inflated the dinghy, brought the anchor from its locker and shackled it to the anchor chain. There is no Port Control to call to request permission to enter the bay.

"Go on, go on," I urge Robin, "it's your turn now." Just to please me he goes below to shower and dress in his clean gear, although we still have at least three hours to go.

I stand alone on deck, tears streaming unchecked down my face. Robin promised, and has brought me through this ordeal. While I reflect over the past five weeks, a ruggedly beautiful remnant of an ancient volcanic eruption materializes before us.

This must be heaven and I'm not sure I'll ever leave.

Land! Nuku Hiva

11

Colours, Perfumes and Chicken Jacket
Nuku Hiva, Marquesas

I am breathing deeply and slowly to calm the pounding in my chest. Velvety, blue-green mountains take on greater and greater definition as we approach, burgeoning into a dense mantle of exotic vegetation covering the jagged peaks and spires as well as the deeply-clefted valleys between. The scent of wet forests, damp red earth and heavily-scented tropical flowers extends its arms to welcome us.

With *Orca* still on autopilot, we drop and lash all sails and motor gently into Taiohae Bay, Nuku Hiva—a huge anchorage sheltered by the hills and mountains on all sides except to the south where it is open to Pacific swells. The Marquesas Islands have no large, fringing reefs nor coral-clad lagoons; just massive extinct volcanoes offering a savage beauty. We're entering another world.

"Can you see a good spot to anchor?" Robin asks.

I scan the bay with binoculars. There are about 30 other yachts peacefully at rest; their bows pointing out to sea and sterns to land.

"Let's anchor to the seaward side of them, to give us room to swing." I suggest, never wanting to be in a difficult manoeuvring position.

We choose our area, well away from other yachts and lower the anchor. A man in a little green rowing boat is pulling hard on his oars and heading in our direction.

"Hi there!" he shouts. "We all put out a stern anchor here, to stop swinging and give everyone more room. Let out a lot of anchor chain on your bow anchor, give me your stern anchor and I'll row round and drop it for you. Then you can pull in on your bow anchor chain to set the stern anchor."

Sounds simple. We gently lower the stern anchor into his boat, to avoid piercing the bottom and he manfully sets off rowing as I pay out the line. There is a breeze in the anchorage and despite his best efforts, he's not having any success dragging round the stern of *Orca* to get us perpendicular to the waves rolling in from the ocean. To be fair, he has no idea *Orca* weights 40 tonnes and there isn't time to give him the vital statistics.

Taiohae Bay

Things are getting stressful as it's not going well. I'm agitated and Robin is not in a very good humour. By the time we've got the anchors set, we are well and truly broadside to the Pacific swells and rolling like a sonofabitch. "Ah well," I say in hopes of defusing the situation, "we've just spent the last 36 days rolling, a few more won't make any difference."

"Thanks for your help." I shout to the man as he rows away. He would have been happy to try again to reset the anchor, but we're just keen to turn off the engine.

"We made it Rob!" I run up and hug him. "Thanks for getting us here safely." He grins and gives me a bear hug. We both just stand for a moment, soaking up the peace and tranquillity exuding from these warm shores.

It's still well before midday, so we launch the dinghy ready to go ashore. Robin jumps down into it and steadies it as I get in, clutching the knapsack carrying our precious papers. The motor starts at the first pull and we gently proceed ashore and secure the dinghy. First stop—the Gendarmerie.

What a weird sensation! As we walk along we're both lurching from side to side, to counteract the non-existent swells to which we've become so accustomed. The world about us is constantly tilting. It takes about three days for us to regain our land legs.

The Gendarme, in his typically French police uniform complete with peaked pill-box hat close by, is less impressed with our miraculous deliverance from the ocean than we are. Judging by the number of yachts in the harbour, he sees far too many of us, all requiring paperwork and he treats us with barely-concealed ennui. It is only the beginning of June and there have been 700 yachts through already. He is not bothered when we say we haven't enough cash in hand to pay the required 'bond'.

The bond is an amount of money equivalent to the air fare from Papeete to one's home port (Grand Cayman in our case). It is held by the officials against one's good behaviour and eventual departure from French Polynesia. It can be reclaimed from certain administrative centres when leaving, minus a percentage kept for administration purposes. It suggests that too many people have arrived on these idyllic shores and refused to leave. We offer to pay the bond when we reach Papeete, whereupon he grants us a 3-month visa. Our school-type French serves us well enough, which he seems to appreciate in his polite, aloof manner.

Apart from our inability to stand motionless, the most striking sensations upon reaching land are accorded to our senses of sight and smell. After five weeks of endless blue horizon, mixed with salt, clouds and sun, this is sensory overload. Tropical vegetation crowds every metre of the mountains, heavily studded with coconut palms, breadfruit and banana trees. Every shade of green is displayed, from pale and bright green, through blue-green, olive green to dark forest green. The truly heady scents of gardenia and frangipani blossoms intoxicate us with their strength.

"It's like smelling a rainbow, Robin." I can't breathe in deeply enough and am almost light-headed with the effort. The red-brown loam also has its own rich aroma, smelling freshly washed.

Our next visit is to the Post Office, to call one of our family members to advise them of our safe arrival. They can then spread the word for us. My sister Di, in England, is ecstatic that we have arrived in one piece; she hates the idea of us being out on the ocean.

At the west end of the bay on the hillside, is Rosie's Bar at the Keikahanui Hotel, which is the recognized hangout for yachties and where we can pick up mail.

"A couple of beers please and is there any mail for the yacht *Orca*?" The Hinano beer is good and we look through a couple of bits of business mail and read the birthday card and letter from my father. We don't chat with any of the other yachties yet. So much excitement in one day leaves us exhausted and we return safely to *Orca*, our home and refuge. We winch up the dinghy and swing it on board—our equivalent of pulling up the drawbridge.

"Let's crack a bottle of wine," says Robin.

I wholeheartedly agree. After weeks of abstinence, it feels an appropriately relaxing thing to do. We sip as we munch the last of Robin's bread and some cheese from our stores.

"Tonight we can both sleep all night through and in peace—no three-hour watches to keep. It's going to be heavenly, Robin."

It is a calm night. We wake periodically out of habit, to hear the wavelets lapping the hull and to remind ourselves that we don't have to go on watch, then turn over and slumber again.

Early morning is bright and clear. I sneak out of our bunk without disturbing Robin, put the kettle on for tea and slip on deck to inhale this beautiful land. It is cool, barely light and everything is at peace. I make a cup of hot tea and gently wake Robin.

"What's up?" He immediately sits bolt upright out of habit.

"Nothing! It's a beautiful day and I've brought you some tea."

Robin slides back onto the bunk and exhales. "Still rolling, I see."

"Shall we have breakfast now? It's cereal, I'm afraid, until we can get fresh fruit and French bread to go with our butter and marmalade."

Shopping is at the top of the list today. "Hopefully we can refill one of our propane gas tanks too," Robin says.

Before long, we're ready to go ashore and have written a wish list for groceries. Just as we're launching the dinghy the little green rowboat draws alongside, with a young boy in it.

"Hi," I say, "how are you?"

"Can we do a book swap? We've read all of ours," says Neil, the 9-year old rower.

"Oh sure, but we're just off to town. When you see our dinghy back, come on over."

"OK. See you." He glides away in his boat, a skilled oarsman.

After securing our dinghy to the jetty wall and scrambling up the slippery metal rungs of the ladder cemented into the concrete, we set off for Maurice's General Store. The main road is hard-packed red earth, which turns to slick red mud when it rains. Inside we ask for Maurice Fitzpatrick, but are directed to his son, a big man with a dark beard and long hair.

"My father doesn't speak much English," he explains.

"Several weeks ago," Robin says, "we wrote and asked the fuel supplier to deliver 800 litres of diesel here for us and we wondered if it had arrived."

"Yes, it's here, but there's only 600 litres."

"Oh well, we'll take what there is," says Robin.

We make an appointment for a couple of days' time, to take *Orca* to the commercial wharf at high tide, so that the fuel can be pumped into the tanks.

"I have another question," Robin continues, "can you fill our propane gas tank?"

"Sure, we can, bring it in the back," says Maurice's son.

We follow him through a rear door of the store into an open-air storage area where he looks at our tank fitting. "This is a different fitting from ours."

"It's a British tank, it came with the boat." I say.

"One moment." Maurice's son busies himself with hoses and connectors. "We can't use the high pressure propane tank, but I can partially fill it from one of my small tanks, if I use some frozen chickens."

I think maybe I have misheard. He suspends a full propane tank upside down from the rafters above our tank. He then connects a hose from his tank to ours. "Now for the chickens," he chuckles and retreats into the store. He returns with a garbage bag full of frozen chickens, which he drapes over the shoulders of our tank. Next he opens the valves on both of the tanks.

Robin laughs and explains to me what is going on. "Connecting the tanks like this will partially fill our tank as the liquid propane trickles down. But when the pressure is equal in both tanks, no more will flow. By reducing the temperature and thus the pressure of our tank, more liquid can enter. Normally, the vapour from our tank would be vented back to the main tank, but we can't do this because our connectors don't fit. So, reducing the pressure in our tank by cooling is the only way we can get more liquid in—by gravity."

"You'll have to leave it here all day," we're advised, so we enter the store to see what goodies we can find. I look back with a wry smile at our tank with its chicken jacket. I have discovered for the first time the resourcefulness of the inhabitants of these remote islands.

It is fun to be able to shop again but we only buy essentials. Naturally, in French Polynesia baguettes are cheap and plentiful. The tasty tinned processed cheese is subsidized by the French government, so together these items form the backbone of our diet. Meat, vegetables and fruit are available but are prohibitively expensive. We buy a meagre selection to form a balanced diet. Supplies arrive on the island on one of the last tramp steamers to operate, the *Aranui*. It connects these far flung islands with the rest of the world.

We stroll the unpaved streets, as Land Rovers and other 4x4s drive back and forth filled with Polynesians in gay attire, waving to each other and stopping to chat. They've probably just had a bone-jarring drive from across the island over the rough, rutted mountain roads; just a few kilometres, but it will have taken them a couple of hours.

"What do you suppose these people do?" I ask Robin.

"I expect the main industry is copra: selling dried ripe coconut for the oil to be extracted."

"It looks so fertile I imagine they can feed themselves pretty well without any problem."

"I think they do a fair bit of stone and wood carving too, there's probably quite a trade in tourist goods."

"Do you think it's time to collect our propane tank?"

"I should think so, I'm ready to go home."

At the store Maurice's son takes us through to the back. He removes the chicken jacket from our tank and carries it into the store. The chickens are no doubt being returned to the freezer section, having amply fulfilled their duty. I wonder whether they're going on sale, or perhaps he keeps these chickens for that very purpose. He returns and unhooks the hose and we have a tank about two-thirds full.

"Thank you so much, merci, merci beaucoup, that was ingenious!" I am most impressed with the result.

After we have put the tank in our dinghy, we go to scrutinize the commercial dock and work out how we are going to manoeuvre into position for the refuelling.

"Look at that surge," Robin points to the water heaving up and down the side of the concrete jetty, "we'll need all our fenders to stop us being rammed against the wall."

A burst of adrenaline surges through me, as I imagine all the difficulties we could encounter because *Orca* is not very manoeuvrable in confined areas. It will definitely have to take place at high tide. The commercial dock was built for boats which are much higher off the water than we are. I hope we can get it into reverse and don't ram something.

Shortly after we arrive on board, the little green rowboat arrives. "Hi," says Neil, "I've come to swap books." I lead him below. His eyes light up at the selection. He looks at them with a practiced eye and rapidly selects a bunch of newish novels. "I read a lot," he says by way of a nine-year-old's explanation. He packs the books into a plastic bag and hands me his bag of books in trade. I spread them out on the bunk revealing a moth-eaten selection of old novels and far too many romances that we won't read. I wouldn't think they are his choice of reading either. I don't have the heart to tell him that I don't think it is a very fair exchange. I will just have to learn from the experience.

"What else do you do apart from reading?" I ask.

"Oh, I meet up with kids from other boats sometimes when we're in port."

"Don't you miss school?"

"No, I've never been to school, I've lived on the boat since I was born. I do all my schooling by correspondence courses."

What a lonely life for a kid, I think. No siblings, no school and living in an adult world. I bet his seafaring and world knowledge is vast, though.

Thanks to our hard work in Panama correcting all the boat problems during our six-week stay, we have no serious jobs to tackle. This is good, because there isn't a boat chandlery in Nuku Hiva and there are no boat haul-out facilities, so tomorrow we've decided to pack a picnic and hike up into the mountains for the day.

It's already warm and humid when we set off early up a red dirt road, each carrying a knapsack with food and drink. Robin shoots out his arm to stop me and gestures to be quiet. A big black pig is wallowing in a cool ditch sheltered by a fern-covered bank. We're particularly fond of pigs, having raised some several years ago. She is totally unconcerned as we pass by.

Further ahead we hear some snuffling and grunting and stand still as a large sow breaks cover from the brush. She charges across the road shortly followed by eight scuttling babies not more than a few days old. After an upheaval in the underbrush and much indignant squealing, things go quiet. Mother has probably succumbed to the demands of her offspring and is letting them nurse.

"Oh my goodness!" I say. "They are *delightful!*"

We hike the valley bottom and lower slopes, passing palm-thatched dwellings with yards full of coconut palms, breadfruit trees and rainbow-coloured hibiscus bushes. Under a gardenia tree perfumed white flowers have fallen to the earth. I pick up a fresh blossom and put it behind my left ear, to show that I am happily spoken for. The fragrance is heavenly.

Mother pig

As we ascend the hillside, habitation is sparse but there are many remnants of old stone walls covered in vegetation, often with a stone-carved tiki—a Polynesian god—set in the corner. He is a squat, heavy figure, with hands clasped over a protuberant belly. A tiki is believed by the Polynesians to be the powerful ancestor who created the human race.

"I think we go this way," Rob says, "towards Mount Muake."

We strike off the main track and follow the narrow path, climbing steeply. Dappled sunlight filters through the jungle affording us some respite from the sun, but not the heat. We climb and scramble for a long time. It gets increasingly hot and sticky as midday approaches and we push through thick, scratchy branches and bushes, longing for cool breezes.

"It's funny how we expect each bend to take us to the top, but there's always another hill," I say, as our climbing rate slows. Eventually the tree canopy above our heads thins, so we must be nearing the peak. After a while we scramble up to a narrow knife-edge ridge, the pinnacle of this mountain.

"Look at that!" Rob says as we gaze down and the mountain falls away. "It's worth the climb."

Every peak and prominence is covered in vegetation, looking bluish in the distance. The ridges and folds sweep down to the sea, meeting up with a large, semicircular bay. It is edged with creamy-white sand running down into a line of turquoise water before the deep blue of the Pacific. We are on Mount Muake looking to the NE at Haatuatua Bay. We stand still for a few minutes and gaze at the stunning panorama, trying to absorb it all.

"What a perfect spot for lunch, I'm starving!" I say. With difficulty, we find a patch of ground with a view and just large enough to spread out our meal without being enveloped by the bushes and without fear of anything toppling over the edge. It would be nice to stretch out and snooze after lunch, but Robin has other ideas.

"We'd better start straight down," he says, as we pack our belongings. "It will be a few hours before we get back to the yacht." The descent, as always, is more rapid than the ascent and within a couple of hours we have reached the wide track to town.

"I love the wild pigs," I say, "but I'm disappointed that we haven't seen any wild horses, cows or goats that are supposed to inhabit the interior."

We hear a vehicle coming down the track behind us and step aside to allow it to pass. It's an open-topped Land Rover carrying a good-looking young Polynesian couple.

"Bonjour!" They wave as they pass, and then slow to a stop. When we get alongside the man and woman are smiling. "Would you like a ride to town?" he offers.

"Yes please, that would be great!" I look at Robin and shrug my shoulders. This was meant to be a walk, but we've done a lot of walking already and there's a long way to go yet. Besides, it would be churlish to turn down their kind offer.

We scramble into the back of the Rover and set off down the track, bumping and lurching our way to town, while the beautiful breezes course over our hot bodies. We attempt a mixed language conversation, but the noise of the truck on the rock-strewn road soon stops our efforts, so we sit back and enjoy the ride down through the subtropical jungle. At the town, we hop out and bid farewell, with profuse thanks. The happy couple wave again and drive off.

As we walk back past Maurice's General Store, Robin spies a battered, elderly Land Rover parked outside and wanders over to take a look. He loves Land Rovers and we used to own a Series II for years. Leaning up against the body is a little man.

"Hello, you speak English!" he says.

"Yes, we're Canadian."

"My name is Tau."

Tau is an atypical Polynesian. Not well-muscled, not god-like, not covered with tattoos. No leis of flowers circle his head or neck. No blossom is tucked behind his ear. He's thin, with matchstick arms; his legs are overburdened with large knobbly knees. Brown, crepe-like skin stretches over a meagre frame and his short grizzled hair stands to attention. I think he needs the Land Rover for support.

"Where did you learn English?" we ask.

"I was in the US Army. I've served in *two* armies," he boasts, "the French as well."

It is hard to imagine this wizened little gnome in US fatigues, as he stands before us in bare feet, ragged shorts and stained T-shirt.

"I love to practice the language, but there's no one here who speaks it," he laments, "you're from a yacht?" His powers of deduction are remarkable, since it is almost the only way to get here and we don't look like wealthy tourists. "Come and visit me in my bay, the Bay of Cannibals," he chuckles, "and come to my house for lunch—I'll give you fresh fruit!"

Visions of green bananas hover before us and we need no further bidding. I brush off a second's foreboding. Cannibalism is forbidden now, isn't it?

We agree to visit, and say adieu.

With time to spare we saunter across the road and sit for a while on the grass by the waterfront next to a big stone carving of a tiki.

As we watch the world go by, we can see some stunning examples

Taiohae foreshore

of the young Polynesian males' tattoos. Some practically covering their beautiful bronzed bodies—a sign of their strength and virility. According to a few of the other boaters, who have been brave enough to acquire their own tiny tattoo, it is an incredibly painful process, using the sharp edge of pieces of shell. I, for one, am impressed with the strength and endurance of the young males.

"Look over there!" I whisper to Robin while discreetly nodding towards three people walking towards us down the street. "That's got to be Nancy." Indeed it is, chattering away and although the trio pass right by us, there's no recognition.

I see a familiar face from another yacht and pass the time of day. I mention that we've just seen Nancy and am told that she now calls herself Clancy and is looking to crew on another yacht. She doesn't mind where it's going as long as it's not America. For some reason she can't go home. We're glad we didn't get involved with her.

We make our way back to *Orca*, to start preparing for sailing.

After we pick up fuel tomorrow, we'll sail out of the bay to the east, to locate Taipivai, Tau's bay.

Early in the morning we set about raising the two anchors. It is a glorious bright day, just a few puffy clouds in the sky and already quite warm. The engine is idling smoothly and with the aid of the genoa winch, we wind in the stern anchor and secure it on deck. Then comes the laborious task of winding up the bow anchor using the hand windlass. It is a tedious process, but the anchor is ultimately secured and we motor slowly towards the wharf.

Four, fat fenders hang over the port side of the yacht as we approach, to protect us from 'wharf rash' and I stand at the bow with the port mooring line in hand. The minute we are close enough, I scale the safety line and leap onto the wharf to wind the line around a mooring bollard then race along to catch the stern line which Robin throws to me and secure that too. The surge of the Pacific forces us against the wall, squeezing the fenders flat but fortunately doesn't rupture them.

Three drums of diesel stand on the quay, with a man holding a hand pump on the end of a long hose. "Wow!" I say to Robin. "I wonder how long this is going to take." In fact, my scepticism is unfounded. The diesel is quickly transferred to our tanks and the tank caps screwed down into the deck. Now we have an additional 600 litres, but at a very high price, US72¢ per litre. Hopefully, we will have enough now until we reach American Samoa, where fuel should be unlimited and much cheaper.

Our Polynesian helper casts off the mooring lines and throws them to me on board. Robin eases the throttle forward to move us away from the dock. I finish hauling in the fenders and secure them so we're ready for the ocean. *Orca* heads out of the bay to a kilometre or so off shore before turning east and then north. Even on short voyages, we observe our self-imposed safety rules and wear our safety harnesses clipped onto safety lines.

I'm glad we're not tackling another long voyage yet and it will only take a few hours to reach Taipivai. Being out on the ocean again is actually quite exhilarating. Lured by images of green bananas, we head for the Bay of Cannibals and our very own grizzled cannibal in his Garden of Eden.

12

Tau the Cannibal gets Cantankerous—Taipivai Bay, Nuku Hiva

Our passage to Taipivai is smooth, motoring all the way using the autopilot. There is no point raising sails for such a short distance as we're constantly changing direction. We just dial up each waypoint on the autopilot—a far cry from our experience from Cayman to Colon. We haven't bothered with sea-sick pills this time and find we are still acclimatized to the motion.

I make a cup of tea and we sit in the sun enjoying the breezes and admiring the craggy scenery. Once again the fruity scents and warmth of the island reach out to us and two beautiful turquoise and yellow mahi mahi, about a metre long, leap in and out of our bow wave. By the middle of the afternoon we motor in through the Baie du Controleur heading for the middle finger of the three-fingered bay.

Taipivai is at the tip of the long bay which offers shelter from all directions. There are only a couple of boats here. I watch the depth sounder as Rob selects a spot to lower the anchor. We pay out plenty of chain to hold us on the bottom. Easy.

Tucked into the mountains like this, there's only the barest hint of air movement and soon the disturbance we created has disappeared and the surface returns to an oily calm. Some distance ahead of us is a neat trimaran yacht and an elderly man gives us a cheery wave.

"Come on over and say hello," he calls.

It sounds like fun, so we launch the dinghy and row the short distance. He is a tall, distinguished-looking man with silver-grey hair and helps us aboard. "My name is Jim and this is my wife, Rea."

We shake hands and introduce ourselves.

"Will you have a glass of wine?" Rea is a petite lady whose smooth pretty face and boyish haircut belies her age. They are retired and Jim, in his early 70s, used to be School Superintendent on the

Marshall Islands. Rea is an artist and takes us below to show us her studio and examples of her art. She is particularly keen on watercolours of flowers and produces striking work.

A couple of glasses of wine later, having swapped stories and experiences both boating and non-boating, we take our leave. Jim would like to accompany us tomorrow on the trek to find Tau. Rea gracefully declines, because she's allergic to mosquito bites. She will stay behind and guard the vessels.

At 8:00 a.m. it's already hot and humid; the heavy blanket of air tinged with exotic flowers. We have breakfasted early on cereal, tea and baguette.

"Tomorrow, with any luck, we'll have *fruit* for breakfast." Robin smiles in anticipation.

We slip the inflatable dinghy over the side of *Orca*. On contact with the water, it drives the perfect mountain reflection into ripples. Jim is watching for us as we motor gently towards him. At the water's edge we run the dinghy up onto the white coral sand beach and leap out. "What the hell's that?" I squeal as we all start hopping up and down, slapping at our legs.

"Sand fleas," says Jim, "get off the beach!" We haul the dinghy high above the water line, drag socks over damp sandy feet, jump into trainers and run into the sub-tropical jungle. "Mercifully they confine themselves to the beach," Jim informs us.

There is no breeze and we are perspiring freely. Despite this, we are in good spirits and start along the only track running inland. The going is difficult. Sticky, red earth clings to our shoes and the track is littered with rocks and large puddles. It winds its way past two small square dwellings, made of whitewashed cinder block. A little brown pony with a long ginger mane is tethered alongside one cottage. It lifts its head to inspect us for a moment before returning to grazing. The other cottage is surrounded by an ordered vegetable garden.

Half an hour later the track broadens into a clearing. Ahead is a 12-metre wide shallow river with a concrete weir where currently the water is only 2 cm deep. We gingerly step through the flooded part and turn right, following directions towards the beginnings of a tiny village. Pretty, miniature whitewashed houses with tin roofs peek out from the lush vegetation.

Taipivai ford

"Look at all the fruit." Jim's eyes are shining.

We can see breadfruit, coconuts, football-sized grapefruit, limes, lemons and bananas. I think we're all salivating. Spurred on, we follow the earthen road as it sinuates its way up the mountainside.

"Is this the right track?" I ask some time later. "We've been climbing for hours and I've got a blister on my heel."

"Of course it is," says Robin, "can't be far now."

"If I can find someone," I say, "I'll ask directions." Naturally it will be up to me to ask—I'm accompanied by two men and asking for directions is not in their genetic makeup.

The temperature is still rising towards its daily peak and several mosquitoes, oblivious to the dusk-dawn rule, sound like miniature band saws as they home in on our salt-laden, carbon-dioxide-producing bodies.

I catch sight of a little grey-haired lady in a shapeless cotton dress, tending her garden on a steep hillside. "Excuse me Madame, do you know where Tau lives?" I appeal in my best schoolgirl French. Her hands fly to her mouth and then a toothless grin bisects her leathery face.

"Oh! C'est mon mari! My husband! My husband! I am

Catherine!" She is ecstatic. So am I. It is already 10:30 a.m. She rushes down a hairpin path to greet us and guides us up to their little hut, sprouting like a mushroom from the side of the hill. Their dwelling is fashioned from cinder block and corrugated iron sheets; a glassless window cut into each wall allows breezes to pass through.

Catherine leads us past a few busy chickens scratching in the yard, past a low lean-to room which houses a pig and into an adjoining lean-to. This serves as washhouse, kitchen and dining area. I linger a moment to speak to the pig. It looks up, but sadly I have no scraps for it so it returns to dozing. Tau is sitting inside at a picnic table; in front of him a well-fingerprinted half-full tumbler stands beside an empty, red-wine bottle. Tau has obviously foresworn the taste of human flesh and taken up a blood substitute.

"Hello, hello! Bonjour! Ça va?" We're all talking at once. Tau, smiling, pushes himself to his feet and we are privileged to glimpse a few brown stumps erupting from his gums. Tottering forward, he hugs me and sundry grey bristles sprouting from his cheeks rasp my face as I am enveloped in a heady wine vapour. He shakes hands with Robin and Jim and I shake my head clear.

"I need your help," Tau states. Without more ado, he guides us into the main living area. It is a bedroom/sitting room. A strip of cloth hangs on a nail beside each of the two glassless windows, to serve as a curtain when hooked up to its partnering nail. The room is furnished with an iron-framed bed, two wooden chairs and an old sea chest. Nails in the wall support wire hangers with an assortment of faded cotton garments draped over them. On small nails at the head of the bed is Catherine's jewellery, which she proudly displays.

Incongruously, an enormous television set dominates a corner of the room. Tau produces a remote control and waves it at us. "I can't get any picture on my TV," he wails, peering myopically at the remote. "I can't see so well." He passes the remote to Robin—but he might as well have passed a book of poetry written in Cyrillic script. I look at Robin—we've never owned a TV with a remote controller.

"Let me have a look." Jim volunteers. Gratefully Robin hands over the instrument and Jim settles on the end of the bed and starts to manipulate the buttons.

I fish in my backpack and bring out a pair of strong reading glasses and hand them to Tau. "Perhaps these will help."

He seizes them enthusiastically and perches them on his nose, peering around. His eyes light up as things close to him zoom into focus. Tau returns to his table, scrutinizes his tumbler through his new spectacles and pours the remaining mouthfuls of liquid down his throat. He reaches into a box on the floor and pulls out another bottle. "Come and talk with me." he instructs Robin.

Catherine guides me to the chest which contains her treasures and photo albums. Together, we spend a companionable hour looking at the photos. Beautiful sepia prints of indistinct people; her family and others, whom she obviously adores. She is exceedingly proud of Tau in his army uniforms.

After a long time of button-pushing and TV menu interpreting, Jim succeeds with the TV. Tau had zapped every button to extreme, with disastrous results. Jim patiently tries to explain how to work the remote and I write down the instructions as he dictates them to me. Tau is more concerned that he's finished off the second bottle and uncorks another. Is this a bottle for a celebration? I wonder. But it's not to be. No more glasses appear. "I'm thirsty." I whisper to Robin, who steadfastly ignores me.

Tau continues his foray into the depths of the grape.

"I'm so sorry," Catherine says in French, "I don't have anything to offer you to drink."

"We're not thirsty," we lie, not wanting this sweet lady to feel embarrassed.

However, she rummages around in a rust-coloured freezer behind Tau and produces a bottle of frozen water. "Soon it will thaw," she says and smiles coyly.

It is way past noon. I'm dying of hunger and thirst and believe that the fruit may just have been a mirage. I don't think the men are ever going to say anything.

"Well, I think it's time to leave," I say and start to get up.

"No! You haven't got any fruit yet, go with Catherine and cut some bananas," Tau orders. It is obviously women's business.

I am amazed as this little old lady brandishes her machete and starts hacking at the massive stem of a green banana plant. We're apparently not just getting a few hands of bananas, but a whole stock. This translates into at least thirty hands of bananas, the total weight of the stock being something over 20 kg. Her mission accomplished, she swings the mighty object onto her shoulder and marches towards home. "Wait here." she instructs and soon returns and starts severing another stem.

"Catherine! This is far too much." I protest thinking also of our two-and-a-half-hour walk home.

Unfazed, Catherine cuts a third stock. "You can hang them on the boat and eat the bananas as they become ripe," she says. This time we both haul a stock back to the house and Catherine disgraces me by trotting ahead in sprightly fashion. Then we take bags and collect grapefruit, papayas and lemons.

Inside, Tau has drifted into a snoring slumber by his bottle. It is now about 1:30 p.m. and I really want to go home to the boat.

"You can't go yet," Catherine insists, "you must have some lunch." We are indeed very hungry and thirsty. After searching in the freezer, Catherine withdraws an unwrapped solid fish, weighing about ten pounds. She slides it onto the table and uses it to prod Tau in the ribs. He rallies and together they scrutinize it—Tau sporting his new spectacles—and declare it too solid to thaw in time. Thank goodness, now perhaps we can go. But no. Crooning happily to herself, Catherine finds a block of frozen meat, which I *think* she says is beef, and chops several chunks off with her machete. She beams at me—she's enjoying having some company.

Now she sets a big iron cauldron to boil on the old range and flings in some handfuls of rice, the pieces of meat, some beans and a few other unnamed ingredients. Tau's head slumps onto his chest, but his hand still reaches periodically for the glass, until the red wine has yet again disappeared. Never mind, there's always another bottle. By this time I feel like grabbing it and taking a swig to quell the rumblings of my stomach. The bottle of ice has long since disappeared back into the freezer.

I'm thinking of pretending to faint and excuse ourselves that way. But no, Robin would never forgive me, that would not be polite. By 3:00 p.m. the meal is ready and we each receive a bowl of truly delectable rice, meat and beans. Tau, however, declines. He doesn't eat at this time of day. To look at him, I don't think he ever eats.

"This is absolutely delicious!" We all wholeheartedly agree and Catherine is thrilled with our praise. Fortified by the meal, we insist we really must be leaving. We have a two-and-a-half-hour walk ahead of us, each carrying 20 kg of bananas. I can't imagine how we're going to do it. We're heading for the doorway when Tau rallies and indistinctly informs us that he will come down the mountain with us, because he wants to see our yacht. Catherine doesn't mind. I'm waiting for one of the men to take command of the situation and dissuade him, but nothing happens.

"Tau," I say, "you are not going to be able to walk all the way down the mountain." Tau glowers at me, he is not used to being instructed by a women. In his world *they* do man's bidding. I can imagine he is already wishing he could put me into a cauldron. He is now even more determined to come.

Catherine is now fussing like a mother hen. "Put on your long pants and long sleeved shirt," she warns, "and long socks and shoes, you are allergic to mosquito bites."

Oh great! I think, now we might have a *sick* drunk on our hands.

Tau, by this time is truculent and equally adamant that he will *not* wear long clothes. Because sweet Catherine is getting upset we agree to help and attempt to feed Tau's spaghetti legs into his jeans. We have to pull up long socks and get his flailing arms into the shirt and button it to the neck. Even after this ignominious procedure, Tau still wants to come.

We are an unlikely caravan trekking down the mountainside. Tau, carrying nothing, is meandering back and forth across the track while we take a straighter path with our burden of bananas. Robin and Jim also have backpacks of fruit. It is 4:30 p.m. and dusk arrives early in these latitudes, between 6:00 and 6:30 p.m.

"This is bloody great," I moan to Robin, "we'll only be halfway home when it gets dark—that's if I make it that far." My bananas are cutting into my shoulder and getting heavier with every step, although the men folk don't seem to show any signs of discomfort. They daren't, they could have taken a positive stand against Tau who, pathetically, is now sitting down by the roadside saying he's tired.

"What the hell does he think we're going to do, carry him?" I am barely under control when we hear a vehicle behind us. It is a long-wheel-based Land Rover. I march into the middle of the track. Adrenaline seems to have sharpened my memory of French.

"Please, do you think you could take us down the mountain?" I beg. "We need to get to the bay." The man looks at us, at the bananas and then at Tau—they exchange threatening glances.

"I want to walk." Tau says with a pout.

I want to heft my banana stock at his head. Instead I say, "Good. *You* walk, *we're* going to ride."

We pick up our fruit and climb into the back of the truck. It's not many seconds before Tau scrambles to his feet and lurches towards the vehicle. "*I* will sit in front."

Poor driver, I think. Jim and Robin at this point are not sure who should be humoured, Tau or me, but for the moment the situation is defused.

As we chat with the driver he tells us that we're in the 'School Bus' which takes the children living on the mountain to and from school every day. A delightfully swift and bumpy ride takes us down the twisting track. Tau is getting restless, like a squirming child. The bumps are playing havoc with his bladder, yet he asks if we have any beer in our backpacks.

"If we had any beer we'd have drunk it by now." Robin tells Tau.

Tau is gesticulating wildly and telling the driver he must stop the Land Rover by a group of houses. It transpires that one of the wooden shacks sells beer. Well, after all, it's at least 30 minutes since Tau's last liquid refreshment. It doesn't look promising, though, as the hut is boarded up. After relieving himself against the wall and a few other items that get in his way, Tau bangs on the door. No answer. Undaunted and driven by desire, Tau staggers off to another house, and then another; hammering on doors until he locates the hapless store owner. With bullying gestures he coerces the man to open his shack and sell Tau some beer. It is, they know, the only way to get rid of him. I resign myself to whatever fate has to offer.

In a few moments Tau is back at the rear of the Land Rover, babbling incoherently.

"Have you got money?" we eventually manage to decipher.

Oh yippee! Now he wants beer but can't pay for it.

Tau is not leaving without the beer; the shop owner is not letting him have it on credit; the driver doesn't want to be stuck with Tau; and we don't want him to start fighting. Sighing, Jim, Robin and I empty out our pockets to see what we can find and subsequently a 6-pack changes hands. The driver has seen it all before.

Tau clambers back into the Land Rover and rips the pull-tab from the first can. Because I'm parched, I'm considering the possibility of taking Tau in a head lock and wrenching the beer from him.

The driver wants to set us down by the weir to walk for the last half hour. I plead with him, very politely, to see if he could *please* take us right to the beach. Reluctantly he agrees. I think for fear of being stuck with Tau, who now doesn't intend to walk anywhere. At the beach we thank the driver profusely and he is glad to be on his way. Dragging the stocks of bananas, the fruit and Tau, we locate the dinghy.

I have one last attempt to be rid of our little cannibal and say, "There you are, there's the yacht. Thanks for the fruit—see you another day." But no luck. Tau installs himself in the dinghy beside the bananas, clutching the three remaining cans of beer.

Jim's wife Rea is delighted to see us back, fearing we'd been put in the missionary pot. She accepts our invitation to join us on the yacht for a glass of wine and some supper. We moor alongside *Orca* and have to bodily haul Tau up to deck level. His arms and legs are like wet noodles. It is after 6:30 p.m. and already quite dark. Tau investigates every centimetre of the boat, chaperoned by Robin, and then joins us outside. We've drunk copious amounts of water and are now enjoying a glass of wine with supper.

I look up. Despite everything, it is a magical night; billions of glittering stars are set in a black velvet heaven. Tau once more is refusing to eat and works his way through the rest of the beer. He gets up frequently and unsteadily to pee over the side of the boat. Soon he asks for wine.

"Sorry, we only had one bottle and that's gone." I lie without compunction.

Jim and Rea regretfully say goodbye, somewhat concerned about leaving us with Tau. We assure them we have everything under control and they motor off to their trimaran.

"Tau, we must take you back home now." Robin is firm.

"*NO!*" he pouts, defiantly folding his arms across his chest. "I will stay on the boat tonight."

Over my dead body, I think. That last pee didn't reach its destination and I'm certainly not having him down below.

"OK Rob, lets get some flash lamps, we'll take him back to the village."

We lift him bodily over the side into the dinghy, pry his hands from the yacht rail and roar off to prevent him scrambling back on board. Tau is fuming. In moments we draw up to the beach and help him out of the dinghy and start off along the track. Tau is hanging back, dragging his feet. He finds the first muddy puddle on the track and stomps in it in his best trainers to register his displeasure. I have a moment's urge to slap his legs.

"I'm *not* going!" He reiterates.

"Oh yes you are. Here's a flash light," says Robin, taking command and giving Tau the biggest lamp we possess. With Rob in the lead, Tau in the middle and me at the rear, we march the petulant Tau-child along the track until we reach the river. The going is rough and difficult by flashlight.

I am so happy when we see the twinkling lights of the village. At the weir a couple of Polynesian teenagers greet us good humouredly, then snigger when they see our companion. "Tau!" they say, looking at the dishevelled little man.

"Can you see that he gets home?" I ask. They roll their eyes heavenward, in the universal exasperated gesture, but nod. "Thank you, Merci!" I am genuinely elated.

"Keep the flash lamp Tau and take these gifts to Catherine," Robin says, pressing a bag into his hands for his long-suffering wife. It contains a couple of gold chain necklaces and some treasures I don't need. The youths stroll off, cajoling Tau, as we retrace our steps.

A load the weight of a small cannibal has been lifted from my shoulders. As always, everything has its price—I hope the bananas are worth it.

Banana stocks

13

Boobs, Barnacles and Rocks
Anaho Bay, Nuku Hiva

After two more days at Taipivai we head to Anaho Bay on the north coast of Nuku Hiva. No rivers run into the bay which is renowned for its beauty. The yellow sand and clear waters are perfect for snorkelling and swimming. The beach, however, like Tau's, is infested with 'no-nos'. Shaped like the toe of a boot, the bay is completely sheltered. We'll be able to make some sail repairs and check out the hull—chores which aren't possible in Taiohae Bay because of the constant rolling motion.

Anaho Bay

Once *Orca* is 1 km offshore we head north, motoring because we are pointing into wind.

"Look over there!" Robin hands me the binoculars from his neck. "Midway between the island and us—a big male killer whale!"

"He doesn't seem active," I say, "I reckon he must be snoozing." The straight dorsal fin, the male's trade mark, stands erect from his back which is just above surface level. Gradually we pass him, as he continues his rest.

Despite the engine running we are surrounded by a pod of small pilot whales, leaping in and out of the bow waves in formation. Sparkling diamonds of spray catch the sunlight and bounce off their sleek backs. It looks like they're playing and having wonderful fun.

Pilot whale

Orca turns south at our final waypoint down the leg of the boot into the toe which forms a huge circular anchorage. There are not many vessels here and we have lots of room.

Boaters, I feel, may do anything on board their vessel so long as it has no adverse effect upon fellow sailors. I am wondering if this is the motto of a small neighbouring yacht flying the Norwegian flag. On deck is a bewitching woman with an hibiscus blossom tucked behind her left ear. She is as brown as burnt almonds and uncluttered by any shred of clothing. She gives us an expansive, welcoming wave, her ample breasts swaying with the rhythm.

"Well, now there's a comely wench!" I say.

"Hmmm," Robin agrees, "but don't look her way again, she might want to invite us over for a glass of wine!"

"Perhaps she's found this is the best way to keep people away."

We make supper and take it on deck to watch the day fade, and sit facing away from the Norwegian boat. The hills obscure the horizon, so we can't watch the sunset and the gathering dusk comes quite early in this enclosed anchorage.

"I think I could get used to this—sailing by day and anchoring in the evening," I say, "and sleeping every night is just wonderful." Robin smiles in the half light, but makes no comment. I sip my wine and deeply inhale the evening air.

"What *is* that awful smell?" I wrinkle my nose at the sickly odour.

"It's copra, the islanders' gold. That's the smoke from the fires they build under it to speed the drying."

What would I do without my human almanac at my side?

Little lights start twinkling on the other vessels and a sprinkling appear on the shore. As it darkens, the millions of stars in the sky become intense. My mind, never at rest, returns to the present. I break the spell.

"Tomorrow, if it doesn't rain, we must start repairs on the sails, there's a lot to do."

Robin maintains his reverie, savouring the last of our inactivity.

Early in the morning it is fresh and comparatively cool. After breakfast we take the 83-square-metre mainsail off the boom, following the same plan we used on the ocean. It is less trying this time. For one thing we don't have to be harnessed and clipped onto the lifelines, so have more freedom to move around.

We spread out the heap of sailcloth on the deck section by section, crawling all over it, marking the areas for repair. I write down dimensions for the patches I must prepare, from our stock of spare sailcloth.

"Are you ready for the sewing machine now?" Robin has run the long power cable to the generator and lugs the machine into position for me.

"I can't say I enjoy this," I say, "but it's a lot easier than nearly falling off the deck into the ocean." After sewing on a dozen patches, we are satisfied with the results and it just remains to reinstall the battens and the sail.

"Come on," I encourage, although Rob looks a little fatigued, "let's finish and get it back in place."

By mid afternoon it is reinstalled and we both feel pleased. "Perhaps we should make some baggy wrinkles to tie on the shrouds at the chafe points." I suggest.

"Yes, maybe, but that's a long job and we're not starting now. Let's have a swim before supper."

"Sure, we can look at the hull," I say, already considering the next job.

We don snorkelling gear and lower ourselves into the clear water. After swimming slowly round the perimeter, we dive down and inspect the hull.

"It's a garden," I say when we surface, "it's covered with goose barnacles. They look like little fingers hanging down!"

"Pretty impressive, aren't they," says Robin when we're back on board, "they've been growing all the way across the Pacific. They probably started in the Peruvian current from Panama, and I bet I know what you've got organized for tomorrow, a spot of weeding in our underwater garden."

"Yes, but I think we'll do it with scuba tanks on. I suppose we should harvest the barnacles and eat them, they're a delicacy in France."

"I think I'll just be happy to have a clean hull," says Robin, "we're slow enough without all those little sea anchors to slow us down."

Next day we arm ourselves with plastic scrapers, dive knives, stiff nylon-bristle brushes and pot scourers to tackle our uninvited guests below the waterline. Robin stands on the edge of the boat in his scuba gear and makes a giant stride entry into the water. When he has cleared the area I follow. We give each other the OK sign and, releasing air from our buoyancy compensators, we slip below the surface and start work. The barnacles are tenacious and we need to remove them carefully without taking off a lot of the bottom paint.

The dozens of square metres of the hull are horribly familiar and it feels strange to be working on it underwater in scuba gear. We are fortunate to have such excellent visibility in this bay and can see the local fish tackling the barnacles with gusto. Beside the barnacles there is the green film that started covering the hull as we crossed the Pacific, but this comes off easily with a light brushing. I take the opportunity of checking the log impellor again to see if it has grown anything since my last inspection.

Robin fins round to my side of *Orca*, points to his eyes and then points away in the distance. I follow his direction and see a huge turtle, comically swooping up and down in the water, using its great paddle feet. I can't help smiling, and that lets water seep in round my mouthpiece.

The results of our morning toils are pleasing and after lunch we decide to snorkel in the shallows of the bay for recreation. We motor around in the dinghy to select a spot over rocks and lower our tiny anchor. Rob has his underwater camera and takes shots of magnificent spotted eagle rays, turtles and an abundance of small multi-coloured tropical fish.

The evening is balmy as we sit on deck. "Now we've finished the boat work, let's go ashore tomorrow and do some exploring," suggests Rob.

"Great idea, I can pack a picnic."

In the morning we dress in long pants, long sleeved shirts, hats and stout trainers. We carry bug spray and rain gear for the trek, to cover every eventuality. Nothing is to mar this day off. We hope to find a track over the mountain into the adjacent Hatiheu Bay, four kilometres west as the crow flies.

Beyond the sandy foreshore, the track meanders past some small dwellings with thatched palm roofs. Breadfruit trees, coconut palms, and flowering shrubs obscure the walls. Some have modern-looking white plastic siding and white front doors.

They all have fertile gardens, with an abundance of fruit bushes, papayas, lemons, limes and bananas. Occasionally we see the owners, keeping their heads bent as they work. They are naturally shy and value their privacy. It must be very tedious with inquisitive visitors from all over the world prying and taking photos.

Thatched roof

Further along the shore, we see a little tent with a camping stove and other paraphernalia outside, but we don't meet its occupant. In between the trees, blue smoke drifts into the air from the copra-drying fires.

We discover a drying platform 10 metres long, a metre wide and a metre off the ground, above a smouldering fire. It has a sophisticated arrangement of corrugated iron which can be pulled over the copra to keep off the rain.

Copra-drying rack

The path starts to climb through dense vegetation and leads over old stone walls and rocks covered in lichens and mosses—eventually we seem to be climbing up a streambed. It's warm and damp and the going is rough. In a couple of hours, however, we reach the apex and start descending towards our destination, breaking out of the bush onto the foreshore. Everywhere there are beautifully groomed lawns and flowerbeds filled with blossoms and carved tikis. We spot what looks like a little restaurant set back from the footpath.

"To heck with a picnic," I say, "let's see if we can have lunch!"

"My very thoughts," says Rob, as he leads the way. The sun has disappeared and it is threatening to rain.

There are half a dozen tables, set on a raised wooden platform, and covered with cloths bearing Polynesian geometric designs in black, brown, red and orange. Overhead is a thatched pandanus roof and giant hibiscus blossoms decorate the centre of the tables. It looks so inviting we stroll in and sit down.

A beautiful Polynesian lady in a colourful pareu comes to see us.

She has a gardenia blossom behind her left ear—she, too, is happily spoken for. We order two cold Hinano beers.

"Now *this* is paradise," Robin says, relaxing in his chair and looking about him and out over the bay. "We've lost the good weather, though." As he speaks, the first large raindrops plop onto the pandanus leaves and roll down to the ground.

It's a choice between shrimp or lobster for lunch. Robin chooses lobster, so I go for shrimp. Before long our food appears on a serving dish, surrounded by small potatoes. I think perhaps we should have ordered one dish between us, it is so large. A feast indeed, for $10.00 each.

The seafood is perfectly cooked and we devour as much of it as we can while listening to the tattoo of raindrops. We are the only occupants of this delightful restaurant and our attendant hovers in the background, but we can eat no more. Reluctantly we leave and retrace our steps.

"Well, we were lucky this morning," I say as the rain comes sheeting down, "but at least it's not cold."

We follow the dry streambed, wondering how much rain has to fall before it becomes a stream again. Everything has become slick and I slip on a round, wet boulder and fall heavily on another.

"Oh shit!" I say.

"What have you done now?" Rob asks.

I refuse to wail as I look down at my leg. I've ripped my pants and blood is gushing out of my shin. No good hoping for sympathy, as an egg-sized lump rapidly rises. I say nothing.

"Why aren't you more careful; is it really bad? Do I have to carry you?"

"No of course not," I say bravely, "I'll be fine." I find a clean handkerchief and tie it round my leg to stem the flow, before setting off again. Of course, we haven't brought a first-aid kit.

Back on the track at ground level the rain is still pouring down. I stop to talk to a stringy, brown pony with a straggly black mane. It has appeared from nowhere. Despite universal evidence of horse manure, this is the first one we've seen and it's not the least bit wild. It allows me to stroke its muzzle.

"Wild" pony

As we walk back through an ancient, overgrown orchard, we find a couple of citrus trees bearing small lemons. We pounce on them with delight and can't resist the urge to fill a knapsack. They'll make a wonderful addition to our stores —we've really missed citrus fruit.

I'm glad to get back, my leg is throbbing. I have to submit to having it examined, but it is so sensitive I can't bear to bathe it. We pour on hydrogen peroxide and allow it to fizz and pop and do the cleansing. I have a 4-centimetre gash on my shinbone. Robin offers to close the wound with steri-strip plasters, but I don't want it touched. Instead we cover it with a clean pad and I drink a couple of beers.

After an uncomfortable night, I get up and try to stand. It is excruciatingly painful to put any weight on my leg. I look down and am sickened. From thigh to ankle it is swollen like a fat sausage.

"Oh Robin," I groan, "you're not going to be very happy with me. I think my leg must be infected." I support myself, using the sides of the cabin as crutches, to get to the galley where he is making tea. He turns round and a horrified look appears on his face.

"We aren't going to be sailing far with that, are we? We'd better get you round to the hospital in Taiohae Bay."

We had been contemplating setting off for the Tuamotus islands in a couple of days, but now that will be on hold. I try to help Robin prepare the boat for the trip back round to Taiohae Bay, but there's not much I can do. The cloud has blotted out the hills: it is raining steadily and we can barely see across the bay.

Robin starts the engine and it is running smoothly in idle. I stand at the helm, easing the throttle forward every now and then, to take the strain off the anchor line while Robin winds it up. We must be right over the top of the anchor now and he is having a terrible time. Something is wrong. I feel the familiar panic rising—more, I think, because I know Robin will be furious and somehow I feel responsible. From my position at the helm under the doghouse I can't see what is happening up at the bow. Robin comes stomping back along the deck, looking like thunder.

"We've hooked a bloody great chunk of limestone; it's caught on one of the flukes. It's a couple of metres in diameter and must weigh half a ton. Keep motoring round the bay very slowly, while I try to chip it free."

It is at this time that it starts to rain hard, really hard—a white-out.

"Put your harness on." I remind Robin as he goes back down the deck with hammer and chisel. He ignores me. I step aside from the helm for a moment and watch him climb outside the safety lines to wedge himself between the bowsprit and the side stay. He starts hammering and chiselling the enormous rock. Meanwhile, I'm blindly creeping round the bay with *Orca*, struggling to see ahead so that I don't run into anything. The limestone is swinging like a pendulum and I won't even know if Robin slips and falls into the bay and I run over him. Visibility is about 25 metres and I curse loudly through the sheeting rain.

It seems an age before Robin returns. "We're free," he says. He takes over the helm, checks the compass and heads for what should be the channel out of the bay. We still can't see the sides of the passage. When we are well offshore we retrace our passage to Taiohae Bay.

The squall blows over, leaving us with a hot sun and a glistening, sweet-smelling world. We've left behind the overpowering smell of copra and our decks have had a great freshwater wash and are now gently steaming.

"We're not using two anchors," Robin states, as we enter Taiohae Bay and he selects a spot well away from all the other yachts.

The little hospital looks deserted, but we find a Polynesian nurse and I am fortunate that she speaks excellent English. She puts me in an examination room, one of many small rooms off an open quadrangle, somewhat like my old school in England. She cleans the wound and sutures it—I can hardly tell *her* not to touch it—and goes for the doctor. He is Parisian, working for a couple of years in French Polynesia. We manage to converse in schoolgirl French and schoolboy English and I explain that I fell during a hike over the mountain. He checks my vital signs, the temperature of my hands and feet and questions me about pain. He voices concern about the rapid swelling and the possibility of septicaemia plus the compound risk of tetanus. He hooks me up to a substantial-looking dose of IV antibiotics and gives me a painful anti-tetanus shot in my buttock on the side of my good leg.

"You might as well go and walk around for a while," I tell Robin when the nurse lets him into the room, "it's going to take half an hour for this IV and then I'm going to be kept here for an hour or so, to see if I have any adverse reactions to the anti-tetanus."

"OK, that's a good idea, I'll be back later." Robin has never been fond of hospitals, so is happy to be relieved of caretaking duties.

The nurse flits in and out as I rest and we chat about inconsequential things. She divulges that she is hoping to continue her studies to become a doctor one day. I tell her she'll make a good one and she smiles bashfully. When Robin returns, the doctor comes to check me. He allows me to leave, with a prescription for oral antibiotics.

"Thank you so much for seeing me and treating me with such good care," I tell him.

"C'est rien, it's nothing," he smiles, "but look after that leg." I promise to rest, with only a slight twinge of conscience, knowing I will do no such thing. The hospital pharmacy fills my prescription and when I ask about paying, the pharmacist tells me it is free—courtesy of the French government.

Nuku Hiva has been home for three weeks and we love it, but it's time to move on. The feeling of desolation I had being at sea for such a protracted journey, has faded as all painful things do. Our marathon voyage is behind us and the rest, as Robin says, will be 'a piece of cake'.

If given the choice of what to do on this particular day, it probably would not have been sailing, but at least our next leg is only two to three days—hardly anything at all. We depart Taiohae for Ahé, in the Tuamotus on 26th June, 1994 my 47th birthday.

14

Jewels for Joules and Little Man in Big Green Pants Ahé, Tuamotus

It promises to be a brilliant day. The gear below decks is safely stowed and prepared for ocean voyaging; anchors, fenders and the dinghy are lashed on deck. There's enough wind to raise all sails and we experience our first textbook sailing, 10—15 knots of SE trade winds and we are sailing on a broad reach, making 7—8 knots.

"This is more like it!" I exclaim, as *Orca* slices through the sparkling ocean. "I'm beginning to realize why some people like sailing when there are days like this."

Robin smiles and sits down to read a couple of chapters of his book. Currently, everything is running smoothly and behaving normally, so he can relax and transport himself into another world for a while. I busy myself about the yacht. In our stateroom I look for a new book to read, but can't quite decide which one to start. I'd intended reading the *Lord of the Rings* trilogy, but found it too slow to keep my mind off sailing thoughts. I return to the deck empty-handed and find some line ends which I can whip with waxed sail thread.

By night we are back into our three-hour watches and enjoying them. There's a velvety comfort about being on an untroubled ocean at night. Only a small red glow emanates through the hatchway from below decks where there is a low-wattage red lamp by the chart table. The moon, just past full, casts a shimmering silver trail across the water. For a fleeting moment I catch myself thinking it's a pity we will have to stop soon to make landfall.

For two and a half days, sailing is sheer delight. No engine throbbing, just the fluid swooshing of water against the hull. *Orca* is heeled over, but steady. Gone forever, I hope, is the rolling motion of the Pacific. The autopilot knows its business, so there's no need to helm. In fact we give both autopilots a turn to keep them in trim.

"No boat traffic, five dolphins and I've identified Saturn and Mars!" Robin reports happily. He hands me a cup of tea and the Night Sky guide and, yawning, disappears below to his bunk. He will be asleep in seconds. I scan the horizon and gaze up at the heavens before taking a stroll round the deck to check the sails. My harness tether follows along, clipped to the jack-line. Everything seems to be in good order. At the stern I sit on the lazarette and tilt my head back to absorb the vastness of the night sky—zillions of tiny pins shining in a giant pincushion. I never tire of looking at them. This is our last magnificent night of sailing before landfall tomorrow.

"I'll start the motor and we can drop the sails," Robin says, "Ahé should be coming into view soon." In stark contrast to our approach to the Marquesas where the land rises hundreds of metres, the highest point of the Ahé atoll struggles to 3 metres above sea level. The lagoon measures roughly 21 by 8 km, but there are only a few dotted islands, or motus, strung around the ancient volcanic rim, so we could be virtually on top of the reef before we see it.

"You'd better stand on the cabin roof with the binoculars and let me know if you can see a line of foam, or breaking seas or some palm tree tops—any indication at all," says Robin. The GPS can give an accurate fix of our position, but the coordinates of the islands were charted before such accuracy was available and are often quite a long way out.

"Damn," I hear below me, "the GPS screen has just gone blank— it's searching for the satellites again."

A knot of nervousness ties itself in my abdomen. The Tuamotus weren't called 'Les Iles Dangereuses' without good reason. We must find a passage through a reef that we can't see and now we've lost the GPS.

I scan the horizon, binoculars glued to my face. "I think I can see some surf ... and I can see a boat!" I gleefully shout. "It looks as though it's coming straight through the surf."

Robin pushes open the throttle and takes over from the autopilot. "It obviously knows where the pass is, so keep your eyes on it."

At 4:00 p.m. we arrive at the entrance to the renowned Reianui pass and it's more or less slack tide, although there are still lots of breakers crashing over the rocks. At least we shouldn't be pushing against a full 6-knot outflow.

"I can see the markers now, on the rocks—we're OK."

At slack water, maximum depth in the pass is 3.5 metres, so with our 2-metre draft we don't have too much to spare. Robin lines up with the markers. "Here we go!"

I peer over the side and can see the bottom as the water surges and sucks around the rocks. It's so clear it looks much too shallow. Robin powers *Orca* through and I grit my teeth. Thank God there are no grating sounds. Once through the reef, Robin relaxes and I can breathe normally as we motor unscathed into a massive lagoon.

"The village is at the SW corner," Robin says, heading in that direction, although we can't see across to the far side.

"Is that the first marker?" I point to a small pole sticking up away in the distance. "Visibility's not very good."

The four-mile passage across the lagoon to the village should be shown by markers about one mile apart. I climb back up onto the main boom to my lookout position. Errant coral outcrops are pretty unforgiving to the careless and the unwise.

"Yep. It's definitely the marker," I say and we continue with more confidence. As we close on the first one, I scan the horizon for the next. "The markers are on big chunks of rock, so don't cut it too fine or we'll run aground."

Section by section, we thread our way through the corals to where the diminutive village squats precariously on the rim of the extinct volcano. On one side it is sheltered by the reef and lagoon and open to the Pacific on the other. I make a mental note that we should do this sort of manoeuvre in the middle of the day, in future, when the sun is overhead and visibility is best—but then it might not be slack tide.

Dusk arrives with us at the anchorage and we are met by a well-meaning yachting guide in a dinghy with an outboard motor. He indicates for us to follow him and proceeds to race inside an inner reef, where there are already about 10 snugly-fitted boats. We lose him momentarily after weaving in and out in an effort to follow, executing our version of racing turns, before finally escaping to the outer lagoon to anchor in the dark in 15 metres of water.

"We'll have to check the anchor tomorrow," Rob says, "we'll hope for the best with coral heads. What do you say to a tot of rum?"

By the light of our headlamps we complete the securing of the sails, then sit out in the mild darkness with our rum allowance, musing on our superior sailing skills.

Early next morning I gingerly crawl over Robin to get out of the

Shallow lagoon in Ahé

bunk, anxious to get on deck and have a good look at our surroundings in daylight. Judging by the comments, he seems to believe I've woken him, but he makes tea and joins me.

"Idyllic," I say, soaking up the scenery. White coral sand beaches, coconut palms laden with coconuts, rainbow coloured flowers, blue skies, sparse cumulus clouds and turquoise lagoon. "It's hard to picture these motus as tips of the rim of a gigantic extinct volcano."

"That reminds me, I'll just check the anchor and then we can go and explore after breakfast."

After tying up the dinghy at the concrete jetty, we take a leisurely stroll through the village. The Ahéans smile and nod as we walk down the main street which traverses the island; small children play games in the sand or chase around on bikes. The coral sand street is impeccably clean—raked and swept every day as an extension of their own yards. I'm not sure what they think about us as uninvited guests, but I feel we're invading their privacy.

Small white houses hide behind flowering shrubs and coconut palms in pocket-handkerchief gardens, some bordered by picket fences. Building materials of choice are white-painted cement block or woven pandanus walls, and either corrugated iron or thatched roofs. Windows are mostly functional rectangular holes in the walls to allow for the passage of breezes, although a few houses have glass panes. There are perhaps, two hundred people living here in the village covering 20 acres and a few others in a scattering of homes and black pearl farms on motus around the lagoon.

"What do you suppose *those* people are doing?" I indicate with my shoulder as we approach a house. A gaggle of individuals are standing in the doorway and an overspill is peering in at the window.

As we pass, we catch the flicker of a TV screen. It seems this is one of the few houses with a TV monitor and video player and they are showing a movie.

"What do they use for power?" I ask.

"Free-standing diesel generators—look there's one behind the house."

Ahé boasts a church, a school, a post office—which doesn't sell stamps but can sometimes patch through a telephone call; a bank and two stores. Apart from a few canned goods, there's not much to offer at the moment at either of the two stores. Presumably the vessel we saw coming through the reef was the boat to collect copra, not the supply boat which arrives with goods every two to three weeks.

On the Pacific side of the island, an unsightly hill of garbage has grown. One of today's most indestructible items, the 'disposable' diaper, festoons the area. Sadly, they'll still be here long after the tin cans and old pieces of machinery close by have rusted and become one with the coastline. The garbage pile also attests to the wealth of the locals. All sorts of mechanical devices are given up for dead; things like fridges, outboard motors and generators.

Despite a simplistic lifestyle, many islanders are very wealthy as they culture black pearls—highly treasured in the Pacific and the rest of the world. A perfect specimen fetches around US$1,000.

Our circular island tour takes less than an hour. Back at the jetty we meet an Australian yachtsman Chris, from *Foam Follower*, taking apart an outboard motor.

"G'day, nice to meet ya!" We shake hands and complete introductions. "There's no shortage of work here if ya like it." Chris tells Robin. "This salt environment plays havoc with their equipment and nobody does anything till it busts." He looks over his shoulder, "don't worry about your dinghy, just the kids having fun. They're pretty harmless."

Some very young Polynesian children are having a wonderful time leaping from the dock into the dinghy, then pushing each other into the water. A nearby adult, when he sees us, reprimands them with mock sternness and smiles at us as we near. This is what makes life fun and worth living, for the kids and for us.

As we're relaxing on *Orca* a day or two later, we see a little boat heading our way. Annie and Tom—the two youngest children belonging to Jo and Rick on the Wharram *Kate Cooley*—are rowing across to us in the outer lagoon.

"Mum says to tell you we've all been invited to a party this evening at Henri's house," says little Annie, about six years old and obviously the spokesperson, "he lives in that house over there." She releases the oar and flaps her hand behind her, before quickly retrieving her oar. "We can take some food. Mum will be there early to help his wife, Hanna."

Supper features poisson cru—sliced raw fish caught this morning, marinated in lime juice with onions and spices. Other delicacies are lobster, cooked fish, rice and yachtie pot-luck dishes. Quite the feast.

Following supper, someone starts strumming a guitar and another person taps the beat on an empty tin.

"Now we all have to play some music!" Henri lapses into peals of laughter as he brings out musical instruments. Other musicians appear from the shadows and join the burgeoning soirée. Everyone is encouraged to contribute. I play the spoons and sing heartily. Robin, who is musically challenged, joins in with a good spirit, shaking tins containing dried seeds.

One amazing young lady—tall, slender and beautiful, looks to be about 25 years old. Not only is she the most nimble-fingered guitarist on the island but she has eleven children!

"When do you suppose she has time to practice the guitar?" I whisper to Robin.

Wherever we go, it seems unusual weather isn't far behind. After a few days in Ahé, winds increase to 40 knots and white-capped waves race across the outer lagoon. *Orca* is tugging and straining on her anchor chain.

"I think we'll put out another bow anchor," Rob says, "we don't want to drag and end up on the coral."

The second anchor, this time on a rope rode, improves the holding. In two days, however, *Orca* completes three 360° turns. The anchor rodes wind themselves up beautifully around a 10-metre high coral growth beneath the yacht, into a double helix, like a strand of DNA. The anchor lines now pull down vertically from the bow.

We put on scuba gear and dive to correct the problem. I hover below the surface, in case Robin needs help. He unshackles the anchor and hauling the line, swims over and around the anchor chain and coral head several times before re-shackling the ensemble. We're ever grateful that we have scuba skills. It's an unexpected bonus that we can get our scuba tanks refilled on Ahé, as Rahiti, who owns the store by the jetty, has an air compressor, but refuses to charge us.

Sitting on deck one afternoon, we see a new yacht entering the lagoon and idly watch her progress from marker to marker.

"Robin, it looks like she's missed the last marker and is heading straight for us, I'd better call her!" I hang up the binoculars and jump down the companionway steps to call on Channel 16.

"*Absolutely Gorgeous, Absolutely Gorgeous, Absolutely Gorgeous*, this is *Orca*. Over!"

"*Orca, Orca, Orca*, this is *Absolutely Gorgeous*. Over!" A beautiful Scottish lilt trills over the airwaves.

"*Absolutely Gorgeous*, we are the yacht off your bow. Although it looks OK to motor directly towards us, DO NOT DO SO. Turn to starboard immediately until you have rounded the last marker, then turn towards the village. Over!"

"OK, thank you, *Orca*!" *Absolutely Gorgeous* turns away just before encountering the reef.

"Well, I guess that's our good deed for the day, Robin. She looks far to good too be shipwrecked."

"I don't know," he says, "there might have been some good pickings!"

A daily run is made by a couple of power boats to Manihi, a neighbouring island, to collect fresh baguettes flown in from Tahiti. Apart from seafood and fruit on their doorstep, household necessities (like diapers) arrive every 2-3 weeks by an inter-island tramp, or sometimes on the copra boats.

"The boat, the boat!"

The cry passes round the village when the tramp is spotted. The large vessel must anchor off in the outer lagoon, like us. Amid great excitement, a flotilla of little boats swarms to its sides to receive whatever has to be unloaded, then ferries the cargo to the jetty.

Surprisingly, large bulky items are deftly manoeuvred onto wobbly little craft and brought ashore without mishap. Jo from *Kate Cooley*, has promised to show me how transactions are conducted on board the vessel.

I pick her up in the dinghy and we raft up to the outer edge of the other small vessels surrounding the boat. We hop from one to another, until we can clamber up the ladder to the topside of the tramp. Here we wait our turn to give our order for supplies through a little hatch opening in the ship's topside. There is no browsing of laden shelves, or anything so gauche. We hand a list through the opening and just wait. If they have what we want, it is brought up to us and we pay through the little window. Jo is returning a sack of flour she bought from the vessel last trip. It has lost all its gluten to weevils and is useless for making bread.

When we finish our transactions, we carefully heave our purchases from one dinghy to the next, until we reach ours and motor home bearing our prizes. It is a joyful occasion when the cupboards are full.

Dog 'n' duck

Today, at the invitation of Henri, we are going ashore to mend a small generator belonging to his father, a revered village elder. On the short concrete jetty a couple of young French Polynesian 'gods' wearing frangipani leis, reach into the dinghy for our heavily-laden tool-boxes. They escort us along the hot sand of the freshly-swept main street. As usual, giggling children accompany us and this morning we have an incongruous couple tagging along, a white duck and a puppy.

Henri's palm-thatched hut is partially obscured by multi-coloured bougainvilleas and hibiscus and the heady scent of gardenia hangs on the air.

"Ha! Ha! Bonjour! Ha! Ha!" Our portly host emerges; flicking long hair from his eyes and welcomes us into the shade of some coconut palms. He sweeps the back of a pudgy hand across his rustic garden table to clear it of wildlife and long-abandoned mechanical parts, which now lay scattered in the sand. Henri lifts the ailing 'Robin' generator onto the bench and gives it a perfunctory wipe with a rag.

"If you mend this," he explains, "my father can use his fan. Now he is old, he finds it very hot."

"I hope we don't disappoint him," Robin whispers to me, "it doesn't look too promising."

The day, however, does look promising for the Polynesians and is blossoming into quite an event. Dressed in gaily coloured pareus, Henri's friends gather round, squatting on their haunches, sitting on boxes and leaning against palm trees to watch the spectacle. The smell of cigarette smoke shrouds the gardenia.

Ahéans are, without doubt, the most jocular people we've met. On this tiny island every situation is just cause for banter and they are frequently consumed with mirth.

I leap backwards in surprise when Robin removes the starter housing from the generator. A handful of crickets explode from their hiding place and shoot into the vegetation as the onlookers shriek with laughter.

"Oh boy," says Robin, peering inside, "I guess this one hasn't been running for a while." He continues stripping down the machine, piece by piece.

"Could we please have something to put the bits in?"

It takes a few moments to convey the request in French, but soon some old tin cans appear. Now at least we have a fighting chance of reassembling the parts, which are currently being closely inspected and going the rounds of the admiring group. I pray they don't drop them in the sand.

Progress is slow, but it doesn't matter, they're not going anywhere and this is excellent entertainment.

Even in the dappled sunlight beneath the palms, it is very hot. We must look thirsty, because a young man brandishing a machete deftly chops the top off two huge green coconuts he's just picked and hands them to us. The liquid contents of the unripe coconut is cool and deliciously refreshing and dribbles down my chin. Encouraged by our obvious enjoyment, he prepares two more and places them beside the others.

"Merci beaucoup! Magnifique!" I say, while calculating that there must be at least a litre of liquid in each coconut and Henri's door-less washroom faces the assembled crowd and we've quite a way to go yet on the generator.

After he has stripped and cleaned the carburettor and the air filter; checked the electrical system and removed corrosion from the terminals, Robin reassembles all the components.

"Here we go," he says, "testing time."

A cheer goes up when, after a few pulls, the generator splutters into life, but Robin is not celebrating yet. There is no output voltage. The crowd remains unperturbed—they now have total faith. Fortunately, altering the speed-setting of the governing device cures the problem. Henri disappears into his hut and produces a fan to plug in. The fan whirrs into action.

He bounds over to Robin and embraces him, then holds up Robin's hand like a champ at a prize fight and announces, "Robin has mended the 'Robin'!"

This sends the men into renewed peals of laughter and henceforth, Robin is known as 'M. le Générateur'.

"Have you noticed what's arrived?" I ask Robin as we pack up our tools.

Robin looks puzzled. "What do you mean?"

"Your reputation has spread." Robin turns round. Four wheelbarrows have mysteriously appeared and they are all overflowing with broken generators. "I wonder if they've been to the rubbish tip to pick these up? You're going to be busy this week!"

Henri tosses one old generator to the ground and commandeers the wheelbarrow to carry our tool boxes to the dinghy. Perspiring freely and grinning as always, he affirms, "My father is very happy and he would like to visit your yacht tomorrow to thank you."

Thirty-knot winds are creating waves in the lagoon. We watch the visiting party flexing their muscles as they plunge their paddles and draw them powerfully through the water. They steady their outrigger canoe and lift Henri's father onto *Orca*. As a village elder he receives due respect.

All seven visitors eagerly accept a tour of our home. Radios, navigation equipment, engine and staterooms are enthusiastically inspected, but the most admired item, which gives rise to more nudging and tittering is, without doubt, the turquoise half-size bath.

On deck we drink tea, eat home-made cookies and enjoy the

considerable breezes while swapping sea stories in French/Polynesian/English. After two hours, polite formalities have been observed and the elder speaks in Polynesian. Jacques, the cousin of Henri, nods and says, "Please bring a tray covered with a soft cloth."

With great ceremony the elder produces a small pouch from the folds of his pareu. Slowly, he rolls out a dozen black pearls, caressing them with his fingers.

"You may pick one pearl," translates Jacques, holding his forefinger aloft, "for mending my uncle's generator." Although Robin did the mending, I must be the one to pick the pearl. It is a solemn occasion and I take time to make my choice. To hurry would be insulting. I explore the shape, size and lustre of the individual pearls, as a connoisseur may explore the depths of a good wine. I make my selection and the old man murmurs.

"He says you make a good choice," translates diplomatic Jacques. The old man's weather-beaten face crinkles into a smile. I think he understands English *quite* well.

The entourage bids us farewell, gently lowers the old man into the outrigger and paddles swiftly to shore. I glance down: my black pearl nestles in my hand, glowing with the green/black iridescence of a raven's wing. It is priceless. An ancient ceremony has been re-enacted—the exchange of goods and services between peoples of different cultures. Each participant satisfied that the trade is perfect.

Black Pearl

Since our arrival at the end of June, preparations have been underway for Bastille Day celebrations on 14th July. We can hear snatches of musical arrangements drifting across the island, as musicians accompany pockets of dancers practicing their dance steps, directed by the ample-bosomed choreographer with generous hips. With the beat of a drum, these hips can swivel mechanically at speeds that defy the eye.

Male and female dances differ dramatically. The girls, while mechanically wiggling their hips at the speed of light, can walk, knees together, in a sensuous way and simultaneously sinuate their arms in the most delightful manner. The men, following the traditions of war dances, take a partially-squatting stance and walking and stomping swing their knees together and apart. It is very strenuous exercise, yet we don't find anyone complaining of arthritis.

As we wander along the street, we see little knots of weathered elderly men in pareus sitting cross-legged on the ground weaving mats and panels from coconut palms, all the while smoking, chatting and joking. We pass ladies preparing headgear, leis and adornments from the local greenery, which will then be bedecked with fresh blossoms on the day. Matching costumes are being sewn from red and white, and green and white cloth. White 'grass skirts' are fashioned by teasing the warp from the weft of burlap bags.

"Do you suppose the storming of the Bastille has any significance to these people?" I ask.

"I should think it's highly unlikely," Robin replies, "but it's a great opportunity for a few days of celebrations!"

Ahé blossoms into festival appearance. The village carpenter erects a juice and coconut concession stand, complete with thatched roof and woven walls. Every pillar and post in sight is dressed with woven leaves.

First thing in the morning on the great day, we 'dress' *Orca*, shimmying up the masts to haul and secure metres and metres of nautical flags. They fly out from the rigging in a large catenary. The Ahéans are touched by the effort.

"Don't take too long," I say to Robin who is making breakfast, "we need to be on shore fairly early. We don't want to miss anything."

Orca in Ahé

The crews from all the yachts have been invited to share in the fun and games. *Orca, Kate Cooley, Foam Follower, Absolutely Gorgeous* and a couple of new yachts that have just dropped anchor. The day is radiant. A summer-blue sky, dotted with small cumulous clouds and no hint of rain.

We exchange the breeze of the lagoon for the heat of the village. Not a wisp of grass, nor a leaf is out of place. The village has been raked and swept immaculately. It's not only the children who are feeling excited and the concession is already doing a roaring trade in free soda pop and coconut milk.

The MC of races is calling the children and lining them up to start. Their little faces have been polished like shiny apples, and they grin and nudge each other, jostling for pole position at the start line.

The day is filled with competitions for adults too. Coconut husking, boules, volley ball, soccer, tug o' war and sack races. Joking and giggling, we are all eager to show off our skills.

"Come on Robin, you can do it!" Robin is jumping along in fine form in his race. What he lacks in speed and distance gained, he more than makes up for in height; springing from the ground like a young gazelle, much to the pleasure of the onlookers.

Sack race

In the evening the contestants are electrically charged for the music, singing and dancing competitions: sparkling with fresh blossoms in their hair, round their necks, arms and ankles. The air is heady with frangipani and gardenia. Onlookers sit in lawn chairs. Several 'chariots des bébés'—a term coined by the girl from *Absolutely Gorgeous* for the wheelbarrows carrying children— arrive, some lined with blankets and pillows for the infants.

The street is lit by smudge lamps, which also serve to keep mosquitoes at bay. Participants assemble in a big group on the 'dance floor' outside the post office, receiving last minute instructions from the choreographer. Everyone is smiling and they look radiant: young maidens and young warriors surreptitiously eye each other. They are going to perform their best tonight.

Chariots des bébés

"Oh my goodness, look at that!" I grab Robin's arm and point to two tiny dancers, about 3 and 4 years old. They pay rapt attention to the directions. The little girl is dressed as a perfect miniature and her hips wiggle just as fast as her older sisters'. The little boy is lost in a big pair of green pants and wears a dangling streamer of greenery over his left shoulder. He's not actually part of the troupe, but that doesn't dampen his enthusiasm for joining in.

Little man in big green pants

The Ahé band

Musicians take their place in a large semicircle in front of the judging table. They are decked out in their most colourful pareus with fresh green wreaths of leaves on their heads. They have guitars and ukuleles; drums of all shapes and sizes, even a blue plastic oil drum as big as the small boy playing it. Large empty biscuit tins are played with the hands; and hollowed-out wooden-log drums, common throughout Polynesia, are played with carved wooden sticks. Just about anything that can make a noise is used.

The resulting mixture is the sweetest melodic Polynesian music and the accompanying harmonious singing is enduring. Group by group, participants take to the dance floor. Beautiful maidens first, then young warriors join the dancing. The judging panel of elders scrutinize participants and make notes.

Over their short red pareus worn diaper-style, the young men sport the snowy white grass skirts we saw being made, the waistbands sewn with plant sepals. The result is stunning. Matching white tassels adorn their wrists. The outfits are completed with pink and red hibiscus headgear and greenery necklaces.

Ahé dancers

"I've just realized why the men dance in a squatting position," I say to Robin, "it's so we can see their superb thigh muscles gleaming through the frazzles of their skirts. It's very seductive!"

A celebration is worth naught in Ahé, until everyone is reduced to crying with laughter. To this end, following the serious competitions, they delight in involving visitors in their dancing and they don't even *try* to disguise their mirth at our puny efforts. The worse we are, the better they like it. They get full value from Robin and me as we're choreographically challenged. For such a good-natured, fun-loving bunch of Polynesians, we're happy to be the brunt of their jokes. If you've ever tried wiggling your hips at speeds that defy the eye, or stomping around banging your knees together, you'll know that we haven't developed the required muscles.

Idyllic days pass swiftly in Ahé. We alternate the never-ending boat chores of varnishing, painting and caulking of windows with hedonistic pursuits—visiting uninhabited motus for picnics, where we can pick up ripe and unripe fallen coconuts for our store. We scuba dive and find pearl oysters that have come adrift from their lines and are lying, silt-covered, on the bottom. Not one contains a pearl! We explore the nooks and crannies of the reefs with the underwater camera, in the company of black tipped sharks and gaudy schools of fish which, fortunately, make up the sharks' normal diet. All the while the *Jaws* music *da-da da-da da-da da-da,* plays along with the beating of my heart. It's good to see *Orca* when we surface.

Surfacing from dive

Robin is invited to go fishing with Rick and his boys from *Kate Cooley*, Chris from *Foam Follower* and Henri and friends. I watch them wading in the shallows in a circle. Some with superior skills throw nets to trap the fish. They're planning another party and need supplies for poisson cru.

A few days ago, when we were sorting out our twisted anchor lines, we spotted a large coral grouper, red with blue spots and vowed to go back with a spear gun to claim supper, but somehow it didn't seem sporting to shoot something that would swim up and peer in at us through our masks.

"We can teach you to fish from the boat." Little Annie and her brothers are determined to take us in hand and teach us the art of hand-lining. They successfully haul in several fish, but I think it involves patience. We later learn why these fish hang around yachts and what it is that they actually eat. If we'd known first, we wouldn't have eaten the fish! However, our health remains intact. We'll not be making water with our reverse-osmosis water maker, though, until we are out in the open seas again, where the water will have a lower faecal content.

One day on shore, a middle aged lady called Fetia takes Robin by the arm. Earnestly looking into his face, she says, "Please, please can you help me? I have a Vespa motorcycle but the brakes don't work."

How can Robin refuse? He can't bear to think of her racing up the main street and straight into the Pacific because she can't stop.

Next day he carries his tools and I carry a book to Fetia's house. I settle down to read in the shade of a tree, while Robin works. The brakes and throttle-cable are badly corroded—hardly surprising in this salt-laden environment. He methodically strips and cleans the cables and linkages.

"I've made some lunch for you—come, come and eat it." Fetia points to her back door and leads us into her kitchen where there is fish, rice and papaya laid out on a little kitchen table.

"This is very good," Robin tells her, as she flits around us.

"Yes, it's very kind of you," I add.

"Do you want more fish, more coconut milk?" Fetia asks.

When we can't eat another morsel, we excuse ourselves. Robin reassembles the parts, despite having an overfull stomach and fancying a snooze in the shade. Fetia is hovering again, peering over his shoulder, her hands clasped to her generous bosom. Robin kick-starts the machine, hops on and zooms round her garden, testing brakes and throttle. He makes a small adjustment and all is fine.

Tears trickle down Fetia's face as she embraces Robin. "Thank you, thank you!" She says over and over. Robin packs his tools and Fetia brings him two, half-oyster shells, the size of a saucer. Each has been seeded with spherical and tear-drop plastic inserts between the layers of shell. After a few years the oysters have grown layers of black mother-of-pearl over the inserts, resulting in four large black half-pearls protruding from the shells. They are usually made into pearl pendants. It is a unique gift. She also hangs garlands of shell necklaces round Robin's neck.

He gives her a big hug. "This is very generous of you!" He is rather embarrassed because he considers it such a small thing that he did.

After a month of fun and work, it is time to leave. We spend a couple of days gradually preparing for ocean voyaging. Things are put away and battened down; charts selected and studied and the engine and generator checked over. All is in good running order.

Rahiti is filling our scuba tanks before we leave and a few people have gathered on the dock to say goodbye. Fetia buzzes up on her scooter and hangs even more shell necklaces on Robin. We promise Henri that we'll organize manuals, wiring diagrams and spare parts to be shipped to the island for his big Brush generator. Hopefully, an engineer from a future yacht can reinstall them.

It is difficult to leave this little paradise. The inhabitants have welcomed us into their lives with open hearts. We motor across the few miles of lagoon and through Reianui Pass without mishap. Several new yachts have arrived in the lagoon, so the perpetual cycle of welcoming visitors and exchanging goods and services will continue for the enchanting community of Ahé.

Approaching Moorea

15

Whelk Harvest and Yarns at the Bali Hai Moorea, Society Islands

Once clear of all reefs, we set our course for Moorea in the Society Islands. It is renowned as one of the most scenic islands in the world, blessed with expansive white sandy beaches, shallow coral lagoons and spiking mountains. This magical island inspired James Michener to write about the mythical Bali Hai and was twice chosen for filming *Mutiny on the Bounty*. Everyone talks of going to Moorea's sister island, Tahiti, which is reason enough for us to go instead to Moorea, 19 km to Tahiti's northwest.

We set a reefed genoa, mainsail and mizzen and are sailing well. Winds are a brisk 25+ knots and we're heeled over to starboard. It's lumpy and uncomfortable, crashing into moderate to rough seas left behind from a serious squall, but we're making good progress.

Lengthy periods at anchor encourage laziness and it's a shock to the system getting back into 3-hourly watches, but we manage and see nothing untoward during the night. In a way it's more fun as we know we'll be anchoring again soon, so even rough weather doesn't dampen our spirits. I enjoy the challenge of getting the last ounce out of our sail configuration and often play around with the sails when Robin is off watch. I'm pleased that I've become quite proficient. I don't do it scientifically, but can just see and feel the right thing to do. By the second day the seas have moderated and the going is easier. We've managed to sail throughout the entire passage again.

TP has become a genuine nauti-cat. She hasn't been off the yacht for five months. I no longer worry that she'll go overboard, because even in port, she'll only come out on the deck for a while and doesn't go forward unless we are there. When we return to the cockpit, she comes flying back. She's obviously taking her job seriously as RRCO, as we haven't seen a single cockroach on board.

"Moorea on the nose!" Robin announces. Its presence is given away by the white halo of clouds hanging around the mountain tops. We head for Cook's Bay, (Baie Paopao), on the north side—one of two deep fjord-like bays which cut in a quarter of the way to the centre of this extinct volcano. As we draw closer we can see dramatic, sharp lava peaks and all but the vertical spires are clothed with thick vegetation.

The sun is warming the rich soil and the breeze wafts intoxicating scents of soil, blossoms and ripe fruit. It's a sensation we never tire of and stirs in me some visceral emotion. Robin starts the engine and we drop the sails and gently motor through Passe Avaroa. We glide between expanses of fringing coral reef where we can clearly see the sandy bottom through the crystal waters. Wavelets trip and dance over the exposed reef, showering twinkling rainbow sprays. As the water becomes shallower, the colour changes from emerald through blue, to turquoise.

Cook's Bay, plunging deep into the interior of the island, offers great shelter. There are several yachts here, but it is an immense inlet. We anchor in 14 metres of water on a good sticky mud bottom and are not surprised to find that the water is murky.

Cook's Bay

"Those coral reefs we passed through look like great places to snorkel." Robin says when the anchor is down and the engine is off.

"Yes, maybe we can find something to eat—perhaps an octopus!"

First things first, though. I'm eager to motor ashore and walk on land. We tie up the dinghy, hoping for its safety and find directions to the Gendarmerie, to report our presence. The heat is palpable on shore and a surly Gendarme is standing behind the counter in shirtsleeves, yet is still wearing his pillbox hat. He gives the impression that he hates visiting yachtsmen—possibly with good cause. He is probably doing a stint in what he may consider to be a remote outpost; a long, long way from the centre of his world, Paris, France.

He is perfectly aware that we haven't yet paid our bond, but he obviously doesn't want to bother with the paperwork and is relieved when we tell him we'll be going to Papeete and perhaps we could do it there. He might have been slightly concerned if we'd admitted that Papeete was to be our last French Polynesian port and there would be little point in paying the bond and reclaiming it the same day. We also don't tell him that we are going to Papeete by catamaran, not on *Orca*. We are operating on a 'need to know' basis.

After the gloomy interior of the gendarmerie the street is blindingly bright. On our way back to the yacht we decide to look in a few of the local supermarkets. We choose a shop under Chinese ownership which seems well stocked and displays the ubiquitous 'Gaz' propane bottles outside.

We haven't bought provisions for a long time, apart from a few things from the supply boat in Ahé, and are particularly relishing the thought of fresh food. There is a good selection of packaged and tinned produce, but prices are astronomical! Baguettes, however, are plentiful and cheap so prove to be our staple carbohydrate once more together with the tinned cheese, of which I'm becoming quite fond. Fresh vegetables are almost prohibitive.

"Are they kidding, $5 for a cabbage the size of my fist?" I say to Robin. "I can do without imported vegetables." We pick up mangoes, papayas and a pineapple more reasonably priced and a couple of bottles of the cheapest red wine. It is outrageously expensive, but we're prepared to pay for our pleasures. Handing over hard-earned money is unfamiliar and painful and we feel the need to retreat to the cocoon-like comfort of *Orca*.

To our dismay, as we motor towards the bow, we discover that we've lost 3 metres of our 5- by 8-cm mahogany rub strip on the starboard side, just back from the bowsprit.

"We must have lost it when we were thumping into the rough seas the first day out of Ahé," says Robin.

"I'm surprised we didn't feel or hear anything when it let go."

"I'm not going to worry about replacing it yet. It's not structural, but tomorrow we'll have to treat the exposed area and fill the bolt-holes in the hull with the Phillybond Blue epoxy we used on *Orca's* keel."

Supper consists of baguettes, butter which we still have in the freezer, cheese and some 'interesting' sharp red wine which we probably could have put to better use as paint stripper. Hopefully we won't pay the penalty tomorrow.

Our day starts off effecting repairs to the starboard side. Robin chamfers in the broken exposed end of the mahogany strip and deals with filling holes.

"Shall we go to the reef now?" I ask when all is tidied.

We launch the Avon and at the mouth of the bay lower the little anchor on a sandy spot to avoid damaging the coral reef. With masks, snorkels and fins in place, we slip over the side, one at a time, into 26°C clear water, gunnysacks attached to our waists and slowly swim along the surface to view the area. Our eyes take a few moments to become accustomed to the muted colours of the sea bed three metres below us.

Drifts of minute, coloured reef fish; electric blue, striped and spotted move as one, darting back and forth and in and out of the corals. A few sea cucumbers repose on the sand and wickedly sharp sea-urchins lurk at the base of rocks. There's also a pernicious bright orange seastar feeding on coral. Robin gives me the 'going down' thumb signal and I watch him dive and fin to the bottom. He picks something up and returns to the surface. "Look!" On his upheld hand is a triangular-shaped giant whelk (trochus), about 10 cm in diameter, covering his palm. "There are lots of them."

"OK, I'm coming." We descend together. The coral reef is surprisingly noisy, emitting lots of cracking and popping sounds. Then the inordinately loud noise of an outboard motor overrides everything when a curious boater comes to see what we are doing. In half an hour we pick up a couple of bags of trochus each and lob them over the side, into the dinghy.

"I've just spotted a track in the sand," I tell Robin, "I'm going down to check it out." Moments later I'm back at the surface and hold up my prize—a beautiful giant spider conch that will make tasty eating and provide us with an unusual shell souvenir.

"Well, we may not be able to catch fish when we're sailing," I say as we head for home, "but at least we can find good free French Polynesian protein when we're anchored."

The rest of the day is spent scrubbing the shells and pressure-cooking the whelks, so we can extricate the edible meat. We've collected about 60—enough for several good nutritious stews. Tonight it's baguette with whelk stew for supper and we freeze the rest in meal-sized portions.

In the morning Jim and Rea's trimaran motors into the bay. We swing by in the dinghy on our way to shore to say hello. We tell them about the trochus; something Jim is familiar with from the Marshall Islands.

"Have you got any muriatic acid on board?" He asks.

"Yes," says Robin, "do you want some?"

"No, but if you use a toothbrush dipped in muriatic acid and keep scrubbing the whelk shell you can dissolve the outer layer and end up with a beautiful mother-of-pearl shell."

"Thanks. We'll try that later. We're going ashore to find out about hiring a scooter to tour the island. Would you guys be interested in doing a round-the-island trip with us?"

"Sounds a great idea," says Rea, "when do you want to go?"

"We thought tomorrow, making an early start. Would that be all right?"

Albert Family Enterprise rents scooters for f3000 ($30) for 8 hours. We reckon that will be quite long enough in the saddle, so book two scooters for the next day.

The scooters are ready at 8:00 a.m. sharp. We stow our belongings in the pannier bags, slap on our helmets and ride off, the men in the driving seats. It is exhilarating to be speeding along with the wind rushing past and we're on land! Actually we're only coasting along gently, so we don't miss too much.

Our first stop is Belvedere lookout point, high in the interior mountains between 1207-metre Mount Tohiea and 898-metre Mount Rotui. It is said this view was reserved for the gods. At the top of an incredibly steep hair-pin track, we reach the lookout point. It is breathtakingly beautiful. On the west side of the arrete is Opunohu Bay and on the east is Cook's Bay.

Belvedere lookout view

We hop back on the scooters, creep down the switchback to the road and continue on our way. Jim, an amateur radio ham, has made arrangements for us to visit a retired American with whom he's chatted many times during his voyages. We arrive in time for coffee and cookies in the dark, cool interior of his house high on the hillside of Opunohu Bay. After coffee we climb the steep ladder to his ham shack in the loft above his carport. Here he spends several hours each evening talking with hams all round the world. It is astonishing to see the amount of electronic equipment and I can't help wondering how he got it all up here.

The heart-shaped island of Moorea has an area of 130 square kilometres and it is possible to do a complete 64-km circumnavigation. Ancient religious tikis and artefacts aren't as evident here as they were in the Marquesas, because they were destroyed by missionaries in an effort to discourage traditional worship. We make good use of our eight hours and return the scooters and helmets intact, although we are more than a bit weary and wobbly.

Thankfully, the dinghy is still secure where we left it. One is never sure that it won't be removed or damaged. A young ex-British army fellow, single-handing on a 12-metre yacht, brought his mountain bike ashore in his dinghy and chained it securely so that he could use it ashore for sight-seeing. It was stolen the first night. Such a shame, but just too tempting. Unfortunately, our western values have become prevalent here.

So far it has been serenely calm in this bay and *Orca* has hardly changed direction. Following our scooter ride, however, we have several days of high, gusty winds and watch the squall clouds marching across the hills bringing heavy showers. The benefit of this is that everything is washed down with fresh water. It also dampens the omnipresent smell of drying copra. Instead, we can inhale the rich aroma of moist, fertile soil and blossoms. Despite the weather, we complete more work on the boat; health-monitoring, maintenance and improvements. I've started chipping away the old paint on the deck and filling spots with Phillybond Blue. It is a massive job, best tackled piecemeal.

Even in bad weather there's something to look forward to. "Hey, it's Tuesday!" I remind Robin. "Happy hour at the Bali Hai."

Twice a week the yachties meet at the hotel. We have to dinghy a long way across the bay and tie up with many other small craft, at the hotel's wooden dock. It's a great place to have a few beers, meet old friends and make new ones. We swap yarns, offer advice and outdo each other with our salty tales.

"Have you ever eaten 20-clove garlic chicken?" Asks the captain of Unicorn, a canoe-sterned vessel. "Straight up," he says, "it's not a joke." How could I not believe him, when he looks like Sean Connery?

We confess that we've never had the pleasure, so he gives me a recipe and indeed, we try it later and it's just fine. His wife, a nurse, displays her very painful ankle tattoo, which we duly admire. Rather her than me. I get quite enough pain on a trip like this without intentionally inflicting more on myself. Their beautiful vessel requires a formidable amount of varnish work topsides, and we often watch the captain beavering away at every opportunity. It's comforting to know that we're not the only ones working. He invites us aboard for an inspection of his spectacular accomplishment.

"How'd you like to fly to Easter Island for a couple of nights?" he asks. "A group of us are going in a few days."

What a temptation! Regretfully we decline. During this poor weather we are once again hampered because of *Orca*'s mass. The fear of our yacht dragging or swinging and hitting someone if they anchor too close, prevents us from leaving her. The repercussions of crashing into another vessel don't bear thinking about. Robin is very disappointed and I suggest he goes alone, but he refuses.

It transpires that the weather is terrible and the trip very expensive and miserable. It rains all the time, of course, and is windy and cold—but that's what one expects on Easter Island isn't it? We're still sorry to have missed an opportunity that will never recur. I remember reading about Easter Island in Thor Heyerdahl's *Kon Tiki*, which I found riveting when I was young.

The series of low-pressure systems finally moves on and the weather returns to being sunny and humid.

Rain in Cook's Bay

"Let's go for a hike," suggests Rob, "I'd like to see if we can get to the top of Mt. Tearai (770 metres) to look over the other side."

The sharp volcanic peaks are virtually clothed all the way to the top with rich vegetation. The lower slopes are cultivated with large vegetable plantations and coconut palms grow everywhere. In gardens along the way we see many breadfruit—so popular in Cayman, and which bleed the most disgustingly sticky, milky-coloured fluid when the stalk is cut. The juice is difficult to remove from skin and impossible to remove from clothing.

The vibrant colours of the bougainvillea; brilliant orange, purest white, intense fuchsia and gentle mauve, vie for our sensory attention with the giddy scents of ginger, jasmine and gardenia. The mysterious blue-grey fields we've seen through binoculars are pineapple plantations. All the pineapples are picked by hand. It must be an odious job and not a little bloody, because the foliage is so savage and only one pineapple is produced per plant.

Once through the foothills, it's quite a steep trek through narrow, overgrown tracks. After a long, sticky haul, we reach the top of the arrete—a narrow ridge running the length of the top of the mountain. We look to the east, down the majestic sweep of green-blue, velvet-covered foothills to the wide bay of Vaiare with its guardian reefs. There, the catamaran 'fast cats' and ferries arrive from Tahiti which is visible in the distance topped with clouds.

Vaiare Bay

As we take in the beauty around us, it is clear why this island was chosen for the filming of *Mutiny on the Bounty*, and Shark's Tooth Mountain—Mount Mouaroa—used as a backdrop for *Bali Hai*.

One day while I'm splicing rope on *Orca* and Robin is catching up on his reading, who should I see but *Absolutely Gorgeous* motor into the bay. "Look who's arrived!" I say. They anchor nearer to the toe of the bay adjacent to the rocky bank. It isn't a surprise when they have to re-anchor after getting blown perilously close to the rocks. Fortunately, they have a charmed life! They don't even ruin their new 12-volt batteries, believing it is OK to run them down to 7 volts before recharging.

Robin is checking his boat spares and supplies. "We're going to need some more Raycor fuel filters," he says. He changes them frequently, usually after a rough crossing when sludge in the tanks is disturbed and fouls the fuel supply lines to the engine. "We can go to Tahiti on the fast cat, do some shopping and have a look around."

"Will we have to go to customs and pay our bond?" I ask.

"Naw," says Robin dismissively, "no point, now."

We research the bus and the catamaran schedules and plan our trip

Shark's Tooth Mountain

on the *Aremiti II* to Papeete. A minibus picks us up at the end of the bay and takes us to the ferry terminal. While we wait to board the catamaran we wander around the little food stalls, like a mini farmers' market and buy ready-to-eat pineapple in polythene bags. Food of the gods! It is so fresh and sweet, ripened naturally, and so unlike the dull, artificial flavour of the ones we buy in supermarkets back home.

The fast cat takes only 25 minutes to cross the 19 kilometres. It's a thrilling ride. As we power through the water, it throws a massive rooster tail in the air behind, causing exquisite rainbows.

Papeete, Tahiti, is a complete contrast to Moorea. Unending hustle and bustle of side-walk cafés, boutiques, video stores, pharmacies, churches, offices, workshops, noise, traffic and people, people, people everywhere. Visiting boats anchor cheek by jowl at the water's edge tied stern-to, to a busy street. It's just like living in a shanty town. UGH! Not for us. I'm amazed to think that those who revel in the solitude of ocean voyaging can enjoy this noisy, smelly, communal living. We're so glad we didn't bring *Orca* here.

We're also pleased we opted to stay in beautiful, non-commercial Ahé for the Bastille Day celebrations on July 14th and didn't come to the French Polynesian centre of commercialization. What a disappointment it would have been, especially since those who rushed here for the grand celebrations say they arrived to unusually bad weather and many events were rained off.

Despite the number of sailing vessels that visit Papeete annually, we are only able to locate three large boat shops: Comptoir Marine, Marine Corail and Sern. They are bitterly disappointing as they are geared to power boats and absolutely useless for sail-boat owners. We found far superior supplies in Colón, Panama. However, there are good tool and hardware stores. We take a long walk via the naval dockyard and are delighted to find our fuel filters.

It is an exhausting trip and the stark contrast of the city makes us feel even happier to be back in Cook's Bay. We stop at the Post Office on the way back, a 30-minute walk from our anchorage, and send a one-page fax home for a mere US$28! Unfortunately, there is no mail for us. Nothing of note must have happened in the world we left.

Sometimes we stroll along the road to visit art galleries and black pearl galleries exhibiting fine artwork and exquisite pearls; their lustre highlighted by intricate settings. The cost, though, is exorbitant. Our co-yachties are handing over hundreds of dollars for a souvenir black pearl. How lucky I am to have the one that Robin earned for me in Ahé!

Dozens and dozens of brightly coloured pareus are hanging in one shop in an eye-catching array of designs and shades. "I think we should buy lots of these," I say to Robin, "they'll make lovely gifts and will be great on the yacht for us, you as well as me."

"Oh, I don't know," he says.

I feel he needs to be convinced. "Oh yes," I insist, "just tie it around you and you're dressed."

"It looks very good!" The assistant comes to my aid and we convince Robin.

"I don't think it would be wise to regard pareus as solely female attire if you are in Polynesia." I say. "I certainly wouldn't want to tell a brawny Polynesian he's wearing a skirt. Besides, they're much more enticing than swimming trunks!" Along with our purchases, we receive a leaflet instructing us in the art of tying pareus and they indeed become very useful aboard *Orca*. They wash and dry in minutes, are cool to wear and shade us from the sun.

Before we leave Moorea, we hear over the radio the voices of Andy and John on *Sara of Hamble*, anchored in Opunohu Bay. We've not seen them since transiting the Panama Canal with them as line-handlers, so we hop into the dinghy to visit. We pick our way gingerly through and over the treacherous coral outcrops at the entrances to both bays.

It's a fun reunion, with coffee and lots of noisy chatter and laughs. John, as usual, is busy tinkering with something mechanical.

A small yacht called *Xaxero* (pronounced Zazero) comes into Cook's Bay and anchors on our port side. Robin hails them. We recognize the name *Xaxero*, because Jonathan and his Argentinean girlfriend Roxanna are good friends of Andy and John. Jonathan produces Windows-based weather satellite data and image-processing software for yachting people and daily gives updated weather reports for everyone's benefit.

They have suffered considerable sail damage. We bundle the sail below into the saloon where I set up the sewing machine. Happily, I'm able to help out with my spare sailcloth although it has not always proven wise to sew new cloth into old. Roxanna helps me while Jonathan, an absolute computer whiz, gives Robin advice with his computer printer problem.

It's difficult to pinpoint, but for me there is something missing from this Island. No doubt generations of western influence has changed the nature of the islanders. Now most are only interested in commerce, as in resorts worldwide. In their Garden of Eden, they've tasted the apple and lost their innocence. Who can blame them? It's just such a contrast to the smaller, remote islands of French Polynesia where people are uncomplicated and so much fun to meet.

After a month we are ready to leave these picturesque surroundings and no longer need worry about paying the bond. We are leaving French waters and are eager to see isolated Niue Island, formerly named Savage Island by Captain James Cook.

16

Behold, Coconuts! and Hana has the Last Laugh Niue Island

The skies are lowering as we leave Moorea on 27th July, 1994, and head for Niue. Almost as soon as our course is set we are assailed by squalls and thunderstorms. It's a compromise trying to make headway against the moderate to rough seas with enough sail set, yet without shredding them. Even with the aid of the motor it is impossible to find a suitable combination.

On the third day out, as soon as it gets light we can *still* see the blob of Moorea from the stern of *Orca*.

"This is bloody ridiculous!" Robin moans. "We're getting nowhere, we've only got 400 litres of fuel left. There's no point wasting it to battle through these seas, we'll heave-to and wait for better sailing conditions."

It's the most frustrating experience, bobbing like a cork with waves coming from all directions while *Orca* rolls, pitches and yaws like a sonofabitch in the pelting rain. There is nothing we can do to improve conditions. Below decks, we wedge ourselves on the seats behind the galley table. One of us goes on deck every 30 minutes to scan for other boat traffic. For a diversion, I tune in to the net to hear the other vessels chatting, some of which seem to be faring rather better than us. However, others are not. The storms have caused the yachts currently in Niue, to swiftly haul up anchor and rush for the open sea.

At the end of the day, the winds drop and the seas start to subside, so we have choppy conditions but no wind. Once again we motor-sail with minimum sails, the bow slamming into the waves.

"At this rate we'll be lucky if we don't rip the rub strip off the port side too." I say.

Robin tears the latest weather fax from the machine. Its forecast is realized as we watch another squall line marching towards us and prepare for a repeat performance. During night watches we curl up miserably on deck in rain gear. Every 15 minutes we scan the horizon and check the compass heading, autopilot and reefed sails. We maintain our custom of preparing hot tea and biscuits for the person coming on watch—it helps to soften the blow.

It is a grossly uncomfortable 1200-mile trip, which takes us 13 days. Finally the frontal system moves on and we arrive at Niue on glassy seas, under azure skies. Good timing. The world seems a different place.

Behold, Coconuts! In Polynesian, 'Niu' means coconut and 'e' means behold. The name aptly describes every South Pacific island. Yet Niue is unique with its limestone cliffs rising sheer from the ocean floor, piercing the sapphire sea and thrusting skyward without even a *hint* of sandy, palm-fringed beaches or protecting reefs.

Niue has no harbour. The only anchorage is an open roadstead on the west side of the island, off the town of Alofi. When the wind blows from the west, it is imperative to leave *immediately* to avoid being driven onto the cliffs. The incautious lose their vessels, if not their lives, with the resulting debris swiftly washed away to sea. At various times several buoys have been set for the use of boaters but they frequently disappear during storms. There are none in evidence when we arrive.

As we slowly motor round the open roadstead, it's quite a challenge to choose a suitable site, although there are only three other vessels here. We finally drop anchor on the limestone bottom, 200 metres from the end of the concrete jetty extending from the rocks where the cliffs stagger to their lowest point.

"Is the depth-sounder giving a false reading?" I ask.

It seems impossible that twenty-six metres beneath us, we can clearly see our anchor through the crystal waters.

"It must be right, look how much chain we've had to pay out." As we stare into the depths a carnival parade passes by; gliding sea turtles, eagle rays, sting rays, pipe fish, gaudy parrot fish, multihued platoons of synchronized fish and wriggling techni-coloured sea snakes.

"It's *magnificent*! I've never seen such clear water, obviously there's no river run-off here."

We drag ourselves from the spectacle and launch the dinghy to motor ashore. We've been warned about the unique dinghy hoist.

Great ocean swells up to 3 metres, surge and slap against the concrete quayside, prohibiting tying up to the jetty. So the Niue islanders have mounted a small crane with the jib overhanging the water, dangling a hook and a thick, knotted rope.

"Fend off! Catch the hook!" Robin yells.

Dinghy hoist

Half standing in the dinghy, I push off from the wall using an oar in my left hand and lunge for the hook with my right. I stab the hook into the dinghy's rope yoke that we use when winching the dinghy onto *Orca*'s deck. At the same time, Robin grabs the knotted rope, makes a 'Tarzan' leap, swings up onto the jetty then madly cranks the winch handle. Like a phoenix from the ashes, the dinghy and I rise from the clutches of the sucking, gurgling waters and swing onto dry land.

"Good!" A smiling young lad watching us, claps.

We look at each other, feeling pretty smug and grin at the boy. "And I suppose all we have to do to launch the dinghy is merely reverse the procedure?" I say.

The Customs and Immigration office is at the top of the hill. He notices we are from Cayman and he welcomes us cordially. It seems his colleague, Fa'ama, from the tourism office has been to Cayman to attend a Commonwealth conference. After formalities we return to *Orca*, to catch up on overdue sleep.

Early in the morning we're sitting on deck sipping tea, when we see a little outrigger canoe. It approaches as the occupant, a large muscular man with a halo of brown curly hair, draws the paddle smoothly through the water.

"I'm Fa'ama," he introduces himself, "I'm the tourism officer. Why don't you come to my office today and sign the visitors' book? We can have a chat."

We do that and Fa'ama greets us warmly and calls us brothers, as we have mutual acquaintances in the Cayman Islands.

"Tonight it is 'Island Night' at the hotel—lots of food and Polynesian dancing!" He gives the universal hourglass gesture with his hands.

"If you'd like to go, I'll pick you up at 7 o'clock on the dock."

True to his word, Fa'ama has a car waiting. At the hotel, there is feasting, followed by a colourful display of local dancing. After a while we are all persuaded to join in and once again our pathetic attempt at native dancing becomes good entertainment for the locals. It's a splendid evening which Fa'ama spends in the bar, patiently waiting to drive us home. I guess he's able to tell his wife that he is 'on duty'. Fortunately, the road from the hotel to the jetty is wide and straight and the car knows its way. Our dinghy is waiting just where we left it, unharmed. It is a treat to be among honest people on these smaller islands, who respect others' property.

The vagaries of the weather, and the open roadstead anchorage limits the number of visitors arriving here by sea. We have to keep a constant watch on weather faxes and reports and the dinghy is on board at all times, ready for a hasty exit if necessary.

With only one small hotel on the island western influence is minimal. The islanders are naturally warm and friendly and will initiate a conversation at every opportunity with a grin and a cheerful, "Hello, where are you from? Come and talk to us for a while."

Niue Power Station

Charlie, who works at the local power station, invites us to sit in his garden overlooking the anchorage and the great Pacific. We chat with him and his wife, Aso, and their ten children, exchanging stories about our different worlds. Niueans are fiercely proud of their island and allow no outsiders to buy land. When we leave, he presents us with an abundance of fruit—coconuts, limes, passion fruit and papaya. The latter grow in such proliferation he calls them weeds. There is enough to supply all four yachts in the anchorage. We promise to meet Charlie tomorrow, so he can show the Cayman Islands power-plant engineer, the Niuean power plant, of which he is justly proud.

One morning, after a papaya breakfast, we are indulging in a favourite pastime, hanging over the side of *Orca* looking down into the water. "Those colours are outrageous!" I say, pointing to the sea snakes. "Look at that one!" We just have to get in the water to check them out. As we snorkel round the yacht, the inquisitive sea snakes wriggle beside us, dressed in their festival costumes: brilliant pink on brown, black and white stripes, green and orange splodges. Among the most highly toxic of snakes, their bite is fatal but their tiny mouths pose no threat to us, unless they can bite an ear lobe or something really small. We don't allow them to swim that close.

Robin fins across to me and attracts my attention. "There are two anchors down there." The ocean floor is a system of mini canyons and fissures in the limestone and slopes sharply to the deepest of blue, where no man should go. I peer into the water, following his direction.

"They must be what boats have left when they've had to cut and run. Perhaps one would make a good storm anchor for *Orca*. Shall we dive?"

Of course Robin is always ready for a dive, so we make a plan. It is 24 metres deep, so we can only dive down for a total of 40 minutes, timing from when we leave the surface to when we start an uninterrupted ascent from the bottom. Allowing that the bottom shelves quite steeply and it's easy, inadvertently, to go deeper than anticipated we agree to start ascending after 30 minutes.

We kit up and check each other's gear before slipping into the water. Robin signals 'going down' and I reciprocate. Slowly we descend, allowing our ears to clear and use *Orca*'s anchor chain as a guide to the bottom. Even at this depth it is quite light as the sun is overhead. Together we fin to the anchors. The first is so encrusted with sea life, it must have been there for half a century. The other looks a distinct possibility—until we get close. The stock of the anchor is longer than Robin's body and half as thick, so our ambitious hopes of raising an anchor don't come to fruition.

The sea bed is fascinating, but there is also a lot of island to explore. To make best use of our time before the weather changes, we rent a motorcycle to travel around. In search of legendary limestone caves, we cautiously drive down a sloping, rocky trail. The track narrows as we fight through a tangle of overgrown branches before coming to a small clearing. As we congratulate ourselves on our fine effort of getting the bike so far, we hear a pop-pop-pop-putter-putter-pop-pop as an ancient 100cc trail bike comes down the steep track. The rider must be the 'Queen Salote' of Niue overflowing the seat. Miraculously perched behind her are two children, clinging to her like baby koalas. They all spill off the bike, which she drops to the ground.

"Hello," she says, "my name is Hana—where are you from?" Dressed in a grubby, pink frock and wearing one shoe and one sandal, she waddles over to us, with a face-splitting grin. "We're goin' fishin'!" Her offspring are shy and hide behind her. She tucks a large woven basket under her arm and the girls, with long straggly hair and wearing shorts and tops, carry the fishing rods. They scramble through the bush and disappear from sight.

"And we thought we were so clever getting here!" I say.

We park the bike, upright and continue on foot the way Hana went, and climb down a rough path to some outrigger canoes lodged on either side in the bush. Below us is an amazing bamboo ladder down which the outrigger canoes are launched. It slopes at an exceedingly steep angle and we clamber down to a wide, rocky ledge beneath, dotted with rock pools.

Outrigger slipway

Hana is not far away and waves to us, so we join her. It turns out the children are her two *nephews* sitting on a rock, fishing. Hana tells us a boy wears his hair long until his rite of passage. Delving into her coconut-frond basket, she states, "I always get so hungry. Look, I have lots of food, have lunch with us!" She extracts a couple of frozen flying fish and tosses them into a salty rock pool, to aid the thawing process. Opening her basket wider she reveals boiled yam, taro and cassava, still warm.

With remarkable athleticism, she bends double and scoops up a flying fish, swishes it in the water and cuts into it at an angle behind the head. She slices out a wedge and proffers it on the end of her filleting knife. We take a piece of the raw fish. It is delicate and sweet. We then accept chunks of boiled starch. Hana continues to deftly carve the fish and gives us more carbohydrates, sharing her regal feast. It is a touching, simple display of friendship.

"This is sooh good," we tell Hana and rinse our sticky hands in a rock pool. She smiles coyly.

"Now I must show you a special spot—a beautiful view." We follow her over the rocks. "Careful," she says, pointing to the slippery seaweed. For the last few steps she directs us ahead of her for a better view. We are standing on a promontory facing the vast expanse of ocean—for that's all we can see—when THWUMP! Hidden from view by the ledge we're standing on, a huge wave slams up against the rocks below sending up a high-pressure spray through a blow hole. It swamps us. Hana and her nephews are convulsed with laughter. I guess we're not the first to be caught by her fun.

"Good spot!" she says, when she can take a breath. We have a brief glimpse of white teeth and flashing eyes before she is enveloped in another paroxysm of laughter. Her beefy arms support her large bosom as she rocks back and forth, her pink frock in imminent danger of splitting.

The gentle, good-natured folk remaining on Niue tell us they are sad, because in the past ten years the population has dwindled from 14,000 to 2,000 inhabitants. Islanders have left lured by the possibility of paid work in New Zealand, of which Niue is a protectorate. Some have found office jobs instead of their previous subsistence farming. This explanation accounts for the many empty houses we see on our travels and the ghost-like quality of the outlying villages. It is even sadder to realize that many who left are supported today by social security in New Zealand. One can't help wondering if they wouldn't be better off with their subsistence farming and no debt worries.

The main street, in contrast to the desolate outlying villages, displays great activity *and* inactivity. Outside the wide variety of busy shops, strategically-placed seats encourage shoppers to indulge in the age-old pastime of gossiping and watching the world go by. Niue restores our faith in warm, simple humanity, after the coolness of Moorea and Papeete.

Once called the Savage Island, Niue has not always had such gentle-natured folk. In days gone by, a child demonstrating any mental or physical defect was simply hurled to its death off the cliffs. An effective remedy for the products of inbreeding, thus ensuring genetic stability in the race. Notably, the child of Niue today is

Limestone cave

remarkably well behaved!

Apart from the notorious cliffs, Niue can boast other remarkable limestone formations. The island is riddled with vast caverns descending through several layers, containing dramatic stalagmites and stalactites. We visit several and are amazed at their pristine condition. Most of the depths, it seems, remain unexplored. It is a spelunker's dream. Also, colossal sculptured sea arches extend into the ocean as monuments to the waves' relentless action on the softer limestone. The sea has also toiled to enlarge fissures in the rocks, creating small convoluted groups of crystal-clear pools. Like the ancient kings before us, we bathe in these pools with the fish.

It is 2:00 a.m. when I gently wake Robin. "It's all right, don't panic." When at sea, being woken in the night usually requires galvanizing into action because of a problem. "Just listen to those sounds."

As the mists of sleep clear his brain, realization dawns. "It's whale songs!"

The haunting sounds of their whistles, sighs and squeaks are transmitted through the hull—our personal serenade. In daylight we watch the enormous humpbacks breaching, fluke-slapping and blowing less than a kilometre away. In the hot sunshine, with a delicate hint of seaweed and fermented krill, 'essence of whale breath' pervades the air.

Pacific Mariner

Gafia II

Orca

Alofi Harbour open roadstead

As we're sunning ourselves on deck after breakfast, we receive a surprise call on Channel 16.

"*Orca, Orca, Orca*, this is the *Pacific Mariner*. Over."

Looking astern we see a large coastal tanker. Robin climbs down the companionway steps to the microphone and responds. *Pacific Mariner* is waiting to come closer to the jetty in order to deliver refined fuel products to the island. The captain's English accent immediately strikes a chord, reminding me of the old country.

There's no alternative but to wind up the couple of hundred metres of chain and move. By great good fortune the anchor isn't snagged in the limestone caverns below, and although it takes several minutes to wind up by hand, the tanker captain is patient. We move a few hundred metres to the north and drop anchor again. Ashore on the cliff top, we watch the intricate operation of delivering fuel through a floating fuel line.

Each time we dinghy ashore, we notice there is a second, larger crane and hook at the dinghy hoist. After talking to the locals we find it is for bringing supplies ashore. Lighters ferry crates of goods from supply ships moored offshore, to the jetty. The crates are secured to the large hook and immediately a tractor attached to the other end of the cable pulley system, literally races across the wide jetty to hoist the cargo into the air so it can be swung onto land. Using this method they even bring ashore 6-metre shipping containers. Simple and effective.

Gafia II, a neighbouring yacht at the anchorage is captained and crewed by two delightful Australians. These unassuming, middle-aged men found the 10-metre Actin cutter, *Sofia*, six months after it had been rolled and abandoned in the notorious Queen's Birthday Storm on 6th June, 1994. The storm tragically overtook some of the yachts in the annual Auckland to Tonga regatta.

The date set for the regatta was chosen to coincide with a perfect weather window. Yet a dreadful, unforeseen weather system, a 'bomb' occurred, wreaking havoc and claiming several lives among the crews in the race and others sailing independently at the time. *Sofia*'s crew was rescued by the French transport ship *Jacques Cartier* from which brave men risked their lives in an inflatable craft to effect the rescue. As drifting vessels are a potential shipping hazard, the captain of the French ship was instructed to shoot the boat out of the water. However, based on political considerations relating to the French sabotage of *Rainbow Warrior* 10 years previously, he refused.

"We found it snagged 230 miles from where it was rolled," say this modest couple, "so we just took it in tow."

The calm weather on Niue lasts six days before forecasts predict a change. We collect our exit papers, choose a few good bottles of wine from the duty-free (what a treat!) and say farewell to this charming island community. *Orca* is heading for Pago Pago and a taste of good old Uncle Sam in American Samoa; infamous for its stinking tuna-canning factories.

Oasis in limestone cliffs

17

Good Fuel and TP goes AWOL
Pago Pago, American Samoa

Despite the threat of poor sailing conditions, initially they are light and pleasant. But in the middle of the night, the weather system overtakes us. A 35-knot wind accompanied by lashing rain catches me with all sails flying in a full-blown squall. *Orca* heels over alarmingly, her port gunwale well underwater.

"ROB!" I yell down the companionway. "SQUALL!"

The deck is washed with light as he flicks on the spreader lights before joining me in his foul weather gear and harness.

"Release the genoa sheet gradually as I winch it in," he shouts.

It's our first priority: the self-furling genoa is 45% of our total sail area. Rob cranks hard on the winch as I slacken the furling sheet, trying to retain some control so the sail won't flap and shred. There's an immediate response and *Orca* stops heeling at such a disquieting angle.

We are on a starboard tack and preparing to head into wind to take the strain off the remaining sails when the wind suddenly veers.

"BOOM!" Rob shouts. I duck. It flies across just above my head with a sickening crack as we make an unintended jibe. He sheets in the mainsail as close as possible to the midline of the yacht and we try to lower the sail enough to tie a reef.

"Yank them tighter," he yells as I'm struggling at my end of the boom to make my cold, wet fingers fasten the reefing ties. There is such a belly of wind in the pocket, however, it is impossible for me to reduce it.

"I can't, we'll have to drop the sail."

This means we must first haul up the lazy jacks to contain the sail as it drops, in order to prevent it spilling over the deck as *Orca* pitches in the seas.

After a second unintentional jibe, we manage to lash the main, set a storm jib and double-reef the mizzen, and then resume our course. Fortunately, throughout this mess we don't see any shipping traffic.

We are soaked and fatigued. It's taken us over two hours to get into a satisfactory configuration. In fact, it is in perfect time for the wind to drop completely as dawn arrives, and we are again left with broken seas superimposed on the swell and not enough wind to sail.

"What a mug's game this is," I complain as we turn the motor on one more time. It seems we can *never* get it right with the weather. How detestably frustrating it is.

Thirty-six hours before our intended arrival at Pago Pago, we pass through another squall and are making 8-9 knots with reefed sails. Much as we love the speed, to avoid arriving in darkness we reluctantly reduce the sail area during the day to slow us down and plan to heave-to about 10 nautical miles off the coast, to await daylight. But the wind drops again to 2-3 knots, so instead of heaving-to we have to motor through the night so we can get into port in the morning. In keeping with the American ideal, the glow of Pago Pago lights is clearly visible on the horizon for many hours before we arrive.

Two consolations in rough, squally weather are the gimballed stove and the pressure cooker. Together they allow us to cook safely in most conditions and to eat really well throughout our trips. It may not be Carolyn's Cordon Bleu menu, but it's good, wholesome, hot food.

As we close on Pago Pago, we talk with the vessel *Kona Star* approaching ahead of us. We discuss the long and difficult entry from the sea buoy to the harbour and the apparent chart errors on the channel entrance.

When *Orca* is 5 nautical miles off we radio harbour control for permission to enter. Despite repeated calls there is no reply. Finally a girl from the harbour master's office informs us that the port captain is attending a meeting and we should raft up alongside several other boats already awaiting customs and immigration clearance. The communication is rapidly followed on Channel 16 by a moan from one of the boats rafted.

"No, No, not *Orca* rafting up with us, she's much too heavy and there are six of us here already!"

This is joined by other voices of protest, leaving us feeling thoroughly rejected. Not that we have the slightest intention of rafting up to any of them.

One helpful yachtie suggests that when we arrive, we tie up at the

Orca at the crippled-boat dock

crippled-boat dock. We reach the harbour at 11:30 a.m. during a white-out. The rain is sheeting so hard we can barely see past the end of the bow as we motor slowly looking for landmarks.

Of course, we have no idea where the crippled-boat dock is located. With our limited visibility, we are greatly relieved when out of the gloom an angel in yellow oilskins appears and waves to us from a little dinghy. He must have been the only helpful guy on the radio. He's come all the way out to the entrance to guide us to the dock—what a champion! He sounds British and probably recognized our accents, though we've long been Canadians. We're just sorry that in all the fun of docking, we lose sight of him and never have a chance to thank him properly for his generous help. Maybe sometime we can return the gesture by helping someone else.

John & Leena from *Kona Star* are on the dock. "Throw us your lines and raft up next to us," they say.

The yacht *S'mine,* which we first met in the Marquesas, is tied ahead of John and Leena's yacht, awaiting delivery of critical engine parts. When *S'mine* moves off, we slide *Kona Star* along the dock, leaving the rear for us.

Initially, the harbour master is full of wrath at our audacity, but we explain our plight that we will be unable to 'hold' on the bottom of the harbour, because of the thick layer of polythene garbage. It helps that we are suitably repentant about our miscreant behaviour so he can be magnanimous. He graciously allow us to stay three days at the dock. Just enough time to reprovision and refuel. I could hug him!

Getting fuel has never been so easy or cheap. The fuel truck pulls up right alongside the yacht and offers us fuel at 74 cents per US gallon. It's the same price we paid *per litre* in the Marquesas. We gladly accept and take on board 2000 litres, much to the surprise of surrounding boats—enough, we hope, to see us to Australia.

The new lines we had for traversing the Panama Canal we now use as mooring lines, but the Pacific surge in the harbour causes them to chafe against the edge of the concrete wharf. Robin prepares split plastic hoses 40 cm long which encase the lines to act as chafe-guards. He secures them with ties. However, with each tide the lines have to be let out or snugged up, so we are constantly moving the guards. No wonder other boats prefer a single-point mooring where they tie up like spokes round the hub of a wheel. There is a second reason for them preferring not to tie up to the dock.

Pago Pago anchorage

"What are all those things for?" I ask a boat owner who has been in Pago Pago for some time. I point to aluminum cones, about 30 cm in diameter which are tied on the mooring lines midway between the dock and the boat, with the mouth of the cone pointing ashore.

"They're rat preventers," she says. "If you don't have them, you can see the rats running along the lines and coming on board." We haven't got time to make preventers, so will have to trust that TP does her work and keeps them at bay.

The next two days are a mad dash cashing travellers cheques and shopping. We take a bus to a store with Alex and Chris from *Foam Follower*, load ourselves with goods—including some vodka in a plastic gallon jug. Prices are good, so we really make the most of it and have to hire a taxi to bring us and our purchases home to Orca. We just fit in the taxi, sitting on each other's laps.

It is *vitally* important, we are told, to remove our purchases from any cardboard boxes, packaging, paper bags or newspapers on the dock side and to inspect everything carefully before stowing it on *Orca*. Otherwise it is 100% certain we will carry aboard cockroach infants or eggs by the hundreds. We take this advice seriously and even remove paper labels from cans, and write the contents on the lids in marker pen.

The propane tank we use for cooking needs refilling and the gas station is across the other side of the bay, so we must take another bus ride. We are warned that we won't be allowed on the bus with a full cylinder, so we put it into a garbage bag so no-one is any the wiser. It's pretty obvious what we have, standing at the bus stop outside the gas station with a large, heavy garbage bag, but there are no comments.

This is the only port of call where TP escapes. Perhaps the lure of the local rodents or the smell of the tuna-canning factories is just too inviting, or maybe she's tired of being a nauti-cat. It is completely out of character, as she's normally so timid.

"*TP, TP, here TP girl!*" Her brindle colours are perfect camouflage. In the early darkness we creep along the dock calling in hoarse whispers, trying not to draw attention to ourselves. Quarantine regulations insist that she may not leave the vessel and we don't want to be charged with illegally importing an animal. We've only one day left and we *can't* leave her behind.

"*Over there!*" Robin whispers as a shadow stealthily crawls along low to the ground. He creeps up on her and employs a long-forgotten rugby tackle to retrieve her. She was way down the dock, heading to a garbage pile in the distance, so she wasn't intending coming home any time soon.

"Thank God!" I say, carrying her inside. I close up the yacht, so she can't escape again.

One wonderful luxury here in Pago Pago is the newly-built shower and laundry facility. I bundle up everything I can: clothes, sheets, towels, and spend several hours ferrying laundry back and forth. I indulge in using as many washers and driers as I need, so that everything is fresh and crisp. It's heaven. In the evening, we sample the fare at a local restaurant with friends, as tomorrow we must leave. However, on the local radio channel there is an announcement for a trip to the Amalau Forest in Vatia to take a 'Walk on the Wild Side' to look for bats and birds.

"We don't need to leave here till tomorrow afternoon," I say to Robin, "let's go along, it'll be fun!"

We are a group of twenty-one, twenty of whom are yachties and we leave the harbour at 7:30 a.m. by bus. All the bats and birds we encounter are identified by the Marine and Wildlife employees. We are lucky to see a white-faced species that feeds during the day, soaring above the trees with a host of other birds.

It's time to leave for the Kingdom of Tonga and we haven't overstayed our welcome at the dock. For a change, visibility is excellent and we motor out between masses of rusty hulks on the foreshore; tuna fishing vessels 40-50 metres in length and long ago washed up from past cyclones. We're also leaving behind the aroma of the fish-canning factories—and I used to think the copra smell was bad!

18

Teeth-Sucking Sam; and The Bishop and the Tandem
Niuatoputapu, Tonga

From Pago Pago harbour we set a southerly course for Niuatoputapu. Although physically closer to Samoa, it is the northernmost island of the Kingdom of Tonga, which is the only South Pacific Island group that has not been colonized by Europeans. Perhaps this is the reason it is an enduringly calm and beautiful place! These friendly, happy people are still ruled by a King.

Shortly after departure a few brief squalls pass over leaving a light south-easterly wind and we can motor-sail quite comfortably making 5 knots.

On our second night I am on early watch. The sky is cloud-free, so I pay particular attention to the sun sinking. It is a deep, blood-orange orb as it slips below the horizon. There are no clouds to obscure it and when there's just a sliver of fire left, WOW! The luminous green explosion of incandescent light flares for a split second, then it has gone. Twice I've been lucky enough to experience this spectacular phenomenon.

The rest of the night is peaceful as we roll along on the swells and we sight land at 6:30 a.m. on a dazzling morning. During this short trip we've crossed the International Date Line and lost one day. Instead of GMT +13, we are now GMT −11.

Niuatoputapu or 'New Potatoes' as some yachties insist on calling it, is an atoll. Three small villages are strung along the northern edge and one hilly ridge runs down the centre of the island like a backbone. It has an exquisitely-marked narrow channel 6-metres deep, leading into the best anchorage for us so far. The large circular lagoon has a maximum depth of 8 metres and gives us lots of room to manoeuvre and swing. It is protected by reef or island from every direction. Only a couple of vessels lie sleepily at anchor.

The Agricultural Officer is the first to come aboard. He waves from the shore and Robin collects him in the dinghy. This giant of a man, over two metres tall, is softly spoken and charming. After checking our provisions and meeting the cat, he completes his paperwork. We invite him to sit and have tea and cookies with us against the backdrop of the extinct volcano called Tafahi, 10 km away.

As we are chatting about various topics, I notice his feet, which command attention by their sheer enormity. I must have been rather

Tafahi volcano

less than discreet because he smiles at me and says proudly, "Yes, all my family have big feet—mine are the largest on the island!" We are in no doubt that he is correct.

So that we can clear customs and immigration, we must walk to the furthest of the three villages, about 45 minutes from the jetty. We return the Ag man to the shore of the first village, Falehau, and continue along the track through Vaipoa village to Hihifo. These picturesque villages are the first we've seen where the inhabitants live in woven palm-frond huts.

The islanders are friendly, but the pre-school children are a nuisance. Someone has taught them to say, "What your name?" "Where you from?" "Give me lolly!" (candies), "Give me money!" It is the first and only time we meet this constant pestering and it quite spoils a stroll through the villages. However, we are acutely aware that it is *their* home not ours. By contrast, the high school students who go to boarding school in neighbouring Manihi are elegant, charming and eager to practice their English.

Along the way pigs, goats, horses and chickens range freely throughout the villages and bush. I'm not sure why the farmers don't lose all their produce to these free-rangers. I notice an industrious lady outside her hut beating a mat. As she does so she disturbs several tiny piglets which scuttle off into the bush.

"Are all these pigs and piglets wild?" I ask her.

"Oh no!" she replies. "They all belong to someone and every morning and evening the pigs come home to be fed. We all know our own pigs."

It is comical to watch a minute piglet ploughing furrows along the shore at low tide, using its well-adapted prehensile ring of cartilage we call a snout, to great advantage to ferret out small edible morsels like crabs, shrimps and other invertebrates.

Piglet on foreshore

Although we trek to his office to fulfil our customs entry requirements, Sam, the customs officer, tells us he must come on board. Shortly after we return to *Orca*, he's gesticulating at us from the shore. Robin collects him in the dinghy and Sam explains that he has to come to check for firearms.

"We don't have any firearms on board," Robin tells him.

With barely a pause for breath, his real reason for boarding is revealed. "Do you have any whisky?" he asks, "Scotch whisky?"

We're rather startled at his question, but with a clear conscience can say, "No! No whisky at all."

He is persistent. "Do you have any other liquor?"

Now he's irritating me and without compunction I say, "No, we don't drink alcohol. We have some tea if you'd like some."

He ignores me and turns to Robin, as the yacht's captain.

"I want you to radio your yachting friends in Pago Pago and tell them to bring some Scotch whisky."

This man is unbelievable.

"And tell them to bring American cigarettes and American food. There's nothing here on the island that I can eat."

During this conversation we discover an infuriating Tongan habit. They suck their teeth when they are displeased. Sam sucks his teeth so often I think he must have a piece of food lodged between his incisors. We tell him we'll see what we can do. We haven't forgotten that this is the man who will be giving us our exit documents and he is Customs, Immigration, Harbourmaster and Postmaster, all rolled into one obnoxious being. It's difficult to throw an official off the yacht into the lagoon however tempted we might feel, especially when it depends upon him to give us exit clearance.

"We'll call to see who's in Pago Pago," says Robin, knowing full well he will do nothing of the kind.

Thatched dwellings

Sam makes two more visits, each time on a different pretext, but in reality to check on the progress of his shopping list. The last visit is late one afternoon. He's trying to catch us supping Scotch whisky, no doubt. When at length he leaves, Robin accidentally manages to thoroughly scare him. In order to avoid a rock that appears from nowhere Robin executes a swift 90° turn in the dinghy. Sam almost flies off the side of the dinghy onto the reef. It curbs his enthusiasm and he doesn't visit us again.

What a contrast to our friendly, undemanding Agricultural Officer! It's rumoured that Sam, who is not an island local, has been sent from the Tongan capital, Nuku'alofa. He has certain airs and graces associated with one who comes from the metropolis, albeit he is here at this 'outpost', as a form of punishment for some misdemeanour he's committed. The locals do not regard him highly.

So that we can see more of the island, Robin adapts his mountain bike for two people. He fashions a saddle from a piece of wood and some sponge foam and fixes it to the cross-bar. He then knots a pair of 'stirrups' out of thick rope, which dangle like nooses from the handlebars. We motor ashore with the bike perilously balanced on the dinghy and manoeuvre it onto the jetty.

A large number of people are milling about, all helpless with laughter at our antics. I am trying to balance on the little seat and keep my feet inside the stirrups yet out of the front-wheel spokes. Robin is struggling hard to mount and push the pedals round, to propel us along. We wobble precariously as he tries to gain momentum and keep us upright, but their laughter is so infections we just have to stop to join in.

"I think we're causing a bit of a disturbance," Robin says, glancing back along the causeway.

Regrettably our trip has coincided with the new Tongan Roman Catholic Bishop's visit to his northernmost flock. He is now standing with his entourage on the end of the jetty looking serious and neglected. Someone draws the attention of the crowd to the fact that the Bishop has just alighted from the boat and he's the real reason they are here. It is not our intention to upstage the Bishop.

We continue our cycle ride and become fairly proficient as we meander along the tracks to see the sights. At Hihifo, we visit the policewoman who is young, tall and powerfully built. She wears a sparkling-white, short-sleeved shirt that displays her police badges. Her flashing smile is engaging, all the more so because of the intricate gold work implanted in her front teeth.

She proudly shows us her office and the 'lock-up' cell. On the walls are several impressive old muskets and the cell has iron shackles embedded in the walls. I briefly have a pleasant but wild image of Sam shackled to the wall, when the locals tire of him. The open window is covered by a substantial set of jailhouse bars yet, incongruously, the roof is thatched.

"Do you have to lock up many people?" I ask.

"No, not for a long time," she says, her smile glinting in the sunlight, "we're quite quiet around here."

We chat for some time and promise her magazines and books to improve her already-good English. We give her a demonstration of our tandem, then wave goodbye.

Despite our recent lack of decorum on the jetty, we are invited to the feast in the Bishop's honour at the culmination of his seven-day visit. The crews of the ten vessels in the anchorage are also invited but not many accept. It is a fiercely sunny day and extremely hot. The Tongans are dressed in their Sunday best.

Ladies wear brightly-coloured dresses with floral and leafy decorations, and *ta'ovalas*—finely woven pandanus skirts. The men dress in crisp western-style shirts, and *tupenus*—tailored wrap-around skirts—covered with ceremonial *ta'ovalas* tied with bark belts. I wish I had dressed more lavishly for the occasion.

The dancers sit in the baking hot sun awaiting the arrival of His Excellency. As honoured guests, we sit in the shade under woven pandanus canopies with the village elders and their families. The vast majority of the villagers sit around watching. A delicious scent of

Seated dancing

blossoms and ripe fruit pervades the air.

In honour of the Bishop two hours of speeches are given then a welcome, in Polynesian, to all the visitors. The dozens and dozens of dancers who have been sitting so patiently in the hot sun now offer their tributes. They perform beautiful examples of Polynesian singing and dancing choreographed by the *punake*, a senior and respected man in the community.

The most important dance, the *lakalaka*, is performed seated by men and women all dressed similarly. Stories are told with the gyrations of the body and the sinuous weaving of arms and hands, in a sensuous, fluid manner. Afterwards, they even perform the *kailao*, the war dance (not seated!) which has been banned on many islands. It is a reminder of the days when the men went on raiding parties to Samoa and Fiji. We are invited to join in the *fakepale* custom, to approach our favourite dancers and tuck pa'anga—Tongan money—into their costumes.

The Bishop's feast

Then it's on to the feasting. I have an irreverent, fleeting thought that I hope the Bishop and everyone else, has a robust bladder. The banquet is of gargantuan proportions. Each of the three villages provides four 'trays' of food, measuring 1 by 4 metres. Wire hoops have been erected over them and covered with mosquito netting, floral decorations and candies. Safely protected from unwanted wildlife, each tray has 8 to 10 roasted suckling piglets, together with roasted and baked vegetables including yams, cassava and breadfruit. There is also coconut, fish and lobster, noodles, rice dishes, trifles, juices and soft drinks. Everything is lavishly decorated with leaves and flowers.

Only the elders, their families and visitors feast initially, so we don't make a great impact on the food. After this celebration is over it is the turn of the villagers. They will take the abundant remains of the food trays—which they have prepared over many, many hours—to their respective villages for the real feasting to begin. This will last long into the night.

It is heart-warming to be involved in a genuine non-commercial Tongan festivity. However, being unused to sitting cross legged for over four hours, my knees will be reminding me of it for some days to come.

The reef encircling the lagoon beckons us and we snorkel around happily for hours in the warm water, watching the wildlife. Some of the reef is covered with water only waist-deep, so we can walk along peering down with just our masks submerged.

"I've found a pile of empty shells!" I call Robin over. "Look there, I think it could be outside the entrance to an octopus hole." It's pretty much a giveaway. When an octopus finds a meal and takes it back home to eat it just discards the empty shell outside its front door.

We both submerge and peer into the hole near the sand, using a diving flashlight.

"You're right!" Rob says as he pops his head up. "I saw an eye. I'll see if I can catch it."

He squats down below the water's surface and plunges a gloved hand into the hole. Immediately, clouds of ink obscure everything. I watch the top of the rocky outcrop because there may be an exit hole here. Little puffs of ink emerge from time to time. Luckily Robin can just lift his snorkel out of water to breathe, because he's having quite a struggle. He has a hold on the octopus, while two of its tentacles are climbing up his forearm to his armpit. The others cling to the den. Robin positions himself so that he can dispatch it with a plunge of his diving knife.

"Got it!" Robin holds up the large octopus, its tentacles half a metre long.

Later, when he is cleaning it, Rob says, "I almost didn't do it when I looked into its eye and saw it staring back, but food is food after all."

We freeze half and cook half into a delicious stew and invite Alex and Chris from *Foam Follower* for a seafood supper.

Sam is not the only demanding Tongan on this island. During the evening a small local boat comes alongside. The occupant would like fuel for his outboard motor. Apparently another yacht captain in the anchorage has told him we have plenty and it's difficult to explain that we have diesel, not gasoline. This doesn't deter him and he says he will return at 10:30 a.m. to collect. That settles it—we decide to move on first thing in the morning, since we have our exit papers.

At 7:00 a.m. we leave the lagoon, motor out through the reef and set course for Vava'u, Tonga. There's a stiff breeze, the sea is choppy and we are feeling less than robust.

19

Little Tsunami and Big Knickers—Neiafu, Vava'u Group, Tonga

For the first time on our trip we are sea-sick—both of us. Unfortunately, we broke our golden rule, *never party the night before leaving port.*

The sails are flying to make good use of the 25-knot winds in lumpy conditions and the bow is crashing into the waves. It would be just bearable if we were going in the right direction, but we're sailing too far to the west. Our preferred heading, of course, is directly into wind.

Heeled over

Robin and I behave like zombies and can do nothing to change our situation. It is a classic case of sea-sickness. Apart from the obvious discomfort of throwing up over the side rail, we are mentally incapable of working anything through. The autopilot we're using is competent to steer in heavy conditions and works hard. We mechanically take our watches. Luckily there is no conflicting traffic to require swift or calculated action. *Orca* is doing her part much better than we are, but as the day drags on, our livers metabolise the toxins and we slowly recover. Along with our recovery, comes awareness.

"We'll drop the sails and motor!" my born-again captain instructs.

"Great idea."

It's still uncomfortable in the rough seas, but at least we're getting closer to our destination. Sea-sickness is frightening and debilitating, but we are in good health before arriving at the Vava'u Group of islands.

How majestic is the approach to Neiafu Harbour flanked by towering limestone cliffs scattered with fissures and caverns! I stare over the side into the depths and am mesmerised by the navy-blue water rippling away from our hull. I pull myself from my reverie when Robin calls Harbour Control to notify them of our arrival.

"*Orca, Orca, Orca,*" a familiar voice from *Sara of Hamble* calls. "Welcome to Neiafu!"

Officially, we shouldn't use the radio calling channel for flippant chatter, but it's nice to be welcomed instead of rebuffed, as we were in Pago Pago!

This exquisite Neiafu anchorage is entirely sheltered—a natural fjord-like harbour over 60 metres deep in the centre, rising steeply to a rocky ledge along the sides where boats may anchor. True to tradition, we choose a point furthest away from the many boats crowding to be within spitting distance of the jetty and are positioned off the Paradise Hotel. We don't have to run up the Q flag, as we've been cleared in Niuatoputapu.

"Isn't this beautiful? It feels like coming home!" I'm excited to be meeting friends again and hearing of their exploits.

We dinghy ashore to the small-boat jetty which is crowded with dozens of craft. Clambering across several boats, we pull our line with us to tie it off to the dock. The Bounty Bar is our first stop, to collect mail and have a beer. It's full of happy chattering people, but we manage to find a couple of chairs outside in the sun on the deck. Sipping our 'All Malt Royal Draught Beer,' we look at our mail from family members. I open a parcel containing a treasured new pair of reading glasses from my sister, Di, to replace the ones I gave to Tau in the Marquesas.

"How neat," says Rob, after we've left the bar and are walking towards the jetty, "sashimi!" Two large Tongan men are sitting with their legs dangling in the water—a great slab of raw tuna in one hand

and a whole loaf of bread in the other—a hearty and sustaining Tongan meal.

Neiafu is a colourful, bustling town and the anchorage is a haven. Many boaters stay long-term to avoid cyclone seasons; some stay for years and set up business here. I don't need to stay for ever. I've lost that desperate feeling of wanting to be anywhere but on the seas. I love our yacht, over which we toiled for so long, and the security it provides us. I now enjoy knowing that we can bring our home with us, and whatever happens in the world, it's always our home once we're cocooned inside.

After sleeping soundly, we rise early to breakfast on deck and absorb the atmosphere. I turn on the VHF radio. It is 2nd October, 1994, and the following announcement swiftly brings us back to reality.

"An earthquake northeast of Hokkaido, Japan, has been reported measuring 8.3 on the Richter scale. A Tsunami warning has been issued for the Pacific."

The anchorage is buzzing—should we pull up anchor? Should we head out to sea—the safest place in a tsunami? As we've only just arrived we're reluctant to move. The general consensus is that we'll stay and await further reports.

With lunch, Robin opens a bottle of wine and we relax. If we are to be affected, the first thing we'll notice will be the water being sucked out of the harbour, then it will return as a tidal wave—not that we'll be able to do a thing about it.

There's a further announcement on the radio and Robin goes below to catch the details. He's soon back on deck.

"Thank goodness we didn't go out to sea again," he says, "this time we got it right, the tsunami here measured 5 cm!"

The Vava'u group of islands is perfect for cruising and is home to Moorings' fleet of Bénéteau yachts; available for hire with or without a skipper. There are dozens of idyllic anchorages within a day's sailing, and Moorings has published an informative *Cruising Guide to the Kingdom of Tonga*, principally for the use of their clients. They have numbered all the suitable anchorages and provide details and hazards of entering each area. This guide is enormously helpful for the independent yachting community too and we all refer to the anchorages by the Moorings' numbers.

Number 10 anchorage in the cruising guide is Aisea's Beach where we anchor to attend one of the regular Saturday night feasts. At the appointed time, a bonfire is burning on the beach and underground umu ovens are cooking lobster, tuna, crayfish, pork, chicken and root vegetables. It is an excellent cooking method, which seals in all the flavour of the food. There is also an array of tropical fruit, some steamed in coconut milk. All is beautifully arranged on banana leaves decorated with blossoms. Once we've eaten our fill, we watch dancing displays, where the young Tongan girls are covered with coconut oil, so we can stick pa'anga notes to the skin of favourite dancers. We also have the opportunity of buying a very large tapa cloth, made from the bark of a mulberry tree.

Tapa cloth

On Sundays the only activity allowed in Tonga is attending church. They are a deeply religious people and although we are not, it is delightful just to hear the legendary singing delivered to the full extent of their lungs. Robin decides against it, being neither religious nor musical, so I attend Aisea's church with Andy and John from *Sara of Hamble*, along with their guests, Mike and Mair.

The Tongans really do 'make a joyful noise unto the Lord'! The pastor welcomes us warmly and after church, Aisea invites us to lunch with him and his family. He lives in a modest house comprising two rooms. The front is where he entertains us to a delicious lunch as we dine cross-legged on the floor. It is an excellent way to use the remains from the previous evening's feast and cement international relations. The womenfolk disappear into the back room when not serving us. It is interesting to note that the walls of his room are decorated with pages from quite unsuitable magazines.

In many of the anchorages, local boats frequently come alongside to trade goods and fruit. As we remain anchored off Aisea's Beach for a few days, we get to know some of them. One morning, while painting the cabin exterior before the sun rises too high in the sky, along comes a wide canoe containing two fat ladies and a little skinny man at the stern with his hand on the tiller of an old seagull outboard motor.

It's Sharpener's mother, Nanihi. Her 7-year old son, 'Sharpener' is so nicknamed because on earlier visits to us, she traded some goods—woven mats, baskets, carvings, bracelets and fruit in exchange for milk powder, sugar, a mirror, T-shirts, drawing books, pencils and crayons. She accepted them gracefully, then said, "Have you got a pencil sharpener for my son?"

"A pencil sharpener?" Robin said, "Can't you use a knife?"

Since then she always refers to the boy as 'my son, Sharpener'.

This time she has brought a friend with her and there's not much room for anything else in the canoe. Everything Nanihi says is accompanied by peals of laughter which seem to ripple through her glowing brown flesh. In response, the canoe rocks from side to side transferring the ripples to the water.

"We'll be leaving soon, to go to Australia," I tell her. She looks at me for a moment, her head on one side, as if considering something. Then she throws her hands in the air, brings them down on her meaty thighs with a slap and laughs and laughs. It seems like her heaving bosom will finally cause the already-stressed bodice of her dress to split at the seams. Her mirth is so infectious, we're all laughing, except for her skinny husband.

"Whatever is it?" I ask her, "What are you laughing about?"

"Well Miss Maggi," she fixes me with her chestnut eyes, "there's something I want to ask you—something I would like you to send back on a boat from Australia," she continues. With lowered eyes she folds her arms demurely across her bosom and strokes her fleshy biceps. "I am a big girl and there's some clothing I just can't get here. In fact, my husband has to make them out of sugar sacks, to fit me and he doesn't make them very well—they're not comfortable!"

She has to break off as an outburst of embarrassed laughter overwhelms her. This time she is joined by her friend. It is a sight to behold. Two fat, beautiful ladies rolling about in a canoe with the little husband hanging on to the outboard to steady himself.

I think we're almost getting to the point of the conversation. When she recovers her composure, I smile at her and say, "Tell me what you want."

"Big knickers!" She bursts out. "*Really* big knickers!"

Orca is back in Neiafu Harbour, so now we can explore more of the town in between bursts of chores. Besides painting the whole cabin exterior, I've been making more Sunbrella covers for the woodwork and feel in need of a break.

"Let's go ashore for supper."

The tiny local restaurant is busy because of its excellent, cheap local fare. There's only one table left and we sit down. A couple of moments later a young couple walk in and look around, so we invite them to share our table. Andy is Canadian and Liz is British. They're back-packing round the world, now staying at the Adventure Backpackers Hostel. We find lots of mutual interest and after a pleasant evening together we invite them on board for a few days, to enjoy some of the outer anchorage locations.

As we sail to anchorage #28 off Ofu Island, we're extremely glad to have two extra pairs of eyes to 'spot' coral heads as we navigate the crooked pass. For three days we snorkel, reef-walk, swim and beach-comb. It is perfect for Liz, who is an inveterate collector of shells, tiny bits of coral, sea fans and anything for later art projects. Every few weeks she packs a box of treasures and ships it to the UK. They are happy to pitch in with the cooking and other jobs including helping to rub off the weed growth that continually grows on the waterline. It's sad to see them leave. Subsequently, we meet up with them several times in Australia, England and Canada.

The wide, sandy expanse of our current anchorage is a favourite with the yachting community for shelling and barbecues, but today we have it to ourselves.

"Shall we hike to the other side of the island for a picnic?" Robin asks.

It's good to get away from the beaten path occasionally; to go where others don't. Beyond the fragrant pandanus trees and the graceful casuarinas it quickly becomes clear that this is no easy hike. The sun is all but obliterated by the tall trees and there is dense underbrush. One fallen tree, termite-laden and crumbling, looks just like the next. Creepers trail in every direction over the ground ready to trip us. We take the easiest route, following a tortuous path round obstacles and leave markers to help us find our way home: two logs pointing; a tripod of twigs, a liana draped across a bush.

The scrub thins out after an hour and we break through the bushes on the far side of the island to a view of the ocean to the west. Looking down from the wall of black rock which drops to a tiny cove and the sea, we see a crevice in the rock face and climb down 10 metres over a slippery tumble of boulders to emerge on the sand. Fresh water trickles out of the fracture into a rivulet and wends its way down the miniature beach to mingle at the water's edge. The silvery sea glints and winks in the sunlight as far as eternity, with ripples advancing and retreating, licking the shore with a salty tongue.

"This is magical!" I unlace my hiking boots and remove my thick socks. Robin props the backpack by a rock and follows suit. The sand is warm, the water tepid. We inspect the stretch of beach, admiring shells and looking into rock pools for sea life.

"Picnic?" Robin asks, heading towards the backpack.

"Umm."

He spreads a tablecloth, glances up and smiles as he sets out tinned pâté and cheeses, along with delicious flaky biscuits, crusty bread and fresh pineapple. He unwraps two wine glasses from a white napkin, polishes them and places the shining crystal on the sand. Sparkling wine bubbles into the goblets.

"To this piece of paradise—ours for a short time," he says as he hands me a glass.

Our burnished bare bodies soak up the sunshine. We laugh as we sip the wine. The cares of the world are far away.

I set my glass down on the sand, lie back and stretch out. My eyes close and a young breeze riffles over my flesh, tightening my skin and sharpening my senses. I inhale deeply; the air has a trace of moist rich earth and salt.

Cool droplets of wine splash onto my skin and Robin slowly, gently, licks them up. The droplets work their way over my throat, across my breasts and abdomen and down my thighs. My heart pounds and I can scarcely breathe, as my back arches reflexively, my nerve endings electrified.

I tip my head back and open my eyes to absorb a fraction of the vast blue sky, the sheltering trees and bushes and the ageless lichens' patterns on the rocks; to imprint the image of this special moment onto my mind.

It is cooler when I awake, the sun lower in the sky. I run my hand over Robin's chest and he opens his eyes. "We must leave soon," I say.

We sit and savour the last moments of our solitude, prolonging the magic.

At the top of the rocky cliff, we turn to gaze one last time at our view of the Pacific.

Before the bush swallows us, we see a tiny bird flitting from twig to twig. As we watch quietly, it enters a hole where a branch has fallen from a tree. In the indentation is a tiny nest with two pea-sized eggs. New life is always blossoming somewhere.

Retracing our steps is more arduous than we anticipate. Identifying the signs we left on our outward route is difficult, so each time we find a marker one of us stands beside it, until we identify the next. The dinghy is just where we left it on the beach and *Orca* still lies alone, peacefully at anchor.

It is while we are in Vava'u that we decide to head for Australia and not New Zealand where all the other yachts seem to be going. A lucky choice as it transpires, because of the horrendous weather off North Island at the time of our passage. As we will need entry visas for Australia we arrange with the High Commission in Tonga's capital, Nuku'alofa, on the island of Tongatapu, to send the forms to us here in Vava'u. We wait and wait, checking the mail every few days. It is certainly no inconvenience to spend a few more weeks here enjoying the beauty of the islands. The only difficulty is deciding between bush-walking, caving, beachcombing, reef-walking, shelling, swimming, snorkelling or diving.

Chris, from *Foam Follower*, tells us about giant mussel-shaped pen shells which one can dig out of the sand and they have a very large, white, scallop-type muscle. We follow his directions to the anchorage, then dinghy to where the water is 3-4 metres deep to locate some shells. They're quite difficult to spot and it takes time to acclimatize our eyes to the bottom conditions. The shells are buried upright in the sand with only the top 4-5 cm exposed—enough for it to open a little to allow water to pass over the delicate brown and yellow mantle for filter feeding.

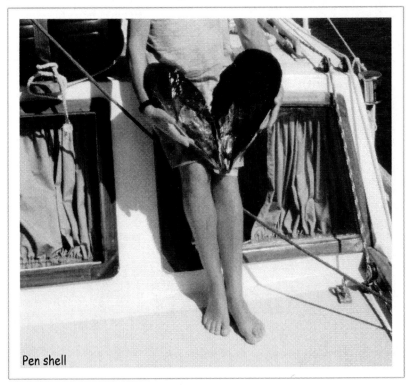

Pen shell

"Perhaps we'll try with scuba gear," Rob suggests, but after blowing away nearly a tank of air each in very short time, we continue using snorkels—much better exercise for us.

We take a big breath, dive down, and using a diving knife or machete, clear away as much sand as possible from the upright shell. Then we hack at the base of the pen shell, to sever the fibrous roots attaching it to the rocks beneath the sand. It takes several attempts of exhausting breath-holding work for each shell, surfacing for air in between sessions. We don't give up and manage to collect several specimens which vary from 30-45 cm long and 15-30 cm wide.

"We've got a good number," Rob says when we're motoring back to *Orca*.

"Yes, but I think these definitely belong to that class of food on which we expend more energy harvesting, than we gain from eating them."

The scallop-like muscle can be sliced thinly and is simply delicious frittered, chowdered or raw in a marinade—well worth the effort. Interestingly enough, the locals seem unaware of their existence, or perhaps it's the amount of work needed to harvest them that makes them unpopular, whereas fishing is relatively easy.

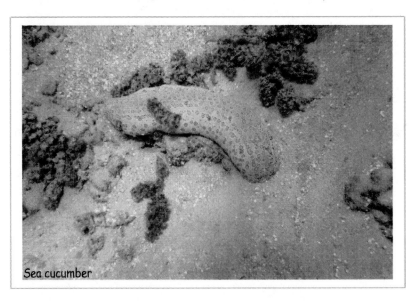
Sea cucumber

Diving is a commercial enterprise here, as well as a sport. Several local commercial divers use the Hookah system, which supplies air through hoses from the surface and enables the diver to walk across the bottom, unencumbered by a scuba tank. A second member of the dive team sits in the boat, to keep an eye on the air supply as the divers pick up the ubiquitous sea cucumbers. It's a profitable venture, selling them to an ever-hungry Asian market. Unfortunately, while we are in Neiafu, a 41-year old local diver drowns. He leaves a wife and 11 children from 16 years of age, down to a small baby.

To help support the fatherless family Diana, an expat Aussie with a heart of gold, immediately organizes a large Tongan feast at her restaurant on Ote'a Island. All yachties are invited, so we go to the anchorage early to help with preparations and decorations.

It is here that we meet Bill and Robyn from *Ramtha*, a 11.5-metre catamaran from Australia, another vessel that had to be abandoned during the Queen's Birthday Storm on 6th June. The *Ramtha* crew was rescued by a 4,000-tonne ship, *The Monowai*, and gave up their vessel for lost. A week or so later, they were stunned to learn that it had been found, upright and in surprisingly good shape. They are cruising again in *Ramtha*.

At the party there are a lot of games and contests, eating and drinking. I enter a conch-blowing contest and come in second. Shame on me, for I used to be a bugler in a Girls' Life Brigade band. It's just a pity the party is for such a sad reason, and particularly emotional when the diver's wife comes in with her 11 children to thank us. All the proceeds of this evening's feast go to the family, plus the yachties donate large quantities of food and clothing. Happily, we raise enough money to keep all the children in school fees and uniforms for the next two years and the food will last for months.

A few of us stay anchored near the restaurant to help clear up after the night's revelries. While we are talking to Diana, she offers to take TP to join her menagerie. She has also just taken delivery of a parrot from another vessel. Sailing with pets on board presents a quarantine problem at most destinations. We agree to deliver TP just before we leave Neiafu.

One last trip is to the famous Mariner's Cave. The only two entrances are 3.5 and 15 metres under water. I practice breath-holding by diving underneath *Orca* a few times, to make sure I'll be comfortable attempting it. There's no place to anchor by the cliffs, so we go with John and Leena on *Kona Star*, and take turns motoring their vessel adjacent to the cave entrance. Robin and I dive down, swim through a 5-metre rocky passageway and surface in a 12-metre high chamber with beautiful rock formations and stalactites. The popular myth is that a Polynesian god once hid his beautiful princess in this cave.

Because of its geological arrangement, an interesting phenomenon occurs. As the cave has no entrances above water the air inside is a fixed volume. Swells surging in and out of the underwater entrances create pressure changes within which cause a moderately thick, local fog to form and then dissipate. This happens with each swell, so one moment it is crystal clear, the next foggy, all within a matter of seconds.

No papers arrive for us from Tongatapu, so regretfully we'll have to sail to Tongatapu to complete formalities for our Australian visas. We bid a fond farewell to friends and especially to TP, our sailing companion who has a new home at Diana's on Ote'a Island.

Goats on foreshore

20

Red Tape and Rain
Nuku'alofa, Tongatapu Group, Tonga

An hour before dusk, Vava'u is well behind us. We are on course for Tongatapu in brisk SE winds when we see a rocky outcrop with sheer cliffs off our starboard bow, about 2 km away. There's nothing marked on our chart and it seems like we will sail past it with ease. When we are adjacent, however, a very strong current is drawing us towards the mass and we can see through the binoculars that around the base of the cliffs there is a virtual 'boiling cauldron' of water, such is the turbulence. Robin fires up the engine.

"What's going on?" I ask.

"The autopilot can't cope with the current and we're getting closer to the cliff."

The engine is on full power, but even so, it's difficult to overcome the influence as we tack and steer away, 90° to port. Adrenaline rushes into my system, but after 15 minutes the current relinquishes its hold and we're able to resume course. I wonder for a moment what would have happened if it had been dark, or if we hadn't noticed, or the engine hadn't started.

Our chart of the area has many comments like: 'discoloured water sighted in the year 19XX', or 'turbulence reported in 19XX'. The next day we see several patches of strange, discoloured upwellings and large chunks of floating pumice. We sail on, maintaining a sharp lookout and wonder what is really happening on the sea bed.

Despite our inauspicious start, we're sailing well and making great time—how refreshing! It means, of course, we'll arrive 5 nautical miles off the Tongatapu northern pass at 10:00 p.m. so we continue sailing then make a reciprocal course to arrive by daylight, whereupon the wind promptly falls off and we motor again.

By the time we're close to the pass, the cloud layer is thick and it has started to rain—light but persistent, *really* persistent. Visibility is exceedingly poor, but we manage to locate the outer marker. It's an intricate passage of about 8 nautical miles through the reefs to Nuku'alofa, and Robin enters all the coordinates of the markers into the GPS, as waypoints.

"Let's hope the darned thing works properly this time," Rob says.

I keep my eye on the GPS below deck, but no luck, the screen goes blank. I switch it off and on again and wait for it to perform a satellite search, to pinpoint our position. Meanwhile, we continue on autopilot in what we think is the correct direction of the next marker.

"It's no good," I tell Robin, who is at the helm on deck, "it just won't work. What if I keep my eye on the marker we've just passed and you keep a lookout for the next. If you haven't spotted the next one before I lose sight of the last, then we'll turn round and go out and wait for better visibility."

"We'll give it a try," he says.

Following this course of action we slowly proceed through the pass into the lagoon but once inside, it is impossible to locate the small-boat harbour. We have no intention of getting closer to a chunk of land we can't see, to search. We head for the edge of the island of Pangiamotu which we know from the chart exists at the far side of the lagoon. This will mean a dinghy ride of 2.5 nautical miles to Nuku'alofa.

Having set and secured the anchor in pouring rain, we don our foulies; Robin in bright orange and me in acid yellow. They are actually insulated floating survival suits which we bought in Canada, the type worn by fishermen, and I'm grateful for the warmth. I carry our documents, wrapped in polythene bags, in my favourite small black backpack. It came from France, years ago and goes everywhere with me. We strike out for shore in the dinghy and I hope we haven't forgotten anything. Robin will be justifiably mad if we have to retrace our steps.

Wham, wham, wham, we bump along in the choppy water with the wind behind us—wham, wham, wham on the back of every whitecap. Wet with spray, we make our way to the Australian High Commission to pick up our visa applications.

"Fingers crossed that we can complete everything today," I say.

Strangely, nobody remembers anything about our telephone call and the promise to send applications to Vava'u. It seems it is impossible to speed up the proceedings and complete the forms here and now. It is Friday afternoon and the office, of course, isn't open on Saturday or Sunday. We must bring back the filled out applications on Monday.

"Shit!" is all Robin has to say.

We have to face the journey back to the yacht, but this time into wind and get totally soaked as the rain makes its way down our necks and through the seams of the suits. The dinghy is shipping lots of water so for the first time ever, I have to bail. Fortunately we always have a bailer attached to the dinghy.

Robin is in the darkest of moods and silent. I'm not feeling any happier, but am cussing.

"Jeez, I hate this—what the hell are we doing here?"

This is the first time we've got close to being cross with each other—apart from when we both wanted to get off, mid-Pacific. It's not because either of us is at fault. If we were, we certainly wouldn't make an issue of it. It's a pity, though, because it would be nice to leave for Australia in a calm frame of mind, but the weather is so lousy and bureaucracy just doesn't work the way we think it should.

Once we're back in our cocoon, drying out, our moods moderate slightly, although we're still concerned about weather conditions. The squalls and thunderstorms are going to continue for some time and we wonder whether we'll be blown onto Pangiamotu. We take turns to check regularly.

"Will you come out on deck?" Robin shakes my arm in the early hours of the morning. I wake up and fly out of bed.

"We've turned 180° and are stern-to to the shore. It's OK at the moment, we just need to line up some markers and watch to see if we're drifting. I'll turn on the engine in case we need to re-anchor."

I dress quickly in foul-weather gear and go on deck. The squally wind is hurling splatters of rain. Our anchor chain is taut and straining, making a noise like grinding teeth with each gust. We keep watch for 15 minutes, but *Orca* seems to remain stationary and we haven't lifted the anchor.

"I don't like this place," I tell Robin. He nods in agreement.

During the stormy days we spend our time below, doing maintenance jobs, reading or cooking. This constant wet weather depresses me. On one occasion when the cloud base lifts a little, we can see across the lagoon. It resembles a dinosaur graveyard, littered with rusting hulks of tankers—solemn reminders of battles lost with past cyclones.

We must make two more trips to Nuku'alofa; one to return our application forms and a third to pick up the visas. We are eternally grateful for the 8 hp outboard motor.

As we may be on shore for several hours on our final trip, it's a good opportunity to fumigate the boat, to rid us of a few cockroaches. Possibly they are descendants of the infants we picked up in American Samoa and now TP isn't here to keep them under control. She was obviously very good at her job of RRCO.

We open all locker and cupboard doors to storage areas and lift floor sections to the bilges. Just before we exit we activate several roach bombs and close the hatch. Once again dressed in fashionable foulies, we safely negotiate the waves and reach shore. It is still raining, so we take a taxi to the High Commission for our visas and to Customs and Immigration to process our exit papers.

Once we have all our paperwork we shop for fresh fruit and vegetables at the supermarket, enough to last three weeks. "Pork sausages!" Robin says, holding up his find. "This will be a treat." Sadly, they turn out to be anything but pork and are absolutely disgusting.

We have one more call to make to buy gasoline for the dinghy since we've used so much lately. The taxi driver takes us to a filling station, then wants us to go somewhere so he can sell us some of his family's handicrafts. We tell him in no uncertain terms that we are *not* purchasing anything more so he reluctantly returns us to the dock.

I wrap our bags of shopping in garbage bags and we are ready to do final battle with the elements, back to *Orca* in the dinghy.

"There's no change in the weather yet." Robin sounds disheartened as he hands me the latest weather fax to study.

Frustratingly, the storms persist and we spend another two days at anchor watching for a break. On the short-wave radio we hear terrible reports from our friends and other yachts braving the elements en route to New Zealand.

Unicorn, in Severe Gale Force 9 on the Beaufort Scale, has lost both autopilots, taken a lot of water on board and lost most of its electrics, so is hove-to in lousy seas. *Sarah of Hamble*, in Gale Force

8, has lost main and genoa halyards and also has no engine: hove to. A pan-pan call alerts us that *Kevake*, a trimaran, has been dismasted in Storm Force 10 winds and lost its engine. They have taken a lot of water on board, but are not sinking: hove-to. *Gypsy* has not been heard of for two weeks and has VHF radio only. By contrast, *Xaxero*, a slower boat somewhat behind the others, has sheared its prop shaft and is becalmed in a high, with plenty of fuel it can't use. It has been drifting backwards for two days. Some vessels decide to head for Fiji. We stop complaining about our conditions.

The rain eases for the first time in six days, and as the cloud ceiling lifts a little we make a break for it through the northern passage, eschewing the shorter southern pass. Horizontal visibility is still unreliable and apparently that channel is only variably marked—more by wrecks than markers.

"There are so many shipwrecks!" Rob says, as we enter the northern pass. As far as the eye can see it is strewn with debris ranging from small yachts to vast tankers. One tanker is frighteningly close to the channel and we didn't even see it when we entered.

"Thank goodness we kept close to the marker buoys," I say, "and didn't wander outside the channel."

Once clear of Tongatapu and its surrounding reefs, we sail on broken seas, employing the usual variations of sail and motor. Winds vary from 5 to 30 knots, so we keep quite busy.

"Yes, yes, yes!" I dance around and shout as we catch our very first fish at last; using the steel trace we bought in Tonga. It is a 10-kg, brilliant turquoise and yellow mahi mahi, with an ugly blunt head, one long continuous dorsal fin and a jack-like tail.

What a messy business processing is! Blood and scales everywhere as we clean and cut the fish into thick steaks and bag them for the freezer. When we finish, the winds are around 30 knots. Flying so much sail, we are heeled right over, but we barely notice the conditions in our euphoric state. Only one-third of the way to Sydney and we have lots of fresh fish. We cook it in every conceivable way from pressure-cooker to BBQ—delicious!

Once again, we are adding too many running hours to the engine log, just as we did from Panama to the Marquesas. Sailing opportunities are infrequent, and when there's no wind, again the swells become annoying. In an idle moment, we calculate we've rolled from side to side over a million times since leaving Cayman.

Keeping ourselves busy can be a challenge. To pass time in the evenings, we tune into the BBC World Service for company and world news. One day, it's a pleasant diversion when we spot a lone Orca killer whale swimming on the surface in the opposite direction. We shout 'hello' and watch its progress for 15 minutes, but it ignores us.

"Look, birds!" Robin points to two specs in the sky. We're approaching Ball's Pyramid: a volcanic pinnacle of basalt rock formed during a massive eruption millions of years ago. It is the world's tallest sea stack and rises *half a kilometre* from the ocean's surface, piercing the sky. Our first sight of land since leaving Tonga is an inhospitable, windswept, bird paradise. A phenomenal solitary object to encounter.

We experience some bizarre, strong currents and are determined to pass to the north of the pinnacle, since our chart of the area states that because of the bullets of wind rushing down the cliffs, approaching Ball's Pyramid from the southeast, *will* result in dismasting—not *may*, but *will*. That's certainly enough to make up *my* mind. We'll pass to the north, no matter how difficult it is.

We're sailing, but going slower and slower as a strong current sets towards the cliffs. To counteract the current we re-trim the sails and point higher, but that brings us closer to wind and so we slow down more. Robin starts the engine.

"If we don't get moving, we're never going to get past this thing," he says.

We wonder if the problem might be a function of the undersea ridge, causing upwellings and strong currents. With bags of power from the engine we start making headway, then suddenly our boat speed increases by three to four knots and we're steaming. The current has changed and is working with us. Now, there's nothing between us and Australia—somewhere I've always thought of as the other side of the world. Funny, it doesn't feel like the other side, now we are here.

Twenty-four hours away from Sydney we're having a beautiful run, sailing briskly under completely clear, sapphire skies. We'll soon be in a fantastic new country. Robin is sitting on deck. To celebrate I'm in the galley preparing a special lunch: mahi mahi in a white wine sauce, a tin of new potatoes, carrots and some frozen peas. For desert, since we're nearing the end of this leg, I will serve one of Robin's favourite chocolate bars that I keep hidden for emergency morale-boosters.

The casseroled fish is in the oven and the vegetables heating when I hear a loud CRACK like a gun shot, followed by "ALL HANDS ON DECK!" I drop what I'm doing, snap on my safety harness and fly out. It's a gorgeous day and difficult to think anything can be amiss.

"We've blown out the genoa." Robin says. I look forward. Our best natural-power producer is wretchedly flapping and snapping like a whip.

"We can't drop it, because it's back-wrapped itself round the foil. Ease the sheet and I'll furl it."

What a mess. The bottom section of the genoa has ripped off—an 11-metre tear, and the Sunbrella sacrificial strip sewn on in Miami, has shredded. Our progress is markedly reduced.

"What caused that?" I ask Rob when we eventually manage to eat lunch.

Galley

"Clear-air turbulence—no warning and you can't see it."

Luckily we don't have far to go now. I can't imagine trying to unwind that mess and repair it on deck while at sea.

It's 17th December and we are in touch with Sydney Radio. Christmas carols are playing on a commercial radio station. I always loved Christmas carols and am immediately transported back in time to the warm family Christmases of my childhood and with my own children. Just a day ago, all our thoughts were tropical. Now, incongruously, it's Christmas. I'm overwhelmed with nostalgic feelings. What are we doing so far away from everyone?

During the night, the stars disappear and sounds become muted as fog enshrouds us.

Captain's cabin seating

21

G'day Australia!
Drifters on Land and Water
Sydney, New South Wales

By dawn, the fog is eerily thick. Very slowly we motor south-west over the flat seas, in touch with several other vessels by radio, but can see nothing. A cable-laying ship calls alerting us to its position and requesting that we keep clear. We have no desire to tangle so creep forward, eyes straining, occasionally sounding our ship's bell. We consider standing-off if the fog doesn't clear, but don't feel happy hanging around waiting to be hit by another vessel. Finally, a mile from the Sydney Heads—the entrance to Port Jackson (Sydney Harbour)—we make out a vague outline of land. What a relief!

At first we see a few, then dozens, then hundreds of little vessels dressed with flags.

"How nice of them," I say to Robin, "to come out to meet us. What a wonderful country!"

The fog is left behind at sea and we have raised our Q-flag. As *Orca* weaves between the craft in Sydney Harbour, a large customs launch sweeps alongside us. Thoughtfully, he's come to guide us to Neutral Bay where the Customs and Immigration offices are located. Rob has to execute some pretty tricky manoeuvring, steering clear of the racing ferries plying their trade across the mouth of the bay, as well as avoiding two black submarines tied up at the dock. He can finally pull in between the two pilings indicated by the officer. I'm always in awe of how Robin handles *Orca* in limited spaces under stressful conditions.

The Customs, Immigration and Quarantine officers are all most courteous and helpful. "It's not really for you, y'know," the quarantine officer says, "we don't do this for all our visitors. The little boats are waiting for the replica of Captain Cook's *Endeavour*. It was due in at 9:00 a.m. but is delayed until 11:00 a.m. because of fog."

Orca is still tied in Neutral Bay when the *Endeavour* arrives amid a fanfare of horns, bells and whistles. We have a ringside seat as it sails past our stern into the harbour, complete with its flag-decorated flotilla.

Cook's Endeavour

"It feels really *good* to be here, Rob, everything is so alive!"

Sydney Opera House

Robin gives me a bear hug. It's becoming pretty obvious that any piece of land will feel like home to me.

After entry formalities are completed and we've been parted from our remaining meat and dairy products we proceed, as directed, to Ball's Head Bay for short-term anchoring, motoring past the Sydney Opera House, a modern wonder of the world, then under the majestic Sydney Harbour Bridge. It's difficult to believe we are really in Australia—it's magical and so vibrant.

Sydney Harbour Bridge

In Ball's Head bay we anchor, give way to exhaustion and crash out. Everything looks great in the morning. Our first priority is to locate a permanent mooring in the vicinity for a few months and we visit some potential sites from a list given to us by the customs officer. On our return to Ball's Head Bay, the wind is strong. A man, sitting on the shoreline contemplating nothing in particular, says, "I've been watching her—seems like she's dragging." We thank him and race in the dinghy to *Orca*.

The windlass brake has let go, allowing all the anchor line to run out. Thank goodness the end of the chain is securely shackled to *Orca*. The wind is around 40 knots, with bullets of higher gusts rushing down from the hills. A miserable couple of hours ensue when, using the engine, I try to keep *Orca*'s head into wind while Robin operates the hand windlass. It's a near-impossible task with the gusts which cause *Orca* to veer off to one side or the other.

"Keep her steady," Robin yells, "not too far!" He flaps his hand at me, as if to say 'stay back'. Perhaps I'm using too much power and am over-running the anchor line. It doesn't help when we are both at our respective tasks that neither one can see the other.

Robin rushes back, disappears below, then returns to the bow with tools. His problem is compounded because the chain repeatedly twists up—like a piece of string held by the ends and twisted in opposite directions—and locks on the windlass gypsy. He has to knock off each link with a hammer. I know nothing of this at the time and wonder what is going on—why is it taking so long? It transpires that the anchor had fouled on a large piece of steel rod in the bay, so the swivel between the chain and anchor can't function.

When the anchor is at last clear of the bottom, I motor round the bay, while Robin checks the gear before we attempt to re-anchor.

Bullets of wind from the hillside in Ball's Head Bay, apparently, are not uncommon and we register prolonged gusts of 58 knots. Only one more night to endure, then we will be safe on a permanent mooring in Drummoyne that can handle vessels up to 127,000 kg and we're a measly 36,000 kg. It will be wonderful to feel secure, with none of the stresses of dragging at anchor.

Our mooring is owned by John & Peter Minehan, father and son, who run a small family business: President Shipwright Services. Mrs. Minehan is a pretty blonde with an hourglass figure, tight t-shirt and tiny shorts, shapely legs and very high-heeled slippers. I think she keeps the books.

It's Christmas day and we've been snug on the mooring for five days. I'm standing in the galley, roasting a stuffed chicken, to be served with roast potatoes, sprouts, carrots and gravy; Christmas pudding and custard; mince pies and brandy butter. Tears stream down my face and plop onto the counter top as I listen to *Oh Come all ye Faithful* and *It came upon a Midnight Clear*.

On Boxing Day a Seawind catamaran stops by the mooring to chat. The owner of Seawind Catamarans, Richard Ward, is at the helm running sea trials on the pre-production Seawind 1000.

"It's pretty busy here on New Year's Eve," he tells us, "hundreds of boats congregate under Sydney Harbour Bridge to watch the big firework display. Why don't you come on board with us?"

"That would be fantastic, we'd love to!"

What a magical evening it is—Richard, his wife Lindy, two daughters, Rosie and Amber, plus other invited guests.

Familiar only with the difficulty of handling *Orca*, we're highly impressed with the manoeuvrability of the catamaran, as Richard weaves in and out of the other vessels to find us a good spot. The food is excellent, as is the company, and we have a glorious view of the firework display. It's an unusual and exciting way for us to see in the New Year.

Within walking distance of our mooring is Birkenhead Point Marina which looks as if it's been fashionably developed from old warehouses. It's quite upper-crust, with houses, dozens of shops, ship chandlers, taverns, restaurants, supermarket, a food hall and liquor supplies. What could be more perfect? There are also little shops in downtown Drummoyne, our favourite being a sandwich bar supplying the famous and most delicious Aussie meat pies. We often buy them for lunch and walk to a little local park for a picnic. Also, there's a Legion Club close by, where all foreigners have automatic access. They serve tasty, reasonably-priced meals and a good pint.

By chance, we've hit on the most well-appointed location. The only drawback is that telephone calls to the other side of the world have to be made in the middle of the night and we must walk a couple of kilometres to a pay phone.

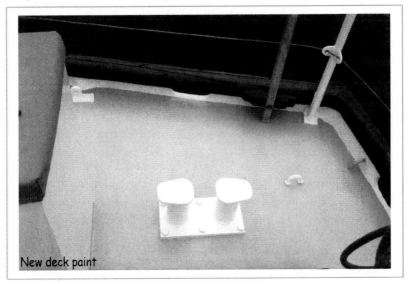

New deck paint

Daily work continues on the boat and we finally finish the deck preparation and painting, including scattering special anti-slip grit on the last coat before it dries. We still have to mend our torn genoa and keenly watch for a windless day to unravel the bits of sail. Once we have the pieces down and measured and the metres of heavy-grade sailcloth ordered, we must find somewhere to effect the repairs. Two hundred metres down the road is another slipway, owned by Big Jim (Jumbo). Across the other side of his slip, is a little park.

"Let's go and talk to Big Jim," Robin says, but I think he means let's go and *you* talk to him.

It's a really busy shipyard, catering to large commercial vessels and there's no slack time to be able to catch Jumbo so we have to barge in.

"Jim," I start, not wanting to be over familiar and calling him either Big, or Jumbo, "we're neighbours—on one of John's moorings."

"Yeah I know, the ferro boat." He smiles.

"We have a big repair to do on our genoa and we need somewhere to spread out and work on it. We could probably manage in the little park, across from your slip and wonder if we could buy some power from you to run the sewing machine? We've got extension cables and a transformer."

"Yeah, course you can, just tell the men in the yard." With that, Jumbo turns to attend to pressing business.

"Thanks very much!" I shout after him. What a great guy and what a load off my mind.

Now for the difficult part. We must transport the bulky sail, the new cloth, the 30-kg sewing machine, a transformer and extension leads in the dinghy to the park. Then we must climb the iron rungs let into the side of the sea wall and heave the gear up onto dry land so that we can lay out all the parts and fashion a new panel measuring 1.2 metres by 10.7 metres. Of course, it's not just a straight strip; it is cunningly contoured and if we get it wrong the sail won't hold a proper shape. Once the panel is attached we'll have to sew on a new leech line pocket and then the repaired 40-cm wide Sunbrella sacrificial edge. As it's not possible to pin the layers of heavy cloth together, it all has to be taped and each piece of tape removed before we stitch over it. This way the sail won't resemble a duct-tape patchwork quilt.

It turns into a monstrous task, just manoeuvring 124-square-metres of sail over the grassy tussocks and through the machine. Not surprisingly, I break lots of sewing machine needles. It takes us four days to complete, working eight hours a day on hands and knees, but we are thrilled with the results. The weather doesn't allow us to carry out the work on consecutive days, which is good, because the delays allow our aching bodies to recover. When it's finished we visit Jumbo to pay him for his power, but he refuses. I think he feels sorry for us.

"I can't believe you sticking at that, mate. Why didn't you just take it to a sail locker?"

"The cost." I reply.

The only thing Big Jim will accept is a slab (24) of his favourite beer. The miniature cans, dwarfed by his sausage-like digits, are his preference. He's been forced to abandon large cans on account of his girth.

It's not all work for us in Drummoyne. We contact several people whose names we have been given and make many new acquaintances. Our social life becomes quite hectic as we accept invitations for meals and outings. Even the quarantine officer and her boyfriend pick us up one day and take us on a riverboat day-trip along the Parramatta River. We are certainly overwhelmed by the Australian hospitality and find ourselves telling our tales over and over again.

If we don't feel like leave the mooring, we can sit back and watch the local sailing club's skiff races. There is some spectacular sailing—and some spectacular ditching, but although they're racing all around us, we are never actually hit—close though.

There is no point in coming all this way without sampling the great outback. Australia is geared for travelling on a shoestring and there's a hot market for old, used vehicles. At the famous King's Cross Car Market in an underground car park in Sydney, we buy a Ford Falcon station wagon, circa 1978, complete with camping gear. This stylish and reliable vehicle becomes our home as we tour New South Wales, Victoria and South Australia.

Two glorious months we spend travelling on land! We avoid cities and visit as many national and state parks as possible. Late each afternoon we set up camp and invariably are the only people there. We see pink, white, green and saffron-coloured parrots, and listen to the haunting, glottal song of the pied currawong. We play with a kangaroo joey in its mother's pouch and watch goannas waddle

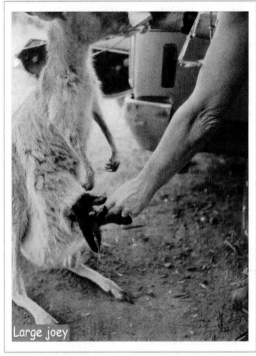

Large joey

about their business and shy koalas in tall eucalyptus trees.

Each evening we build a bonfire, cook supper and drink a glass or two of wine. The campsites are excellent. Some state parks charge no camping fees at all, yet still offer hot showers. We are free to wander a tiny portion of this vast land and marvel at the varied geographical terrains: from the snowy mountains and cold lakes of the Blue Mountains right to the ancient sand dunes and prehistoric river beds of Mungo National Park—complete with prehistoric mouse bones. It is with a slightly heavy heart that I return to the yacht.

The mooring has been *Orca*'s home for seven months and ours for five. In July we will head for Queensland to catch up with Sue and Steve at last before leaving for the North Pacific. Our equipment has been repaired: the GPS, the wind direction indicator, the compass and the windlass. We feel *Orca* is ready to go to sea.

One last job remains; to haul her out to do another bottom job. We are too heavy for most slipways to handle us, but Big Jim promises he'll to try to fit us in over a weekend, between commercial contracts, although he's booked up for months in advance.

Early one Friday morning, Jim tells us to go immediately as he's had a cancellation. We will have to be off the slipway again by first thing on Monday.

We haul up the dinghy, start the engine, slip the mooring rope and set off—or rather, we don't set off. Despite engaging forward gear and employing full revs, we are drifting backwards down the

Parramatta river with the incoming tide. Robin stays at the helm and I quickly re-launch the dinghy and use it like a tug, to keep *Orca*'s head into wind. From nowhere, Big Jim appears alongside in his giant triple-decker launch.

"Come on, what's the matter?"

Rob explains that we have no forward propulsion and need assistance. Fortunately, our shipwright, John, owns a tug which is at this very moment heading off on a mission. Big Jim roars off and diverts it towards us and we are soon trussed up alongside and ignominiously driven to the slipway.

Robin is deep in thought, considering all the potential problems. Is it the engine, or perhaps a broken drive shaft? As *Orca* emerges from the water one possible cause is immediately obvious. The propeller is covered with 2.5-centimetre-long barnacles and resembles a big, fuzzy ball—no wonder we have no hydrodynamics.

By day and by floodlight at night, we work like mad things; cleaning and preparing the hull, applying two coats of antifouling paint and renewing the zincs.

"The part of the keel I recast is holding up well," Rob observes, "and nothing terrible has appeared since we hauled out at the beginning of the year."

As we grind and scrub I add, "I don't know about you, but I feel I know every inch of this keel *intimately*."

There is a niggling worry, however, at the back of our minds while we work, as to whether we have an engine problem.

On Monday at 7:00 a.m. we have the tug standing by on the radio, while we re-launch *Orca*. As we enter the water, Robin starts the engine, we reverse from the slipway and take *Orca* for a run, under the Sydney Harbour Bridge to the Opera House and back and make 9 knots with ease. We are more than happy to pay our slipway fees for the three days.

"Thank God!" Robin says, "The engine's fine, it was just those barnacles on the prop. We should celebrate, let's go out to dinner!"

We are utterly exhausted after our weekend—our hands are lacerated and swollen, our bodies sore and splattered with paint. Nevertheless, we bathe, dress in presentable clothes and go to an Italian restaurant John has recommended. We last until 8:00 p.m.

Our last chore is to fill up with diesel, and what a truly civilized arrangement it is—the fuel barge comes to us!

As *Orca* is now ready for voyaging, we drive our trusty Falcon to Queensland in three days, so we can use it there during our stay. The trip involves re-registering the vehicle in Queensland and we have the name and address of the office. What we fail to take into consideration is that there is a time difference between the states and we arrive a few minutes before they close the doors on Friday afternoon. We are ever amazed at how accommodating the officials are. They wait for us to collect all the papers from the car and process them immediately.

The return to Sydney by bus takes 36 hours. Surprisingly, it is a relaxing and enjoyable trip. We catch up on reading or sleep when we tire of looking out of the window at the vast countryside.

Orca is provisioned with fresh food and we are excited to have a favourable forecast of 15-20 knot winds for our departure.

Inner steering station

22
The Great Australian Current and Queensland's 'Windy' Coast

Jumbo's slipway

There's a light breeze in the harbour. We hoist the mainsail, slip the mooring and for the first time ever silently leave under sail alone, gliding beneath Sydney Harbour Bridge and past the Opera House for the last time.

"Farewell fair Sydney and thanks for your hospitality!"

Outside the harbour, we unfurl our repaired genoa, but instead of kicking up our heels and sailing forth, the wind fades away and we are becalmed. The forecast was just a mirage.

Motoring north, late afternoon sea breezes arise and give us a little help. Towards midnight the steadily increasing wind is approaching 30 knots and we've reefed down several times. Adding a 4th reefing point in the mainsail and a 3rd in the mizzen while in Sydney was a fantastic idea. It makes things much less stressful in strong winds. Sailing becomes more comfortable as we drop from 9 to 7 knots. With the dawn the winds lighten so we increase sail area. Then, as we slow to less than 2 knots, we drop the mainsail to stop the boom flogging from side to side with the swells and finally engage the engine. The pattern repeats itself over the next 24 hours, but thereafter we have varying amounts of NW-NE winds—on the nose again.

"Good job we filled up with fuel, we'll damn well need it." Rob says.

We were expecting the notorious Australian current running North to South, but in places it is racing up to 7 knots and we have to motor flat out at times to make any headway at all. Thank goodness we have a clean hull. Some vessels avoid the current in large part by hugging the shore, but we can't do that and are sailing a couple of kilometres offshore. The engine runs permanently for the next eight days until a piercing, beeping alarm sounds.

"What the heck is that?" I say as Robin rushes below.

"Shit! It's the engine high-temperature alarm." He shuts off the engine and works to identify the problem. I stay on deck to keep a lookout while we wallow in the seas.

"I've got to replace the cooling water pump impellor. It's shredded." says Robin, looking weary.

The impellor has disintegrated. It takes four hours for Robin to clean out all the pieces of hardened rubber and complete the replacement, during which time we are drifting south with the current. I feel so sorry for him stuck with his head in the bowels of *Orca* while she is tossing about, then having to rush up for air to stave off the waves of nausea. I wish there were something I could do to help. The only consolation is that we're not hugging the coast or we'd have the proximity to land to worry about.

If we had no GPS, we wouldn't know how much ground we are losing. However, with the super accuracy of this marvellous system we are able to watch the distance to our destination *increasing* by more than 20 nautical miles before we can again move forward. It is ironic that our GPS is working well for the first time since we left Cayman.

The current strength is hugely variable and at one point while motoring hard against its influence, we are dismayed to find that we are *still* moving backwards. "At this bloody rate we'll be swept round the Tasman Sea, past New Zealand with the current and find ourselves back near Tonga." Robin grumbles.

The night watches are heavy with cloud. As we near the beginning of the Great Barrier Reef, however, the cloud lifts and we see the lights of myriad small fishing vessels. It is exciting and keeps us amused during night watches.

The wind at last swings round to the SE—how we would have liked this for the past week! At least we are now able to fly the spinnaker for a day, well, part of the day, after we work out how to set it up again having used it so infrequently. Our problem is not with the raising or dousing of the spinnaker, because the spinnaker sock I made from a kit in Cayman, works well. It's more a problem of running all the control lines correctly to the cockpit. There are so many snaking back that the deck looks as if it's covered in multicoloured entrails. The spinnaker also helps to reduce rolling as each swell passes beneath us.

"What's the weather forecast for tonight," I ask Robin, "are we leaving the spinnaker up or not?"

"It's supposed to be fair, but do we trust it?"

"No! Let's take it down. I don't want to be caught in a gale flying a spinnaker."

Before nightfall it is neatly doused and stored, but would you believe it? There is no strong wind this night.

We turn northwest, heading inside the outer Great Barrier Reef where we see several hump-backed whales and watch their antics. We are passing through their breeding ground, but we don't seem to disturb them.

We will make port tomorrow and we must be especially alert tonight. There is no moon and we will be passing between the islands of the Great Barrier Reef. Until now we have been able to avoid being close to land in the dark, but tonight we have no choice. Careful not to spoil our night vision, we use one small-wattage red lamp on the chart table. Gradually, one island mass after another looms up and slips by. Because of the tidal influence and greatly confused currents around the islands, we must alter the course of the autopilot continually to accommodate drifting, but we have no close encounters of a disturbing nature.

Spinnaker run

It is Sunday morning, 10:00 a.m. We have eaten breakfast; eggs and bacon, tea, toast and marmalade and we bathe before dressing in our best clothes.

The sun is fierce as we douse the last of the sails and glide into Shute Harbour where our friends on *Trochus* are moored. It has been over 18 months since we last met Steve and Susie in Cayman. We want to surprise them, but they spot us immediately and wave and shout, "Hi *Orca*, G'day Mate!

Where've ya been?"

Shute Harbour is almost full of permanent moorings, mostly for charter vessels. Not one of them is suitable for *Orca*'s size and displacement, so we have to find a spot to anchor on the outer perimeter where it is less sheltered, but is still only 8-10 metres deep.

Our reunion turns into a 'wee party' in the afternoon and we toast each other's health with a couple of bottles of wine. Tonight we will have a long and peaceful sleep after the past 11 nights at sea.

We have been looking forward to wonderful weather on the well-advertised 'Sunshine Coast' of Queensland, but for two days the winds increase until we have a constant 30 knots blowing in the harbour, with higher gusts. The weather report tells us there is a massive high over the southern Tasman Sea with a strong ridge running up the Queensland coast. This high stalls in the same position for more than 30 days. Fortunately, we can't foresee this and each day expect conditions to change.

Despite half-metre waves in the anchorage we manage to get ashore a few times for provisions, soaking both ourselves and our supplies—shades of Tongatapu. As we are stuck on board we decide to go ahead and start our last large job before leaving Australia for the North Pacific Rim: stripping down all 13 window frames to bare wood to re-caulk and re-varnish in order to stop a few leaks and to protect the wood.

In three days we have all the frames bared, the caulk removed and re-caulking completed. It is exhausting work with the boat constantly moving on the choppy water. Then the worst thing happens—it starts to rain—heavy rain. Within eight hours the exposed mahogany frames are acting like blotting paper and every window leaks inside.

I howl with despair. "Oh Robin! Why does it always do this to us?"

Towels are pressed into service to prevent the spoiling of our internal equipment and belongings. It will take days to dry out before we can rub down the grain again and varnish. The rain abates after a few miserable days but the wind remains, so at least this helps the drying-out process. Eventually we start varnishing and get a couple of coats on quickly. There are still 30+ knot winds and every day we have rain showers, so the varnish must constantly be rubbed down and washed with thinners, before applying new coats. It is tedious in the extreme and I've had enough of varnishing after applying only six coats, but this proves watertight for now.

For a relief from chores, we arrange to meet Steve & Susie for a weekend in a sheltered anchorage in Bernie's Bay on Whitsunday Island, to fish, barbecue and generally relax. Remembering our unpleasant time raising the anchor in strong winds in Ball's Head Bay in Sydney, we are dubious about moving in these windy conditions. However, we know the windlass is working well so decide to do a test. The engine springs into life, as always, and this time using very gentle power I creep forward to take the strain from the rode. It seems as though it will work, but we suddenly suffer a 35-knot gust. *Orca* is blown back, snapping the anchor line taut with a bang.

"I think perhaps we'll just stay here," Robin says, "it's not going to be any fun if we have to fight the yacht."

Orca, however, has other ideas.

"Aren't we a lot closer to that yacht behind us?" I ask Robin, feeling the alarm rising in me.

"Oh Hell!" he says. The shock of *Orca* settling back on the anchor chain, enhanced by the gust, is enough to break out the anchor which has been well dug-in for many days. As we bear down on the unfortunate boat behind the decision is made for us. Luckily the engine is still running and Robin eases into forward gear and in double-quick time we continue with our original plan.

I take over the helm as Rob cranks up the anchor and soon we're heading out of the harbour. I race below to check the security of goods which are normally lashed down while at sea. Pushed into crossing a very choppy Whitsunday passage, we are a little ill-prepared. The sum of our loss is two wineglasses—both empty, luckily.

Three hours later, we gain the security of Bernie's Bay just as the light fades. We creep into the wide, shallow bay as far as we dare and set the anchor. *Trochus*, with less draft, is in much closer. Apart from an occasional bullet of wind, which lays *Trochus* right over on her side at one point, it is certainly more sheltered than Shute Harbour. It rains intermittently all weekend, so we fish and barbecue in the wet, but we have good company and are doing something other than work.

"It's not normally like this!" Sue says. Cold comfort.

When *Trochus* leaves on Monday, we decided to stay until the winds drop. Each day I rise at 6:30 a.m. to hear the marine weather forecast, hoping for a miracle, but none happens. The pictures from the weather fax are most depressing. The high remains stalled over the southern Tasman Sea and the ridge still runs up the Queensland coast. It is no consolation to know that it is a most unusual weather pattern.

After a further week the bad weather is *really* wearing thin. We occasionally fish from the dinghy or walk on the beach in between showers.

"I think we should see about getting a berth at Abel Point Marina." Robin says.

"Oh yes! We'll be closer to provisions at Airlie Beach and we'll just be able to step off the yacht onto the quay and can go away for a few days leaving *Orca* safe and secure!" All the reasons for taking a berth just tumble out of my mouth, I'm so happy. I contact the marina by radio.

"What's the matter?" says Robin, when he sees my face.

"No luck. It's the marina's fun-race weekend in 10 days' time, with over 400 yachts racing from Abel Point to Hamilton Island. The Marina is booked solid. They've promised us a berth during the week following the race."

Resigning ourselves to being at anchor yet again, we decide to move to Airlie Beach where we anchor off the marina next to a crane barge. It certainly is much calmer here.

With all the bad weather in Queensland, I sympathize with the people who have rented yachts for holidays in the Whitsunday area of the Great Barrier Reef. It is incredibly expensive and for weeks there is not a single calm, sunny day. Some nervous charterers never even leave their moorings and I imagine there are quite a few people who will never want to go sailing again.

At Airlie Beach, Rob picks up the weekend newspaper to read what has been happening in the rest of the world. It is August, 1995, and the first time we've bought a paper since leaving Sydney. He idly scans the employment section.

"Hey Mags, a New Zealand company is looking for a power plant engineer to send to the Philippines, to act as a consultant to the Philippines National Oil Corporation on three new geothermal plants being built there."

"Give them a call," I say, "it can't hurt." An injection of cash into the sailing kitty would be most welcome.

Within a week Robin is in the Philippines for four days of interviews. I try to keep things in order on *Orca* and hope that nothing goes wrong.

Robin is invited to start immediately but returns to Australia as we'll need two weeks to prepare for a move to Asia.

The great Australian high moves on and we lose the ridge up the coast with all the strong winds. This ensures that we have two weeks of absolutely stifling heat and no breeze whatsoever in the marina, while we're working to get ready for our trip to the Philippines. We must secure *Orca* in her berth; sort out our personal affairs; prepare the yacht for long term storage; flush all systems with fresh water; remove the impellor; make Sunbrella covers for all our newly varnished windows; and sell the Falcon—our trusted friend and second home for two months while travelling 32,000 kilometres of Australia.

After our seclusion on *Orca*, we strike out at a tangent on yet another adventure, this time to the Philippines and culture shock, living in an apartment among 11 million people in Metro Manila.

Orca waiting in Abel Pt. Marina

23

The Crew from Hell and Delay
Airlie Beach, Queensland

The Philippines comprise an outstanding group of islands; the people are polite and charming, even when packed tightly together in the cities and shanty towns. The smaller islands have a pristine beauty where the inhabitants carry out subsistence farming and fishing. Although there are many local languages and dialects English is the second language, so it has been easy for me living in the heart of downtown Manila. The work world has held many more challenges for Robin, but we both feel privileged to have glimpsed the lives of this Asian culture with values so different from ours.

Robin is eager to get back to *Orca* and continue cruising. I returned once to Australia, to stay with Steve's sister, Sue Humphries and know that *Orca* is in fine condition.

We arrive at Airlie Beach on 21st December, 1996, ready to celebrate Christmas eating fresh oysters from the beach and barbecuing yabbies (crayfish) and prawns. All too soon the party is over and it's time to prepare in earnest for our challenging voyage round the North Pacific rim to Canada. While in Manila, we planned the route minutely and will be travelling via the Solomon Islands, Japan, Korea, Russia, the Aleutians and Alaska.

Summer temperatures in Airlie exceed 30°C with stifling humidity and it takes us several days to acclimatize after the air-conditioned Manila apartment. Frequent heavy showers boost the humidity and leave the decks well-washed and steaming. We throw open the hatches to entice a breeze to enter. Instead of breezes, we get mosquitoes, so I must insert the mosquito-screens I made for all hatch openings, but this further impedes airflow. While anchored offshore we were not troubled with mosquitoes, but now I even have to make a fine net tent to hang above our bunk, for mosquito-free sleeping.

Harvesting oysters

Robin's first job is to install the new Marlin electric windlass. What a difficult task it is, requiring holes to be made in the reinforced cement deck. It also involves lots of suffocating work inside the sail locker, where temperatures are often in excess of 40°C, to mount the dedicated windlass battery and run the power cables. When it's finished it works beautifully, no more hand cranking, just step on the rubber pads set into the deck. To complete the ensemble, we buy new anchor chain—tonnes of it.

Next on the list is a Furuno Radar. This necessitates modifying the mounting platform on the mizzen mast to accommodate a large unit, then running cables through the mast and the deck into the yacht interior and waterproofing all openings. We set the radar screen above the chart table and can see it from outside, by peeping down the companionway.

It takes a lot of searching through catalogues to find the right unit to replace our galley deck-hatch which has cracked. It's frightening that it costs so much for one small hatch, but it is a perfect fit and not too difficult to install. I can do it without supervision.

"If we'd had time to search in RV supply shops, I bet it would have cost half the price." I say.

"No doubt. If anything has the tag 'nautical', the price automatically doubles, like engine parts."

Robin turns his attention to the rigging and buys new heavy-duty turnbuckles and replaces some of the shrouds. Everything has to be meticulously measured and fabricated to specification with the correctly swaged ends.

In preparation for voyaging one of the books we've read is Lin & Larry Pardey's *Storm Tactics*. They describe the use of a parachute anchor, whereby a large parachute is streamed off the bow in severe conditions to keep the head of the vessel into wind, thus reducing the possibility of being broached or pitchpoled by giant waves.

"Considering that we're going into the North Pacific, I think a parachute anchor might be invaluable," I say to Robin and he agrees wholeheartedly. "When sea conditions become too uncomfortable, we can deploy it and ride out a storm safely."

We research the correct size for *Orca* check available sources and order a unit from New Zealand which arrives in two exceedingly heavy, large boxes. It is an 8-metre parachute with a self-deploying bag, massive stainless steel swivels and shackles, and 125 metres of 2.5-cm line. We store the line in a compartment in the chain locker where it will be readily accessible and take the parachute anchor down below.

I have to box up and send away our Avon dinghy to an agent for the seams to be re-glued, as some are leaking. We need everything to be working perfectly for the coming months—nothing left to chance.

"Do you think it would be a good idea to pack some of our treasures and things we won't need on this trip and send them home to Canada?" I ask Robin.

"Not a bad idea. We could probably send our Tongan tandem. I don't suppose we'll be doing much cycling. It will just be a few days in each port so we can get through the Aleutians and Alaska by September." Robin has the route printed in his mind.

It takes a few days in the roasting heat of the cabins to sort and select goods we won't need: books, good linen, cutlery and dishes we've had on board since Cayman. I also send treasures we've picked up along the way: the 3-metre square tapa cloth; carvings and war sticks from Tonga and our black-pearl shells from the Tuamotus.

While we're busily working we are watched carefully by some other boat owners in the berths. Marinas are always good places to meet unusual and colourful characters. Of course they're the colourful ones, not us.

"For Chrissake, stop working and come and have a drink with us," says Brownie, from a vessel called *Big Wheel*. "You're making us feel bloody tired, just watching you."

Big Wheel is a pontoon 'party' boat, especially on Friday afternoons, for all who want to relax with a slab of beer. It doesn't take much to entice us. It's a jolly gathering of unlikely souls with a common theme—relaxing and bending the elbow and we swap wild and unlikely tall stories, each one better than the last until we no longer understand a word they're saying.

It's not long before we'll have finished refitting and leave these shores, so an opportunity to visit Eungella National Park, the oldest subtropical rainforest in Australia, is not to be missed. *Orca* will be safe at Abel Point Marina. Steve and Sue have booked a picturesque cabin in the forest at Broken River Mountain Retreat where we barbecue, picnic, hike and explore. It's the first time I've encountered leeches while walking through the damp underbrush—fortunately on Steve's leg, not mine. Eungella is one of the few places to see the shy, duck-billed platypus, which live in the banks of the stream, right by our cabin.

"How tiny they are!" I say to Sue. "They're no bigger than a kitten."

"Yeah, that's right!"

"But I thought they were much bigger creatures, like medium-sized dogs without legs!"

"Oh Na-ah," she says, "they're just wee things, Mags."

Steve and Sue must return to work. Rob and I decide to stay for another couple of days but even this idea fails. It's raining hard and in the late afternoon the owner knocks at the door.

"If you don't want to be stuck here a week or more you'd better leave now—the road is washing out down the mountain."

It's an exciting ride, racing the water down the hillside and at the bottom driving through a few hundred metres of a 40-cm deep flooded valley.

"It's seeping in though the door!" I tell Robin, whose foot is gently, but firmly, on the accelerator.

"We can't stop now, we have to keep going."

We pass several other vehicles that have come to a soggy standstill.

"Oh my goodness, what's happening!"

I can't keep my feet flat on the floor because the carpet is billowing under them like a big water balloon.

It takes hours to dry out the hired car, even though we keep it an extra day. We even have to extract some tell-tale weed from one of the headlights. It must have been forced there from the bow wave we created, while wading.

"I don't think the car will ever be the same again," I say to Robin, "and I reckon it will smell for weeks."

Robin looks at me sheepishly, grins and shrugs his shoulders.

Our last chore is hauling-out, bottom-cleaning and antifouling. We've booked a slot at the local slipway and are allowed to sleep on board for the few days while we do it and soon *Orca* is back in her berth.

Somewhere along the way we make a really, *really* bad decision. The wife of a colleague manipulates her way into our lives. She wants to cruise for 10 weeks in the South Pacific. We refuse, but give her the possibility of one leg—from Australia to the Solomon Islands. She is really forceful and we are too polite to squash the idea at the outset.

Madelaine convinces us she will be a great sailor and learn fast. She will work hard, is an excellent cook and eats anything; she promises to take her turn with watches and sail trimming and generally make life easier for us. She will be an asset to the ship's complement. Although we're unhappy about it, we feel snared and give in to her persuasive powers, mainly out of respect for her partner. To be honest, we don't believe she will really come.

We both hope she will change her mind—there are many months to go before the trip and anything could happen. Lots of people 'talk' about crewing, but usually that's all it is—talk. A selection of the conversations we've had so far with Madelaine could be entitled: 'What I've done', 'Who I know', 'Where I've been', 'My operation', 'My hobbies', 'My domestic arrangements' and 'My ex-husband'. She's probably already weaving tales in her mind for the benefit of others about, 'My time on *Orca*', 'Sailing the South Pacific' and 'How I was indispensable on *Orca*'.

It's definitely our fault, but I don't think she really has any idea of what life is like on board. She's probably imagining soaking in hot baths every day and lounging around in casual wear waiting for dinner to be served on the poop deck.

I put it out of my mind, certain that we'll receive a polite excuse from her when the time comes. But no. We badly underestimate her. She's determined.

The dreaded day arrives and we collect Madelaine from the bus station. She's been in Australia visiting an aunt. Standing in a broad-brimmed sunhat and carrying big sunglasses (she's just had laser surgery on her eyes), she squints myopically out of habit, looking for us. She runs manicured hands over her crumpled, pink and blue plaid shirt and yellow flowered shorts. Her polished toenails peek from her strappy sandals.

"Aah there you are!" She says, and kisses the air by our ears.

As luggage is unloaded from the bus, she points to two enormous matching brocade cases, then turns and gets into our waiting taxi. Robin looks at me, shrugs and we each pick up a case. The 16-hour bus journey has been tedious for her. She's been forced to sit in a cramped seat next to a man with a strong odour and weak opinions. He hasn't been interested in her stories.

"Isn't it hot!" she says as we board *Orca* and go below to her cabin. "There isn't any air in here."

"There'll be plenty out at sea." Robin tells her.

She settles into the forward berth to unpack, then we show her the workings of the galley and the bathroom. When she's completed her toilet, she says, "What's for lunch?"

"Lamb, fresh green peas, carrots and new potatoes," I tell her. I want to start her off on good wholesome food. Her mouth stretches into a Hollywood smile.

"I must have a green salad every day—and rice is so much nicer than potatoes, don't you think?"

"What the bloody hell does she think this is, a hotel?" Robin whispers to me. It does not auger well. He takes her on a tour of the deck, but she's not really listening. I fit her up with a safety harness and explain its workings.

"And I'd suggest you wear running shoes, or deck shoes, instead of sandals with no support or protection."

Oops! Too late. She trips over a neatly coiled line on deck and is sitting, nursing her foot.

"I've twisted my ankle," she wails.

"Do you need to go to the doctor?" I ask. "We leave the day after tomorrow and customs have already cleared us for departure."

"No. If you could just bandage it, I'll rest."

Madelaine spends the remainder of the day in the shade on deck, with her foot up. She's a little distressed that we won't stop work to keep her company. Robin explains, as if to a child, what it is we are doing and why we have to do it.

"Tomorrow we're provisioning with fresh food and the next day we're leaving," he reminds her. She sighs and continues some touch-up work on her varnished nails.

Steve and Sue meet us at the marina. We've arranged to have a farewell supper together at a local restaurant and they can meet our crew member.

"Are you going to be able to walk there?" Robin asks Madelaine.

"Yes, if you support me," she says with a little sigh.

Holy shit! I say to myself, *What have we let ourselves in for?*

Steve walks ahead, Madelaine leans heavily on Robin's arm, while Sue and I follow behind.

Sue looks at me with a wicked grin and whispers, "She's a bit of a whiner, ain't she Mags?" Then she frowns. "You're not really going to take her are you?"

She has vocalized the misgivings that Robin and I have.

"No." I decide on the spot. "I'd throw her overboard during the first day, sitting around like the Queen of Sheba expecting to be waited on. We'll tell her later this evening that it won't work. We're just not compatible."

We all sink a few beers, while Madelaine regales Steve and Sue with her life story. It's strange; Steve and Sue are usually ready for a party but are yawning freely and leave early. Not the fun farewell together we'd envisaged. Madelaine hobbles back to the marina and we all say goodbye.

Steve takes me by the elbow and mutters, "Good luck Mags. It won't work. She never stops talking for one thing and Robin couldn't handle that."

On board, Robin and I confront Madelaine.

"We can't take you," Robin tells her, "we can't sail with an injured crew, and we must leave in two days to take advantage of the weather window."

"And we have to face it," I add, "we're just not compatible. Life would be much too tough for you on board."

Madelaine dissolves into tears. "But I've come all this way!"

"Yes," I say, feeling resolute at last, "but it's much better to find out now and not when we're on the ocean. Tomorrow we'll arrange a flight home and take you to the airport."

Unhappily it takes two days to get Madelaine a flight. Meanwhile, she's chirping away as if nothing's happened. In fact the day we put her on the plane is the very day we should be leaving Australia. We also have to visit Customs and Immigration in Mackay to delay our departure date and take her off the crew list, but what a relief—now we can rely on each other without the burden of another body.

For weeks since we've been back on board, we've been checking weather faxes and forecasts. The usual strings of lows are now moving across at higher latitudes. In recent history Queensland has not had really adverse weather at this time of year, although, there is always a slight risk until we are north of latitude 5° South. We are not the only ones watching the weather. The largest joint military exercise in history since D-Day has chosen this time of year for its *Operation Tandem Thrust* in Queensland. This US/Australian manoeuvre involving 150 warships, 50 aircraft and 25,000 personnel is under way.

Our Marina dues are paid; we have all our visas and permission documents in place and a multitude of navigation charts. We're stacked with provisions: dried, tinned and fresh, including six dozen fresh, free-range eggs—probably enough food on board to last us for a year. We also have thermal clothes for northern climes and a multitude of gifts for islanders we will meet. *Orca* has never been so well equipped and carries a huge supply of spare parts. Robin and *Orca* are ready to sail home to Canada via North Pacific ports, and best of all? I am looking forward to sailing too.

24
MAYDAY!
Orca Abandoned to the Coral Sea, Australia

Leaving Airlie Beach

In the early morning cool of 4th March, 1997, *Orca* slips quietly from her berth at Able Point Marina. We motor-sail south, inside Australia's aptly named Great Barrier Reef, running North-South, parallel to the Queensland coastline: sixteen hundred kilometres of extraordinarily beautiful coral islands and submerged reefs spreading 60 km from shore. It takes us two days to reach the entrance to the only large outlet through the reef, the tortuous 120-km-long Hydrographer's Passage leading into the Coral Sea. We heave-to and wait so we can exit the passage to coincide with the slackest tide rather than battle the 6-8 knot currents.

Over the SSB, on Nandi Radio, we hear mention of a cyclone over

Fiji. Robin calls Townsville Radio to see if there is anything brewing in the Coral Sea. He is reassured that they have no information on the development of any cyclone. While we are hove-to, a 12-metre diving catamaran returns from the Coral Sea through the passage. Robin calls the vessel on VHF Radio, talks to the skipper and asks about sea conditions. He also has not heard of any cyclonic development, but says that the seas are a bit bumpy. 'A bit bumpy' is not a problem for *Orca*.

At first light on 6th March, we safely exit Hydrographer's Passage and set course for the first of our several waypoints. The autopilot steers. It is still necessary to avoid isolated patches of reef that exist many kilometres out to sea. In the 25-knot SE winds, *Orca* picks up her skirts and flies along—perfect conditions for her.

By evening, the mercury in the barometer is falling steadily.

"It's a bit breezy." Robin says as we change watches. It is an understatement and we both know it. By midnight it is obvious that a serious low-pressure system is approaching. Winds rapidly increase to Gale Force 8 and drive the seas into a churning, heaving mass.

Mounting seas

In the pre-dawn darkness of 7th March, I shiver and shrink into my yellow foul-weather jacket. The rising winds lash steel pellets of rain in my face, plastering my hair to my head, as I cling to the mizzen mast. In the Coral Sea, one hundred kilometres outside Australia's Great Barrier Reef, we're bucking crazily in a frenzy of 4-metre storm-whipped waves.

The yellow beam from my flash lamp slices through the darkness, picking out Robin, not only my husband and mentor, but my best friend for 29 years, as he strains to raise the stiff, heavy storm sail on the main mast. His 1.7-metres is dwarfed by the 20-metre mast, swinging like a metronome as *Orca* rolls and pitches while we struggle to prepare her for the worsening storm.

Orca plunges through the waves, still steered by the autopilot. With the storm sail secure, we climb down the steep companionway steps into the warm mahogany glow of the inner steering station to discard our soaking clothes. Rain trickles down Robin's short, silvering hair and beard and drips onto the chart table as he reaches to tune in the radio.

The 6:00 a.m. weather forecast explodes into our lives like a grenade.

"… a monsoonal low in the Coral sea has deepened to become Tropical Cyclone 'Justin', its centre at latitude 17.5°S, longitude 151.2°E …"

Robin turns towards me, his face ashen. "That's right in our path," he says.

My ears ring, my heart thumps and I fight for breath as I sink onto my pink and green upholstered seat, trembling.

"Oh God," I whisper, "we're trapped."

Images of cyclones race through my mind. *Hurricane-force winds, moving at twice the speed of an express train with seas as high as a 6-storey building.* I fight to control my quavering voice. "We'll never get back inside the reef for protection."

Robin springs to the controls on the port side of the cabin, switches off the autopilot and fires up the engine. Only 100 km out from the Great Barrier Reef, we could easily be blown by the winds, or swept by the currents and dashed onto the coral.

"Steer from outside," he says, "and keep us diagonally across the seas. We've *got* to motor further out to sea, away from the reef."

On the after deck I clench my teeth, brace my legs and use all my weight to wrestle the helm; heaving the wheel this way and that in an attempt to steer *Orca* east across the huge swells to take us further from the reef. My safety harness tether is clipped to the mizzen mast behind me, so I can't be thrown off balance and catapulted into the sea.

"Please be careful," I beg Robin, as he secures his tether to the jack-line and unsteadily moves forward over the deck that alternately rises up to meet him, or falls away from his tread. I don't want to lose him and would never *want* to survive alone on the yacht.

Body crouching, head bent against the driving rain, he grasps the rope safety-line running through the stanchions around the perimeter of the vessel. He cautiously works his way along, checking the security of the rigging and lashing down sails in preparation for the nightmare of a cyclone we can't fully envisage.

Throughout the morning the seas build to 10 metres with crumbling crests as I continue to fight the helm. Occasionally I catch a glimpse of Robin labouring on the foredeck. Miraculously, *Orca* rises, teeters on the peak of each wave and then plummets down the back into the following trough. If I don't keep her bow pointing in the right direction we could easily be rolled over by the breaking peaks—I don't think we could survive that, not in a ferro-cement vessel. My concentration is intense.

At 1:00 p.m. after completing his arduous circuit, Robin yells as he clambers below. "I'll check our position on the GPS."

In moments he bounds back up the companionway steps, wearing a satchel of tools, his brow heavily furrowed.

"We're not moving away from the reef," he shouts, "we're being dragged northwest, deeper into the cyclone!"

Despite our powerful 165hp engine, we are already caught in the spiralling winds, racing at 5 knots towards even stronger winds, circling the calm eye.

"WE'VE GOT TO SET THE PARACHUTE-ANCHOR NOW," he yells above the screeching winds, "TO SLOW US DOWN."

I thrust the engine into idle, leaving *Orca* tossing like a piece of flotsam at the whim of the seas, and mentally run through the steps to set up our new parachute-anchor, our last line of defence in untenable conditions. *Attached to a 125-metre nylon line off the bow, the 8-metre parachute will fill with water creating tremendous drag and should act like an anchor to oppose the great wind forces blowing the yacht, and so slow down our crazy progress into the cyclone.*

"This won't be easy." I say. Hot tears course down my face. I hope they're mistaken for rain.

"We'll be OK." Robin promises. He checks to see that my harness is fastened securely and gives me a bear-hug before dropping to his knees and crawling forward on the see-sawing deck, dragging the 25-kilo parachute assembly between his knees. I follow close behind pulling the flotation buoys we will attach to stop the parachute from sinking.

Exposed on the foredeck near the bow, we are at the mercy of the sea as we kneel to attack our self-preserving task. In all directions waves peak and break; spume flies through the air in long strings. The rain-laden wind screams in our ears making verbal communication impossible. Each time the bow bites deep into a wave we cling to each other and the safety line, holding our breath as tonnes of seawater sluices us to the extent of our tethers against the perimeter safety lines. Each time we laboriously crawl back into position to continue the painstaking assembly of the equipment.

The parachute-anchor line is stored at the bow in the chain locker accessed by a hatch in the deck. I start hauling out a few metres at a time. Robin, spread-eagled on the pitching deck, feeds the line over the bow, under the side-stay of the bow sprit and back onto the deck, ready to shackle it to the stainless steel swivel protruding from the parachute-anchor bag. Each connection has to be meticulously locked with stainless steel wire, using pliers.

Kneeling beside Robin, I clutch his harness in one hand and the jack-line in the other as we wash back and forth, knees bleeding from continually scraping across my new, anti-skid coating of the concrete deck. Hawk-like, I watch his every move. We have only one chance to get it right. With 15 metres of the line pulled out like spaghetti on the foredeck, we force the bagged parachute and its attached flotation buoys under the side stay into the sea.

Almost instantly, the bag pops off, the chute opens and *Orca*'s bow jerks into wind. Metre by metre I haul the rest of the line from the locker and Robin controls it by leaning back with all his weight as it runs out, snaking in a double figure-of-eight round the two 20-cm-tall metal mooring posts set in the deck. Seawater-soaked, the brand-new line stretches and a fine, acrid-tasting chemical mist emanates and blows over us.

"WHAT'S THAT?" I cry, blinking and making an ugly face as it stings my eyes, nose and throat. Robin just squeezes his eyes shut and shakes his head, water flying off his beard.

When all the line is payed out, *Orca* is 'anchored' to the sea's surface. With her bow into wind, her gyrations have reduced to a more tolerable level. But a major problem remains. The nylon line passing over the steel bow roller that usually carries the anchor chain, will constantly rub back and forth as the wind gusts, and wear through within hours. The line is now stretched as tight as a metal rod and we can't slide the chafe guard between the line and the bow roller.

After two exhausting hours, daylight is fading as we despondently drag our battered, soaked bodies back along the deck, climb down into the security of the cabin and bolt the hatches. I fall into Robin's arms, crying with pain and fright.

"My eyes are burning." I sob. I turn to look at the radar screen but can see only a bright green blur. "I can't read the instruments, what's happened to my eyes?" Desperately hoping that Robin is not afflicted, I ask, "What are yours like?"

"They're not good," is all he will admit.

"Please don't turn the engine off," I beg. Having it purring beneath my feet, gives me a feeling of security. I imagine that if the parachute anchor fails, we may at least have some control.

Grabbing the cabin walls for support, I lurch into the bathroom to flush my eyes, but the water makes them sting more. I collapse onto the bunk in our polished mahogany bedroom unable to stem the flow of cathartic tears. If the parachute anchor line wears through now we won't have a chance. We can't read the instruments, so we can only sit by, helpless, waiting for the worst.

Some time later I hear a bang and pull myself off the bunk and peer into the cabin as Robin, wet and bedraggled, is fastening the hatch behind him. He climbs down the companionway steps to join me.

"Where have you been?" I quiz, angry and terrified that he's been outside alone.

"I've shackled a length of anchor chain to the end of the parachute anchor line to take the chafing over the bow roller. Now you won't have to worry about it wearing through."

I feel a rush of love for him. By some Herculean effort he has accomplished what seemed a physical impossibility. Exhausted, he retreats to the bedroom to change into something dry.

As the storm rages through the night we wedge ourselves together on the seat in the inner steering station, close to all the instruments and the chart table; our feet braced against the wood panelling to prevent being flung across the cabin.

"We can't do any more now. Just hope that the cyclone moves on quickly." says Robin, putting his arm round me.

"At least the children don't know what's going on." I reply. "When they hear about this it will all be over, one way or another."

I think bleakly of the reunion we'd planned for when we arrive home. Our family has not been together for six years, since that first Christmas when we were so excited with our new yacht. Lisa and Pete, now married, work on Vancouver Island, not far from our destination and Billy will fly from Halifax, Nova Scotia, with his young wife whom we've never met.

All through the night we resist the forces of gravity and listen to the protestations of the boat. The winds have reached demonic proportions: 60 knots sustained, gusting 80. A macabre orchestra is plucking at the rigging like giant cello strings. At any moment I expect a mast to come crashing down through the cabin roof. Occasionally one of us stumbles forward to read the radar and GPS, but our damaged eyes still will not focus. Increasingly waves break over the yacht and race along the decks, but the parachute-anchor holds firm as *Orca* climbs up the watery mountains and slides down into the steep abysses.

A slight lightening in the cabin shows that we've passed many hours in a trance-like state and the long-awaited day is breaking. Mercifully, the burning sensation under our eyelids is easing although I still can't focus. Robin stands and grasps the sides of the chart table for support, staring hard at the instruments.

"My eyes are getting better, I can just make out the GPS!" he says, and busily transfers the details of our position onto the Coral Sea chart using dividers and pencil. He remains silent.

"What is it?" I urge.

"Well, the parachute-anchor has cut our drag rate from 5 to 2 knots," he says, "but we're heading straight for Malay Reef and it's the only reef for miles around."

I feel the now-familiar surge of adrenaline flooding my bloodstream as my heart hammers and my ears sing. I fight back a wave of nausea.

"The cyclone is sure to start moving through soon and then we'll get a shift in wind direction," Robin reassures me, "don't worry, we'll miss it."

In frustration I scream at the elements, "THIS CAN'T GO ON."

But go on it does. The day takes on a nightmare quality. The constantly screeching wind maintains its strength. As the broken tops of the 13-metre seas crash against our cement hull and swamp the decks, a new problem appears.

Pressure from tonnes of seawater over the deck compresses the hatch seals and litres of saltwater spurt into the cabins each time a wave sweeps across. Our shiny, cork-tiled floor is awash and slick as ice making it treacherous to move, so we fling down towels and start a constant round of exchanging them and ringing out the water.

"We've got to keep the electrics and instruments dry so we can still use the GPS and radios." Robin says.

I find a large polyethylene drop sheet and drape it tent-like over the instrument panels to divert seawater onto the floor. Frequently the electric bilge-pumps kick in, to pump out the water collecting beneath the sole. The seals on the chain locker hatch set in the deck at the bow, must be suffering the same fate and the locker will be filling with water and giving us a heavy, nose-down attitude.

I half-heartedly mention food. We've eaten nothing since supper two days ago, but have no appetite. We force ourselves to drink a box of juice. My last attempt at boiling a kettle resulted in it spilling and scalding my wrist.

Incredibly, the barometer continues to fall. At midday on 8th March, thirty hours into the cyclone, our nerves are strung as tight as piano wire when we tune in to the latest weather forecast.

Last picture

"... Cyclone Justin has intensified ..." the meteorological report is barely audible above the external cacophony, *"... "from Category I to Category II, but has given no indication of movement ..."*

I am numb. If the winds don't change, we will founder on Malay reef in 34 hours. But cyclones *always* move. We must trust that the winds will soon shift and allow us to clear the reef.

Yet Justin's fury continues unabated, repeatedly slamming us with 80-knot gusts. We are tossed about the cabins like rag dolls, collecting bruises as we labour mechanically through a second sleepless night, to keep up with the ingress of water.

It barely grows light on 9th March. At 9:30 a.m. as I stand wedged in the galley wringing out wet towels, I hear a rumbling roar, like a massive landslide, obliterating all other sounds. Something monumental is happening and I know it's not good.

I am hurled across the galley as *Orca* slams onto her port side. I watch in horror as a grey-green waterfall like a huge elephant trunk explodes into the galley, centimetres from my face. The 30 x 13 cm galley port light has gone.

For several seconds the water torrent flows then slows to a dribble, as *Orca* sluggishly rights herself and cold air blows in. I am ankle-deep in water and an icy hand tears at my entrails. *Cement vessels don't float well, full of water.*

"GALLEY!" I scream to Robin who is already leaping down the two stairs from the inside steering cabin. We slither around on hands and knees in the salty water feeling for the window pane which, amazingly, he finds intact. I pull myself to my feet, skid across the floor and jam it back into the splintered wooden frame, leaning on it with all my might as a stream of cool seawater runs down my arms.

My heart is pounding and my throat stings. *What will happen if one of our large windows is smashed in?*

Robin sloshes across the cabin to his tool cupboard and returns with hand-drill, screws and wooden battens to secure the pane in place. A flashing red light on the cabin control panel shows that the electric bilge pumps are working overtime. It takes an hour to complete the temporary repair.

"I've got to go outside," Robin says, heading for the stairs with a heavy waxed-cotton tarpaulin, "to lash this across the window for some protection."

"Please be careful!" I beseech, as he closes the hatch behind him. I wish he didn't have to go on deck alone.

Orca continues dragging towards the reef. The winds have increased to 65 knots, gusting to 90, but we cannot give up hope that the cyclone will start moving.

At 2:30 p.m. *Orca* suffers a second spine-chilling attack. Following a mighty roar, she is bulldozed through the sea and crushed once more onto her port side under hundreds of tonnes of green water. She shudders under the impact then in slow motion majestically rights, pulled upright by her large, heavy keel. Dazed, Robin picks himself up from the floor.

"What have we hit?" he says, expecting the worst as he pitches forward to look out of a porthole.

"I don't think we've hit anything," I say, "I think it was a rogue wave that hit us."

We ricochet from cabin to cabin in our haste to check the hull for leaks below the waterline, but it is intact. Back in the cabin Robin looks out along the deck and realization dawns.

"Oh God," he says, "I can see right across the deck, the dorades have all been sliced clean off!"

We stumble again to the forward cabins and this time look upwards. Water from the last wave is funnelling in through eight 8-cm holes in the deck where the dorade air-vents had been. I feel sick.

"Quick," says Robin taking command, "get wooden bungs and some sailcloth, I'll hammer them into the holes from outside."

He buckles on his safety harness and slides the companionway hatch back just enough to reach out to secure his safety line before squeezing through. I thrust the equipment at him then turn and stand on the companionway steps, with just my head poking out, to watch him. I'm not letting him out of my sight now. With bowed head he claws his way forward to the holes, then turns and faces me as he works.

I stare beyond him at the grey, horizon-less scene fearful of another giant wave. Something is wrong. The stanchion safety line is slack and a couple of stanchions dangle uselessly. Although Robin's harness is clipped to the jack-line, he often braces himself against a stanchion when the boat rolls. I gesticulate wildly to gain his attention and will him to look up.

"STANCHIONS GONE—NO SAFETY LINES."

He can't possibly hear me—he is 7 metres upwind but he glances up, immediately understands and nods.

At 3:00 p.m., once more in the womb-like security of the cabin, we no longer feel the bruises as we are flung against the interior of the vessel. We look around and take stock. The last repairs will be no match for the forces of the sea and at any time a large port light could be punched in. The barometer is still falling and reads 968 millibars as we approach the severest weather circling the cyclone's calm eye. We are taking on water in a cement vessel. For 53 wretched hours we have been dragged unswervingly towards isolated Malay Reef. At this rate it will only be 8 more hours before we founder. We have to accept that Cyclone Justin is not moving and we possibly won't make it.

Frowning heavily, Robin reaches for the microphone to call Townsville Radio, the closest Queensland Marine Radio station. "We should update them on our latest position and the weather conditions. If we don't come through this they can inform the children."

His thumb closes on the transmit button.

"Is this a life-threatening situation?" quizzes the radio operator after he has taken our details. We no longer struggle with denial. I look at Robin and nod.

"Yes," Robin admits, "this is a life-threatening situation."

It is surreal. At 3:10 p.m. on 9th March we listen while Townsville Radio broadcasts our personal distress to the shipping community on VHF Channel 16.

"*MAYDAY, MAYDAY, MAYDAY. All ships, all ships, all ships, we have a MAYDAY situation. A sailing ship is breaking up at 18°09'S, 149°22'E. Any vessel in the area call with your location and intentions. All other ships keep clear of this channel until further notice. Repeat, there is a MAYDAY in progress.*"

"I'm sorry," Robin's voice is husky and quivers as he reaches towards me huddled on the companionway steps.

"It's not your fault." I move into his arms. "We went into this together. We'll just keep working until we can do no more—we may still get a wind change."

The unmistakable smell of electrical burning reaches us both at the same time.

"Oh no, the electrics!" Robin says, snapping open breakers on the electrical panel. He pulls his multimeter from a drawer and starts testing circuits. Salt water has seeped into one of the light sockets and shorted the lighting system. Tonight we will be reduced to flash lamps. The last thing we need is a fire on board—the ultimate dilemma.

Orca's radio sparks into life at 4:30 p.m. We both lean close to listen.

"S/V *Orca*, this is MRCC (Maritime Rescue Coordination Centre) Canberra, we are coordinating a rescue attempt. Do you have an EPIRB emergency beacon and flares on board?"

Unbelievable! Are they really going to try to reach us? I dare not allow myself too much hope.

"Affirmative." Robin's steady voice replies. "Over."

"Good. Activate your EPIRB. Tie it to the vessel and drop it in the water. Stand by for further instructions. Over."

Robin is swallowed by the storm as he ventures on deck to release the emergency beacon from its clip outside the companionway. I peer through the stern porthole, watching as he ties it to a line and drops it overboard. It bobs up to the surface, a bright reassuring strobe-light flashing before it disappears in the churning foam.

Back inside *Orca*'s cabin the radio crackles again. It is 4:50 p.m.

"S/V *Orca* this is MRCC Canberra." We strain to catch every word of the message. "A US Navy Hercules has been diverted to locate your position for the Queensland Rescue helicopter which is 50 minutes away from your location. Both pilots will contact you on VHF Channel 16. Stand by the radio at all times, over."

Things are happening fast.

"I can't believe it," Robin says, "a US Navy Hercules?"

So this is really it? 50 minutes to sort through six years with Orca and say farewell. My pulse is racing. Abandoning wringing out wet towels and with my head buzzing, I jump down into the stern stateroom. *Think! Think! What should I be doing at a time like this?*

It feels inappropriately like packing for a short holiday ashore. Incongruously, I first pull out a clean, dry set of clothes for us and lay them alongside our survival suits. Next, I collect the waterproof package containing boat papers, passports, credit cards and legal documents, always ready to hand, and stuff it into my black backpack.

I open cupboard after cupboard and feel the warm clothes and new gear we bought specially for the voyage round the North Pacific rim. I leave them spilling onto the bunk—no point in folding and stowing them now. Books, photos and treasures, will all have to be left behind.

One item, however, I am desperate to save—my new laptop computer. I pull it carefully from its secure stowage area, zipped in its carrying case, and treble-wrap it in new garbage bags twisting the neck of each bag securely, then put it into the back pack. I grab our new camera, the hand-held GPS and finally put in my small jewel box containing the black pearl Robin earned for mending the generator on the tiny atoll of Ahé. I ram it all in. Six years of our lives reduced to a backpack.

I change into my clean clothes; bright yellow survival suit and safety harness and pull on my backpack. I am ready. We sit holding hands for a few moments in the dark cabin trying to cope with the enormity of what is happening.

If we abandon Orca, we will no longer have any claim on her. If someone finds her, they will have salvage rights. Everything we've worked for over the past few years will disappear the second we leave the hull. We have no insurance to claim. It was impossible to insure a ferro-cement vessel for ocean voyaging, only coastal work. Sometimes abandoned vessels have been found intact weeks later, should we hang on and hope for the best? No, we're taking on water. Perhaps the helicopter won't find us in time. Perhaps the rescue won't be successful.

At 5:30 p.m. MRCC Canberra makes its final call to update us. "The Hercules should be in your area now, can you hear an aircraft?"

My mind is jerked from its turmoil into the present.

"That's funny!" I say, with a wry smile. We can hear the wind shrieking though the rigging; rain and spray cracking like pebbles thrown on the windows, and the roar and crash of giant seas, but an aircraft? No.

"I'll go and look for the Hercules," I tell Robin as I clamber up the companionway steps, glad to be doing something active. "You stand by the radios." I open the hatch just wide enough to squeeze my arm through and secure my lifeline. This is not the time to be washed overboard. I climb out in my cumbersome survival suit and slam the hatch shut.

I am on deck for the first time in 50 hours. It is a different world.

Hugging the mizzen mast I clung to three days ago, I look around as *Orca* thrashes from side to side and jerks up and down in her frantic dance. White-topped waves like tower buildings rumble in different directions. Long trailing tendrils of spume stream through the air like foaming spider webs. Mesmerized, I stare at the source of the two damaging waves. *Please don't let us have another one now.*

At 5:35 p.m. the Hercules briefly appears through the black racing clouds. One massive wing seems to trail in the water, the other dragging through the clouds. I wave wildly, watching the plane buffeted by severe gusts.

"IT'S HERE—IT'S FOUND US!" I scream, tumbling back down the companionway steps into the cabin. As I wipe the water from my face, the calm reassuring voice of the American pilot calls on the radio.

"S/V *Orca*, this is Captain Spratt in US Navy Hercules *Nalo 817*. We have had a brief sighting of you and marked your position for the rescue helicopter. It should be here in 30 minutes. We will stay in the area as long as necessary. Over."

We are later to find out that the pilot's calm voice belied his feelings. After reporting visual contact to the rescue helicopter, he prepared his crew to lower the ramp door. He did not expect a successful rescue and lingered in the area so he could make one final pass over the stricken yacht in near darkness, to throw out anything that could possibly make life more tenable for the short time left to the souls below. "*God Bless them,*" he said to his men.

Ten minutes later an Australian voice breaks through on the radio.

"S/V Orca. This is Captain Hope in Queensland Emergency Service Helicopter **Rescue 521.** *LISTEN CAREFULLY. We are twenty minutes away from your position. I am flying at the extreme limit of my range and very low on fuel. We will have only twenty minutes to attempt a rescue before heading home. Can you dismast so I can lower a man on deck? Over."*

An image of our 20- and 13-metre masts whipsawing through the air flashes through my mind as Robin replies, "Negative, it will be impossible to effect a controlled dismast in these conditions. Over."

"OK, then you must abandon the vessel and we'll pick you up from the sea. Do you have a dinghy on board?"

"Affirmative."

A moment of silence, then the pilot's voice returns.

"Follow these instructions EXACTLY. Prepare the dinghy for launching off the stern. Attach it to the boat by a line of at least 15-metres. Retrieve your EPIRB and STRAP IT TO YOU. Bring only what you can stuff into your pockets. There's no room for luggage. DO NOTHING MORE until I call you. I must first approach to assess if I can hover. Stand by the radio. Over."

"Message understood: standing by. Over." Robin replaces the microphone and pokes his head out of the companionway hatch. Miraculously, the 3-metre roll-up inflatable dinghy is still lashed to the cabin roof. He attaches his safety line and eases out of the opening to crawl forward and retrieve our vital means of escape. Waiting below, I start when I hear a voice on the radio and pick up the microphone with trembling hands.

"What is your current position?" the helicopter pilot calls on Channel 16. His reassuring voice is clear. I force myself to take a deep breath and read off the co-ordinates from the GPS in a quivering voice that seems to belong to someone else. I replace the microphone in its clip, then turn to peer out through the stern porthole.

Robin crawls into view dragging the rolled up dinghy between his knees, his T-shirt and shorts clinging to his drenched body. He re-fastens his safety tether and ties the dinghy to the mast before unrolling it along the after deck. He pulls the foot pump from its bag and stuffs the inflation tube into the valve.

As *Orca* rolls from side to side, Robin hangs on to the mast with one hand to keep his balance on the pitching surface and stamps up and down on the foot pump. Finally he lashes down the inflated dinghy to prevent it becoming an airborne dirigible. He leaps down the companionway steps, his chest heaving as he strips off his soaking clothes and takes my proffered dry towel.

"Will you man the radios now?" I plead. "And get into your gear, I'll go and pull in the EPIRB." I am already halfway up the steps, still wearing my back pack. *It's fairly small and I'm not very heavy. Perhaps together we make the weight of one person?* I leave Robin at 6:02 p.m. as he waits for final instructions from the helicopter. I never again see the inside of *Orca*.

Clipped once more to the jack-line I kneel, wedging myself between a stanchion and the companionway. Hand over hand I haul in the wet line and swing the oblong, one-kilogram brick-shaped EPIRB on board and secure it to the front of my harness with many un-nautical knots. Feeling calmer, I stand with my back to the driving rain, as the relentless wind whips my collar in my face. I scan the dirty, ragged skies for the helicopter, every few moments peering down at Robin dressing in his bulky bright orange survival suit waiting for instructions.

A pinprick of light appears in the sky astern and grows steadily larger. My heart sings as the helicopter materializes out of the clouds. I spring to the extent of my tether and scream down the companionway, "ROBIN, ROBIN, THE HELICOPTER'S HERE!"

I turn to watch the helicopter rising and falling, attempting to hover. A smoke flare streaks down into the water behind us to give the crew a visual indication of wind direction.

The last radio message ever heard on *Orca* barks out loud and clear at 6:06 p.m.

"S/V ORCA GO! LAUNCH THE DINGHY AND GET IN NOW!"

Like a greyhound from a trap, Robin springs from the companionway to join me on deck. Together we wrestle to untie the fat, wilful, inflated dinghy and force it through the narrow stern opening in the handrail. It sticks fast. We pummel and push with monumental effort until it finally pops out like a champagne cork and lands upright on the water.

Robin hangs on to the tether line to snug the dinghy against *Orca*'s stern. I jump down 1.5 metres and clip my safety harness to a rope handle, stand, then try to hold the dinghy against *Orca*'s stern for Robin to drop in, but it is impossible. The violent pitching motion rips my hands free.

Adrenaline lends wings to Robin's heels. Immediately he releases the line, he makes an Olympic leap as the dinghy races astern. Somersaulting, he lands inside on his back. In seconds the 15-metre tether pulls up tight with a massive jerk and Robin, unattached, flips sideways into the sea.

"NOOOOH!" I scream. *After all we've been through together he can't be lost now.* He bobs to the surface, buoyed up by his thermal suit, his outstretched hand in the air. Hanging over the side, I reach and grab his jacket and fumble in the water to find his harness tether. He must be stunned, he's not reacting. "Clip on," I shout, "you can't just hang there."

The rescue paramedic drops from the helicopter on a steel cable and plummets into the sea only 3 metres from the dinghy. With massive determination, he lunges forward to the body in the water, throws the rescue strop over Robin's submerging head and drags his arms through. Robin's eyes open wide and his mouth gapes in abject horror.

Crouching low in the dinghy, watching his anguish, I know exactly what he is thinking.

What are they doing? They can't take me first and leave Maggi down here.

"IT'S ALL RIGHT. I'LL BE FINE. I LOVE YOU!" I shout, but my words are lost to the screaming winds. In seconds, with arms and legs entwined, the rescuer and Robin rise, like the phoenix from the ashes, and soar skyward in the gathering darkness. I hold both sides of the dinghy and lean my head back, straining to see upwards through the lashing rain and gloom.

I don't notice the avalanche roaring down behind me. Over and over the dinghy flips, dragging me under, through the churning salt water. *Don't panic.* Ignoring the pounding in my ears and my aching chest, I concentrate hard on what I was taught when I first learned to swim, just a few years ago. *Don't breathe in when your head's under water.*

I seem to be watching myself from afar. *Am I drowning? NO! I promised Robin I'd be all right. I won't let him down.*

An eternity passes before I feel wind on my face. I heave in lungs full of air and salt water, coughing and retching as I kick myself upright, gripping the handle of the capsized dinghy. *I'm alive! I'm all right!*

My safety tether is still attached and the flashing EPIRB is floating beside me. I lay back gasping, feeling strangely calm. I idly watch my jacket cuff abrading the skin from my scalded wrist. There's no pain. Squinting into the sky, I can just see the skids of the helicopter and can make out a dark blob descending again. Like a human pendulum the rescue man is swinging and twirling on the winch wire. *I knew he'd come back for me!*

He drops into the sea 10 metres away and disappears from view on the other side of a wave. After spinning on the wire, it's amazing he knows in which direction to swim. He must be catching glimpses of *Orca*. Occasionally his head or arm is visible as he claws his way through the turbulent water, dragging the restraining winch line. He is approaching the far side of the upturned dinghy. To save time, I unclip my harness and haul myself round the dinghy. *Here I am!*

I reach out to grab him. But my hands don't close on his wet-suited body. His arms fly into the air and he disappears backwards. *What's the matter? I don't understand. Why isn't he taking me?* He has been hauled backwards by his winch wire and stupidly, I've unclipped myself from the dinghy.

My mind shuts down, unable to cope with the concept that I'm free-floating in a cyclone, in near darkness in the Coral Sea.

Shortly, something grabs my shoulder with a vice-like grip and abruptly snaps my mind into the present. *He's back!*

He drags the rescue strop over my head and pulls my arms through, hugging me with one arm and raising his other arm with a 'thumbs-up' to the winchman 30 metres above in the hovering helicopter. Nothing happens, then a crashing wave rolls us together in the foam. We struggle to right ourselves. *Why is it taking so long to winch us up?*

Suddenly we are ripping through the water before breaking free and flying into the air as the helicopter takes off vertically, snatching us from further danger. The wind is whistling in my ears as we twirl round and round and round. *I'm free!*

My exhilarating ride lasts only a few moments. My head bangs on a skid then hands drag me inside the belly of the craft, remove my back pack and lay me on the floor. The rescuer is hauled in behind me and the helicopter is already moving off before the side door is closed.

"Say goodbye to *Orca*," someone says and I raise my head. Through the open side of the helicopter I catch a glimpse of her mast light describing twinkling arks beneath us, her white hull just visible in the gloom as she thrashes wildly on the end of the parachute anchor, like an animal caught by the neck in a snare.

We gain altitude, already en route for Townsville as the winch-man pulls in the hoist and secures the sliding door. He then deactivates the EPIRB—denoting the official end of the Mayday.

Dripping puddles, I am strapped behind the pilot in a low-slung canvas seat next to Robin. He looks at me, squeezes my hands and beams. We are together and safe. Nothing else matters.

Already wearing a headset, he waits while mine is secured. Without it, communication is impossible above the whirring of the rotor, the whine of the engine and the howling, buffeting winds.

As the two crewmen finally settle themselves the pilot's voice is clearly heard through the headset.

"Townsville Control, Townsville Control, Townsville Control. This is *Rescue 521*. We are departing the sinking vessel at position 18°07'S, 149°19'E. We are very low on fuel and request a straight-in instrument approach. Please amend our flight plan to reflect we have *five* persons on board, repeat, *five* POB."

"We're safe Mags," Robin says, "these guys are incredible!"

Robin and the crew are chatting via the headphones. I can hear them somewhere on the periphery of my world. It seems to be raining inside the helicopter, leaking onto the pilot's control console. He's covering it with polythene, just like we did on *Orca*.

Overwhelming relief surges through me. Punch drunk, bedraggled and waterlogged, I'm glowing from an inner fire. Grinning from ear to ear I try to juggle a fresh fluffy white towel, a bottle of water and a Cadbury's *Time Out* chocolate bar—first food for three days, and oh, how rich!

It's so good to be alive!

Cyclone Justin

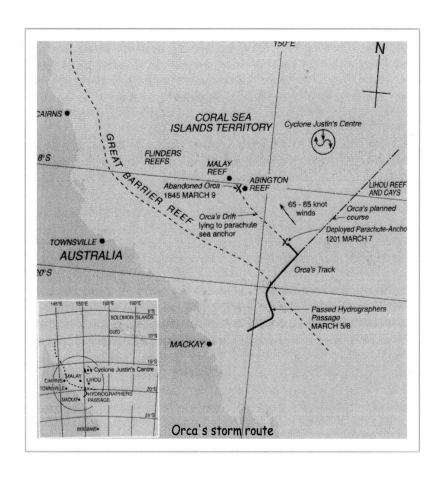

Orca's storm route

25
Survival

Photo: Townsville Bulletin

The rescue paramedic helps us down from the dark interior of the helicopter into a blinding array of flashlights. The media have arrived in force but are not allowed access to us yet. We are first offered a medical check-up at the local hospital but decline, not wishing to further inconvenience anyone.

Still wet, we are ushered into a small room to be interviewed by an unsmiling female Customs and Immigration Officer. We feel like illegal immigrants. I have not been reprimanded by the helicopter crew for carrying my knapsack and am so glad we have it, containing our passports. Fortunately for us, there are a few days remaining on our Australian visas.

Photo: Townsville Bulletin

The media are hungry for interviews and we comply as best we can in our shocked state, giving the Queensland Rescue Services its well-deserved publicity. It is a bizarre sensation, feeling alternately depressed and euphoric. At last the questioning ordeal is over and we are released.

A kind, elderly gentleman has been patiently waiting to meet us. He's the local Red Cross representative, his arms full of clothes in various sizes so we can change into something dry.

"I had no idea whether you were huge or little!" he laughs. It is a supremely considerate gesture on the part of the Red Cross.

How dashing we look in our new clothes! I'm wearing a dress with exotic floral designs and Robin has an Hawaiian-type shirt and beige polyester pants. We both have flip-flops.

"What do you think?" I ask Robin, as I twirl around.

"Cute." he says, "and me?"

"Dashing!"

When we arrive at the Travelodge in Townsville it is too late to order a meal so we have sandwiches and a beer delivered to our room. Apart from the wonderful chocolate bar in the helicopter, it's the first solid food we've eaten for days.

We discover that Robin's brother, Paul, was the first person to know of our ordeal. As soon as the 406 EPIRB was activated by

Robin throwing it into the water, the first satellite passing overhead picked up our pre-registered information and relayed it to a ground station which in turn relayed it to the EPIRB centre in Maryland, USA. Each successive pass by a satellite gave details of our longitude and latitude. Paul, our registered next of kin, was immediately telephoned in the UK, to verify our location to eliminate the possibility of a false alarm.

The Canadian High Commission calls us, offers regrets at the loss of Orca and tells us they have notified our son, Billy, who is serving as helicopter crew on a frigate off Puerto Rico. We speak to him during the evening and assure him we are OK and he doesn't need to fly to our aid. We call Lisa, our daughter, as soon as possible from the hotel, to report the news before she hears it via the media. Everyone is in shock.

The equipment in my backpack which has been submerged for some time in the ocean has fared remarkably well. The computer, the camera and the hand-held GPS all fire up. The garbage bags I used for the wrapping have done sterling work.

All through the night messages of support and requests for interviews arrive. Not only from newspapers, radio and TV stations in Australia, but also Canadian papers and radio stations. Several of today's familiar CBC names appear on the notes pushed under our door: Kathryn Gretzinger, Judy Madrin and Don Genova. Robin speaks to a few people, but we are exhausted and need to sleep. The Toronto Sun places our story on the front page; the Toronto Star, on the front and back page.

On 10th March, 1997 we wake somewhat refreshed, order breakfast in our room and attempt to sort and respond to the dozens of notes that have accumulated during the night. There are even calls from total strangers, offering us accommodation. Later, our rescue paramedic, Angus McDonell, gives us some cash and takes us to buy clothes and then on to the Townsville Water Police where we fill out incident reports.

The next day, Ian Callaghan gives us a guided tour of Townsville, before our flight to Canada. Everyone is sympathetic, attentive and considerate and we are overwhelmed at people's generosity of spirit.

A few days later, back in Canada, we are contacted by more people. Although we are getting tired of talking about it, Robin is happy to give an interview to Rafe Mair and we are pleased to give

Victor Shane details for his Drag Device Data Base—a book of case histories of boats coping with untenable situations at sea.

~~~~~

Many sailors are superstitions, although we are not. A frequent comment has been that we should not have re-named the boat. Perhaps the superstitious believe we got our just deserts—it's certainly ironic that *Orca*'s original name was *The Tempest*!

~~~~~

We believe our survival was attributable to several things. It is impossible to say, of course, how grateful we are for emergency rescue services. When the Mayday was received by the Queensland Emergency Service, Captain Peter Hope, the Pilot, swiftly made calculations then the crew, jointly, decided to attempt a rescue. The interior of the helicopter was stripped of all non-essential items to reduce weight. Long-range fuel tanks were fitted to give them sufficient fuel to reach the site, allow 21 minutes for the rescue and return to base before fuel ran out.

We were also extremely fortunate that American Navy Hercules Pilot, Lt. Cdr. Robert Spratt and his crew heard the distress call and volunteered to fly into the cyclone, to pinpoint our location for the helicopter, to save precious time.

Being properly equipped with a correctly-registered 406 EPIRB was essential. Also, having the vessel in good condition with strong rigging so we were not dismasted, which would have meant the loss of aerials and radios; having a good-sized parachute anchor and installing it properly and using the chain for chafe protection, and also maintaining the electrics and electronics on board, allowing communication with land and aircraft. All increased the chances of a successful outcome.

Finally, according to the helicopter crew, responding exactly as told during the rescue and not panicking, so it could be completed within the 21 minutes' allowable time, with one minute to spare.

Two of our rescue crew are devout Christians. I believe their faith in the prayers of their families and friends during the dangerous and seemingly impossible mission gave them the strength and courage to act so positively.

People have questioned why Robin was air-lifted first. As Captain Peter Hope said in an interview, "There's no room for chivalry in rescue. The priority of any rescue is to take the first body in the water, not to interview each potential victim to see who qualifies to be rescued first." Robin was free-floating when the down-the-wire rescue paramedic dropped into the sea, so naturally he was secured first. I was attached to the dinghy and had the EPIRB. I was calm and knew he'd return for me.

A rescue of this sort involved not only the helicopter and Hercules crews, but also masses of other people and agencies including: Townsville Radio; Maritime Rescue Coordination Centre, Canberra; Flying Doctor Service, flying above the cyclone at 17,000 ft with life rafts; Australian Army Black Hawk Helicopter on standby; Australian Navy Warship on standby; EPIRB Centre, Maryland, USA, and many, many nameless volunteers and workers in the background. For this we feel very humble and grateful.

On our return to Canada, we stayed with our daughter Lisa and son-in-law Pete, who then worked at Campbell River, BC. Subsequently we spent several weeks staying with different friends and family members, while we tried to sort out the direction of our lives. This experience did impact our lives. Instead of seeking more high-powered jobs, we chose a simple, healthy lifestyle, running a small farm on Vancouver Island, B.C. We'd always thought of doing that when we retired—it just came a bit earlier than expected.

We haven't abandoned dreams of cruising. The Inside Passage between Vancouver Island and the mainland of BC is next on our agenda—in a *smaller* yacht. Who knows, maybe one day!

~~~~~

Epilogue

During 53 hours on the parachute-anchor, *Orca* was dragged 165 km and abandoned 16 km from Malay Reef. For several days she was broadcast as a potential drifting hazard to shipping. No trace of her has ever been found.

US Navy Lt. Cdr. Robert (Jack) Spratt and his crew, who flew the Hercules aircraft into the cyclone to locate *Orca* for the rescue helicopter, were decorated by the US Navy for their *Outstanding aeronautical skill and professionalism—in keeping with the highest tradition of the US Navy.*

Queensland Emergency Services Senior Pilot, Peter Hope, skilfully piloted the rescue helicopter into the cyclone and hovered above 15-metre seas. It was the first time Rescue Paramedic, Angus McDonell, had made a sea-to-helicopter rescue, having recently finished his down-the-wire training. Aircrew Officer/Winchman, Ian Callaghan, was a veteran at air-sea rescues. They unselfishly carried out their exacting tasks—an example of perfect teamwork.

Rescue Paramedic
Angus McDonell

Pilot
Peter Hope

Winchman
Ian Callaghan

Golden Hour Award

For their bravery they received commendations from the Australian Government and bravery awards endorsed by Her Majesty, Queen Elizabeth II.

In February, 1998, in California, the crew were awarded Helicopter Association International's *Salute to Excellence, Golden Hour Award*, for the most outstanding helicopter rescue of its kind world-wide, during 1997. We were invited to attend the gala occasion in Anaheim and were reunited with the rescue crew.

Reunion with rescuers

In June, 1998, they received Heroism Awards from *Rotor & Wing, Aeronautical Magazine* in Washington, DC.

~~~~~

Tragically, In 2003 in a freak accident, Senior Pilot Peter Hope was killed when his helicopter overturned on take off as he was conducting a check-ride for another pilot at the controls.

~~~~~

It is possible for anyone to underestimate the potential for harm, no matter how many considerations are taken into account. Cyclone Justin also caused the mass evacuation of 150 aircraft, 50 warships and 25,000 personnel from the Queensland coast: participants in the largest combined military exercise since D-Day, US/Australian *Operation Tandem Thrust*, under the leadership of Brigadier Ian Bryant of the Australian Defence Force.

It was the largest cyclone in 20 years—500 nautical miles (1000 km) across, and remained stalled off the Queensland coast for an unprecedented 15 days before moving ashore and hitting Townsville and Cairns on 22nd March, causing millions of dollars worth of damage. On 10th March, the day after our rescue, a small trading vessel was lost off the coast of Papua New Guinea with all crew. On 18th March a Mayday was received from a 14-metre schooner *Queen Charlotte*. Despite extensive searching only debris, life jackets and a life raft were found. Five crew members perished.

~~~~~

Example of how a parachute anchor works   Photo: Para-Tech Engineering Co

Glossary

Anemometer	A gauge for measuring wind speed
Antifoul	To paint with cuprous oxide paint to reduce the rate of marine growth
Arrete	A sharp-crested ridge in rugged, usually volcanic, mountains
Astern	Behind the vessel
Autopilot	An electronic or mechanical steering device
Back	A change of wind in a counter-clockwise direction
Backstay	A wire support leading aft to the deck from the top of a mast to prevent it bending forward
Baggy wrinkles	Tassels of unravelled line that are lashed around chafe spots to minimize chafing on sails
Barnacle	Saltwater mollusc that attaches to vessel's bottom
Batten down	Close and secure all vessel's openings for a storm
Beam reach	A point of sailing with the wind directly off the beam
Beaufort scale	An international scale of wind speed from 0 (calm air) to 12 (hurricane [cyclone])
Becalmed	No forward motion from lack of wind
Bilge	The rounded, lower part of a vessel's hull. The space in a boat beneath the cabin floorboards
Bitt	A cleat or object around which a rope is wound
Boat hook	A pole with a hook on the end
Bollard	A strong post on a dock for holding fast a mooring line
Bomb	A rapid reduction in atmospheric pressure resulting in sudden storm-force conditions
Boom	A spar used to extend the foot of a fore-and-aft sail
Bosun's chair	Canvas or wood seat attached to a halyard to raise and lower a person working on the mast

Bow wave	Standing wave created by the bow passing through the water
Bowsprit	A spar projecting forward from the bow to which the foremost sail (jib) is attached
Brightwork	Varnished woodwork or polished metal
Broach	To slam over violently toward the wind and lose steering, a 'knock down'
Broad reach	A point of sailing with the wind abaft the beam but not so far astern as to make the vessel run before the wind
Bulkhead	A vertical structural wall within the hull of a vessel
Bullet	A dangerous, high-speed blast of descending air usually encountered near mountainous shorelines
Buoyancy compensator	An inflatable device worn to control diver's buoyancy
Carabiner	A clip, sometimes lockable, for connecting a line to a fastening point
Celestial Navigation	Position determined by an observation of the sun, moon, stars and planets
Chafe guard	Material used to protect lines from wear and chafe
Cockpit	The deck area, usually towards the stern, where the helm is located
Companionway	Passage to below-decks area of vessel
Coordinates	Latitude and longitude position of a vessel
Crow's nest	A partly enclosed platform high on a vessel's mast for use as a lookout
Cyclone	Rapid inward circulation of air masses about a low-pressure centre, circling clockwise in the southern hemisphere, with heavy rain and winds moving at 73-136 knots (12 on the Beaufort scale)
Deadhead	A water-soaked floating log at or beneath the surface of the water
Dismast	To remove or destroy the mast of a vessel
Dog house	Covering that serves as a shelter for the helm
Draft	The depth of the boat below the waterline
EPIRB	Emergency Position Indicating Radio Beacon

Fast cat	High speed catamaran
Fender	Inflatable device hung over vessel's side to protect it during docking
Flake	To lay back and forth in an orderly manner
Forestay	Wire running from the top of the mast to the end of the bowsprit to which the jib is fastened
Furl	To wrap a sail around a furling spar
Genoa	Large foresail with clew abaft the main mast
Gordian knot	An intricate knot with no apparent ends
GPS	Global Positioning System. A system for navigating using satellite signals to fix a position
Gunny sack	A sack made of a coarse heavy fabric (canvas or burlap)
Gunwale	The upper edge of a vessel's side
Gypsy (windlass)	A drum or pulley with specially-shaped notches used for hauling up an anchor chain
Halyard	Rope used for hoisting a sail or flag
Ham	Amateur radio operator
Ham shack	Den of amateur radio operator
Harness	Webbing straps fitting over shoulders and round waist or around waist and thighs for securing crew
Haul out	Take vessel out of water for maintenance
Heave-to	To stop forward movement by hauling in sail and heading into wind
Heel, heeling over	To tilt to one side from wind forces on the sails
Hove-to	Lying head-to-wind with backed sails—stopped
Hurricane	Rapid inward circulation of air masses about a low-pressure centre, circling counter-clockwise in the northern hemisphere, with heavy rain and winds moving at 73-136 knots (12 on the Beaufort scale)
Jack-line	Line that runs along the deck between bow and stern used to attach a safety harness tether
Jib	A foresail that does not extend behind the main mast
Jibe (gybe)	To turn a vessel through wind, the wind coming from astern throughout the manoeuvre

Keel	The bottom of a vessel supporting the frame
Ketch	A sailing vessel with two masts, the main towards the bow, the shorter mizzen towards the stern, forward of the rudder post
Knot	A unit of speed of one nautical mile per hour (approximately two kilometres per hour)
Lazarette	Storage space in a cockpit—often forming seating area
Leeward	Toward the lee side: away from the wind
Lighter	A large, usually flat-bottomed barge used especially in unloading or loading vessels at anchor
Line	A rope, e.g. dock line
Log	A device for determining the speed and distance covered by a vessel: an official 'diary' of vessel activities
Mainsail	In a ketch, the larger sail set on the main mast
Mayday (m'aidez)	Verbal distress call equivalent to S.O.S. in Morse Code
Mizzen mast	In a ketch, the mast closest to the stern
Mooring bitt	Deck posts around which ropes or cables are wound and held fast
Motoring Cone	An upside-down cone raised to indicate a sailing vessel is proceeding under power
Motu	Polynesian small island
Nautical mile (mile)	A nautical mile is based on the circumference of the Earth. If you were to cut the Earth in half at the equator, you could pick up one of the halves and look at the equator as a circle. Divide that circle into 360 degrees. Then divide a degree into 60 minutes. A minute of arc on the planet Earth is 1 nautical mile. This measurement is used by all nations for air and sea travel.
No-nos	See sand fleas
Outrigger	A wooden frame rigged from the side of a canoe to prevent tipping
Pandanus	Leaves from the pandanus tree used for weaving anything from baskets to roofs

Pan-pan	An urgent message concerning the safety of a vessel, aircraft or other vehicle, or persons on board who require immediate assistance. Thus, Pan-pan indicates urgency whereas Mayday indicates distress
Pareu	Colourful material used as wraparound skirt for men and women
Pay out	To ease out a line
Pilot	Person who directs or steers a vessel in or out of harbour or designated waterway
Pitchpole	To flip a vessel end over end
Port	The left-hand side of a vessel, when facing forward
Port light	An opening in the hull or cabin of a vessel with a fixed, translucent pane
Porthole	An opening in the hull or cabin of a vessel which may be openable. It can be opaque or translucent
Pulpit	Rail around bowsprit platform to protect sailor from falling overboard
Q flag	Yellow quarantine flag displayed to indicate a vessel is newly arrived from a foreign port and requires health, customs and immigration clearance
Raft, raft up	To tie up alongside another vessel
Reef	To reduce sail area. A ridge of rock or coral at or near the surface of the water
Reefing points	Points where short lines are attached as the means of tying down a reefed (shortened) sail to the boom
Rigging	The system of masts, stays and shrouds on a sailing vessel
Rode	A line or chain connecting an anchor to a vessel
Rogue wave	An abnormally large wave often coming from another direction from that of preceding waves
RRCO	Resident Rodent Control Officer
Rub Strip	A sacrificial strip that protects the hull of a vessel from impact damage

Sailing Directions	A set of pilot books containing pertinent data about seas, weather, ports and anchorages of the world
Sand fleas	No-nos, no-see-ums. Tiny biting (actually stinging) insects. Can attack in vast numbers and prolific in many areas
Sheet	A rope, attached to a sail, which controls the set of a sail
Sheet in	Haul in on the sheet of a sail to bring it closer to the centreline of the vessel to allow the vessel to sail closer to the wind
Shroud	A set of ropes or wires stretched from the masthead to the vessel's side to offset lateral strain on the mast
Slipway	A sloping dock or shore area fitted with rails or skids, used to haul a vessel out of the water
Sole	The floor of a vessel
Spinnaker	A large triangular, baggy headsail used when running before the wind
Spreader	A horizontal strut on a mast used to lead the shrouds outboard and provide lateral support to the mast
Squall	A brief, violent wind, usually with rain
SSB—Single Sideband Radio	A radio transmission system specially suited to long range marine communications
Starboard (starb'd)	The right-hand side of a vessel, when facing forwards
Stay	Rigging used to support the mast forward or aft
Staysail	A triangular sail set from stays
Stern	Rear
Storm jib	A small strong jib sail used in heavy weather
Storm trysail	A small strong sail set in place of the mainsail, but not attached to the boom, used in heavy weather
Strobe Light	Electronic flashing brilliant light
Tack	To change direction through wind, the wind coming from ahead throughout the manoeuvre
Tapa cloth	A fabric made from pounded paper mulberry or breadfruit tree bark
Tether	Webbing strap with clip for attachment

Toe rail	That part of the hull that extends above the deck
Topsides	The part of a vessel's side that is above water when it is afloat
T-panel	Standard configuration of basic instruments required for flying an aircraft
Trades	A wind, in the tropics, that blows steadily
Trade winds	towards the equator from the northeast north of the equator and from the southeast south of the equator
Transom	The vertical or near-vertical flat or flattish surface that forms the stern of a vessel
Travelift	Self propelled lifting device for removing vessels from, and returning to, the water
Trough	Canyon or valley between large waves
Turnbuckle	A threaded adjuster to tension stays and shrouds
Veer	A change of wind in a clockwise direction
VHF	Very high frequency line-of-sight FM radio communication
Wake	The lateral waves caused by the passage of a vessel through the water
Weather boards	Boards that keep a sailor in his bunk in rough weather
Windlass	A ribbed conical drum on a horizontal axis around which the anchor rode is wrapped to haul in the anchor
Windward	The direction or side from which the wind is blowing
Zincs	Sacrificial anodes attached to the underwater steel components of a vessel to reduce electrolytic corrosion

About the Author

Maggi Ansell, an editor and writer, is published in *Reader's Digest* in Canada, Australia and New Zealand, and in *Sail Magazine*, USA, *Yachting World*, and *Practical Boat Owner* in the UK, and *Cruising Helmsman*, Australia. She has written for the heavy-weather sailing 'bible'—K Adlard Coles' *Heavy Weather Sailing* by Peter Bruce, 5th edition, UK; and for the *Drag Device Data Base*, Para-Anchors International, USA.

Travelling with Robin, her engineer husband, she has lived and worked in the UK, Canada, Libya, Cayman Islands, Philippines and Australia. She gained a B.Sc. degree with High Distinction when she was 42, from the University of Toronto, majoring in Psychology.

Maggi has been a teacher, a barmaid, a scuba diving instructor and worked for a publishing company. She holds a private pilot's licence and has sold organic foods at her local Farmers' Market for the past seven years.

Married for 39 years, Maggi and Robin now live on Vancouver Island, BC, on a tiny organic farm tucked under the Beaufort Mountains with their dogs, cat and other farm animals.

Photo: Julie Huot

Maggi's maxims: "If an opportunity arises, take it. Don't spend your life regretting the things you never attempted. If you fall on your feet—good; if you fall on your face, don't stay there!"

ISBN 141209922-6

9 781412 099226